Cat 'n' Dog

Get Retailed

By

Lilli Lea

First published in the USA in 2016
by Treasure Grove Publishing
TreasureGrovePublishing@outlook.com

To my friends and family at 1789 and 3237

Prologue

Tired and weary, Bizmart manager Brian Parker closed and locked the front doors of the store behind him and punched in the alarm code. *ACTIVATED 12:18 A.M.* flashed on the small electronic screen.

He began the long walk across the dim parking lot toward his car, realizing just how exhausted he truly was. It seemed a mile away to the far side where he made all employees park, including himself. He looked up at the large, brightly lit sign on the front of the building. The "Z" had burned out two days earlier. He would have to remember to get that fixed. Pulling his cellphone out of its holder, he chose an app, punched the record button, and spoke into it.

"Get front sign fixed."

He put the phone back into its holder, and continued on toward his car. Normally the night shift would be there to clean and stock the store, but as of midnight it was a holiday and there were no other cars in the large parking lot.

He looked past the employee parking area to the trees by the fence. Had he heard something? The moon had not risen yet and an eerie feeling crept over him. He shrugged it off to the wind and fished out his car keys from his pants pocket.

Just as he was putting the key in the door lock, he heard footsteps come up behind him. He turned to see who it was, just before the bullet slammed into his chest.

Brian gasped for air and fell back, then slid down the side of the car, clutching the wound with his bloodied hand. A herd of sleeping cows startled by the shot ran off into the darkness, mooing loudly.

Brian's cheek pressed against the cold, dirty asphalt. As his eyes drifted shut, he focused on the Bizmart sign reflected in a puddle of water under his car. The darkness where the "Z" had been was oddly sublime now, and he stared at it as his vision faded.

There was the scrape of a booted foot on the asphalt beside him, then another shot.

Two miles away, a black Labrador raised her head off the bed and looked toward the balcony doors. She recognized the loud sound that had awoken her was a gunshot.

She lifted her nose, sniffing and letting the smells of the night sift through her sensitive canine nose. Outside, the air was still. A few moments passed.

Another shot! Her ears perked up. Alert and awake, she rolled over and pushed all four of her feet into the lump under the covers next to her.

"Jet! Stop pushin' me," a sleepy female voice said, muffled by the pillow.

The Lab pushed again.

"What?" Jet's owner rolled over.

"I heard something!" Jet's voice burbled in Alanna's mind.

"What did you hear?" Alanna groggily pushed the dog away.

"Shots! Two of them!" Jet stuck her nose in Alanna's face.

Alanna looked over at the digital clock next to the bed. It said 12:23 AM. She yawned and rubbed her eyes.

"It's probably just someone shooting at a coyote or raccoon. Go back to sleep and give me more room!" Alanna rolled back over, fluffing her pillow.

"What's wrong, Mommy?" a tiny voice mewled in her mind.

"Nothing. Jet heard shooting. Go back to sleep." Alanna pulled the covers up close to her neck. She felt her kitten-sized tabby cat, Abbey, shift position on the pillow next to hers.

"Gunshots?" Abbey lifted her sleepy head to look at Jet.

"Yeah, two of them." Jet replied. *"Mom says it's probably just a coyote or raccoon."*

"I hope it was a raccoon." Abbey yawned. *"Don't like raccoons. They're mean."*

"They can be." Jet touched the cat's striped back with her nose, then placed her head on the pillow next to Abbey.

"She doesn't like them because they're smarter than her," sneered a second feline voice from the cat bed perched on top of the dresser on the other side of the room. *"Of course, the majority of life forms are smarter than her."*

"Ok, quiet, I wanna go back to sleep," Alanna rumbled irritably.

"Snack?" Abbey asked hopefully.

"No snack! Sleep!" Alanna grumbled.

"Snack!" Jet shouted, standing up and jumping off the bed. Abbey followed and the two went downstairs to the kitchen. The stout black and white cat on the dresser put her head down and started snoring almost immediately, as did Alanna.

Chapter 1

Rain fell so heavily on the windshield the wipers could hardly keep up. Her headlights illuminated the slick, black asphalt of the winding highway. She was driving too fast for these weather conditions on this road, but she had to get away. The yellow flashing light on the caution sign told her where she was and that the curves were dangerous. She gripped the steering wheel so tightly that her knuckles were white and the rings bit into the flesh of her fingers.

She glanced in the rearview mirror and the reflection of the headlight behind her blinded her for a second, but a second was all it took. She looked back just in time to see the edge of the highway. She jerked the wheel and slammed on the brakes. The car hydroplaned.

The verge of the road loomed. There was no guardrail at the graveled edge. She screamed as the car went careening over the side of the cliff, and she raised her arms to cover her face as the tree branches burst through the side windows and the windshield. The car flipped over and over. She screamed again as glass, branches and twisted metal cut into her arms, face, and body—

"Mommy! Mommy!"

She could hear Abbey's voice in the distance, but fear and pain consumed her.

"Mom! Wake up!" Jet barked. *"Wake up!"*

Alanna bolted upright in bed, screaming, shaking, and drenched in sweat.

"Mommy, what's wrong?" Abbey stood next to her on the bed.

"You had a nightmare again." Jet sat beside Alanna, licking the sweat from her cheek.

Her father flipped on the light as he ran into the room. Juneau, the black and white cat on the dresser, rolled over in her cat bed and buried her face beneath her paws. *"Bright light! Yelling! Bad humans! Bad humans! This is why I want my own room!"*

"Are you all right? You sound like someone's killing you!" Fintan, Alanna's father, moved Abbey aside and sat on the edge of the bed. He put his arm around Alanna and held her. She was still shaking badly.

"I'm ok. It was just a nightmare."

"You scared the hell out of me," he said, rubbing a hand over his face.

She leaned against him. "Sorry, Dad."

"Was it the same dream?"

"Yeah. The car, the rain . . . the cliff." She put her head in her hands. "Why do I keep having this dream?"

They both heard Fintan's cellphone ring. He glanced at the clock, got up and left the room to answer it. They would not be calling the Chief of Police at 4:27 a.m. unless it was important. He grabbed his cellphone off the nightstand in his room and pushed the Receive button.

"Chief MacLachlin," he rumbled into the receiver. He stood for a few minutes with the phone to his ear listening to his captain explain the situation. The conversation ended with his customary and terse "all right." He punched the button to end the call and switched on the light. Tossing the phone on the bed, he ran his hands over his face and head. He stretched and popped his back. *Ah, to be young again*, he thought wistfully. With that thought, he pulled his uniform on, grabbed his phone and walked back down the hall to Alanna's room.

"I have to go. You gonna be all right?" He stood in the doorway.

"Yeah, I'll be fine. What happened?" She knew that the captain would not have called him in the middle of the night if it were not important. "Is everything ok?"

"Nothing for you to worry about. Try to go back to sleep," Fintan reassured her as he turned to go downstairs. It was going to be a very long day for him, and he knew it.

"Dad?" she called after him.

He came back to the doorway. "Yeah?"

"Be careful," she pleaded, a note of concerned love underlying her words. She did not know what kind of danger he faced this time. She was used to being the daughter of a cop, but that didn't mean she could ever take his safety for granted.

He smiled, the edges of his mustache curling up slightly. "Always am. Love you."

"Love you, too." She sat in the bed, hugging her knees to her chest. Alanna and the animals listened as Fintan descended the stairs. They heard him grab his keys and head out the laundry room door to the garage.

Alanna got out of bed and padded barefoot to the balcony doors on the other side of her room, shadowed by Jet and Abbey. She opened the balcony doors and cool air rushed in.

The three stepped out onto the cold wood floor and crossed to the railing. The night breeze bit right through Alanna's pajamas. She crossed her arms, hugging herself for warmth. She had spent many hours on this balcony watching the sun rise and set, also watching the activity in town and on the lake below her hilltop home.

They watched as her father got into his squad car and drove down the long concrete driveway to the ornate wrought iron gate. He idled patiently while the gate slid open. Once he was through it, he headed down the side of the hill towards town. She watched his headlights through the thick trees. Only when he was almost to the bottom of the hill where their private road met the highway did he turn on his police lights, but he left his siren off. Alanna knew he was trying to avoid one of the city's reporters catching a whiff of trouble and following him to a crime scene. He picked up speed once his tires hit the county road.

She watched the flash of her father's lights go through town. Past the dock shops he drove, past Mulligan's Pub & Grill, the gas stations and the residential area on the other side of town. Then she saw his destination. It was the superstore on the outskirts of town. She watched her father come to a stop and turn off his lights.

She grabbed her high-powered binoculars off the bookcase next to the balcony's French doors, and returned outside where she focused them on the scene. She was at a higher vantage point and what she saw made the hairs rise on the back of her neck. There was a yellow plastic tarp laid out on the parking lot and she knew what that meant. Someone was dead.

"Someone's sleeping. They put a blanket over him." Abbey was on the railing by her elbow, feeling sorry that humans had such bad eyesight.

"He's not sleeping. He's dead," Alanna stated.

"Dead? Are you sure?" Jet stood up on her hind legs, put her paws over the railing, and sniffed the air. The breeze shifted. She smelled deer, coyote, rabbit and Abbey.

"Yeah. The paramedics would be a lot busier if he, or she, was still alive." Alanna lowered the binoculars. "Whoever it is, I want to know what happened."

She spun on her heel and stepped back inside. After closing the balcony doors and returning the binoculars to her shelf, she headed downstairs, flipping the hall lights on as she went. In the kitchen, she started a pot of coffee and grabbed a thermos out of a cabinet. She went back upstairs and turned on the light in her bathroom.

Juneau opened one green eye and peered at her over the lip of her cat bed. *"Breakfast?"* she asked, twitching an ear indolently.

"No, not yet," Jet groused, sitting down by the bed. They watched Alanna get dressed in jeans and a faded sweatshirt. *"A human is dead."*

"Oh. Well, wake me for breakfast. Or any other significant *event."* Juneau closed her eye and buried her face in her paws.

Alanna tied her shoes and went back down to kitchen. She waited for the coffee maker to finish, filled the thermos with coffee, and grabbed her keys before going to the garage with Abbey and Jet still trailing in her wake.

"I want to go!"

"Me, too!"

"Fine, but no matter what happens you have to stay in the truck. Ok?"

"Ok."

"'k."

Alanna opened the back door to her midsize SUV, and Jet jumped in. She sat Abbey next to the lab, but she didn't stay there. By the time Alanna got in and put the thermos on the seat next to her, Abbey was already standing on her hind legs looking out the passenger door window. Alanna started the truck, opened the garage door, and backed out.

It didn't take her long to get to the road that led up to Bizmart. The streets were still dead at this hour of the morning, and there were very few lights on in the windows of the houses she passed.

Sawhorses and yellow police tape blocked off the entrance to the store's parking lot. One officer stood in front of the blockade. Alanna pulled up slowly and lowered her window.

"Hey, Erin. I'm bringing the Chief coffee," she said to the young female as she approached. She had gone to school with Erin and knew her family.

"Ok, but make it quick, I don't want to get in trouble with him," Erin replied with a smile, moving a sawhorse to let Alanna pass. Fintan looked around and saw Alanna pull up next to his car. She got out and looked over at him, holding up the thermos in one hand.

"Stay there." He held his hand up like the traffic cop he'd been over twenty-five years ago and walked briskly over to her. "What are you doing here?" he said, a note of slight irritation creeping into his voice.

"Just bringing you coffee," she smiled sheepishly tilting her head a little to see around him.

"Uh-huh. And fishing for news, I gather? Well, thanks, but you shouldn't be here, you know that." He knew Alanna had inherited his overwhelming sense of curiosity. He took a deep breath, letting it out in a sigh. "Ah, hell, you're going to find out anyway, Brian Parker's been killed," he said quietly.

"How?" Alanna had known someone was dead, but when she heard who it was she was completely shocked. Brian Parker had been her boss for over two years.

"I shouldn't tell you this, but he was shot twice. Once in the chest, and once in the head." Fintan was aware his daughter had been raised knowing all about what he did for a living, and this wasn't the first time the victim of a violent crime had been a personal acquaintance. He hoped she would be able to shed some light on who might have done this.

"Was it a robbery?" Alanna asked.

"His wallet, keys and watch are all still here. The only thing we can see missing so far is his cellphone. Did he carry a briefcase?"

She shook her head.

He put a hand on her shoulder. "You ok?"

"Yeah . . . yeah, I'm stunned . . . but fine. Just . . . who would do something like this? He has a wife and two kids." She leaned back against her truck. At the open driver's window Jet and Abbey stuck their heads out.

"Told you I heard shots!" said Jet.

Alanna stood up straight. "Dad, Jet woke me up at 12:20 and said she heard gunshots. Two of them. I told her it was nothing, but now . . . I think I was wrong."

"Well, I can't use the family dog as a witness for the time frame. We'll have to rely on the coroner's report for that. Willy's over there now doin' his thing." Fintan gestured with his thumb toward the scene. "We'll see what he says." He dug in his pocket for his cigarettes. Pulling one out he lit it, took a long drag, blowing the smoke away from Alanna. "Any enemies he might have?"

"No. Everyone liked Brian. He's . . . well, he was a really great guy. Always nice and seemed to care about everyone."

"Well, all right then. You should head back home and get some sleep."

"Sleep? I can't sleep now. My boss is dead, Dad." She looked him in the eyes, which always unnerved him slightly. They had the same green eyes. It was like looking into a mirror.

"Go home. Try to get some rest. I know those dreams of yours have been keeping you up at night." He took another drag. "And me, too," he muttered under his breath. "I'm not going to make it to the game today. You three go on without me," he said between drags.

Alanna had forgotten all about the Giants baseball game. Fintan, Nick, Samantha and Alanna had been planning on driving to San Francisco that morning. Nick had plans to propose to Sam at the game. He'd bought a spot on the big screen in the outfield that said "Sam—Will You Marry Me?" It was supposed to have been a wonderful day, full of joy, and fun.

"I can't go to the game now. This . . . this is just . . . ." Words escaped her for the moment. Too many thoughts were running through her head. Fintan opened the truck door for her, shooing the animals back into their own seats. "Go home," he said firmly. "And don't tell anyone what's happened . . . yet." He closed the door after she had got in. "Let me rephrase that. Don't let anyone find out except Sam and Nick." He knew his daughter would be on the phone with her best friend by the time she got home. "We don't want word to get out before we can notify Brian's family. An officer is on his way to their home now."

"Did he put up a fight?" she asked as she started her engine.

"No." Fintan stepped back so he could smoke. "Looks like he was surprised from behind. He was down when he took the second hit." Fintan was always blunt and to the point. "Store was still locked and the alarm was set. Parking lot cleaners found him while doing their routines." He crushed the cigarette butt with his shoe and smoothed his mustache. "I know you work here, but you really don't need to be here right now." There was a firmness to his voice that she knew all too well.

She handed him the thermos. "Let me know if I can do anything, ok?"

"You've done enough." He smiled faintly. "You brought me coffee."

She turned the SUV around and drove back down toward the blocked-off entrance. Erin was talking to a man that Alanna knew was a reporter for the *Aurum Town Crier* newspaper. He was asking questions, but the petite officer was being evasive. He glanced over his shoulder, spotting Alanna in her SUV but Erin waved Alanna by and secured the barricade behind her. Alanna could see the reporter fuming in her rearview mirror.

There was only one main road going in and out of town and that was J19. It ran from one side of town to the other and went past the lake. The closest main highway was Highway 88. The town of five thousand people was still asleep for the most part, which meant Alanna had the road to herself.

The light at the Main Street intersection changed to red and she pulled to a stop. She wished the Aurum Town Council would spring for some motion sensors on the traffic lights. While she waited for the light to change she brought up Sam's number on her cellphone. She was about to call when the light changed to green. She debated about calling her best friend. *It's not like Brian was a close friend. But he was our boss. Who could have done it and why? And what if it was someone we work with?*

"Mom, why did someone kill that man?" Jet put her head on the console between the seats as she lay in the middle of the SUV. Alanna never put up the two back rows of seats. Instead, the entire back of the vehicle was covered in blankets, pillows and comforters which were all spread out. Two cat beds, a covered litter box, a water dish, two food dishes, a gallon of water and small containers of cat and dog food were packed in as well. When Alanna went somewhere, her animals went with her. They liked to travel more than she did.

"I don't know," Alanna said, still deep in thought.

"He made somebody mad," offered Abbey, curled up in the passenger seat.

"Maybe he saw something he shouldn't have." Jet tilted her head to look up at Alanna with her big, chocolate-colored eyes. *"Like when Nemesis read cousin Jenae's diary she yelled at him, 'You little devil! I'm going to kill you and stuff my pillows with your feathers!'"*

"Jenae was mad about that, but would never harm Nemesis. I understand what you're saying but I still can't believe someone killed Brian. He was such a nice man." Alanna furrowed her brow.

"He made somebody mad. That's what he did." Abbey touched Jet's nose with hers. *"I know Juneau makes me so mad sometimes I spit."*

"But mad enough to kill her?"

"No . . . but mad enough to bite her real hard."

"She's your sister. She is supposed to make you mad, that's her job." Alanna pushed the button to open the gate to her home.

Reaching down she used one hand to take turns petting both Abbey and Jet while she waited for the gate to open. "But she also loves you and takes care of you. That's what family's for."

"Family that makes me mad," Abbey said, backing her ears slightly.

Alanna drove up the driveway and into the garage then everyone got out. She started another pot of coffee, and walked slowly through the house, stopping on the huge front porch to look down at the dark, sleeping town below.

Cellphone in hand she brought up her best friend Sam's number and pushed send.

"Al, do you know what time it is?" whined Sam's sleepy voice.

"Yeah, something's happened I thought you'd wanna hear about."

"You ok?"

"Yeah."

"Your dad?"

"We're fine. Sorry I woke you, but it's bad."

"How bad?" Sam perked up a little. Scuttlebutt was always Sam's forte.

"Brian's been shot and killed."

"I'm on my way." *Click.* The line went silent.

Through the trees Alanna saw a light come on in the area of Sam and Nick's apartment down by the town square. She stood on the front porch looking over the immaculate, dimly lit grounds of "Treasure Grove". That was the name her great grandparents had given the estate when it was built in 1936. When her Grandmamma Bermann passed on, Alanna's mother Eva had inherited the estate and part of the vast fortune that had been divided between Grandmamma's three children: Vivian, Nevin, and Eva.

Eva and Fintan's dream had been to update the big house and grounds and fill it with lots of children. They'd succeeded in updating the house and grounds, but two years after Alanna was born Eva had found out that she had ovarian cancer. She battled hard for many years. Some years were better than others, but she eventually lost the fight when Alanna was twenty. Now Alanna owned the estate, and she wished every day that she had her mother back instead.

Chapter 2

Samantha McPherson and Nick Hayman pulled up to the large gate at Treasure Grove and pushed the button on the controller inside their car. The gate slowly slid open, allowing them up the long drive in front of the house. They didn't knock or ring the doorbell but just walked right in, as usual. Sam had always felt more at home in Treasure Grove than in her own parents' house.

"Al!" Sam yelled. "Al, where are you?"

"In the kitchen," Alanna called out.

Jet met them at the door and led them into the kitchen, where Alanna was seated, drinking a cup of coffee.

"What happened? Are you sure it was Brian?" Sam's tone was sleepy but curious as she sat down at the table across from Alanna. Nick poured coffee for them both.

"Yes, I'm sure." Alanna shivered a little. "He was shot. Twice. In the parking lot at the store."

"Holy crap! I can't believe it!" Sam took the cup of coffee Nick handed her.

"Do they know why he was shot?" Nick asked, sitting down next to Sam and yawning.

"He made somebody mad," Abbey intoned from the kitchen floor.

Alanna glanced at her. "That's your opinion."

"What'd she say?" Sam asked, reaching down to pet Abbey.

"She thinks he made somebody mad, and that's why they shot him."

"Tell 'em about the shots I heard! Tell 'em! Tell 'em!" Jet sat by Alanna's chair wiggling all over with excitement. Alanna scratched her head and ears.

"About 12:20 this morning Jet woke me up saying she heard gunshots. Two of them. I told her it was probably nothing and not to worry. But I was wrong. Maybe if I had said something . . ." Alanna sighed.

"Al, you couldn't have known," Sam said. "People shoot at everything around here. Everybody has a gun. Farmers and hunters are always shooting at something. Not a week goes by I don't hear a shot or two. We live out in the country."

"Bernie shot himself in the foot three weeks ago cleaning his gun," Nick chimed in with another yawn. "Drunk as a skunk—lost a toe because of it." He rubbed his eyes. "He acted all unconcerned about it saying he didn't care about that piggy. That it was the one that went wee, wee, wee, all the way home. But it was stupid and had to hurt like hell."

Both women stared at him.

"What?" He shrugged. "I'm just saying there's no way you could've known those shots were different from any of others that we hear, so don't blame yourself for not realizing." He covered another yawn.

"From what Dad described, chances are they couldn't have done anything for him anyway," Alanna said.

"Do they know what happened or who it might have been?" Sam asked.

"No, just that someone surprised him from behind and that the only thing missing is his cellphone." Alanna leaned back in her chair. She felt tired; her dream had exhausted her.

"Abbey might be right," Nick said, looking down at Abbey's cute, furry face beside his chair.

Both women looked at Nick, and Abbey raised her head giving him a cat smile, making her whiskers turn up.

"If it wasn't a robbery then chances are it was someone he knew." Nick took a drink of coffee.

"What makes you say that?"

"Well, statistics show that 76 percent of violent crimes occur by someone the victim knows. Is this decaf?" He yawned again.

Alanna shook her head. "No, it's not, and I can't think of anyone that disliked him that much. Can you?" Alanna looked at Sam.

"Crazy Dave comes to mind."

"He's not a killer. He's just . . . out there." Alanna defended the maintenance man who swept the parking lot, emptied the trash and fixed everything around the store. "Granted, he thinks everything is a conspiracy theory, and he thinks the FBI is watching him, but I don't think he'd kill anyone. Especially Brian. He liked Brian. Brian hired him when no one else would."

"He's weird! And he's got that crazy hair and eye thing going on." Sam shivered visibly. "And he smells funny."

"He has a lazy eye. So what? You don't have issues?"

Nick and Alanna both looked sternly at Sam. "Well, he gives me the creeps. Ok?"

Nick and Alanna glanced at each other as they drank.

"Dad said they were on their way to tell Karen. I feel so sorry for her and the kids." Alanna knew what it was like to lose a parent. It was a horrible feeling.

"I wonder which Church she'll call first," Nick said.

In the town of Aurum it was well known that the mortuary, cemetery, and monument company were owned by a family named Church. So it was always said that when a person died in Aurum County that "the last place you go is to Church". Old man Church owned Church Cemetery; Church Senior owned Church Mortuary; and Junior owned Church Monument Company. Even Willy the coroner was a Church, which meant that the family had a corner on death in Aurum.

"Brian isn't from here. He's from Lodi. I don't even know if they'll have the funeral here. They'll probably have it down there." Alanna got up to refill her cup.

"I can't believe he's dead." Sam leaned on her elbows putting her chin in her hand. "Of all the people in our store to die. Brian?"

"I just hope Dad catches whoever did it. I've been thinking of who could be that evil. I know there was a lot of controversy when the store opened. You know, the whole superstore taking over the town thing. Town council knew that if they didn't build it here then they'd build it just a few miles down the road, and then the state would get the revenue not the city." Alanna sat back down. "Then they passed that zoning law to prevent other superstore business from coming in, and now everyone avoids saying Bizmart's name out loud for fear they might offend their neighbor or friend. Politics!" she huffed.

Sam looked at her. "Hey, we do the same thing. I always just say 'the store'. And you do too. This town has a lot of issues."

"Yeah, everyone's like that around here." Nick drained his cup. "Like our little town would ever be overrun by big stores, but some people wanted it and some didn't. Nothing like small town politics. But my dad was up in arms about it, and still is if you mention it by name. I think he even started one of the petitions to keep it out."

"But why go after the store manager? If you want to get at the source, why not go after Beatrice Martin herself? She's the 'Queen Bee' that owns the entire company, so why not go after her? She's in the news every day. Can't go a day without hearing something about her."

Beatrice Martin's father had started the company, and when he'd passed she'd taken the reins. In business terms, the Aurum store did well on day-to-day sales. The town and surrounding communities consisted of about 7,000 people, but on the weekends and holidays Aurum could swell to over 20,000. Tourists came to see the old gold mines and lumber mill restaurant, shop the antique stores and see the squirrels. Aurum had a large population of squirrels. Every May, the town had a Squirrel Festival. It had started back in the 1840s as a cooking contest to see how many different ways there were to make squirrel palatable. Over time the festival had transitioned into a county fair and squirrel was removed from the menu although almost every booth and balloon still had something to do with squirrels. And the tourists lined up to see the many squirrels that lived throughout the town.

The store capitalized on these tourists. Bizmart's building planners had known that its location on the edge of town would make the most of the influx of tourists on their way to the lake, festival grounds and Gaslight District (what the local Aurumites called The Tourist Trap).

"Remember when the Queen Bee herself came to our store last year?" Sam held out her cup to Nick and he filled it. "She was very . . . diplomatic. She viewed us like a general doing a troop review. She seemed fairly nice, though."

"She stopped by my jewelry counter, looked at my displays, and tried on a ring," Alanna reminisced as she got up and started making another pot of coffee. "I liked her perfume, and the bee ring she had on was very large."

Alanna had been Jewelry Department Manager for a year. She liked her job, but it was just a job to her. She'd graduated a year ago from college with her B.A. in history. Alanna enjoyed retail, but it was demanding, frustrating, and kept her busy for the holidays. When her mother passed Alanna did not feel like celebrating holidays so working retail seemed like a good idea. Mostly Alanna liked her customers. She knew almost all of them by name.

"She seemed to really care about the employees and the customers. At least that's how she came across to me," Alanna said.

"I didn't get a chance to meet her. I was in the back trying to find a certain size shoe for a customer." Sam had been Shoe Department Manager for three years. "Ms. Queen Bee was in and out of there so fast all I saw was the tail end of her stinger."

"Sam, don't you think this is really weird? I mean, the Lodi store just lost their store manager last year. I wonder how their store handled it. Losing their manager like that."

"I don't know." Sam shrugged. "How're we going to handle it? Brian was killed right there in front of the store. You know that's going to mess with some people's heads. I know it messes with my head! I don't wanna go to work tomorrow knowing that."

"Well, at least the store isn't open today with it being Easter. Dad will have an easier time securing the crime scene. He told me that he wasn't going to the Giants game with us today."

Nick shot Alanna a look. The expression on his face was a mixture of worry and panic. "We're still going, right?" he asked, trying to act as though it didn't really matter.

"I'm not," Sam stated firmly. "I'm staying here to see what they find out."

Nick's face fell. He had been planning this day for months. Alanna had helped him pick out the perfect ring. They'd gone to Sacramento a few weeks ago to find it. He'd called and gotten the spot on the big screen in the middle of the third inning. He'd told his family to watch the game and he hoped that the TV station wouldn't cut to commercial. He'd wanted to propose to Sam for months and now this?

"We can still go. There won't be anything on the news anyway until tonight."

"Nick! Our boss has just been killed! There's a crazy person out there with a gun. I'm not going anywhere." Sam got up and opened the door to the refrigerator, leaning to look inside. "Besides, Al's dad will be the first person to know anything."

"Alanna, tell her there's no sense in just sitting around waiting all day. Besides, we have a great day planned."

"Well . . ." Alanna wasn't sure what to say. She wanted to help Nick make his proposal happen, but she also wanted to stay and find out any details that might surface. She looked at the clock . . . 5:34 a.m. "We do have lots of time to make it to the game."

"I can't believe you people can think about baseball at a time like this." Sam started pulling eggs, bacon and other breakfast fixings onto the counter by the stove.

Just then Juneau sauntered lazily down the stairs. She stretched when she got to the bottom.

"Oh, good. Someone finally got the memo. Breakfast."

Sam and Alanna prepared breakfast and fed the animals. As they ate the sun began to rise. It was going to be a beautiful California spring day. One of the French doors in the kitchen was open a little, leading out to the backyard. They were almost done eating breakfast when Nemesis flew onto the back porch and landed. He walked his funny side-to-side raven walk into the kitchen.

"Your aunt wants you," he informed Alanna in his raspy voice. Alanna always thought he sounded like a parched, little old man.

"She could have used the phone." Alanna gave him a little piece of toast as he flew up onto the kitchen table. He crunched it noisily.

"Could have. Didn't. Why use a phone when she has me?"

"Hi, Nemesis." Sam gave him some of her bacon.

"Can I go?" Abbey hopped up on a chair and sniffed Nemesis. He tilted his head to get a better look at her. He wore a thin leather collar with a small rose quartz crystal hanging from it. His sleek black feathers lay over it, so people couldn't really see it unless they knew where to look.

"Me, too!" Jet put her head in Alanna's lap.

"Aunt Vi wants you?" Sam slipped Nemesis some more bacon, glancing at Alanna.

"Yeah, guess she knows." Alanna stood up, putting her plate in the sink. "That doesn't surprise me. Nemesis, what did you see?"

"Mistress said this mornin', 'Blood on the moon last night, Nem. Go fly and see who's found their fate'. Didn't take long. Smell of blood. Lots of humans around the carcass. Stayed on the fence by the trees most of the time. Herd of cows got woken up and spooked by the shots. They're a yappy bunch of old broads." He took a drink of coffee out of Alanna's cup and walked to the edge of the table. *"One of them kept complaining about bees."* He flew to the door. *"Went back and told Mistress what I saw. She told me to come fetch you. My task is fulfilled,"* he said with more than a trace of irony as he flew away.

"What did he say?" Sam inquired.

"That there're a lot of people there now and something about cows and bees."

Alanna grabbed her cup off the table and put it in the sink.

"You two go. I'll clean up. You cooked." Nick stood up, put his own plate in the sink, turned on the water, and opened the dishwasher.

"Thanks, Nick." Alanna walked into the backyard with Sam, Jet, Abbey, and Juneau on her heels.

"Mother, could you get my book? I'd like to read awhile," Juneau asked. Alanna smiled and retrieved from the house a hardcover copy

of *The Art of War* by Niccolò Machiavelli. When Juneau was just a kitten Alanna discovered that she loved to read. Where she'd learned to do so was still anyone's guess. Alanna laid the book on the cushion of one of the patio lounge chairs, opening it to where the bookmark was. Juneau jumped onto the chair and held the book open with one paw.

"Thanks." Juneau used her fangs to flick the bookmark to the side.

"You're welcome." Alanna joined the others, who were already walking toward the south wall. She opened the small, wrought iron gate, which was covered on one side in black mesh to prevent any animals from getting through. As she closed it behind them she looked back to see Juneau turning a page with one claw. A shaft of sunlight was making her black spots shine. She smiled. Juneau was the most unique animal she'd ever known, and she loved her dearly. Even though she was cantankerous and somewhat spiteful at times.

They walked on a well-worn path about a block long until they came to a gravel one-lane road. The smells and sounds of the forest around them were very invigorating. Everything was still fresh with morning dew, the air crisp and clean. The sunlight filtered through the thick, interlinked tree limbs overhead.

They continued about quarter of a mile before they came to a two-story house set well back into the trees. The house looked older than it was because of all the foliage on and around it. It was covered in flowering vines. There were all kinds of wind chimes and garden art spread about. A large Celtic stone cross sat in the middle of what would be the front lawn if it had grass. The front door and windows were all open. The smell of baked pumpkin reached their noses. The wind blew gently and the billowy curtains fluttered outside the screenless windows with the wind chimes playing softly. Jet and Abbey took off, running around to the back of the house.

"Apollo!" Jet yelled with a bark.

"Artemis!" Abbey meowed. Apollo and Artemis were Aunt Vi's two ferrets that loved to play hide and seek.

Alanna and Sam walked in through the open front door, making their way to the kitchen. Some people would have stopped to look at the symbols beautifully etched into the door frame. Vi had protective runes and other symbols around all her doors and windows. The house might be somewhat disconcerting to a stranger, but to Alanna it was her second home. It was clean and neat, but there was stuff everywhere. It looked like a well-lived-in antique store. There were lots of books and curious items that could occupy a person all day.

The kitchen was open, airy, warm and inviting. There was a huge atrium off to the side, where Vi grew all her own herbs and spices. It smelled of lavender, rosemary and other assorted herbs.

"Aunt Vi!" Alanna called.

A curvaceous woman with beautiful, striking features came in through the back door. Her auburn hair, curly and full, was pulled back by a long purple scarf tied around her head. She had on a flowing skirt and blouse, lots of jewelry, and she used scarves as a belt. She set a basket of what looked like leaves and twigs down on the kitchen counter.

"No need to shout, dear. I know when you're here." She pulled off her gardening gloves, walking over to Alanna to give her a gentle hug. "Good to see you. Sit, sit, sit."

Sam and Alanna sat down at the large, well-used and scarred claw-foot oak table.

"You must have some of my muffins. I just made them."

"We just ate," Alanna protested.

"Ok," Sam said at the same time.

Vi smiled, setting a pumpkin muffin overflowing with walnuts on a small plate in front of each of them. Then she got a pitcher of juice out of the fridge and poured two small glasses. She put them on the table and made herself a cup of tea.

"So, tell me dear, who was the man from your work that was killed?" Her gaze was level and steady.

"It was the store manager, Brian Parker," Alanna answered.

"Oh my, this will cause a stir." Vi sat her cup down on the table leaning back in her chair. "Do they know who or why yet?"

"No, just that they don't think robbery was the motive." Alanna picked at her muffin, eating little bites.

Abbey came barreling through the back door. She jumped up and climbed into Vi's lap, then rubbed her face against Vi's cheek. *"Hello, Auntie,"* she purred. *"I've missed you. I'm hiding. They're seeking."*

"I've missed you too, love." Vi stroked Abbey's silky fur. "It's been far too long. Almost two whole days." Abbey curled up and laid down in Vi's lap. "Do they know who did it?"

"I think it was Colonel Mustard, in the library, with the candlestick," Sam stated.

"I think it was the pissed off person, in the parking lot, with the pistol." Abbey was oblivious to Sam's sarcasm. She was looking up at

Vi with her eyes squeezed shut in contentment.

Alanna and Vi smiled. "Abbey might be right." Alanna sighed. "Maybe he did make someone mad. But I've known him for two years, and he always seemed real nice."

"Well, you never really know someone unless they want you to, my dear."

"Yeah, but you can't sneeze in this town without someone on the other side saying 'God Bless You'." Sam reached for the rest of Alanna's muffin as she pushed it towards her.

"True enough. It is hard to keep a secret in this town." Vi and Alanna shared a private smile, thinking of their own family secrets.

"And people jump to all kinds of conclusions at the drop of the hat." Sam finished her juice. "They embellish and exaggerate *everything*. How many people around town think that you're a witch or sorceress?"

"I have been called a lot of things over the years," Vi replied with a sigh. Then a hint of a smile crossed her lips. "I think I liked 'enchantress' the best. When I opened my shop fifteen years ago people thought I was a devil worshipper or that I practiced black magic." Vi made a dismissive gesture. "People are very narrow-minded." She absently rubbed her large tiger's eye pendant with one hand and Abbey with the other. "Movies, television and the Internet taint people's minds. People fear what they truly don't understand."

Vi owned The Mystic Eye, a unique gift shop in the Gaslight District. She sold crystal balls, incense, tarot cards and books on the supernatural, amongst other things. The tourists liked it, and the store was successful. Vi and her daughter, Jenae, ran it. Her husband, Bob Dalton, owned the only health food store in town. It also did very well. Uncle Bob had always been good at guessing what the newest food craze would be in the health-obsessed state.

Wanting to change the subject, Vi looked over at Sam. "So my dear, how are you feeling?"

Sam nearly choked on a piece of muffin. "Fine. Why?" She firmly believed in Vi's psychic powers.

Alanna looked at her aunt with wide eyes. She hadn't told Vi of Nick's plans to propose but Vi probably already knew.

"No special reason. Just . . . are you taking a trip soon?" Alanna's aunt asked.

Sam looked at Alanna, alarmed. Alanna held her tongue.

"We were going to San Francisco today for the Giants game, but with Brian's death and all, I've decided not to go." Sam stared fearfully at Vi. "Why?"

"You should go." Vi sipped her tea meditatively. "Something wonderful awaits you there."

"Really?" Sam's face lit up. "What?"

"I don't know, but something very special." Vi winked at Alanna. "It's going to be a game that I wouldn't miss if I were you."

By 12:35 p.m. they were in their seats at AT&T Park in San Francisco, waiting for the game to start. Alanna had called her dad to let him know they were still going. She could tell by his tone that he was in no place or mood to talk.

The scene when they drove out of town past the road leading to the store had been a madhouse. People and cars were everywhere. Both the Aurum police force and the county sheriff's deputies were working on holding the crowd of onlookers back. There were now three reporters and two news crews.

Nick was sweating even though it was cool outside and their seats were in the shade. Alanna made sure to take Sam to the restroom with her during the second inning so she wouldn't leave before the big moment.

Before long it was the top of the third inning. Nick was so nervous that he was pale and shaking. Then it happened. The huge advertisement board lit up with the words, *"SAM, WILL YOU MARRY ME?"*

Nick brought Sam's attention to the board, and as she read he got down on one knee, which was not easy with the stadium seat beside him, with the open ring box in his hand. Sam realized what was going on when she saw herself and Nick on the big board. She was stunned and overwhelmed, the cameras cutting in for a close-up. She looked at Nick with tears in her eyes and nodded. Yes! The whole stadium erupted in cheers and clapping. He slid the ring on her finger, kissing and hugging her.

When they finally sat back, Sam was still crying. Alanna was crying, too. She was so happy for them. They'd been close friends for so long, and Alanna wanted only the best for both of them. She had recorded the whole thing on her phone just in case it didn't get broadcast.

Sam rounded on Alanna. "I can't believe this! How long have you known?" A smile covered her whole face.

"About two months." Alanna looked over at Nick. "And believe me, it wasn't easy keeping it from you!"

"I just can't believe this." Sam kissed Nick again. "Did your dad know?"

"Yeah, he really wanted to be here for it, but with everything . . . hopefully it got recorded at home so he can see it." Alanna dutifully admired Sam's ring. "Yeah, at a time like this all we could think about was baseball."

Nick drove the long way to get back to Aurum, so they wouldn't have to go by the scene at the store on the other side of town. He wanted the mood to stay focused on their engagement. During the ride home Sam asked Alanna to be her maid of honor. Alanna happily accepted. Sam bubbled over with ideas for the wedding. Nick made sure to keep his bride-to-be down to earth, interjecting his opinion of some of her more fanciful ideas.

As they pulled in through the gate to Treasure Grove, they noticed Emma's car parked in the driveway next to Fintan's empty spot. She was usually off on Sundays, but Alanna could guess why she was there. Emma Hoffman had been the MacLachlin's housekeeper, cook, and friend for twenty-four years. Emma was that port in the storm that everyone needed in their life, and they weren't surprised that she would anticipate the Chief's wishes.

As the three friends opened the front door, the expected aroma of corned beef and cabbage wafted out to them. It was Fintan's favorite. Anytime Emma expected Fintan to have an overly stressful day she made it for him.

"Emma, we're home!" Alanna called.

"Good, because dinner's ready," Emma called back.

Emma was a tall, thin lady with salt and pepper hair pulled back into a no-nonsense bun. As they entered the kitchen Alanna noticed that all three of her animals were on the floor, a small plate of corned beef in front of each of them.

"Yum. More?" Jet had finished hers and was waiting to see if Abbey left any.

"Your father should be home soon. He called about thirty minutes ago," Emma informed Alanna, checking the cabbage. The kitchen table was set for five. Sam rushed over to Emma.

"Look! Nick proposed! Isn't it gorgeous?"

"Well that's wonderful!" Emma wiped her hands on her apron and hugged Sam. Then she gently took Sam's hand and admired her ring. "I'm so happy for the both of you. It's about time." She went over and hugged Nick. "Your parents are going to be so happy."

They heard the sound of the front door opening and closing. A tall, older gentleman with a large gray mustache, fedora and ornate cane walked into the kitchen.

"Grandpa!" Alanna rushed over to give him a hug as she took in a deep breath. She loved the smell of the mixture of his cologne and his pipe tobacco.

"Didn't think I'd miss corned beef and cabbage, did you?" Ronan MacLachlin took off his hat and sat it on the kitchen counter. Sam came over to him.

"Look, Grandpa! Look what Nick did! We're engaged!" She held out her hand.

"Well. It's about time that boy made an honest woman of you." He hugged her.

"Nick, my boy, you've got your hands full. She's a stubborn one." He slapped Nick on the back and shook his hand. "Congratulations!"

"Thank you, sir."

They all sat down at the table, where Emma had just finished placing the steaming bowls of food. She set a foil-covered plate in the oven and took off her apron to hang it on the hook in the laundry room where her purse sat.

"There's a chocolate cream pie in the fridge." She opened the garage door. "I'm late for church." She was gone before everyone could get their "goodbyes" out.

They were just finishing their pie when Jet jumped up and ran to the laundry room. A few minutes later Fintan came in through the garage door. Jet jumped to greet him, wagging her tail. She trailed beside him on his way into the kitchen.

"Evening." His voice was worn.

Alanna got the warm, foil-wrapped plate and put it at the head of the table while he changed upstairs. Ronan got up at the same time and went down the hall to the den where the bar was and came back with a shot glass full of sour mash whiskey and a cold frosty mug of beer. He set it by Fintan's plate as he came down stairs in his usual outfit of T-shirt, boxers, and slippers. The family was accustomed to his unusual fashion choices, including the wearing of boxers (with briefs underneath) whenever he wasn't in uniform.

Fintan sat down heavily and downed his whiskey in one gulp, then took a bite of corned beef. He let out a long sigh, leaning back and chewing contentedly. He savored every bit of flavor while an expectant silence lay over the room.

"So, I understand congratulations are in order." He looked at Nick and Sam. "Three different people told me that they saw you on TV today."

"Yes, look!" Sam held her hand out. "Isn't it beautiful?" She beamed.

"Yes, it is." Fintan smiled tiredly. "I'm very happy for both of you."

As Fintan ate, the conversation picked up again; the upcoming wedding, the baseball game and the Giants season ahead being the main topics. Once he had finished his dinner and pie, Fintan leaned back in his chair and sipped his beer. His brow furrowing a little, he cleared his throat and they all looked at him.

"We weren't able to see the killer clearly on the security footage," he began without preamble. "He or she wore all black. Couldn't get a good look due to the angle of the camera. The killer surprised Brian from behind as we thought. We found a bunch of cigarette butts by the side of the store, but that could have been some husband waiting on his wife to shop. We'll see what the lab has to say."

"How's Karen?" Alanna asked.

"She's in shock. She insisted on seeing the body." Fintan stood up and grabbed his cigarettes, lighter and beer before walking out onto the patio. The rest of them followed and seated themselves around the table without saying a word. Ronan lit his pipe and puffed on it. Fintan blew out smoke, watching it mix in the air with his father's. The evening sky was a beautiful pinkish orange and twilight was starting.

"Don't know why the killer wanted his cellphone," he continued quietly. "Brian was talking into it when he was walking to his car. The killer may have the phone, but it's not turned on. We're hoping it will get switched on so we can use GPS to track it." He looked over at Alanna. "He was killed between midnight and 12:30."

"See!" Jet was lying beside Fintan's chair. She raised her head and looked at Alanna. *"Told you!"*

"We feel it was definitely premeditated. We speculate that the killer waited until Brian was the only one left at the store. Also the killer didn't try to get into the store, so robbery wasn't the motive. We interviewed all the other management today." He looked over at Alanna and Sam. "You two have any idea who might want to do this? Any talk around the water cooler?"

"I don't know of anyone who'd want him dead."

"People get upset and say they'd like to see him get off their backs, but then some people just don't like being told what to do. Not even by the boss," Sam replied.

"Was Brian having an affair?" Fintan took a drag and watched the two women's expressions.

"Not that I know of." Alanna looked surprised. "That's not something that would be talked about at work; at least not by any reliable sources."

"I never heard anything about an affair," Sam shrugged, her eyes wide at the thought. "He was always talking about his wife and family. He seemed pretty devoted to them."

"Can you remember anyone saying anything about him taking a trip soon?" Fintan asked.

"No. Why?"

"He had a packed suitcase in his trunk, with his passport in the pocket."

"Well . . . I know he goes to Alaska for salmon fishing with our district manager once a year," Alanna mused, watching her father's face. "But I'm not sure when they go."

Fintan crushed out his cigarette in the ashtray on the table. "Pretty close then, Brian and his boss?"

"Yeah." Sam nodded her head. "They've been friends for a long time. They went to college together, I think. He gave Brian the Aurum store when it opened. Before that Brian was manager of the Lodi store."

Fintan touched the pack of cigarettes in his T-shirt pocket, but refrained from lighting another one. Alanna would protest. He took a deep breath. "I understand Brian worked for that store for over fifteen years. Why didn't he climb the corporate ladder?"

"He told me once he liked running a store because he could go home each night, and not have to be on the road all the time," said Sam.

Fintan shot Alanna and Sam a look. "Do me a favor. Keep your ears open, and let me know if you hear anything. Even if it seems unimportant. Let me know what's being said around the store over the next few days. Ok?"

The women nodded in unison.

"Well, it's been a long day. I am going to go in and watch the game." Fintan stood and collected his stuff before heading back into the house.

"Yeah, I'm tired too," Nick said with a yawn. He stretched and stood up. "Come on, babe. Let's go home." He extended his hand to Sam to help her up.

"See ya in the morning," she said to Alanna as they walked back into the house.

Alanna remained outside, watching the stars come out. Ronan puffed away at his pipe. They sat for a while in companionable silence.

"He'll catch the killer, don't worry," Ronan said between puffs. "Your papa loves puzzles, and this is a whopper, but he'll solve it."

"I just hope he can find all the pieces. It bothers me that it might be someone I work with," Alanna replied, watching Jet pretend to stalk a deer from the other side of the ten-foot wall. "I don't know why anyone would do this."

"People do bad things all the time." He tapped his pipe on the ashtray, emptying the contents and putting it away. "In their minds they have reasons for what they do, reasons we'll probably never understand. If everyone understood each other there'd be no need for politics, war, shrinks or lawyers. Everyone would just agree and get along." He stood up and smiled down at her. "Wouldn't that be a wonderfully boring world to live in?" He leaned over and kissed the top of her head. "Goodnight, Pumpkin."

"Goodnight, Grandpa." She smiled up at him.

She sat outside for a while longer, thinking and watching the night sky.

Chapter 3

Alanna pulled into the parking lot of the store early Monday morning. She noticed Brian's parking spot had been roped off by upturned shopping carts with yellow police tape laced through the wheels. Already the murder site was surrounded in flowers, cards, candles, stuffed animals and balloons, all left by friends and coworkers who wanted to show how much Brian had meant to them. Alanna was touched when she saw a small boy leaving a bouquet of flowers while still holding his mother's hand. The mother crossed herself and bowed her head in prayer. Alanna recognized her as a cashier whom Brian had hired last Christmas.

Alanna passed a small group of cows standing at the fence, chewing their cud and watching the human activity with a typical bovine patience that made her smile. As she entered the store, she glanced at the newspaper rack by the door, where the glaring headline *BizMart Manager Killed on Eve of Holiday* jumped out at her in 24-point type.

Alanna walked through the crowded store to the employees' area, where the time clock and lockers were. Stuffing her purse into her locker, she made her way to the break room for the five minutes before her shift started. Sam was already sitting there at a table with two other coworkers. They were talking about the groups of people clustered throughout the store, obviously out of morbid curiosity rather than a need to shop.

"Hey, it's pretty busy out there, huh?" Alanna commented as she sat down next to Sam.

"Yeah but most of them are here to gossip and gawk, not shop."

"Yeah, people can be real vultures." Lorraine, one Alanna's friends, looked at her. "Do the police know anything new? The news and paper didn't give a lot of details."

Alanna had read the paper. The reporters were having a field day with the murder. In a quiet little town like Aurum, a grisly killing was going to be the news of the year.

She shook her head. "What's the word around here?"

Sam shrugged. "People are just saying how horrible it is, and how they feel for his family. I noticed a couple of people kind of broken up about it. Give it a day or two, though. You know how the grapevine is around here. There'll be all kinds of speculation by tomorrow morning."

"I heard we've got a temporary manager. Corporate sent him in this morning," Lorraine put in.

"That was fast."

"They want someone here to man the ship and keep us from running amok," Charlene, another one of Alanna's coworkers, said in a conspiratorial voice. "They say he's a real . . . well, let's just say he weeds out the slackers real quick."

"We're having a meeting right at seven," Lorraine said, finishing her coffee. "I guess we'll see what's up then."

A group of three men walked into the break room heading for the smoking area at the far end.

"Hey, Alex," Sam greeted one of them. "Met the new manager yet?"

"Yeah, he looks a little like Clint Eastwood. Acts like him too." Alex put his fingers on his hips like guns and walked bowlegged, whistling the theme from *The Good, the Bad and the Ugly*. The other two guys laughed as they closed the smoking room door behind them.

"Is that a good or bad thing?" Sam asked everyone at the table.

"I don't know, but *that* was ugly," Charlene snickered.

Alanna looked up at the clock and stood. "Well, time to go find out."

The others followed her out into the hallway. As they waited in line for a chance to punch the clock, an announcement came over the speakers asking for all available workers to report to the meeting room.

A few minutes later the entire morning shift was gathered in a room down the hall. A tall, thin man with reddish graying hair and mustache walked into the room flanked by two assistant managers. The assistants started the meeting off by assuring everyone that they were going to try to answer any questions that the employees might have. They announced that the police would be conducting interviews, which surprised no one. Once the funeral time was announced, they would post the details by the time clock and anyone who wanted to go would be allowed the time off from work.

Then the stranger stepped forward and introduced himself as Ed

Beckman, the temporary replacement store manager. His manner was sympathetic and understanding, but underneath the pleasant exterior was a very business-like persona. Any questions customers or reporters might have about what happened, he informed them, would need to be directed to management. He went on to tell the assembled employees that a grief counselor would be sent to the store soon to help employees deal with the trauma.

At that point Cecilia Collins, the store's accounting office manager, blew her nose theatrically and dabbed at her eyes with a silk handkerchief. Beckman's eyes briefly rested on the short woman before he went on to assure the assembled group that a fund would be set up to help Brian's family. After opening the floor to questions for five minutes, he closed the meeting, and the somber group dispersed to their respective jobs.

Alanna noticed that Cecilia was the last one to leave and walked over to her.

"Cecilia, are you ok?"

"No. I just can't believe he's gone! I mean, I thought I'd be all right, but then I went into his office this morning as usual to give him the sales reports and he . . . he wasn't there. That's when it really hit me that he . . . he's gone." She blew her nose loudly again, great tears running down her quivering cheeks.

"I know it's hard," Alanna said sympathetically, putting an arm around Cecilia's shoulders. "All we can do is to remember him and everything he did for us."

"Brian did so much for me. When this store opened he let me transfer here, which really helped me. I was going through my divorce at the time, and the move gave me a fresh start in a new town. He was a good man." She paused then intoned in a strident voice, "The heavens themselves blaze forth the death of princes."

"You and your Shakespeare, Cecilia." Alanna patted her shoulder as they walked down the hall. Cecilia quoted Shakespeare like some people quoted the Bible. "I'm sure they would let you go home for the day if you feel it's too difficult to be here."

"No, I'll be ok, I have a lot of work to do. And someone has to put on a brave face as an example to everyone else." She opened the door to the accounting office. "But thank you, Alanna. Your concern means the world."

Alanna turned to walk down the hall and spotted Beckman watching her from the doorway of the manager's office. His eyes rested on her face for a minute before he gave her a small nod and returned to the office.

A little unsettled, Alanna walked out to the jewelry counter to begin her day. She was in the process of getting watches out of a drawer to fill the empty spots in the showcase when she heard a sound behind her.

"Pssst!"

Startled, she spun around to find Dave the maintenance man standing by her counter, leaning against his dust mop. His hair stuck out at all angles, and his left eye wobbled in its socket before coming to rest looking somewhere off to Alanna's right.

"Morning, Dave," Alanna greeted him, recovering her composure.

Dave leaned across the counter, cupping a hand around his mouth to stage whisper in her ear, "I bet it was the CIA that offed Brian." He glanced around nervously.

Alanna sighed. Over the years she had listened to many of Dave's theories. Probably because she was one of the few people who still bothered to give him the time of day, he made a point of sharing all his conspiracy theories with her. "What makes you think that?"

"Well—" he leaned further in, close enough for her to see his whiskers trembling with excitement "—the news makes it sound all straightforward, but you and I know it was just a cover up. After all, the bugger took his cellphone." He glanced around quickly, lowering his voice even further. "That's how they track you."

"Don't all cellphones have GPS tracking nowadays?"

"Yeah, and that's why they wanted it back. So the police wouldn't find it. Wanted their equipment back. Can't let our local blues in on their dirty little secrets. I had to clean up that mess out there this morning. I wanted to take down the carts and police tape, but people had already left a lot of flowers and junk, so I just left it. But I cleaned the asphalt, new guy said it had to be done before we opened. He's CIA too . . . I can tell." He laid a finger against the side of his nose and winked at Alanna with his good eye. Then, spotting another employee over her shoulder, he started whistling and continued down the aisle with his dust mop.

Alanna had a chance to meet the replacement manager later on that day as Sam, leaning against her counter, filled her in on the gossip making the rounds. Beckman walked up behind her as she was sharing the tidbits she'd heard from her shoe associates.

"Hello there, I'm Ed." He extended a hand to Sam, who hastily straightened up, trying to look industrious.

"I'm Sam, Shoe Department Manager." She shook his hand.

He turned to Alanna who extracted her hand from the showcase. "Hi. I'm Alanna, Jewelry Department Manager." She shook his callused hand.

"If there is anything you ladies need, just let me know. I'll be getting together with all the department managers." He leveled a piercing look at them. "Meeting's tomorrow at one. Have a good day." He walked away, looking down at the papers in his hands and marking off their names from a list of employees. He wanted to introduce himself to each and every one of them individually so they knew that he, and the company cared.

Alanna spent the rest of the day fielding customers' questions and taking special orders. A little before her shift ended a familiar face showed up at her counter.

"Hello, Alanna," Detective Mark Holmberg greeted her. He'd always thought the Chief's green-eyed, red-haired daughter was a real looker. Fintan always joked that if Holmberg had been younger and a single man he might have let the detective date his daughter . . . with appropriate supervision, of course. And no handcuffs allowed.

"Hello, Mark. Anything new?" She knew he wouldn't tell her anything but she asked anyway.

"Not yet. We're going to start interviewing workers. Anyone in particular I should start with?" He gave her a half smile. He had worked with her father for years and the two men shared a respect born of hard work and enthusiasm for their jobs.

"Yeah, there's a really weird one over there." Alanna pointed across the aisle at Sam, who was straightening some shoe boxes on a shelf. "Watch out. That one's pretty hostile."

Mark waved at Sam, who waved back. "She looks vicious. I heard she and Nick Hayman got engaged."

"Yeah, they're really happy."

"Know where I can find someone in charge?" Holmberg glanced around.

"I'll get Mr. Beckman for you. He's our temporary manager." She picked up the phone and made a call.

Beckman showed up at the counter in less than two minutes. "Ed Beckman," he said, shaking the detective's hand. "Chief MacLachlin said you'd be coming."

The temporary manager suddenly whipped around to look at Alanna. "MacLachlin. Any relation?"

"My dad."

Holmberg smiled at her over the manager's shoulder. "And definitely one half of where she gets her smarts."

Beckman turned back to the detective, but not before giving Alanna a long, evaluating look. As the two men walked back to his office, Alanna reflected that the temporary manager was just as intrigued by the small-town happenings as any of the native Aurumites. And, she'd wager, just as sharp as any of its uniformed problem solvers.

That afternoon after work, Alanna stopped by the fence bounding the nearby cow pasture. She held her cellphone to her ear in case any customers or employees were watching. She'd noticed the cows before, but Nemesis' comment about them yesterday had sparked her interest. She thought it just possible that the herd might have seen or heard something.

The cows were lying in the shade of the trees that ran along the fence.

"Hello," she said to the herd in general, leaning against the fence.

The cow closest to her looked over at her. "*Look. That silly human is talking at us.*"

"*She must be lonely,*" another cow opined.

"I'm not lonely. I just wanted to say hello," Alanna corrected them.

They all stopped chewing in unison and stared at her.

"*Can you hear us, or was that a lucky guess?*" the first cow asked, tilting her head.

"I can understand you." Alanna smiled.

"*Really?*" The cow slowly got up and walked to the fence. "*Then could you please get those dandelions over there for me? I just love dandelions.*"

"Sure." Alanna walked over and picked the five dandelions growing between the trees. She passed them through the fence, where the cow used her long, rough tongue to swipe them from her hand. "*Thank you. Dandelions are so good!*"

"*Beth, you shouldn't eat those. They give you gas.*" The other cow giggled.

"*Shut up, Lois! So does everything else. And here humans think that there's a gas shortage! Gas shortage, my ass!*"

"*Definitely not there!*" Lois laughed. The whole herd laughed, Alanna chuckling with them.

"So were you ladies here by chance when the human was shot?" Alanna spotted a few more dandelions and gave them to Beth.

"Yes." Beth said between bites. *"We were sleeping right over there when the bang woke us. We ran towards the barn, but the gate was up and we couldn't get to it."*

"Then that giant bee came after us," Lois reminded her.

"Don't pay any attention to Lois. She's banged her head against one too many fence posts, if you know what I mean," Beth stage whispered to Alanna.

"Shut up, Beth!" Lois got up and came to the fence. *"There* was *a giant bee!"* The rest of the herd murmured amongst themselves. A couple of them giggled. *"There was! I swear!"* Lois turned her head toward one of the other cows. *"You believe me, don't you Grace?"* Beth looked at Grace then swished her tail and looked up at the sky.

"Well . . . I was really frightened, and there was a lot of confusion. I couldn't say for sure." Grace continued to chew her cud slowly.

"I did hear a really big bee!" Lois turned back to Alanna. *"It came out of those trees and flew towards that hill. It was really big and loud."*

Alanna looked over at the large hill on the other side of the highway and mentally noted the trees the cow was talking about.

"Did you hear anything else?"

"Yes, Iris tripped in a rabbit hole when we were running, and fell down." Lois looked over at one of the other cows. *"She used really bad words when it happened."*

"Bees don't fly at night, Lois!" Iris yelled. *"So the only buzzing you heard was in your head."*

"Was not!"

"Was, too!" three of the cows said together.

"Well, I know what I heard!" Lois stormed off away from the herd, twitching her tail angrily as she went. *"I know what I heard."*

Alanna watched Lois trot off towards the barn. "Did any of you see or hear anything else?"

"It was dark and when we get startled we just run and follow the leader," Grace said. *"By the way, Iris, you should really try to stay on the path when you run."*

"IT WAS DARK!" Iris bellowed. *"I didn't let the stupid rabbits in the pasture. Good thing we're vegetarians, that's all I can say."*

The herd giggled.

"Ok. Thank you, ladies. I guess I should be going." Alanna turned to leave, concealing a grin.

"*Stop by and say hello again anytime,*" Beth called after her. "*Dandelions pop up every day.*"

"I will. Thanks again."

"*She's lonely,*" Iris remarked to the herd.

"*Well, good bulls* are *hard to come by,*" Grace replied.

"*Mm-hmm,*" chorused the herd.

Chapter 4

Alanna pulled through the iron gate of Treasure Grove and Jet came running out to meet her. She parked in the garage and got out, reaching down to rub Jet's ears.

"Mom, I'm glad you're home. Did they find who did it? Do they know who killed him and why?"

"No, they're still looking. Mark came in today and interviewed a bunch of people."

"Did he interview you?"

"No, he didn't say much to me."

They walked into the house to find Abbey sitting on top of the refrigerator watching Emma make dinner.

"Hey, Emma."

"Hello, how were things at work?"

"Busy."

"I'm not surprised. People are usually that way, wanting to look around and speculate."

"Hi, Mommy, Emma's making chicken!" Abbey said, licking her whiskers.

Alanna reached up, grabbing Abbey gently. "Hello, baby." She petted Abbey as she snuggled her, listening to her purr. "Did you have a good day?"

"It was ok," Emma said. "The upstairs toilet in your father's bathroom keeps running."

"It wasn't my fault. I didn't do anything." Abbey looked Alanna in the eyes.

"I called Nick. He's going to come take a look at it." Emma put the chicken in the oven and washed her hands.

"I'm going to go change." Alanna walked upstairs to her room. She sat Abbey down on the bed next to Jet who had jumped up on it, wagging her tail.

"Are you going to go for a run today?" Jet asked hopefully.

Alanna changed into jeans and a T-shirt. "No, I think I'll relax a little and read."

"Will you read to me?" Abbey asked. *"I like it when you read and sing to me."*

"Yes, I'll read to you, but it has to be what I want to read and not *Cat in the Hat*."

Downstairs in the den Alanna picked up the book she'd been reading. Juneau was watching a show on the nature channel lying on Fintan's easy chair with one paw close to the large-buttoned remote. She looked up at Alanna as she reached down to pet her and scratch her under her chin. "Hello, Juneau."

"Mother, did you know that porcupines have been known to chew on automobile tires and wiring because they crave the salt that gets coated on them from rock salt? Also, they don't shoot their quills at predators, they back themselves into the predator and more or less stab and hook their quills into them."

"I didn't know that." Some might think Juneau's television and reading habits unusual, but to Alanna it was just part of everyday life. So was being called Mother by her four-legged brood. She had rescued each of them when they were merely weeks old and each one had imprinted her as their adoptive mother. She liked being called Mother by them and she loved them like they were her own children.

"I knew that," Jet said. *"Not the thing about the salt, but the thing about the quills."*

"What is pork pine?" Abbey asked.

"It's an animal that has sharp pointy things on its butt and it's not anything you want to make mad," Jet told Abbey.

"Do we have pork pines?"

"I've never seen one." Jet looked up at Alanna. *"Are there porcupines around here?"*

"I've never heard of any being around this area, but I'll ask Uncle Justice when I see him."

Alanna took her book out to the back patio, opened it and began to read aloud. After a few minutes Abbey laid her head down. In five minutes Alanna stopped reading aloud because Abbey was asleep. Emma came outside and set a glass of iced tea down on the table next to Alanna.

"Thank you, you read my mind."

"Dinner will be ready in about an hour and a half. I'm going upstairs to do some dusting. If Nick shows up just let him know I jiggled the handle and it didn't help."

The sky was bright and clear, and the sun was wonderfully warm. Alanna took a deep breath. The air was extremely fragrant with the woods and flowers. In the wintertime the air was always heavy with the smell of wood-burning stoves and fireplaces, but in the spring it was blissfully mesmerizing. She read for a little while longer until Jet jumped up and ran around to the front of the house.

"Nick!"

A few minutes later Nick came walking through the patio doors with his toolbox in hand.

"Hey, Alanna," he said, setting his toolbox down on the ground. "Emma called about the upstairs toilet running."

"Yeah, in Dad's bathroom," she said setting her book down on the table. Abbey woke up and jumped on the table stretching and arching her back. "She doesn't know what caused it. This is like the fifth time this has happened."

Nick lifted his baseball cap, running his fingers through his hair. "I'll check it out."

"How was your day?" she asked him.

"Dad got in a whole shipment of water heaters he didn't order. He's not happy; and I'm not happy either. I had to find room in the warehouse for them until we can ship them back. But, if I know Dad he'll yell and scream and they'll give him a good deal, and then next month we will have a big water heater sale." Nick's father owned Hayman Hardware. "Do you need a new water heater?" He smiled, knowing she didn't.

"You know I don't." Alanna laughed. She didn't have a water heater. Her great-grandfather had been an amateur inventor and there were all kinds of things around the house that were a bit unconventional, but worked really well on either solar, air, gas or water.

Her Uncle Nevin was the only one that could fix the things if they had problems. He had gotten the inventing bug too and her home's hot water came from a box in the basement that heated it as it flowed through the pipe going through the box. Gramps had blown two holes in the side of the barn before he had perfected the gadget. Grams told him to heat the water in the barn first and if it worked for a year without burning it down then he could put one in the house. The barn never burned down, and they had an endless supply of hot water. Alanna didn't have a clue how it worked and she didn't want to, but Nick was fascinated by the strange gadgets in her home and worked in conjunction with Nevin to learn about all of them.

Nick picked up his toolbox and headed into the house, Abbey following him. Alanna continued to read, trying to tune out the chattering of the birds in the trees around her. She put her book down when she was distracted by a group of agitated tiny voices.

"You're pushing!"

"Stop hogging it all!"

"My turn!"

"Stop touching me!"

"Get your butt over!"

"Hey, you slobbered everywhere!"

It sounded to her like a bunch of elementary kids. She stood up and walked around the corner of the house. There, hanging on the eaves was a hummingbird feeder that was almost empty, and about twenty hummingbirds were jarring to get to the four feed slots. She went a little further down the walk to another hummingbird feeder that was completely empty. She lifted it off its hook and carried it into the house. She was in the process of cleaning and refilling the feeder when she heard Nick yell.

"ALANNA!"

She started to run upstairs, hands still wet, when she intercepted Abbey running down the stairs with a shiny new toilet chain and hook clenched in her jaws.

"Treasure!" Abbey tried to slip past Alanna but she reached down, trying to hold onto the cat as she squirmed.

"Abbey!" Alanna tugged on the chain. "What are you doing?"

"Mine!"

"It's not yours." Alanna gently removed it from her mouth. "Nick has to have this, it's not a toy." She sat Abbey down, climbing the rest of the way up the stairs. Nick was in the hallway holding a pair of pliers.

"All I saw was the chain and her tail disappear out the door. Little sneak!"

"Sorry," Alanna smiled. "She loves shiny things." Abbey rubbed against Alanna's legs.

"That was mine! I want it back!"

"You can't have it. He needs it."

"I need it!" Abbey meowed.

Nick looked down at Abbey, shaking the chain. "If you want one I'll bring you another one, but I need this one." He went back into Fintan's bathroom and Abbey followed him.

"When? Want one now!" she meowed loudly.

Alanna went back downstairs and finished filling the

hummingbird feeder. She carried it outside and hung it to joyful cries. *"Yippy! Yahoo!"*

Nick came down a little while later to find Alanna on her laptop at the kitchen table. "Ok, I think I fixed it." He sat his toolbox down taking a seat. "The chain was too short and kept getting hung up, and I think one of your animals is flushing the toilet just to watch the water." He looked down at Jet and then at Abbey.

"Wasn't me." Jet said. *"I don't drink out of toilets, and don't imply that I do. That's just nasty."*

"What is flush?" Abbey asked, tilting her head up at Jet.

"You might think about having someone look at the floor around that toilet. The tile is cracked and chipping around the base, and there are also a couple of them in front of the shower."

"Great. If it's not one thing, it's three. Well, thanks for coming out and taking care of this. You know where to send the bill."

"You're welcome. How was work today?"

"Really busy. We got a new temporary manager, but I know the rumors will start soon."

"From what Sam says about the rumor mill in that place there'll be talk before the day's out."

"It's true. If you say something when you walk in the front door it'll get to the back before you do."

"I'm sure people have their own opinions on what happened."

"Opinions and theories don't make fact."

"Spoken like a true cop's daughter."

"Yeah, yeah."

"Well, I've gotta get home to the little woman," Nick said, standing and picking up his toolbox.

"Listen to you sounding all domestic."

"I'm surprised my phone hasn't rung yet," he said, looking down at the cellphone clipped to his belt.

"Well, I have it on good authority that you're being made a special dinner tonight."

"Oh goodie . . . mac and cheese and hotdogs!"

"Hey, she does what she's good at."

"Just please don't let her try to broil anything again." He looked up toward the sky.

"I remember that night, Filet Mignon à la hockey puck." She laughed.

He turned to leave. "Say, do you want me to get hold of Atherton Flooring to fix that tile?"

"Might as well."

"I'll call and get them out here." Nick started to walk away.

"Ok, thanks. Have a good evening."

"You too."

She screamed as the car went over the side of the cliff, raising her arms and covering her face as the tree branches burst through the side windows and the windshield. She screamed again as her flesh became slashed and bloody. There was so much pain and terror streaming through her.

"Mom! Mom!"

Alanna sat up in bed waking as she came upright, throwing her arms up over her face in an involuntary reaction to the last images in her mind.

"Mom! Wake up!" Jet barked. *"Wake up!"*

Alanna put her arms around Jet who was sitting next to her. She hugged Jet while trying to calm herself. She was still shaking as fear lingered in her nerves.

"It's ok, Mom. It was just a dream." Jet put her head down against Alanna's shoulder, hugging her back with her muzzle.

"Mommy?" Abbey stood up on the pillow next to them. *"You ok?"*

"No, she's not ok," Juneau announced angrily, pulling her head down into her paws and covering her ears. *"If she was ok we'd still be sleeping."*

Fintan appeared silhouetted in the doorway. "Are you all right?"

"Yeah, just the same stupid dream again." She let go of Jet, pushing her way out of the bed and going into the adjoining bathroom to get a cold, wet washcloth.

"I'm worried about you. This is the sixth time you've had this nightmare. I think you need to talk to someone about it." He leaned on the doorframe, rubbing his tired eyes. "If your mom were here she'd know what to do, but all I can say is that you need to make an appointment and talk to someone. I don't know how to protect you from these nightmares."

"I'm fine, it's just a dream." She rubbed the washcloth over her face and neck.

"Alanna, promise me you'll talk to someone." The stern look he gave her was illuminated by the bathroom light before she flicked it off.

"Ok, ok." She sat down on the bed. "I don't like them either."

"Now, go back to bed. It's late, or early depending on how you look at it." He turned, running his hand over his groggy face.

She held the cloth to her face and mumbled. "Sorry, Dad."

He stopped in the hallway out of her view. As a father he only wanted to protect her, but he knew she couldn't help what was happing to her. "I love you," he said softly.

"I love you too." She lay down next to Jet and Abbey, holding and petting them until she fell asleep.

On Tuesday Alanna went to work and the grapevine gossips had started, with "Well, I heard Brian . . . (then whatever they wanted to start a rumor about)." There was also a notice about the funeral which was going to be on Thursday in Lodi. Sam and Alanna signed up to be off that day for the funeral. Sam saw it as an opportunity to shop and get ideas for the wedding. Alanna saw it as an opportunity to pay her respects and maybe get information about Brian from his old store. Sam also wanted to visit her grandmother who was in a nursing home in Lodi.

Her work day went by quickly, and on her way home from work she stopped by Atherton Bookstore. It was the only bookstore in town and it was located in the Gaslight District, a section of town that was ten blocks long and one block wide. It was the oldest part of town and most of the buildings had been built from 1849 to 1851 during the gold rush. It emanated heritage and historic charm. Large hitching posts still sat outside the store fronts along the red brick street. There were wooden planked sidewalks and verandas on each building to add to the allure. The Historic Society went to great lengths to maintain the look and feel of the era in which the town was built. From ten in the morning until five in the evening, dozens of tourists covered the sidewalks and browsed at the shops which were mostly antiques, art, clothing, crafts and gifts, as well as jewelers and Native American hand-crafted works. Each store was unique and as it was only four blocks from the docks of Lake Oro, tourists swarmed in at weekends and holidays. Wives shopped while husbands fished.

Alanna found a space not too far from the bookstore, parked and fed the meter. She went into the store and found Mr. Atherton ringing up a customer's purchase. She smiled and waved as he smiled back, continuing through the store until she found the section she was looking for.

"Have anything to eat?" the very rotund long-haired black cat with green eyes asked from the top of the bookshelf behind her. His

overly fluffy tail was dusting the book spines below him. She ignored Spook when she saw Mr. Atherton come up the aisle to find her. She only let those closest to her know of her ability to hear animals speak, but it was hard not to react sometimes. Especially if an animal was hurt or scared.

"Hello, Alanna." He'd known her since she was a small child as this had been a favorite haunt of her mother's.

"Hey, Mr. A. I need a wedding planner."

"Ah, yes, I heard about your friends on TV." He smiled and reached to a high shelf. He was very tall, almost six-five. "You will also need this." He handed her a book on how to be the best maid of honor. She smiled as she thumbed through it.

"Yes, I think I will." She looked over the other books he was pulling off the shelf. There were all kinds of different wedding planners. She chose one that looked like a school notebook and had pockets for all kinds of samples and things. She handed him back the books and followed him to the register. Spook stood, stretched and followed them along the top of the bookshelves. Walking across specially installed boards from section to section he got to the built-in shelves behind the register, where he became an animated bookend.

"Sad to hear about your employer."

"I feel for his family." She handed him her card.

"It's always hardest on the children."

"How's Mrs. A and your kids?"

"They're good. The Missus still wants to sell both businesses and move to Florida."

"Why Florida?"

"Her sister and brother live there. They keep telling her how wonderful it is."

"And you, do you want to move to Florida?" She took the bag he handed her.

"I'd miss it here, and most of my most of my family's here." He sighed. "All our kids live close to here. I want to stay close to them, but her sister's all the family she has left, and she says we'll never retire if we don't move."

Alanna smiled "Have you ever been to Florida?"

"Yes, we've flown there a few times. It's nice . . . warm, very humid, but nice."

"Well, I hope you don't decide to move. The bookstore wouldn't be the same without you."

"That's nice of you to say." He smiled and waved as she started to open the door. "Have a good day."

"You too." She closed the door behind her then noticed Aunt Vi sitting at one of the small bistro tables at the café next door. She was reading the newspaper. Alanna walked over and sat down in the chair opposite Vi.

"Hello, love," Vi said from behind the wall of newspaper. "I understand you're not sleeping well."

Alanna put her bag on the table. "Did Dad talk to you?"

Vi put the newspaper down. "No, should he have?" She peered at Alanna over the rim of her reading glasses.

"I've been having nightmares."

"Umhmm." Vi took her glasses off, letting them fall to the end of the chain that hung from around her neck. "And what have these images revealed to you?"

Alanna took a deep breath. "Death."

"Are you certain? Are you sure you're seeing everything that the dream has to offer?"

"It all happens so fast. I don't have time to really see anything. It's so frightening."

"Is it the same dream over and over?"

"Yes, it's always the same."

"Then you're not looking at it right."

"How else can I look at it? I'm behind the wheel of a speeding car, it's raining and I go over a cliff." Alanna leaned forward. "I'm scared," she admitted softly.

Vi patted Alanna's hand. "Now, now, do not fear . . . Auntie Vi's here." She smiled.

Just then a young boy and his mother walked by, and the boy pointed at Vi and said "She's a witch, isn't she, Mommy? Adam said she was a witch."

"Billy!" The woman's eyes were wide with embarrassment. "You shouldn't say those kinds of things!" The woman grabbed the boy by the shoulder. "I'm so sorry."

Billy stared at Vi who sat up straight, smiling a very malicious smile. She pointed one long, well-manicured finger at Billy, and in a growling English accented voice said, "A pox on you, young William Hogat. A pox on you!" with an evil laugh.

The woman let out a small scream. "Oh, heavens!" She grabbed Billy, and ran to her car as quickly as she could while not looking back.

"You know, you don't help people's view of you by doing things like that," Alanna scolded her aunt.

Vi gave a devious smile then giggled. "That was funny." Then she laughed out loud, pleased with herself until she noticed the look on Alanna's face. "Oh, come now, Alanna. People are going to believe whatever they want."

"We have to live here you know."

"Did you not notice the small red marks on the boy's face and neck? He obviously has the start of chicken pox. His mother just hasn't noticed yet."

"And when he wakes up tomorrow with a full-blown case of chicken pox who do you think they're going to blame?"

Vi chuckled. "The little girl next door?"

"You're fueling the fire and if we weren't in the twenty-first century, they would be gathering wood right now for your burning."

"Yes, yes, yes. Now where were we? Ah, yes . . . your dream. You need to get a different perception of the things around you in the dream and what they mean. Next time, look around and see where you are, what's around you. Don't focus on the accident. Focus on the things around you."

"But it all happens so fast."

Vi reached into her pocket and handed her a small yellow velvet sachet and a plastic bag of what appeared to be tea leaves. "Here, take these. Put the root bag under your pillow and drink the tea before bed. Make sure you drink it all."

"And this will do what?"

"It will help, dear. It will help." Vi reached over and gave Alanna a pat on the hand and then stood. "I must get back to the store. Oh, and give this to your father . . . he'll need it." She handed her a small insulated lunch bag that had been sitting on the table by the newspaper.

"Ok."

And with that Vi walked directly across the street to her store, The Mystic Eye.

Alanna looked into the lunch bag. In it was a bag of frozen peas, still frozen. She grabbed her shopping and headed home.

When she pulled up to the house she noticed an unfamiliar truck parked by the garage, and a tile saw and other tools around the open garage door. Jet had not come out to meet her. As she entered the house, she heard noise coming from upstairs and Fintan was sitting at the kitchen table.

"Hi, how was your day?" Fintan said looking up from the papers in front of him.

"Fine. What's going on upstairs?"

"They're fixing the tile in the bathroom."

"That was fast. Where're the girls?"

"They're all upstairs watching."

"Here, Aunt Vi sent this to you." She handed the lunch bag to him. He opened it and looked inside.

"How'd she know . . . never mind." He took the frozen peas and pressed them to the large red goose egg on the side of his temple.

"What happened? Did you hit your head?" Alanna stepped forward to examine his injury.

"Yeah, about five minutes ago I was getting a cup of coffee and forgot to close the cabinet door. Ran right into the corner of it." He closed his right eye, leaning into the frozen peas. "It smarts. Right on the temple. I'm glad you're home."

"Me too, I'm tired." She sat down looking at the paperwork in front of him. "Anything new?"

"Not yet. Anything happen at work?"

"The 'I heards' are going around."

"Anything noteworthy?"

"Not really. Nothing I'd put stock in anyway. I'm going to go change." When she reached the top of the stairs she saw Jet, Abbey, and Juneau all lying by her father's bedroom door.

"Hi, Mom." Jet said, running over.

"Mommy, they're tearin' stuff up." Abbey rubbed against her legs. *"And makin' a mess."*

Juneau stood up and stretched. *"Good you're here. These men are very noisy and one of them smells. You should make them leave. Now!"*

"Hello, ladies." Alanna reached down to pet Jet and Juneau, and picked up Abbey.

She went into her room, closed the door and changed, then walked back into Fintan's room to take a look at what was going on. The toilet had been removed and temporally placed in the shower stall while they laid a new section of tile where it usually sat.

"Hello," she said to the two men kneeling on the floor in the bathroom as they both looked up at her.

"Hello," they both said.

She recognized one of them as Derek Atherton. His father owned Atherton Flooring, and his uncle, Roger, owned the bookstore. She'd been two years behind Derek in school and remembered he'd been on their high school football team.

Derek leaned back, looking around at the new tile in front of him. His long, dark blond hair was pulled back into a ponytail. He looked up and something flicked behind his eyes as their eyes met for a second, then he looked quickly away as if not wanting to reveal what it was.

"We'll be done here in a few minutes," he said. "We replaced seven tiles. You had extras in the barn, so the match is fairly good. They'll have to set up overnight. Then I'll come back tomorrow and grout them. Once that dries I'll reset the toilet."

"It's fine. Dad can use the hall bathroom for now." She leaned in the doorway, looking at the tiles.

Juneau was right. Derek's helper smelled strongly of body odor. "Looks good, thank you for getting to it so fast."

Derek continued to work. "Things were kind of slow today. Nick called just at the right time." He glanced over by Alanna's feet and noticed Abbey sitting there. "That little one there keeps stealing our tile spacers." He held up a small piece of plastic in the shape of a cross. "So if you find them around, you'll know why." He risked a brief smile at her. He'd been captivated by Alanna since he'd seen her at the county fair, but she was from a wealthy and prominent family and he was just a flooring contractor.

"Abbey!" She looked down at the spot where Abbey had been but she was now gone. "Sorry, she's a kleptocat."

"My dog does that kind of thing too." He kept on working but glanced at her with interest.

She turned to leave. "Thanks again."

"You're welcome," Derek answered, watching her go and sighing as his attention was lost for a second.

Alanna walked down the hall and saw Abbey hiding beside a chest. "You little thief."

"What is thief?" Abbey watched Alanna go downstairs. Jet and Juneau stayed by the doorway.

Derek's helper looked over at the doorway Alanna had just vacated. "Wow, she's really pretty."

Derek glanced over his shoulder. "Yeah, she's one of the best lookin' women in town."

Barry ran a hand over his dirty hair. "Sooo . . . you think I'd have a shot?"

Derek laughed. "Go for it, if you think you're all that."

"I wonder if she's dating anyone."

Juneau and Jet overheard this and Jet ran down the hall to find Abbey. *"Go tell Mom that they're talking about her."*

Abbey perked up. *"What'd they say?"*

"That they think she's real pretty, and wonder if she's dating anyone."

Abbey ran downstairs as fast as she could and found Alanna sitting at the table opening her mail.

"Mommy, those men think you're pretty and want to know if you're hating anyone." Alanna stopped opening the letter and looked down to see Abbey turn and run back upstairs as fast as her swift little feet would go. Abbey got back to the top and Jet was there waiting for her. *"The smelly one wants to know if she likes wrestling because he has tickets."*

Abbey sailed back downstairs, jumping up on the chair by Alanna. *"The smelly one wants to know if you like to wrestle and he has ticks."* She jumped down, running back upstairs as Fintan looked over at Alanna.

"What's going on?" he asked, watching Abbey take off back upstairs.

"I don't know. They're relaying messages to me, but I think Abbey's getting it wrong. At least I hope she is."

Jet met Abbey at the top of the stairs. *"He thinks she is out of his league."*

Abbey ran back down jumped on the table in front of her.

"He thinks you're out of beans."

"Ok, stop. That's enough."

"Don't you want to know what they are saying?"

"If they want me to know they'll come and talk to me."

Just then Jet ran downstairs and looked up at Alanna. *"They're coming!"*

Derek and Barry came down the stairs carrying tools and a large trash can. Barry glanced sheepishly at Alanna then continued on out the door. Derek stopped by the door. "I'll be back in the morning to grout the tile, then that will have to set for at least twenty four hours."

Fintan glanced over. "Ok, Emma will be here to let you in. Thanks, Derek."

Juneau came lazily down the stairs. At the bottom she sat down and sneezed, and sneezed again. *"Dog lover."* She glared at Derek.

Jet looked over at her. *"What's wrong with that?"*

"He isn't intelligent enough to have a cat."

"Having a dog is better." Jet wagged her tail.

"Cats are better, always will be." She got up and walked towards her water dish. Jet raced over, getting between her and the dish.

"Dogs are better." Jet lowered her head, letting out a little growl.

"Cats!" Juneau hissed.

"Dogs!" Jet barked. Juneau swiped at Jet, then ran out the back door, Jet running after her.

"Looks like they don't get along so well," Derek said, watching them run out.

"Sometimes they fight like cats and dogs, and other times they act like best friends," Alanna said, watching Abbey jump off the chair to run after them. "Just depends on their mood I guess."

"My dog only has only one mood and that's stubborn." He smiled and hesitated a moment like he wanted to say something but didn't. "Well, have a good evening." He left, carrying his tools.

She watched him leave, wondering if he had been the one that thought she was pretty. She'd never really taken a good look at him until now. He was tall, very handsome and built really well. She shook her head, dispersing any thoughts like that and continued to open her mail. "I talked to Aunt Vi about my dreams."

Fintan looked up from the paper in his hand. "What'd she say?"

"That I'm not getting the message that the dream is sending."

He sighed. "Your Aunt Vi is . . . unique."

"Yes, she is."

That evening Fintan and Alanna had a wonderful dinner of pot roast, roasted potatoes and carrots that Emma had prepared. Jet, Juneau and Abbey enjoyed it also. Later that night Alanna was getting ready for bed when she remembered the tea and root bag Vi had given her.

She made the tea and fetched the root bag.

"Smells funny." Abbey sniffed the bag as Alanna placed it under her pillow.

"She says it'll help. This tea tastes bitter." Alanna forced herself to swallow the contents of the cup.

That night the dream came but it came in slow motion.

***

She saw the rain splat drop by drop on the windshield. She saw the headlights reflect on the wet, slick road in front of her, and the slow beat of the flashing yellow light. She looked in the rearview mirror. Light reflected into her eyes, blinding her for a second. She closed her eyes.

When she opened them she wasn't in the driver's seat she was in the passenger's seat. She turned to the driver. It wasn't her! It was a woman with blond hair and brown eyes. She was crying, tears and mascara running down her cheeks. Alanna didn't recognize her. The car skidded off the road. Branches began to crash through the windows. The woman threw her hands and arms up to cover her face. Alanna looked around at the car and the woman. It was a sporty car, tiny, foreign maybe? In the distance Alanna heard a beeping sound. She looked down just as the car began to flip. The woman's handbag flew past Alanna into the backseat. There was that beeping again. It sounded oddly familiar. Branches and glass slashed as blood began to cover the woman from the cuts she was getting. More beeping. What was that? Alanna felt a weight on her stomach as the roof of the car was torn apart by the trees. The beeping grew louder and louder.

Alanna opened her eyes, slowly adjusting them as she felt and heard Emma.

"Alanna, your alarm's been going off for twenty minutes. You're going to be late for work." Emma gently shook her. Alanna tried to sit up . . . so not a good idea. Her head pounded and she dropped back down onto her pillow.

"Alanna? Are you all right? Don't you feel well?" Emma leaned over the bed, feeling Alanna's forehead. "You're not running a fever."

The room was spinning as Alanna closed her eyes. She started to slip back to sleep.

"Alanna!" Emma leaned over her. "Answer me, are you ill?"

She slowly opened her eyes. Emma looked closer than she was and very distorted. She blinked. "I . . . don't know."

"Are you drunk?" Emma pushed her eyelids up looking into her eyes. "You're acting like you're drunk."

"I don't think so."

Emma picked up the cup beside the bed and sniffed it. "I'll go get you some coffee."

Alanna slowly sat up, putting her face into her cupped hands. She separated her fingers a little. The room was still distorted and swaying slowly like a gentle wave.

"Mommy, I tried to wake you." Abbey sat on the bed next to her.

"Thanks." She tried to get out of bed but sat back down. Gravity was very strong right now, too strong. She just wanted to go back to sleep.

Emma walked into the room with a cup of coffee. Alanna was slumped on the side of the bed, sound asleep.

"Alanna!" Emma set the cup down on the table. "Child, you need to wake up."

"I know." Alanna awoke with a jolt trying to sit up. "I'm just so sleepy."

"Should I get your father?" Emma said with concern.

"No." Alanna stood trying to walk cautiously to the bathroom. "I'm up, I'm up."

She leaned against the counter by the sink trying to focus on her swimming image in the mirror. Emma placed the cup of coffee in her hands. "Here, maybe this will help."

"Thanks." She took a sip. "I need a shower."

"Are you going to be ok?" Emma placed a gentle, concerned hand on her shoulder.

"Yeah, I just need to wake up."

Emma left and continued making breakfast. She would stare at the ceiling every once in a while, listening to the sounds coming from upstairs. Twenty minutes later Alanna came downstairs. She was showered and sloppily dressed for work. Her hair was pulled back into a wet ponytail which was not normal. She took a seat at the table and Emma refilled the cup in her hand. Fintan folded the newspaper, noticing her disheveled appearance. "You look sick, what's wrong?"

"I drank some tea Aunt Vi gave me to help me sleep. I think it was a little too strong."

Emma noisily dropped a pan into the sink. "That Vi! I should've known." Emma set a plate of bacon and eggs and toast in front of Alanna. "Here, eat something."

"Well, it worked." Alanna said taking a bite of toast. "I feel kind of strange and I had a hard time waking up but I slept really well. I had that dream again but it wasn't me driving the car. It was some woman I've never seen before." She smiled slightly.

Fintan's brow wrinkled. "Let me get this straight. Your aunt drugged you, you have a hangover and you're happy about it?"

Alanna shrugged. "Yeah."

Chapter 5

Wednesday morning was hard on Alanna. She got to work on time, but just barely. Sam was the first to inform her that she looked like something the cat had dragged in. She told Sam the truth, but everyone else that asked was told that her hairdryer had broken. She bought a new one after work just for appearance's sake.

That day Mr. Beckman fired two people: one for stealing and the other for using foul language on the sales floor, which provoked the worker to curse and yell obscenities all the way out the front doors as he left for the last time. Mr. Beckman turned and told the customers not to pay any attention, it was just that the man suffered from Tourette's syndrome. One customer wanted to know if it was contagious.

Cecilia reminded Sam and Alanna that she was having a ladies' game night at her house on Friday. Alanna told Sam she would pick her up in the morning around nine. It was at least an hour's drive to Lodi.

After work Alanna got into her SUV and drove downtown to Aunt Vi's shop. The Mystic Eye was directly across the street from the Atherton Bookstore. Alanna parked as close as she could and fed the meter. She walked into the shop, noticing her cousin Jenae sitting behind the counter on a stool, reading a book.

"Hey, Jenae." Alanna stepped up to the counter.

"Hey, cuz." Jenae set her book down.

"Is Auntie around?" Alanna leaned over the showcase in front of her, looking at the rings on display.

"Nope, she's gone to get her hair done, but she told me to give you this." Jenae reached to the shelf behind her and grabbed a plastic bag with more tea in it. She handed it to Alanna. "Mom said to only put only two teaspoons into eight ounces of water and if you wake up with a headache, use a cucumber."

"Eat a cucumber?"

"No. Put the peel to your forehead. It helps relieve the pain."

"Ok, anything else?"

"Yeah, she wanted to know, and I quote, what was revealed to you?"

"It wasn't me behind the wheel of the car."

"Well, that's good, isn't it?"

"Yeah, but I don't recognize the woman . . . haven't got a clue who she is."

"At least you know it's not you in danger."

"Yeah." Alanna turned to leave. "Tell her 'thanks' for me."

"No problem." Jenae stood up as two ladies walked into the shop and started to look around, and Alanna left the shop for home.

Alanna arrived home knowing it was Emma's night off this week. She and her father usually went out to eat on those nights. It was what they considered father-daughter time.

She walked into the house with Jet at her heels.

"Hi, Mom. Did you have a good day?" Jet wagged her tail. *"Did ya? Did ya?"*

"My day was really long, and I'm tired." Alanna said with a sigh as she reached down to pet Jet.

"Mine too," Fintan said, sitting at the kitchen table, papers in hand.

"Anything new?" Alanna thumbed through the mail on the counter.

"Not yet. Still turning over stones and seein' what scatters."

Just then Abbey ran into the room. *"Mommy! You're home. Play with me!"* She rubbed against Alanna's legs.

"Hello, baby." She picked her up, scratching her under the chin.

"Derek came and finished the tile in the bathroom this afternoon."

"How's it look?"

"Good."

"Mulligan's tonight?" Alanna asked, sitting down at the table and placing Abbey in her lap.

"Yeah, about that." Fintan shifted in his seat. "I'm not gonna be able to go tonight. I have a meeting."

"Ok, I'll stay home and we'll just eat something here."

"Order pizza!" Jet said anxiously *"Pleeease?"*

"Pizza? Yuck, I hate pizza." Abbey said, pushing her ears under Alanna's scratching hand.

"Or, maybe I'll order a pizza." She smiled down at Jet. "I'm really tired."

"Yes! Yes!" Jet jumped up running over to the counter where the phone sat. *"Pizza!"*

"You can still go." Fintan leaned back in the chair. "Call Sam and take her and Nick out to dinner."

"They're going to a movie tonight."

"Well, go with them." He shrugged.

Alanna tilted her head to the side. "Ok, what's up?" Her eyes narrowed a little. "You haven't sent me off to the movies since I was a little kid. Do you have a date?"

Fintan cleared his throat. "No, I have a meeting, but I need to have it here, and without anyone around."

Now Alanna's curiosity was in full swing. "Why?"

"It's someone who has information for me and wants to meet away from prying eyes and ears." He leaned one elbow on the table. "It's important, so could you please go to dinner and a movie tonight?"

"Male or female?"

"What?"

"Your guest, is it a male or a female?"

"I don't see what that . . ." Fintan sighed. "Male, ok?"

"Ok, Dad. I'll run off to the movies like a good girl."

"Thank you." He picked up a folder of papers and began to read through it.

"Do you want me to bring you home something to eat?"

"No, thanks. I'll find something here."

"No pizza?" Jet was still sitting close to the phone.

"No pizza." Alanna went upstairs to change out of her work clothes. "Sorry, girl."

"Awww." Jet and Abbey followed her up the stairs. *"I wanted pizza."*

"Shrimp. I want shrimp." Abbey ran past them to the top.

"Pizza." Jet raced towards her.

"Shrimp!"

Alanna stopped at the top of the stairs. "How about shrimp pizza?"

They both stopped and looked up at her.

"Just kidding."

Thirty minutes later Alanna was in jeans, sweatshirt, and a Giants baseball hat driving down Treasure Grove Way. When she got to the bottom of the hill where it met the county road she stopped. She turned left to drive the short distance into town and turned off onto the gravel road that led up to Aunt Vi's house. She did a slow U-turn, stopping close to the end of the road; near enough to be able to see any cars coming, but far enough back that they couldn't see her for the trees. She parked and waited.

Many cars passed. Ten minutes later she saw who her father was meeting. She recognized him as he drove by. Then she leaned forward and saw him turn onto Treasure Grove Way. It was Ed Beckman, so now she assumed the meeting had something to do with Brian, and his death. No wonder her father had wanted her gone.

She pulled out onto the highway and drove into town. She had called Sam when she'd gone upstairs to change and Sam invited her along to the movie when she found out Fintan was "busy" as Alanna had put it. Sam and Nick met her in front of the theater and they went in to see the latest vampire movie, Alanna noticing Derek was there at the theater, too. Two rows in front of them . . . alone.

Chapter 6

The movie was really good and Sam, Nick and Alanna continued to discuss it as they got up to leave. Alanna went to put her empty soda cup into the trash can when it fell to the floor and began to roll down the sloped floor. It hit Derek's foot as he was walking up the aisle. He stopped and picked it up.

"Thanks," Alanna said as he walked up and tossed it into the trash. She noticed the large Nordic-looking ring he had on. He hadn't been wearing that the other day.

"You're welcome." He tossed his trash in also. "So, what'd you think?"

"I liked it. Especially the twist at the end."

Derek smiled nervously. She was so beautiful she even made an old, worn sweatshirt look sexy. "I meant what did you think of the tile?"

"Oh." Alanna changed course. "It looks great. You did a good job."

They began to walk toward the exit doors as he tried hard to think of something to say.

"Thank you. The tiles you have in there are a very soft stone. It looks good, but they're very fragile. They crack and break really easily. You should think about replacing that whole floor before too long." He held the door for her. Sam and Nick were waiting outside.

"My mom and dad picked that pattern out years ago when they renovated the house."

"Hey, Derek." Nick shook Derek's hand. They had been on the school football team together. "How ya been?"

"Good, I hear you got engaged. Congratulations."

Sam hugged Nick's arm, beaming. "Thank you," they chimed together.

"Have you set a date?"

"Not yet." Nick glanced at Sam. "But we're narrowing it down. It's more complicated than we thought."

"There's lots of things to consider," Sam pointed out.

"What's so complicated? Pick a date. Tell people to be there," Alanna chimed in.

"It's not that easy."

"Well, just don't try to please everyone. It can't be done. My sister tried that," Derek said.

"Sam won't try to please everyone," Alanna sneered. "Just every other female involved."

"That's not true," Sam defended. "Just me, my mom, Nick's mom, my sister, my aunt, Nick's grandmother . . ." Sam's face contorted in thought.

"I rest my case."

Nick and Derek laughed as Sam furrowed her brow in annoyance. Nick turned to Derek. "We're gonna go get something to eat. Wanna join us?"

"Well?" Derek glanced at Alanna. More than anything he wanted to spend time with her; he seemed to be drawn to her in a very compelling way, but he was a little nervous.

"Dude . . . food, drinks and two women going on and on planning a wedding. What more could you want for an evening?" Nick joked.

"Ok." Derek didn't want to sound too anxious, but inside he wanted to leap at the chance to be near Alanna. "You make it sound so appealing. How can I refuse?"

They walked the short distance to a Chinese restaurant, found a booth in the corner and ordered.

They talked about the baseball game, proposal, movie, and music. They joked and laughed for hours. Derek and Nick reminisced about high school, long ago football games and a coach that used to yell, "You inferior weenies!" when they messed up a play.

During the evening, Derek discovered that Sam snorted when she laughed too hard. This made everyone laugh so much they disturbed the tables around them.

Alanna admired Derek's ring and he told her his grandfather had left it to him and that it'd been in his family for generations.

Wedding plans were not mentioned. It was an agreement the ladies had made with the men from the beginning. They all had a very relaxing and enjoyable time. When the check finally came they each paid their part and hated to see the evening come to a close.

As they left the restaurant Nick and Sam walked to their car and Derek walked Alanna to her SUV. They said goodnight and he watched her drive away. It was the most fun he'd had in a really long time. He took a deep breath and smiled; he could still smell her perfume. In that moment he made a decision.

***

Alanna had forgotten about her father's meeting until she pulled up to the iron gate at 9:45 p.m. She walked into the kitchen and noticed that not many lights were on. She found her father asleep in the den in his easy chair and Jet asleep on the rug in front of the fireplace. Juneau was asleep on the back of the couch and Abbey was nowhere around.

She looked for a good five minutes before she finally found her lying on the floor in front of the double doors that led to the ballroom. It was the largest and least used room of the house.

"Abbey, what're you doing?"

"The door took my treasure." Her paw extended under the doors swiping back and forth reaching under as far as she could.

Alanna opened the doors and switched on the first two rows of large crystal chandeliers. Abbey rushed in, playing hockey with a plastic tile spacer across the highly polished, beautiful inlaid wood floor. The sounds she made echoed in the overly large and silent room. Alanna looked at the floor by the doors. There were about a dozen tile spacers, a safety pin, three paper clips and a thimble as well as a large number of small rubber balls and marbles . . . all of Abbey's favorite cat toys and many other small items.

"Abbey! Look at all of this stuff!" She bent down and started picking them up one by one.

"Mine!" Abbey ran over, pawing at the hand holding the items. *"Treasure!"*

"Yes, I know, but Emma could slip and fall on these. I can't leave them all over the floor like this."

"Mine." She rubbed her body over Alanna's arm and shoulder as she bent over.

Alanna flicked a tile spacer with her thumb and middle finger, causing it to sail across the slick floor.

Abbey raced over, then slid to a stop on top of it and grabbed it in her paws. *"Got it."*

Alanna knelt down on the floor and slid each item across the floor and Abbey chased after them. This game continued for about five minutes. Alanna retrieved some of the items and Abbey batted some back to her as Juneau sauntered into the room.

"Who's winning?" she asked, stretching and arching her back.

"I am." Abbey beamed triumphantly.

"Humph, not any more," Juneau jeered, taking position to intercept the next item.

"Not fair, my game." Abbey squeaked, crouching down and pouting.

"You both can play." Alanna flipped an item in one direction, then another item off to the other side to separate the cats.

"I'm faster," Abbey boasted to Juneau. *"I'm always going to be smaller and faster."*

"Smarter is more important than faster. And I'm always going to be smarter than you."

"Smaller faster! Smaller faster! Smaller faster!" Abbey taunted as she ran over, grabbing the items that slid past Juneau. She got close to Juneau's side and Juneau rolled over, grabbing her and biting and kicking her playfully. They scuffed and stalked each other. Juneau had Abbey on the floor and Abbey held her off with one hind foot pushed into Juneau's chest. Juneau stared down at her with her ears back.

"Smaller is not always better," Juneau exclaimed, launching herself onto Abbey.

During all of this, Alanna was picking up items from the floor and watching to make sure Juneau didn't get too rough. The thought of her father's meeting came to mind.

"When Dad had his meeting tonight did either of you overhear anything?"

"Faster, faster, faster!" Abbey taunted, jumping away and arching her back as they went around in a circle.

"Girls? Did you hear anything?"

"Yes, it was about bubblegum." Abbey said lowering the front of her body to the floor, preparing for attack.

"Bubblegum?"

"Yeah, bubblemint." Abbey launched herself. The two collided, rolling over and over.

"Bubblemint?" Alanna walked over, looking down at the two cats intertwined at her feet.

"And ports," Abbey said, backing her ears, biting into Juneau's neck while kicking with her back feet.

"Ports?" Alanna was confused.

Juneau broke free walking a few feet away and sat down to begin cleaning her front paw as an indication that she was either done playing or preparing for a sneak attack.

"What she means is embezzlement and reports." Juneau stopped cleaning, stood up and looked up at Abbey. *"Smarter is always better."* Then she sashayed out of the room, holding her tail high.

***

On Thursday morning Alanna awoke and was pleased to find she'd slept through the night. She got up and did her daily chores which consisted of feeding the animals, and tending to the litter boxes and water bowls. She made sure the bird and squirrel feeders were full. Then she sat down at the table and enjoyed a big breakfast. She showered and dressed for the funeral.

She arrived in front of Sam and Nick's apartment on time but Sam was already waiting at the curb, standing by a parking meter, bridal magazines in hand. The trip to Lodi was about an hour and they talked about the wedding and the dinner from the night before. Alanna didn't mention Fintan's meeting or what the cats had heard, but she mulled it over in her mind as they drove. She wondered if the embezzlement that they'd talked about had to do with Brian. Maybe that's what got him killed. Sam kept showing Alanna pictures of bridesmaids dresses.

"What do you think of this one?" Sam held up the open magazine.

Alanna glanced over, not wanting to take her eyes off of the road. "It's ok, I'm not real fond of ruffles."

"Yeah, I know what you mean." Sam glanced over at Alanna. It was the third time in five minutes.

"Ok. What is it? My hair? My makeup? What's wrong?"

"Nothing." Sam flipped the magazine pages. "You look fine."

"Well, you've got something on your mind. What is it?"

"I want to ask a favor." She sighed and put down the magazine. "Well, Nick and I have a favor ask."

"Anything. You know that. Sam, you're like a sister to me. I love you. Anything you need I'm there for you . . . you know that. You've never hesitated before. What is it?"

Sam took a deep breath. "Well, you know how much I admire your house?"

"Yeah."

"Nick and I were hoping you'd let us use the ballroom for our wedding." Sam turned in her seat a little, launching into a long pleading explanation. "I know it's always been your dream to get married at Treasure Grove and I don't wanna take away from your dream wedding, if and when it ever happens, but I love your ballroom. It's so beautiful. Your great-grandmother had such wonderful taste, and the floor in there is absolutely gorgeous. I promise it won't be a huge wedding and . . ."

Alanna cut Sam off, smiling and saying, "I'd love for you two to have it at my house."

"Really?"

"Yeah. The ballroom hasn't been used since before Mom died. I think it's time we pulled the sheets off the chairs and dusted off the bandstand." Alanna meant what she said, but there was a note of melancholy in her voice.

"Oh, Al, thank you!" Sam exclaimed. "It means so much to us."

"But, you get to tell Emma and just so you know, my dream wedding would be an outdoor wedding on the grounds with the reception in the ballroom," Alanna mused.

"So, there's hope for your love life after all?" Sam raised an eyebrow.

"Not looking. Not wanting any entanglements. Too much work."

"How about Derek? He's hot! I mean like you could oil him up and put him on a calendar hot! You two got along great last night. He's hunky, funny, and sexy. I wish Nicky would grow his hair long like that. Mm-mm-mm."

Alanna gave Sam a scolding look. "What would Nick say if he heard you talking about another guy like that?"

"I can look, I just can't touch." Sam wiggled her eyebrows. "You should go out with Derek, he seems nice."

"Nice, huh? That's what you said about that guy you wanted me to date last year!"

"How was I supposed know he was an illegal pot farmer?" Sam began to thumb through her magazine again. "Good thing your dad knew him."

"My point exactly. You don't know how people will turn out. Besides, trust is something I am not willing to dole out right now."

Sam looked over at her with a sigh. "I know how much Chris hurt you, but not all guys are like that. Not all guys cheat. Look at Nick, he's a great guy. I'm so lucky I found him, and Mr. Right is out there for you. You'll find him, someday."

"You keep saying that."

"Someday you'll believe me."

"I like being alone. It's easier."

"Your negativity is very apparent when it comes to men."

"How did we get on the subject of me? I thought we were talkin' about your wedding."

"Ok, ok. Hey! Didn't your parents get married there?"

"Yeah, and my grandparents." Alanna laughed. "Aunt Vi refused to. She insisted on a Celtic ceremony under a full moon in Scotland with her Highlander."

"Your parents' wedding picture you keep in your room, that was taken on the front staircase wasn't it?"

"Yes, but that was before the house was updated. They pulled the carpet runner and runner rods off and refinished the all the wood and banister. I think it looks a lot more elegant now with its curves and polished wood."

"You never use it."

"It's at the front of the house. We always use the back stairs."

"I remember sliding down the back stairs on sleeping bags when we were kids."

"And piling pillows up at the bottom to cushion our fall."

"I remember you broke a spindle with your foot and tried to fix it with silly putty."

Alanna laughed. "It held for what? Two seconds?"

"Your dad wasn't mad, but your mom gave you the look and sent us to your room."

"I got that look a lot." Alanna smiled sadly. She missed her mother giving her that look.

"Yeah, you did."

They pulled into the parking lot of the funeral home and parked. They went inside and found seats toward the back. It was very full and they recognized members of management from Bizmart who were sitting with Cecilia, closer to the front. It was a good service making Alanna feel for Brian's wife and children even more. As they were leaving to go the cemetery Alanna noticed an elderly woman in a wheelchair being pushed by Brian's wife. After the graveside service, she was introduced to Alanna and Sam as Brian's mother. Sam thought she'd seen her before, but she didn't know from where. After the cemetery they went and had some lunch. They had a favorite Japanese restaurant that they always went to in Lodi.

After lunch they went downtown and checked out one of the bridal shops. Sam wanted a traditional wedding dress. She saw one she really liked, tried it on and looked absolutely stunning in it. Sam loved the dress and Alanna tried to get her to buy it, but Sam said she wanted to look a little more. She felt it was much more than she wanted to spend. They then decided to go to the Lodi Bizmart. It looked the same as theirs, but a little older and needed some updating. They were walking past Customer Service when Alanna noticed a picture on the wall with a memorial plaque under it. Alanna rushed to it. It read: *Lori Morgan, Store Manager, Respected and Missed.*

"Sam!" Alanna stared at the picture. "That's her!"

"Her who?"

"The woman in my dream."

"Are you sure?"

"Yes, absolutely!"

"Says here she died last year in a car accident." Sam and Alanna read a framed newspaper article next to the picture.

"Well, that's what I keep seeing . . . a car accident."

"Why would you dream about that?"

"I don't know, but that's her!" Alanna tapped the picture. "If she's already dead then I don't have to worry about the dream coming true. It's already happened."

"That's weird . . . you dreaming about a dead woman."

"Yeah, I know." Alanna studied the picture. "Why would I do that?"

"Hey, you're the one with the extra talents, you tell me."

"I don't think this has anything to do with that."

"It might. Your mom could see and talk to ghosts so maybe you can too."

"This isn't a ghost. This is a dream."

"Maybe it's a ghost dream."

"What?"

"Maybe it's a ghost making you have the dream."

"That's just crazy."

"Ok, Doctor Doolittle, then you come up with a suggestion."

"Don't call me that."

"Hey, look! There's Cecilia's daughter, Zara." Sam pointed toward the customer service desk.

They walked over to the desk. "Hey, Zara." Alanna said to the thin brunette girl.

"Hey, Alanna, Sam." Zara smiled. "What're you doing here?"

"We came for Brian's funeral." Alanna noticed the rings she had on her thin hands.

"Oh, that's right. It was today. Such a shame about him being killed."

"Yeah, it was." Alanna motioned toward the picture on the wall.

"You lost your store manager last year didn't you?"

"Yeah. It was a real tragedy. She'd just had a little boy about nine months before it happened." Zara shook her head. "Her daughter, Kristina, is one of my best friends. It really hurt her to lose her mom. Now it's just her and her father trying to raise little Cameron."

"That's so sad." Sam sympathized.

"Her father is a truck driver for our company and Kristina started working her here part time after her mom passed," Zara sighed. "It's hard on her because he's on the road a lot."

"The article didn't say what caused the accident."

"They said it was due to wet roads and that she was going too fast."

Alanna glanced at Sam. "It was raining?"

"Yeah, she lost control and went over a cliff. It happened on Red Tail Hawk Ridge Road. She was coming home from the casino on the other side of Lake Oro. I know where it is because Kristina put a cross with flowers by the road on her mom's birthday."

"Did Lori work here before she became the manager?"

"No, she transferred here when Brian got the Aurum store a few years ago."

"Are you still working in the accounting office?"

"Yeah, like mother like daughter. I'm just covering the service desk for a minute."

"Well, it was good to see you." Sam pulled at Alanna's arm to leave.

"Good to see you too."

Chapter 7

Alanna and Sam left Bizmart and went over to the nursing home where Sam's grandmother lived. They went inside, checking in at the front desk. As they walked down the hall to Nana's room they passed a lady sitting in a wheelchair with her back to the door. They reached Nana's room and went in. Sam's grandmother suffered from Alzheimer's and didn't recognize Sam most of the time.

"Hi, Nana." Sam walked over to the bed and looked down at the small, frail, white-haired lady lying in the bed who kept her head turned toward the window.

Sam took her hand and gave it a gentle squeeze. Nana turned her head, focusing her weak eyes on Sam.

In a small, feeble voice Nana said, "Are you here to take me to church?"

"No, Nana. It's me, Samantha." Sam smiled. "Your granddaughter."

Nana turned her head and looked out the window again.

"Nana, I have wonderful news. Nick and I got engaged."

Nana turned her head away from the window and looked up at Sam again and said, "Are you here to take me to church?"

A single tear ran down Sam's cheek. "No, Nana. I'm here just to see you and let you know how much I love you."

Nana turned her head back to the window. Sam sat down in a chair next to the bed and still held her grandmother's hand.

Alanna stepped out of the room, wanting to give Sam a moment alone with her grandmother. She walked down the hall toward the waiting room when she once again passed the room with the woman in the wheelchair. She recognized the woman as Brian's mother.

She knocked on the open door. "Hello, Mrs. Parker?"

"Yes." The woman turned slightly to see who it was.

"My name is Alanna MacLachlin. I worked with your son Brian."

"Oh, hello. Have a seat. I was just looking at old photos of him."

Alanna pulled a chair up to the small table in front of the wheelchair and sat down.

"I'm so sorry about Brian, Mrs. Parker." Alanna shook her hand.

"He was a wonderful person. He will be greatly missed."

Mrs. Parker smiled. "He was a good boy. He was my oldest son." She showed Alanna a family photo with nine men, eight women and ten children. She recognized Brian, his wife and kids, his mother, and presumed the older gentleman was Brian's father.

"This photo was taken the year before my husband passed. This is my middle son, Robert, and my youngest son, Steven. My daughters are Donna, Kathy, Kelly and Marie."

"You have a beautiful family."

"Thank you." She smiled fondly. "I'm very lucky, I see at least one of them every day. Brian would come to see me two or three times a week."

Alanna picked up another photo from the pile. It was a family photo from when Brian was just a teenager. Mrs. Parker sat in the middle of the photo with her right arm crossing her chest and her right hand resting on top of her husband's hand which was on her shoulder. She was looking up at her husband and smiling.

"This is a nice shot." Alanna showed her the photo. "You look so happy."

She laughed. "Yes, this is one of my favorites. The photographer got mad because I moved. He told me to look at him but I couldn't take my eyes off my George."

"You must have loved him very much."

"Oh, yes, very much." She smiled. "He always made me laugh. No matter how tough times got, he always made me laugh." She kissed the tip of her finger and touched it to the man's face in the photo.

"That is a lovely ring you have on. I've never seen one quite like it. Are those garnets?" Alanna pointed to the ring on her hand in the photo.

"Yes, there are nine of them. George made that ring for me right after our last child was born. He was the best jeweler in town. See, the middle stone is the largest, and the ones on the sides get smaller as they go down the sides. He knew I loved emerald and channel cut stones, and garnet is my birthstone. He said each stone represented a member of our family and that I was the largest middle stone that held it all together. I wore that ring until the day I came in here." She glanced around to the door. "Things disappear in here right, left and center." She looked back at the photo. "I didn't want to lose it so I gave it to Brian for his daughter." She sighed. "He looked so much like his father."

Just then Sam appeared in the doorway. Alanna looked up and nodded her head.

"Thank you so much for sharing your memories with me, Mrs. Parker. I just wanted you to know how sorry I am for your loss." Alanna stood and put the chair back against the wall.

"Thank you for coming by."

She shook Mrs. Parker's hand and said goodbye.

Sam and Alanna drove most of the way home in silence, each caught up in their own thoughts. She dropped Sam off in front of her apartment and was met by Jet as she arrived home.

"Hi, Mom. Did they bury him?" Jet followed her into the house.

"Yes, they did."

"Good."

"Why is that good?"

"Things must be buried." Jet sat down looking up at her. *"That's the way it is."*

"Ok." Alanna smiled, rubbing Jet's ears. "Whatever you say."

"Are you going to run today?" Jet asked, hopeful.

"Yeah, I think I will." She picked up a note on the counter. It was from Emma.

Went to store.

"I could use a little fresh air."

She went upstairs and changed into her exercise pants, T-shirt and running shoes. Jet was wiggling all over with anticipation. Juneau was asleep in her cat bed. Abbey walked into the room and stretched just as Jet and Alanna were leaving.

"Where going?" Abbey followed them down the stairs.

"Running." Jet stood anxiously by the open back door waiting for Alanna to grab her cellphone, earbuds, and jot down an answer on the note from Emma.

Went for run.

"Me want to go!" Abbey followed them out the door. *"Me go too!"*

"Ok, but first you have to have the spray." Alanna walked to a bench by the door retrieving a spray bottle of flea and tick spray.

"Dr. Stucky says you have to have this on your legs and belly when you're out in the woods." She began to spray Jet's legs and underside. Jet stood still, even raising her legs for Alanna. She was happy to do whatever she needed to do to go for a run.

"No spray." Abbey sat down. *"Don't like spray. Taste bad."*

"No spray. No run." Alanna finished with Jet and turned to Abbey.

"Abbey, it will keep the hitchhikers off you." Alanna got one squirt on Abbey's front paw.

"There spray on now we go." Abbey tried to pull away. *"Done!"*

"No, not done." Alanna grabbed her and continued to spray.

"Don't have hitchhikers." Abbey squirmed in protest.

"I know you don't have them. That's because I give you a monthly flea and tick treatment, but this keeps them off you when you run. Hold still." Alanna finished with Abbey and then sprayed some on her own pant legs and shoes. She hated ticks and fleas. She plugged her earbuds into her cellphone and put them in her ears. She pushed the play button on the phone's MP3 player, and then put it in her pocket, zipping it up to hold it in. One of her favorite songs began to play. She stretched a little then she jogged down the driveway to the large iron gate. She pushed the red button on the wall panel, making the gate slide open. She jogged up to where the asphalt ended and then continued on the dirt trail up the mountain, through the dense trees. Jet ran ahead and Abbey brought up the rear, stopping to investigate things as they went.

"Faster." Jet would stop and look back. *"Come on. You can do it. Faster."*

Alanna stayed on the well-worn route. She'd run this trail a thousand times before.

"She can't hear you," Abbey said. *"She has those things in her ears."*

"She chooses what she wants to hear." Jet stopped in her tracks looking off to the south. *"I sense a deer."*

"Have to stay with Mommy."

"I know." Jet fought the urge to run off and find the deer.

They jogged through the woods for a good five minutes when Alanna saw that a very large tree had recently fallen across the trail, taking down three other trees.

"Look at that big tree!" Abbey ran past Alanna and jumped up onto its trunk. It covered the trail and branches blocked any way over it. Alanna veered off the trail and jumped up onto the tree. When she came down on the other side of the large trunk there were a bunch of loud cracks. Boom! All of a sudden the ground beneath her gave way and she fell through a large hole. Dirt, leaves and branches had been covering old board planks. She fell a very long way and hit the ground with an extremely painful thump, landing on her side and hip. She

rose up, looking around. It was pitch black. There was no light except that coming in through the top of the hole a long way up. Alanna stood up, shaking the dirt off, and felt the sides of the hole. Roots from the trees pushed through the sides of the dirt walls. She pulled the earbuds out of her ears.

"Mommy!" Abbey leaned over the open hole, crouching down. *"Mommy, you ok?"*

Jet's head appeared at the open hole next to Abbey. *"Mom! Mom! Mom!"*

"I'm ok." She pulled her phone out of her pocket, turning off the music.

No signal.

She held it up towards the opening of the hole . . . still no signal. She used the phone as a light source to look around. She was in some kind of shaft or well. She knew there were mine shafts all over this mountain, but most of them were marked. She looked up at Abbey and Jet's faces. Her hip and shoulder hurt from the fall.

"Don't get too close. I don't want you two to fall in. Jet, run home and get Emma to call Dad. Abbey, stay here and close to the hole so they can find me."

"Ok, Mommy," Abbey said as Jet took off as fast as she could.

Alanna tried to pull herself up the wall using the tree roots. She got about ten feet from the bottom when the root she held broke and she fell back to the bottom. This time she hit her head on a rock. She sat up rubbing her head as she felt around the ground. That rock was the only one down there. She used her cellphone as a light source to take a closer look at the rock and used her hand to clear dirt away from it.

Abbey looked down from above, her eyes adjusting to see. *"Mommy, do you need to use the litter box?"*

Alanna looked up at the small, cute, furry face.

"No, I don't. Why?"

"You're digging like you need to use the litter box."

"I think I found something."

"Treasure?" Abbey asked excitedly.

"No, not treasure."

Alanna was using her fingers to clear away more dirt when her finger pushed into a hole in the rock. After a few seconds of digging, she realized it wasn't a rock at all.

It was a human skull.

***

Jet ran as fast as she could through the woods. She reached the gate and jumped up at the panel with the buttons. After a second jump she hit the right button and the gate began to open. She didn't wait for the gate to open all the way but wiggled her way through as soon as she could. She didn't see Emma's car, but ran to the back of the house and in the back door.

"Emma!" she barked as loud as she could. *"Emma! Emma!"*

Juneau came lazily down the stairs.

"What are you barking about? Dinner's not for an hour or two."

"Mom's in trouble!" Jet paced back and forth. *"She fell down a big hole! She needs help. WE NEED DAD!"*

"Is she hurt?" Juneau began to look around, trying to decide what to do.

"She said she was ok but she can't get out. It's really deep."

"Ok. Ok." Juneau thought for a second. *"You run into town, try to get someone to follow you back here. Run all the way to Dad's office if you have to."*

"K!" Jet was out the door as fast as she could go.

"What would Mother do?" Juneau sat down and looked up at the phone on the counter. *"She'd call Dad. What would Dad do? He'd call for help if he couldn't do it alone."* She walked into the room that Fintan used as an office and jumped up onto the desk, the one place she knew she wasn't allowed because of the important paperwork. She looked down at the phone on the desk . . . it was the only one in the house that had a cord that ran to the handset. She'd played with the cord when she was a kitten and once pulled the handset down onto the floor. She remembered hearing a dial tone from it.

Jet ran as fast as she could along the paved county road the half mile into town. She was running, looking for someone, anyone, but focused on getting to Dad's office when she heard her name.

"Jet!"

She skidded to a stop and looked around.

"Jet!"

It was Derek! He was filling up his truck at the gas station pump. She ran over to him panting and barking anxiously.

"Mom, fell in a hole! Come quick! She needs help! Now!"

"Hey girl, what are you so excited about?" Derek removed the gas handle, put it back into the pump and closed his gas cap.

"Mom is in trouble! Come with me! Now!" she barked, running a

few steps back toward the house, then back to him. She continued to run back and forth barking.

"What's wrong girl? Did Timmy fall in the well?" He smiled down at her and laughed.

"Who's Timmy?" Jet stopped, cocked her head, then began to bark and run again. *"Now! Follow me now! Now! Now! Now! Now! Now!"*

"Ok, ok. I think I understand. You want me to go with you?" Derek opened the door to the truck and climbed in.

Jet barked even faster and took off as fast as she could, barking all the way.

"Yes! Yes! Yes! Follow! Follow! Follow! Now! Now! Now!"

Derek drove, following Jet the short distance to Treasure Grove. He was going to pull up to the gate when he saw Jet run past. He followed until the asphalt ended and only stopped when the road was too narrow for his truck. Jet kept barking and running, coming back to make sure he was still following her. He shut off the truck and followed on foot. A few minutes later Abbey could hear Jet.

"Mommy! Jet's coming!" She looked down the hole.

"Good, I hope she found someone." Alanna's head, shoulder and hip hurt.

Abbey began to meow as loud as she could.

"Jet! We're here! Jet! Over here!" She jumped onto the trunk of the tree and stood as tall as she could. *"Here! Under the tree!"*

Jet came into view, followed by Derek.

"Mommy, Jet brought the dog lover that messed up the floor."

"Derek?" Alanna looked up.

Jet ran to the hole and barked, leaning down.

"Ok, ok. This had better not be a rabbit or something stupid like that." Derek climbed over the tree trunk and spotted the hole broken through the boards.

"Hello. Anybody down there?" he yelled towards the hole.

"Derek?" Alanna yelled up. "Oh, thank goodness."

"Alanna?" He cleared away some of the branches and leaves to find the edges of the boards. "Are you all right?"

"Yeah, a little bruised, but fine."

"Hold on. I'll get you out. I have to go to my truck and get some rope."

"Ok."

He looked over at Jet. "You're a good girl." He patted Jet as he headed back toward his truck. Hearing a siren down the road, he jogged the short distance back towards the house just in time to intercept the fire truck coming up Treasure Grove Way. He waved it down, Jet by his side the whole time.

"What's the emergency?" the fireman asked.

"A woman fell in what looks like an empty well further up the mountain."

"Show us the way."

The fireman pulled the truck up behind Derek's truck and stopped. Fifteen minutes later, by lowering a harness and rope, Alanna was pulled from the well. She thanked everyone and hugged her animals. They wanted to use a stretcher to get her back, but she insisted on walking. Her father pulled up behind the fire truck when they were putting their equipment back.

"What happened?" he asked, getting out of his squad car.

"Chief, your daughter fell in an old air shaft. She's a little banged up, but she's ok. She's in the house."

"Thank you so much for helping her." He got back in his car and drove to the house just as Emma pulled up.

"Fintan! What's going on? I passed an ambulance on the road."

"I'm not sure, something about Alanna falling in an old air shaft."

They both rushed inside to find Alanna and Derek sitting at the kitchen table drinking iced tea and Alanna holding the bag of frozen peas to her shoulder.

"Are you all right?" Her father came over to her, touching her head gently.

"I'm ok, just a few bruises." She smiled down at Jet, and over at Abbey and Juneau. "Thanks to my girls and Derek."

"What happened?" Fintan took a seat at the table as Emma came over and hugged Alanna.

"You need to eat." Emma stated as she pulled a roasting pan from the oven.

"I went for a run like always, but a large tree had fallen, so I veered off the trail to get around it. Then boom! I fell through some boards and found myself in an old air shaft."

Derek leaned forward on the table. "I saw Jet running into town and she led me straight to her. Smart dog."

"I got called out of a meeting; because they said a 911 call had come from our house."

Alanna looked over at Juneau who was cleaning her paw in nonchalant fashion.

"I tried my cellphone . . . that must have been it," she theorized, hoping Derek didn't ask too many questions.

Fintan looked over at Juneau who winked one eye. "I'm just glad you're safe. Thank you, Derek." He reached down, petting Jet. "And thank you, girls."

"I helped." Abbey jumped into his lap. *"I stayed still. It was hard."*

Alanna smiled. "All my girls were wonderful."

Derek smiled at seeing Alanna with dirt and leaves still in her hair, hugging her animals.

"Yes, they are." Fintan petted Abbey.

Emma started setting plates of roasted pork and vegetables in front of everyone, and she also gave each animal a nice piece of pork.

Chapter 8

Alanna and Fintan both thanked Derek again for his help as he was leaving.

After he was gone Fintan turned to Alanna and hugged her gently.

"Are you sure you're ok?" His brow furrowed with concern.

"I'm really sore, but good. I was worried it would get dark before anyone found me."

She closed the door behind them as they walked back into the kitchen.

"Dispatch called me and said someone had called 911 but didn't say anything. Nothing. No sound, but the line stayed open." Fintan leaned against the kitchen counter while she put the bag of peas back into the freezer. She looked at the bag. It was the same one Aunt Vi had sent to Fintan.

"Juneau used the phone in your office and punched 911. Then she laid next to the receiver and listened to the person on the other end. She wanted to make sure they didn't think it was a prank call."

"Protocol. All 911 calls are investigated. Some people pass out after they dial." Juneau walked into the kitchen and sat down. "You're a pretty smart cat." Fintan reached down, picking her up.

"Ooh, don't manhandle me. I hate to be held. Put me down. Tell him to put me down!"

He cuddled her and began to scratch her head and chin.

"How did you learn to use the phone?" He kept scratching.

"Don't . . . ohh just a little to the left . . . ahh yeah . . . higher . . . ok, that's enough."

She forced her way out of his arms, jumping down.

"It's just like pushing buttons on the TV remote. It only takes one strong claw, and the corner of your car says '911 for help'. It doesn't take a genius to figure it out . . . Even though I am." She sat down, licked her paw and began to smooth the fur he had ruffled.

"She says she's a genius and you should bow to her intellect." Alanna grinned.

"Really?" Fintan raised an eyebrow. "How does such a big ego fit in such a little thing?"

Abbey came running into the room jumping up onto Fintan's leg.

"She not little, I little." Fintan reached down, lifting Abbey into his arms.

Juneau glanced up from her fur. *"Speaking of the size of your brain."*

"Dad, I need to talk to you about that air shaft." Alanna took a seat at the table.

"Ok." He sat down across from her, setting Abbey down on the floor at the same time.

"I found something at the bottom."

"What was it?"

"A human skull."

Fintan leaned back in his chair and smoothed his mustache. "Just the skull? Any other skeletal remains?"

"It was buried halfway, so I'm not sure."

"Hmm." He continued to stroke his mustache. "Did the fire crew see it?"

"No. I had them lower the harness and they pulled me out, then covered the hole with plywood from Derek's truck along with a blue tarp. Nobody else went down into it." She rubbed her shoulder. "They told me I had seventy two hours to cover the hole properly since I was the property owner."

Fintan glanced at his watch and then got up, reaching for the phone on the counter. He punched in seven digits and waited.

Andy's gruff male voice answered. "I was watching the news." Sheriff Andy Douglas was Fintan's oldest and closest friend.

"Sorry, Andy, but I've got something for you."

"Has it got Sapphire gin in it?"

"No. I need you and your boys to take a look in an old air shaft on our property."

"I heard that call on the scanner today." The volume of the television at the other end of the line lowered. "Is she ok?"

"Yeah, just bruised, but she found human skeletal remains at the bottom of the shaft."

There was a pause on the line. "Anyone you know?" Andy teased.

"Not that I know of."

"You sure?"

"Andy," Fintan said with discontent. "No."

"Just askin'."

"I'd like to keep it quiet, if possible."

Andy cleared his throat. "Gonna be hard to keep the media out."

"It's your jurisdiction."

"All right. Can't start on it tonight, we'd draw too much attention with the lights. We'll be out first thing in the morning."

"Go back to your news."

They hung up. Fintan and Andy both knew that finding human remains on the chief of police's property was not a good thing. Fintan grabbed his cigarettes, heading towards the back door.

"Andy will handle it. I'm curious as to how long it's been down there."

Alanna stood up and stretched. *Ouch.* "I'm going to take a shower and go to bed. I feel absolutely filthy."

"Ok, honey. I know you've had a hard day."

"Night, Dad."

"Night."

On Friday morning Alanna awoke with pain everywhere, at least that was how it felt. She slowly got out of bed and dressed for work, then she went to the kitchen for breakfast.

"You should stretch, Mommy. I always feel good when I stretch," Abbey said. Arching her back, she put her front legs forward, lowering herself to the floor.

Alanna tried to stretch a little, but found it very painful.

"What you should do is find a nice warm sunny spot and allow your muscles to soak up the warmth. That's what feels good," Jet said as she rolled over on the kitchen floor where she was lying in a nice warm ray of sun coming through the window of the back door.

Juneau looked up at Alanna from the cat's food dish. *"Painkillers,"* she said between bites. *"Lots of really good painkillers. That's what I suggest and so does every pharmaceutical company with a decent advertising budget. And that reminds me, why do human males feel the need to enhance themselves? Every other ad on TV is for male enhancement."* She continued to chew. *"I don't understand, they should just be happy with what the Almighty Cat gave them."*

Jet sat up, looking over at Juneau. *"Almighty Cat?"*

"Yes." Juneau began to clean her face. *"Maker of all."*

"You mean Dog."

"No, I mean Cat."

"It's Almighty Dog."

Juneau stopped in mid-lick. *"Oh, please. You have to be kidding!*

Cats have been revered and worshipped by humans for centuries . . . even they know."

"Dog!" Jet stood up to add force to her statement.

"Cat!" Juneau stood, raising her shoulders and back in defense.

"Dog! Dog! Dog!" Jet leaped for Juneau, nipping playfully.

Juneau ran for the stairs with Jet close behind. They made a lot of noise running around upstairs.

Abbey lay down, taking over the warm sunbeam Jet had abandoned. She looked up at Alanna and squeezed her eyes shut. *"What is enhance?"*

Alanna sipped her coffee as she got up and went to the bathroom for some painkillers.

When she left for work, Andy and two of his deputies were there and Fintan was taking them to the air shaft. Jet wanted to show them the way so Fintan let her go with them. After clocking in and getting behind the jewelry counter, Sam walked across the aisle and Alanna told her quietly about falling into the air shaft and finding its contents.

"Do you think someone knew the body was down there when they boarded it up?" Sam asked.

"I don't know but Andy will let us know what he finds. I hope he finds out who it is."

They stopped talking when Cecilia walked up.

"Alanna, could you clean my bracelet please? I got correction fluid on it and can't get it all off." Cecilia handed Alanna her silver medical alert bracelet.

"Sure." Alanna read the printing on the back of the bracelet as she began to clean it. "I didn't know you had allergies."

"Just to Benadryl and Epinephrine." She rolled her eyes and overly gestured with her hands. "I can't even walk down the Benadryl aisle here without breaking out in hives."

She tapped her long fingernail on the glass counter top looking down at a ring display. "That's a pretty ring. I may have to get it next payday. Now, don't you two forget about ladies' game night tonight." She wagged a single finger in the air. "And don't be late . . . 6:30, ok?"

Alanna noticed that Cecilia had a ring on every finger.

She wore a lot of large diamonds, and how did she type and run her adding machine with of all those?

"So, you don't have allergies except to allergy medication?" Sam asked. "That's strange."

"Yes, it's a very rare and unusual condition," Cecilia said pursing her lips. "A rarer spirit never did steer humanity; but you gods will give us some faults to make us men."

Sam looked at Cecilia like she was speaking Greek, but realized it was actually Shakespeare.

"Don't worry, we'll be on time," Alanna said handing Cecilia her sparkling clean bracelet. "Here, you go. That's a nice clasp you have . . . very strong."

"It kept falling off so I had a stronger clasp put on." She put the bracelet on and looked at her nails. "I must get my nails filed soon. They're starting to look a little tacky." She turned to go the back office. "Thank you. See you tonight."

Sam waited until Cecilia was gone.

"Don't be late," Sam imitated in a whiny voice. "She can be so irritating sometimes."

Just then a petite, white-haired lady walked up to them. "Good morning, Alanna."

"Good morning, Mrs. Douglas. How are you today?" Alanna had known Sheriff Andy's mother all her life.

"I need a new battery for my watch. It stopped and I have to have my watch or I'll be late for bingo."

"Ok, it'll just take a minute." Alanna started to work on changing the battery.

"Do you play lots of bingo?" Sam asked.

"Oh my, yes! My friends and I play every day. We have a lot of fun. My Harold, God rest his soul, he only went once and afterwards he said 'Helen, please don't ask me to go again'. He wasn't very good at it. I had to play his cards part of the time because he couldn't hear the caller and he said there were too many to keep track of."

"Here you go," Alanna said, handing her the watch back, running and with the time set. "That will be $4.57." Alanna smiled, noticing Mrs. Douglas still wore her wedding ring after all the years since Harold had passed.

"How's your father?" Helen dug into her tote bag for her wallet.

"Good. He's working with Uncle Andy today." Alanna remembered that Fintan still wore his wedding ring too.

"Those two." She handed Alanna the money. "Inseparable." Helen smiled fondly at Alanna. "Those boys got into a lot of mischief growin' up, yes they did. But Harold, Lord love him, never got excited about anything. Just said 'Dirt and blood are part of raisin' boys'. They almost gave me a heart attack or two that's for sure. I remember this one time when they were young 'uns, Fintan climbed up on top of our big barn and told Andrew that he could fly . . . been reading too many comic books I suppose. Anyway, Harold came out of the field about that time and saw Fintan up there with one of my good bed sheets tied to his neck, head up high and his arms out like he was going to dive off. Harold, never one to get excited, walked up to the barn and said 'Hey, boy. Whada'ya think . . . ya can fly?' He said Fintan looked down at him and said 'Yes, sir. I dreamed last night that I could and I really think I can.' So Harold crossed his arms and said. 'Well, this I gotta see.' He stood there watching while Fintan built up his nerve, and just about the time he thought the boy was actually going to jump he said, 'Better not tear or stain that good sheet or my missus'll have your hide.' He said that's when Fintan changed his mind about flying. Said he didn't want to make me mad." She laughed. "Fintan never did jump off that barn and Harold never scolded him or yelled at him when he came down. Just said, 'Better put that sheet back where you found it.' Then he turned and went into the barn and that was that." She looked at her watch. "Well, I have to get going. I can't keep the girls waiting; I'm driving today." She patted Alanna's hand as she turned to leave. "Tell your father I said hello."

"Ok, I will. Good luck at bingo."

Sam smiled at Alanna. "Bed sheet as a cape," Sam giggled.

"Oh, I am so giving him a hard time about this one," Alanna plotted.

A delivery girl was walking up the aisle carrying a large bouquet of mixed flowers when Sam spotted her.

"Oh, maybe Nicky sent me flowers?" she said with excitement.

The girl approached the counter.

"Excuse me. The front desk told me I could find Alanna MacLachlin back here."

Sam's eyes widened as she looked over at Alanna.

"That's me," Alanna said.

"These are for you." She set the bouquet down on the counter. "Have a nice day." She walked away.

"Flowers? For me?" Alanna began to turn the vase, looking for a card. She found it and opened it.

"Who are they from?" Sam leaned in a little to get a look at the card.

Alanna's eyebrows went up. "Derek."

"Derek?" Sam grinned widely as Alanna showed her the card. "Ummm."

"Nothing else, just his name." Alanna put the card back into the envelope.

"He likes you," Sam teased. "You have a not so secret admirer. Let's see, you saw him on Tuesday, Wednesday and yesterday he rescued you, the damsel in distress."

"Well, he—"

"I bet he's going to ask you out," Sam trilled. "He is really handsome, tall and totally hot. Great hair and those sexy brown eyes. Yeah, I can see you with him."

"Stop." Alanna twisted her mouth as she thought.

"He's funny too. You should go out with him. We could all go out as couples."

"I don't want to date anyone."

"Al." Sam let out a long sigh as she leaned against the counter. "In two months you're going to be twenty five. Life is short. You have this large wall not only around your house but your heart. You should think about chipping at that mortar a little bit." Sam smelled one of the roses mixed into the bouquet. "These are beautiful and he seems like a nice guy. Give it some thought. See you at lunch." She walked back over to the shoe department.

Alanna smelled the flowers, touching the petals of one of the roses.

Dave pushed a dust mop past the counter. "Those for you?" he questioned.

"Yes."

He stopped, leaning in a little, and in a hushed tone he said. "Bet they're bugged. Don't take them home with you and be careful what you say around them." He continued on up the aisle.

All day Alanna had trouble concentrating on her work. Her mind and eyes kept drifting to the flowers. She kept asking herself why he had sent them. And, if he did ask her out, what would she say? As Sam said, he did have sexy brown eyes; smoldering was more like it. She also liked his hair, his voice and his laugh. She shook her head. No, she wasn't good at relationships. It was always in the back of her mind. "Does he like me, or my money?"

In two months, when she turned twenty five, she would inherit the rest of her trust fund. She had fulfilled all of the stipulations of the trust. One, to receive a four year college degree or higher. Two, to be employed full time at least two years continuously by someone who was not related. Three, to spend at least two hours a month doing charity work. Four, to retain ownership and maintain the buildings and lands of Treasure Grove. She had to admit, when Grandmamma Bermann had enacted the trust, she knew what she was doing. Those four things had taught Alanna responsibility, patience and an appreciation for others. Her mother and father had taught her thriftiness. Although her mother had loved to shop for clothes and shoes, Eva had never been extravagant. Being a school teacher, she just liked to look good behind her desk. No high fashion except for the few charity balls that she went to before she became ill.

Alanna was snapped back to reality by her name being called behind her. Detective Mark Holmberg was standing at the counter.

"Oh, Mark, I'm sorry, I didn't see you there."

"Your mind is on who sent you those flowers?" A twinge of slight envy stung him.

"Ahh . . ."

"They were sent to you on Wednesday by Derek Atherton. They tried to deliver them yesterday but you weren't here."

"Wow, you can tell all that just by looking at them? That's some nice detecting."

"Well, it helps that my busy-body wife works at the flower shop."

"Yes, that would help."

"Is Mr. Beckman here?"

"Yeah, I'll get him." She picked up the phone and made a call. "He said to go on back to the office."

"Thanks." He turned to leave.

"Hey, Mark. Did you mention the flower thing to my dad?"

"No. Why?"

"Oh, I was just wondering what he might think of Derek."

Mark grinned a little. "He's your dad. No one is ever going to be good enough. But, I do know that the only time Derek ever spent time in our jail your dad helped to get him out."

Alanna's eyes widened furrowing her brow. "When was that?"

"Have your dad tell you about it, I gotta go." He left heading toward the back offices.

When he was gone all kinds of things went through Alanna's mind. She glanced sideways at the flowers. *Why?*

Chapter 9

Alanna pulled into the garage and removed the bouquet of flowers from the passenger seat. Jet had come out to meet her.

"Are those for tonight? Are the ladies coming here tonight to play games?"

She followed Alanna into the kitchen from the laundry room.

"No, games aren't here tonight. Derek sent me these."

"Why? You have lots of them in the yard."

"I'm not sure."

Jet sniffed the vase in her hands. *"There's no dirt. They're going to die. Why would he kill flowers for you?"*

"It's . . . I said I wasn't sure."

Emma came down the stairs as Alanna was placing the vase on the table. "Those are beautiful."

"Yes, they are."

"Who sent them to you?"

"Derek."

Emma sucked in a short breath. "Oh, are you two dating? It would be so wonderful for you to have a young man in your life." She did not try to hide the hopefulness in her voice.

"No, we're not dating."

"Do you like him?" She poured two glasses of iced tea and they sat down at the table.

"Hadn't really thought about it." Alanna was trying to sound nonchalant.

"Ummhmm." Emma clinked her wedding ring against the glass, her gaze firm. "Sure you haven't."

"Well, I don't know him well enough to say one way or the other."

"That's why people date, so they can get to know each other. Do you want to get to know him?"

"Yeah, kind of, but . . . I like the way things are." Alanna sat back and played with the rim of the glass. "No muss, no fuss."

"I know you do, but that's because it's what you're used to, and it's safe. I know you don't want to be hurt again, but that's no reason to avoid men. You need to get out there and have some fun. Live, love and laugh . . . isn't that what they say?"

"Who are *they*?"

"Those who enjoy everything life has to offer. So now, Derek . . . I know his parents, Jack and Elsa. They own the flooring store in town. He has six brothers and a sister. He's the youngest of them all. He's about 27 maybe 28. I think he graduated with Nick. What do you know about him?"

Alanna leaned forward looking down into her tea. "He has a dog, he doesn't like pickles and he likes older cars. Last night Dad and he got talking about cars over dinner. Dad took him out back and showed him his car from high school."

"Ah, yes, the Mustang. Your father's first car. He's been saying for years that he's going to rebuild it but it just sits in the barn, under that tarp, collecting dust."

"He's also gotta good sense of humor," she said, thinking of the list she'd compiled.

"That's good. What else?"

She looked up. "He has really nice eyes."

"The eyes can tell you so much about a person if you look deep enough."

"I like his laugh and voice. He has a great smile, gorgeous hair and he works out."

"He is very muscular. I like muscular men. He has a nice butt."

"Emma!" Alanna said, shocked.

Emma giggled. "Well, I'm old, not dead."

Alanna laughed. "What would Gilbert say?" She referred to Emma's husband of forty plus years.

"In his day Gil was the best built man in town." Her gaze became unfocused as she remembered. "He was a strappin' man. A mason by trade. His grandfather and father helped build this house and the wall around the grounds. I remember we met one night at a dance. Nine days later we were married. Talk about love at first sight." She smiled.

"Nine days?" Alanna said in disbelief.

"Yes, we went out on two dates that week after the dance and he asked me to marry him the night of our second date."

"And you said yes? After two dates?"

"Yes, I just knew he was the one."

"Wow! That's amazing! I just can't see two people meeting and falling in love that quick."

Emma looked at Alanna. "These days people don't let love work its magic—and it can be magical. But now look at your mom and dad.

They were friends, just friends for years, then she went away to college. He became a cop. Then one day when she was home for summer break, he pulled her over for speeding. She didn't even try to get out of the ticket but he let her off with a warning. The next day she came into the station looking for him, and well, you know the rest. I've never seen two people more meant to be together than them."

"He said she asked him out."

"Eva was a fearless individual. I always admired that about her." She patted Alanna's hand. "Is fear holding you back from spending time with Derek?"

"A little . . . I really hate getting hurt."

"Physical pain heals faster than emotional pain. Emotional pain can last a lifetime if you let it. It's all up to you, sweetie. I see a lot of your mother in you. Fear is something you can overcome so if that young man asks you out, you just remember what I've said."

"You're old, not dead."

"Ha, ha." Emma stood up. "Now I made a nice artichoke and spinach dip for you to take to your ladies' get together. I'm still working on the food for your father's poker night, so do you want bread or chips to go with the dip?"

"Both?"

"Good choice, I'll have it ready in a jiff."

"I'm going to go change." Alanna looked around. Jet was on the floor, but no Juneau or Abbey. "Have you seen the cats?"

"Abbey is asleep in the upstairs linen closet. That little brat scared me to death today. She got up onto one of the top shelves and got back underneath a blanket when I had the door open. I didn't see her get in there and then she jumped out at me when I went to put some sheets on the shelf below. I screamed and she crawled back under the blanket, so I left her there. The doors are still open. Juneau was in the dining room a little while ago."

Alanna walked into the large dining room they used only on holidays when the whole family got together. The first thing she noticed was a set of giant green eyes looking at her. Juneau was curled up inside the very large crystal punch bowl on the sideboard under the window. She was looking at Alanna through the bowl, her eyes magnified by the crystal.

"What're you doing?"

"Just getting a different view of the world."

"And?"

"You look short and fat, and the top of your head is flat."

"Ok."

"I heard you and Emma talking. You shouldn't date that dog lover."

"And why not?"

"Because he's a dog lover."

"I love dogs."

"Yes, but you had cats first."

"He might like cats."

"Doesn't matter, he prefers dogs. Nothing good can come from being with a dog lover."

Alanna threw her hands in the air and turned to go upstairs. "Everyone has an opinion about my love life."

As she entered her room she noticed the linen closet doors were open. She walked over and looked in. She couldn't see Abbey but she could hear her purring. As she pulled the edge of the blanket back, she found Abbey asleep with her nose tucked between her paws. She stirred a little then tucked a paw over her ear, continuing to sleep. Alanna put the blanket back down, then went to her room to change clothes.

At 6:10 Fintan still wasn't home and Alanna left to pick up Sam. Cecilia's house was small but very clean, and well kept. Dozens of rose bushes covered her front and back yard. She grew many different varieties of roses and she'd taken home numerous blue ribbons from surrounding county fairs and flower shows. If you asked her, she could talk for hours about them. She also loved French Provincial furniture, something Alanna didn't really care for, but it suited Cecilia. A large, illuminated oil painting of William Shakespeare hung over the fireplace.

Card tables were set up to accommodate the twelve ladies. They all talked and laughed, whilst eating and drinking the provisions they had brought. Then Cecilia rang the bell and everyone took their places at the tables and began to play a dice game called Bunco. The room grew noisy as each one took their turn with the three dice. The bell rang and they changed tables. About an hour later they stopped for a break and to eat a dessert that Cecilia had provided. Then she rang the bell and the playing resumed.

An hour later, Charlene was declared to be the winner of the $60 pot. Each lady had put in $5 to play.

They began to clean up and help Cecilia put away the tables and chairs. She insisted she would take care of it all, and soon everyone was leaving. Alanna and Sam were two of the last people to go. Alanna dropped Sam off and headed home. When she pulled into the driveway of Treasure Grove it looked like a city hall meeting was being held.

Fintan's squad car was there along with Andy's Sheriff's SUV, the fire chief's car, the game warden's SUV, a car that had the Aurum City seal on the door and, to her surprise, Derek's truck.

She pulled into the garage and closed the door. No animals were around. She knew where everyone was . . . they were in Man Land. That's what her mother and grandmother called the overly large barn behind the house. Her great-grandfather had built the barn to house his inventions. Over the years the barn had been home to many things. Now it was heated, cooled, renovated, and filled with Fintan's tools, fishing boat, riding lawnmower, his first car, and many other manly items. One thing of her grandfather's that remained was a large space on the wall which was tiled and showed the periodic table of elements. Each tile showed an element. Fintan spent a lot of time in the large barn, especially on the third Friday of the month. That was poker night.

Alanna walked across the backyard and up to the double doors on the side of the barn. One of the doors was slightly open and she could hear them talking inside.

"It's to you, Fin. What'cha bid?"

Alanna pulled open the door and walked in. Six men sat around a poker table at the far end of the barn. Thick smoke was illuminated by the lamp hanging over the table. Two of the men puffed on cigars, and ashtrays around the table gave evidence of the cigarettes smoked by some of the others. The smell of beer and garlic was strong. Alanna walked over to the table. Fintan, Derek, Fire Chief Aldus "Buck" Stuglemyer, Sheriff Andy, Fish and Game Warden Justin MacLachlin, and City Superintendent Clayton Bridenstine were all sitting with cards in their hands and stacks of poker chips in front of them.

"Miss Alanna!" Buck looked up, greeting her with a wide smile.

"Gentlemen." She smiled as she placed her hand on Andy's shoulder.

"Lady in the house. Watch what'cha say," Andy said, laying a card down, as Justin dealt him another.

"Glad to see you're still in one piece after the other day," Buck chuckled, sitting back and puffing on his cigar.

"Thanks to your crew." She caught Derek's eye. "And Derek. He led them to me."

He smiled a little. "Jet's the real hero." He glanced down at Jet, who was sleeping behind his chair.

She noticed Juneau perched on the canvas-covered tip of Fintan's fishing boat behind Derek. She was looking down over his shoulder at the cards in his hand. From her vantage point she could see Buck's cards also.

I don't think dog lover understands the concept of the game. He never seems to keep the right cards and Buck bluffs a lot."

Abbey was on the opposite side of the table lying on a shelf with paint cans. She was behind Clay and Justin.

"They had shrimp." She closed her eyes and purred.

Alanna looked at the folding table beside them that had been full of food that Emma had made. It was mostly gone and there were some large shrimp tails on the floor by the leg of the table.

Alanna smiled. "Derek, I wanted to thank you for the flowers. They're beautiful."

Derek smiled up at her. "I'm glad you liked them."

There was an ominous silence and the eyes of the other men at the table all shifted to Derek then to Fintan, whose gaze stayed on the cards in his hands. Then Buck sat up and cleared his throat.

"Flowers? Well now, Miss Alanna, I think you best leave so we can torture and interrogate this young man and find out his intentions." Buck's eyes narrowed playfully as he looked at Derek while blowing on the end of his cigar, making it glow red hot.

Andy reached behind himself with one hand, unsnapping the leather trigger guard on his gun holster hanging on the back of his chair. A faint smile touched Justin's mouth as he pulled the handcuffs off his own belt, laying them on the table.

Fintan's mustache twitched a little as he picked up two chips and tossed them onto the pile in the center of the table. "I call," he said, picking up his cigarette.

"Did you know he sent her flowers?" Clay asked Fintan.

Fintan gave a nod as he took a drag.

Andy tossed two chips from his stack onto the table separate from the pile in the center. "Twenty bucks says if he asks her out she says no."

Justin tossed his chips into the separate pile. "And how! Remember Henry? Poor sap limped for a week."

Three of the men laughed, referring to an overzealous drunk man at the last county fair who kept coming on to Alanna. She'd ended up slamming his foot with the sledgehammer from the ring-the-bell strength game because he got in the way.

Clay tossed his chips in. "Don't forget about Ted." A man she had pushed off the end of the dock into the lake at a Fourth of July celebration for the same reason.

Buck tossed in his chips. "And Tommy."

"Tommy's my friend," Alanna defended. "He came up behind me and scared me."

"You mule-kicked him in the nads!" Buck laughed.

"He forgave me. You make everything sound a lot worse than it was." She turned in frustration to leave the barn, her cheeks bright red, their laughter following her.

Fintan looked around the table and tossed his chips on the pile his friends had started "I'll bet she says yes without bodily injury," he said as he crushed out his cigarette and turned to look at Derek. "If you intend to date my daughter I suggest you go after her now. She'll say yes just to show these guys up."

Derek looked him in the eye. "Yes, sir," he said sincerely, tossing his cards on the table and pushing his chair back. "I fold."

As he started to leave, Buck yelled after him. "Make sure you keep your distance. She can be dangerous!"

They all laughed, including Fintan.

Derek found Alanna on the back patio lying on a chaise longue, looking up at the night sky. Jet had woken up when Derek pushed his chair back and was with him. He walked up to the chair next to her.

"Mind if I sit down?"

"No." She didn't look at him.

He reclined on the chair next to hers and looked over at her. Her auburn hair shone in the moonlight and her eyes reflected the sparkle of the stars. God, she was beautiful. His stomach clenched. He wasn't sure what to say.

She broke the silence but didn't look at him. "So, what are your intentions?"

"Well . . ." He was caught off guard by her directness. "I'm not sure."

"You're not sure?" She gave him a sideways, skeptical look.

"After everything those guys were saying, I'm not sure if I should be wearing an athletic cup or a suit of armor to just talk to you." He smiled teasingly.

She looked back up at the sky. "They dramatize everything."

They were both silent, just looking at the sky for a minute.

"I sent the flowers the day after we had dinner with Nick and Sam. I just wanted you to know that I had a good time and I hoped you did too."

"I did." She glanced over and then back up. "A really good time."

Silence settled again for a moment.

"So, how much did you bet?" she asked.

"What?"

"How much did you bet that I'd say yes?"

"Uh . . ." Now he really didn't know what to say. He didn't want to upset her. "Nothing."

She smiled as their eyes met. "You should've taken the bet."

Chapter 10

Cecilia stood at her kitchen sink, washing dishes. She glanced at the clock. It said 10:45 p.m. She felt the evening had gone well. She liked entertaining and missed the large parties she used to host when she'd been married. Her ex-husband was president of a large bank in San Francisco. He'd left her for his secretary. Karma in action, she thought at the time as once she'd been the secretary having the affair with him. The divorce had been very hard on her and didn't leave her with much. Most of the assets had been his before they'd gotten married. She was used to a better life than this. She sighed, pondering this as she washed a plate. The doorbell rang.

"Who could that be at this hour?" she said, wiping her hands on a dish towel.

She opened the front door. No one was on the porch. She stepped out.

"Hello?" She looked around at the yard and driveway. No cars were parked in front by the curb.

"Anyone there?" She was just about to close the door when she looked down.

There, lying on the porch was a bouquet of a dozen red roses.

"Oh, my," she said as she bent down and picked them up. She inspected the bouquet for a card. Nothing. She gave one last glance around before she closed the door. She carried them to the kitchen and sat them down on the counter.

"I wonder who did this." She reached into the cabinet and retrieved a vase. She began to properly trim and prepare the vase of roses. They had really sharp thorns and she poked her fingers three times during the process, sticking the injured finger in her mouth and sucking the drops of blood from each wound. She wished she had her gardening gloves but they were in the shed. Odd. Any florist would have removed the thorns. She realized this bouquet came from an individual's efforts, not a floral shop. A few minutes later she stepped back to look at her work. She scratched her neck, and cleared her throat.

"They are not the best quality, but nice." She rubbed her chest and neck. She leaned against the counter. Something was wrong. What was happening? She pulled the neck of her shirt open. Her chest and neck were covered with large bright red splotches. That's when she felt her throat begin to constrict. She couldn't breathe!

She began to panic as she fell to the floor. She struggled to reach her purse on the counter. All she needed to do was to reach her medication. She began to lose consciousness due to lack of oxygen. She clawed her way up the cabinet, reached the strap of her purse, and pulled it to the floor, spilling its contents. She fell back to the floor, hitting her head on the hard tile. Dazed, she slowly sifted through the spilled contents. Why did she have so much lipstick? She was searching for the small cylinder-type container. Her eyes began to close. No air. Her lips were blue. No air. Her eyelids were blue. She tried so hard to get just one tiny breath. Her fingertips were blue. She fell back on the cold tile floor, motionless.

She was lying unconscious when the back door opened. The killer walked over, and with a gloved hand removed the medical alert bracelet off her wrist, lifted the roses from the vase and placed them back into the wrapping they'd come in, along with everything she'd clipped off. Dumping the water from the vase into the sink, the killer placed it upside down in the wash rack with the other drying dishes then picked up the telephone receiver and dialed 911, before laying the phone on the floor among the scattered contents of the purse. The killer found the small cylinder Cecilia had been searching for. With it, the bracelet and roses in hand, the killer closed the back door and walked around the outside of the house as the sirens sounded in the distance.

Chapter 11

With stinging rain, sharp branches, broken glass and Lori screaming from fear and pain, the dream came again that night. It seemed to be in slow motion compared to before. Branches crashed through the windshield as Lori put her arms up to protect her face while the car turned over and over. Alanna was in the passenger's seat again looking around, watching everything tumble. Items flew around, passing through her, bouncing off the seat. She tried to remember what they were. Purse, cellphone, travel mug, papers, an open map, calculator, books, and a lot of kid's toys flying from the back seat. She thought to herself that she usually woke up about this time.

The car continued to flip—it seemed to go on forever. Lori's head hit the steering wheel repeatedly. Blood soaked her blond hair, face, clothes and hands, blending with the garnets in her ring and obscuring it completely as she tried to keep from hitting her head again. She screamed as a large branch crashed through the driver's window and slashed her shoulder and chest open. Blood-covered tips of the wicked branch pulled back out of the window as the car continued to flip. Finally, the car came to an earth-shaking halt on its driver's side. It rocked a little, then nothing. No sound. Nothing moved. Alanna looked over at Lori. Her bloody, lifeless body slumped against the car door. Alanna thought she heard something . . . a faint buzzing sound like a bee, maybe.

All of a sudden everything went black. Alanna felt a moment of intense panic. Then something grabbed her by the hand and pulled her upwards. Sunlight filtered through the thick treetops above. She was struggling up and over the edge of the air shaft. Derek had her by the hand. He pulled her up, grabbing her by the waist. He pulled her closer. His face and body were so close. She knew he was going to kiss her. She closed her eyes and leaned in. Then he licked her eyelid. She tried to open her eyes, but couldn't. He licked her eyelid again. It felt wet and rough.

Alanna slowly opened one eye. She was lying in bed and Abbey was on her pillow licking the eyelid of her unopened eye.

"Open your eyes, Mommy." Abbey licked again.

"Abbey." She opened the other eye. "Stop it." She rubbed her wet eyelid.

"Play with me." Abbey pulled on a strand of her hair with her paw and mouth.

She sat up. "What are you doing?"

"Want to play." She jumped on Alanna's foot as it moved under the covers.

"Did you have to wake me like that?"

"You wouldn't talk to me." Abbey rolled over, playing with her own tail.

Alanna leaned forward, putting her face in her hands. "I was asleep."

"Sleep done."

"What time is it?" Alanna rubbed her hands over her face.

"Daytime."

"Al, why didn't you tell me?" Sam came in through the open bedroom door carrying bridal magazines and two cups of coffee. Alanna reached over, plucked the cup from Sam's hand, took a long drink, and leaned back against her pillows.

Sam sat down on the bed, tossing the magazines on the end of the bed. Abbey began to play with Sam's hand as she tried to pet her.

"Tell you what?"

"That you and Derek are dating." Sam took a drink of her own coffee. "I'm your best friend and you didn't call and tell me?"

"Technically we're not dating . . . yet."

"But he did ask you out, and you said yes?"

"Ummhmm." Alanna nodded her head taking another sip. "Last night."

"I'm proud of you."

"How did you find out so fast?"

"Emma. She said your dad mentioned it this morning. You better get moving. It's almost ten."

"Really?" Alanna looked over at the clock. "Wow, I didn't realize it was so late." She threw the covers back and headed into the adjoining bathroom to get dressed. Abbey followed her. *"Play!"*

"Did you have a long night?" Sam made herself comfortable on the bed and grabbed a magazine, thumbing through it.

"Not really."

"So, give me details."

"He asked me to dinner tonight." Alanna raised her voice in the other room so Sam could hear her.

"What made you say yes?"

Alanna leaned around the door jam, a toothbrush in her mouth. "Because, Emma thinks he has a nice butt." She smiled.

"What?" Sam stopped turning pages.

"She's old, not dead."

"I hope I'm that way when I'm old . . . looking at young guys' butts. Seriously, what made you change your mind?"

Alanna went back to brushing her teeth. "I don't know." She looked at herself in the mirror. "Just did."

"So where's he taking you to dinner?"

"He didn't say." Alanna came into the room buttoning her jeans, with Abbey chasing her leg. *"Play now?"*

"I hope you two hit it off."

They walked down the hall to one of the guest bedrooms. Alanna opened the closet doors and walked inside. On the shelves and hanging up were costumes of all sizes and types covered in dry-cleaning plastic. Some of them were for her animals. She had been volunteering for over three years for an organization call "PAWZ". It was an organization of mostly retired school teachers that used their pets to help children learn to read. The animals would lie beside the kids at the library and let the kids read to them. The volunteers would supervise and help the kids if they struggled. The kids learned, and the animals enjoyed the attention. Alanna chose to dress her animals up in costumes because the kids liked it.

"Let's see . . ." She looked through the ones hanging. She heard Jet running up the stairs.

"Can I be the bunny?" Jet asked, running into the large walk-in closet.

"You were the bunny two weeks ago."

"She looks cute as the bumble bee." Sam held up a hanger.

"How about the bumble bee?"

"Ok."

Sam laid the costume on the bed.

"Me be witch." Abbey pawed at the clothing and plastic hanging low to the floor.

"That one is for October. You need to pick a spring one."

"Look at this one." Sam held up a jester outfit.

"That for Juneau, not me."

"That is Juneau's size, not hers."

"Ok, Juneau gets this one."

"This one is cute." Alanna held up a hanger with a small ladybug outfit.

"Me be bug." Abbey batted at the antennae with the fuzzy red balls at the ends when Alanna held it down so she could see and smell it.

"Ok. We're good." Alanna carried Abbey and her outfit downstairs, followed by Sam carrying Jet and Juneau's outfits.

They put the costumes down on the table, then refilled their coffee cups and sat down.

"Good, you're up." Emma came into the kitchen from the laundry room.

"Morning."

"I can make you breakfast. I have a little bit of time before the crew gets here."

The crew was a cleaning crew of about ten people that came every two weeks to do all the deep cleaning that the large house needed. Emma kept up the day-to-day things, but the crew did all the major cleaning.

"Ah, Emma?" Sam took a sip of her coffee.

"Yes? Would you like some breakfast also?"

"Sure, but I need to talk to you."

"Of course. What is it?" She smiled over her shoulder.

"Nick and I would like to use the ballroom for our wedding and Al said we could."

"Well, I think that would be wonderful." She stopped what she was doing. "Have you set a date? I must give the crew enough notice."

"We were thinking May."

"May?" She dropped her spatula. "That's next month, child!"

"Not this May." Sam held up her hand. "Next year."

"Oh." Picking her spatula back up she continued, "Well, that's more than enough time."

"We're not sure of the exact date yet."

"That old room could use a good party. It hasn't been used in over six years."

"Ever since we were little I dreamed of having a big party in that room. Your mom used to have the most wonderful parties." Sam smiled at Alanna.

"And you and I always seemed to get in the way."

"Oh, you weren't so bad." Emma set a plate of toast on the table.

"When Eva had her charity balls, you girls were always so excited; running around looking at the flowers, playing with the decorations and eating the food. When you were supposed to be in bed asleep, I would pass the buffet table and look up and there were your little faces behind the vent that opened into the attic."

"You were so great, bringing us a plate of food from the party."

"We could sit up there and hear and see everything."

"A lot of it was boring, all those speeches."

"But most of the time it was pretty entertaining. I liked the costume balls she used to have."

"Hallowe'ens were so awesome."

"And that one 1920s party was neat."

"Your dad looked cool as a gangster in his zoot suit."

"Speaking of charity work, we better get moving. We have to be at the library at 11."

After breakfast they rounded up all three animals, got them into their costumes and then into the SUV, with Juneau protesting about the outfit they had chosen for her.

"A jester?" She scowled as she rode in the back. *"Do I look like a fool?"*

Sam laughed as she glanced into the back and saw the look on Juneau's face under the jester hat with its tiny bells on each tip.

"I love books. I like libraries. I'm not fond of children and I hate wearing these ridiculous outfits and a harness and leash. It's not right! How did I ever let you talk me into doing this every other week?"

"You've been doing this since you were little. You used to enjoy it."

Abbey looked over at Juneau. *"You were little?"*

"Shut up or I'll squash you like the bug you are." Juneau swatted at Abbey. *"I liked it when I was learning to read. I found it educational."*

"It is educational for the kids."

"Knowing my luck, those little monsters will all grow up to be veterinarians."

They pulled into the library parking lot and found a spot. The library was always busy on Saturdays. As they all got out, Alanna and Sam adjusted the head straps on each animal's head so that their outfits looked right as they went in. Sam carried Abbey and Alanna carried Juneau and held Jet's leash. They entered the library and went over to the children's section. Londa Lewis, the woman in charge of the program, was there with the kids.

"Alanna. Sam. Glad to see you and your furry friends." She smiled down at the five kids sitting on the floor in front of her. "Ok, kids. Get your books and choose a station."

Set up in a circle behind them were blankets and pillows that looked like large bright crayons. Each child had a book that was at their level of reading and they sat down on a blanket in front of a pillow. One by one each child chose an animal to sit next to them. Jet lay down next to a young boy who had a lisp and watched his mouth as he read. She liked the way he talked. The children opened their books and began to read out loud to the animal next to them. The girl reading to Abbey showed her the pictures on each page.

Alanna looked over at Abbey one time and her antennae were tilted sideways, making room for the little girl's hand to pet her. Juneau sat still but thumped her tail impatiently. A few minutes later Alanna heard Juneau.

"Someone stop this child! Stop her now!" Juneau meowed. Alanna walked over and knelt down next to the child.

"Katie, is something wrong?"

"I don't know. She just started meowing."

"Well, let's read this part again." Alanna pointed to the beginning of the page. Katie began to read. After three sentences Alanna discovered the problem. Most people said tom-a-toes, especially in the US, but Katie pronounced it tam-toes. Juneau looked up at Alanna.

"Correct this child. She's endangering her fast food career."

Alanna smiled and helped Katie pronounce it right.

One hour, and cookies and milk, later, they were all back in the SUV. Costumes were removed and they were ready to head home when Alanna's cellphone rang. It was Lorraine.

"Alanna, did you hear? Cecilia's dead."

"What? How did she die?"

"I'm not sure. Charlene just said that the paramedics tried everything but that they couldn't save her."

"But, she was fine last night." Alanna looked over at Sam and put her hand over the phone. "Cecilia died."

"What!" Sam exclaimed. "How?"

Alanna shook her head taking her hand away from the phone. "Is there anything I can do?"

"Zara is at the house now."

"Ok, thanks, Rain."

"What happened?" Sam asked.

"I don't know, just that the paramedics couldn't save her." Alanna sat back in the seat. "She was fine when we left last night. Maybe it was some kind of accident or something."

"We should go see if Zara needs anything."

Alanna remembered when she lost her mother. "Ok."

Alanna started the SUV and drove the short distance to Cecilia's house. Four cars were parked in the driveway and in front of the house. Alanna parked by the curb in between Cecilia's house and the one next door. She rolled the windows down and closed the door behind her.

"We won't be long. All of you stay in the truck. I'll be right back."

"Ok." Jet was the only one that answered. Both cats were asleep in their cat beds. The kids had worn them out.

Jet sat watching Alanna and Sam through the open window as they walked up to the door and rang the bell. A young, tall, blond girl opened the door.

"Hello, I'm Alanna and this is Sam. We work with Cecilia. Is Zara here?"

"Hi, I'm Kristina. She's in the kitchen. Come on in."

They followed Kristina to the kitchen and found Zara sitting at the table with a minister and a woman in curlers.

Zara looked up at Alanna and Sam. "She's gone. I don't know what to do. She's gone." She began to sob uncontrollably. The minister patted her hand and the lady handed her another tissue from a box in front of her.

"Zara, I'm so sorry. Is there anything we can do?" Alanna asked.

"I . . . I don't know what to do," Zara cried into the tissue in her hands. Kristina came over and touched her on the shoulder. Zara stood up, they held each other and cried. "She did everything. She took care of everything. I don't even know where to start," Zara sobbed into Kristina's shoulder. Just then a large, redheaded lady came bursting through the front door.

"Zara! Zara. Where are you?" she yelled in a demanding voice.

"Aunt Ellie?" Zara stepped around the table just as the woman entered the kitchen doorway, almost pushing Sam down.

"What happened?" Ellie grabbed her niece and held her tight as tears began to leak out of her eyes.

"The paramedics said she had an allergic reaction and that they couldn't save her." Zara looked up at her aunt. "They gave her Benadryl. They said when that didn't work they gave her Epinephrine."

"What? Didn't they read her bracelet?"

"They said she wasn't wearing it." Zara wiped her eyes. "When they arrived she was lying unconscious on the kitchen floor. She'd called 911. They didn't know what she was allergic to, just that she was having an allergic reaction. They treated it as such. They didn't know that what they were giving her was killing her!" Zara began to cry again. "She was dead when they got to the hospital and they didn't understand why."

"Didn't they have her medical history?"

"It wasn't in their system. Her doctor's in Sacramento . . . she didn't trust small town doctors." Zara's eyes and nose were red as she leaned against her aunt. "They said they tried but it was too late."

Ellie began to cry. "This shouldn't be happening. She always wore her bracelet and kept her card in her wallet."

"They didn't know to look for the card. They were trying to save her. The admissions nurse found her card stuck to the back of her insurance card, but by then it was too late, she was gone."

Alanna stepped into the living room with Sam. "That's really strange, don't you think?"

"Do you think she took it off to wash dishes or take a shower?"

"I don't know. I think she had it on last night, but honestly I wasn't looking for it so I don't know if she was wearing it or not."

"I wonder if anyone else last night noticed if she had it on?"

"She was so anal about it that I don't think she'd forget to put it on."

"Maybe it fell off when we were playing last night? We should look around for it."

Zara came into the living room a few minutes later as they were looking. "Thank you so much for coming by. It means a lot to me that my mom had good friends."

"We were just looking for her bracelet."

"I looked all over when I got here. I couldn't find it."

"Is there anything we can do?" Alanna touched Zara on the shoulder. "Anything at all?"

"Not right now, but thank you. Aunt Ellie said she will take care of everything. She's talking to the minister now. Mrs. Brown, the neighbor, said she'll help with the house. She's Mom's best friend and landlady. They both have such a passion for roses."

"If there's anything we can do just call. Ok?" Alanna wrote her number down on a piece of paper by the chair and handed it to Zara.

"Thank you." She put the paper in her pocket. "I appreciate you coming by. I really do."

They both hugged Zara, said their goodbyes and left. As they walked to the SUV Alanna noticed that Ellie had parked half in the driveway and half in the street.

Alanna opened her door and got in. Sam opened her door and looked down at her seat.

Muddy cat tracks covered her leather seat and door.

"What the . . ." Sam pointed to her seat.

"Who got out of the car?" Alanna looked around to the back, as she handed Sam a container of sanitary wipes from the back.

"I had to." Abbey continued to lick the mud from her paws. *"Had to poooo."*

"There's a litter box right there." Alanna pointed to the covered box.

"Juneau said no stinky in the car while she's in it."

"It's not that bad; there, all clean." Sam closed the container and went to throw the used wipes in the trash can by the curb. She lifted the lid and tossed the used wipes in. Then she stood and stared down at the contents of the trash can. She reached in and pulled out a long stemmed red rose. She carried it back to the truck and got in.

"She threw away a bouquet of roses."

"You took a flower out of the trash?"

"I pulled it from the middle of the bouquet." Sam sniffed the rose. "Besides, it's Cecilia's trash can, it's cleaner than my car."

"Why would she throw away a bouquet of roses?"

"You know her. She expected perfection from her roses. If these babies weren't up to her standards, then, well I guess they had to go." A thorn on the rose poked her finger. "Ouch!" Sam stuck her injured finger in her mouth and sucked the drops of blood. "It has really sharp thorns."

"Maybe that's why." Alanna started the truck and drove away.

Jet laid her head on the console between the front seats. Sam petted her while they drove through town. She sniffed at the rose in Sam's lap.

"Smells strange."

Chapter 12

They pulled through the gate of Treasure Grove and drove up the long drive. Alanna noticed that Derek's pickup was parked in front of the house along with two white vans from the cleaning company.

"You expecting him?" Sam's smile was a little too revealing of her hopefulness.

"No." Alanna pulled into the garage and got out, unloading the animals and costumes.

"There's another dog here!" Jet sniffed the air. *"Male."* She took off, running through the open garage door, nails scraping on the concrete as she rounded the side of the house to the backyard.

"What's that all about?" Sam asked, watching Jet disappear around the corner.

"She smells another dog."

"Great, another dog," Juneau grumbled as she slowly walked into the laundry room while Alanna held the door. *"I'm going eat and take a nap. Make sure it's gone when I wake up."*

"Yes, Your Majesty." Alanna closed the door behind all of them.

"Me want to see other dog." Abbey ran out the open back door.

"You want me to hang these up?" Sam held the costume up.

"No, lay them on the chair. Emma always takes them to the cleaners first."

"Want some coffee?" Alanna poured herself a cup.

"Nah, I'm gonna head home." Sam got her car keys out of her purse. "I have laundry to do." She sniffed the rose in her other hand. "This poor thing needs some water. I'll call you later."

"Later."

Alanna carried her cup out the back door and over to Man Land. The large, roll-up door on the end was up and she could hear her dad's radio playing. She stepped in through the large opening to see both Fintan and Derek leaning over the open hood of the uncovered Mustang. Fintan rose up, twisting a socket wrench in his hand.

"I think that should do it."

Derek went to the workbench. "Hi," he said with a smile as he walked past her.

"Hi. What're you two up to?"

"Derek is going to help me rebuild her engine." Fintan smiled, patting the car's fender affectionately.

Derek placed the engine lift plate on the intake manifold and started to secure it. "My brothers and I have rebuilt a lot of engines. It's a family hobby."

"We still have a lot of things to disconnect but we should be able to pull the engine by this afternoon," Fintan said. She noticed he had a little sparkle in his eye that she hadn't seen in a while.

A chestnut and white colored dog trotted up to her, followed closely by Jet.

"Well, hello." She reached down, holding her hand out for the dog to sniff.

"That's Tanner, he's my dog. I hope you don't mind that I brought him," Derek said. "He doesn't get to run a lot. My yard isn't that big."

"It's fine, I'm sure Jet would like to have someone to play with." Alanna stroked the smooth, short, shiny hair on Tanner's back. He was a unique-looking dog of medium size, with pointy erect ears, a tightly curled tail, small feet, a long muzzle, wrinkled brow, intelligent eyes and a very proud demeanor. "What kind of dog is he?"

"He's a Basenji. They're a type of hound. They don't bark."

"Don't bark?" She raised an eyebrow. "Never?"

"No, they are the only barkless breed. I got him from a rescue organization."

Alanna looked into the dog's alert hazel eyes. "He's very astute looking."

Tanner sat down in front of Alanna. *"Ello,"* she heard him say in a definite British accent.

She giggled, scratching his chin and head. "Ah, you say you got him from a rescue organization?"

"Yeah, they found him in a pound in Sacramento and saved him. That was almost a year ago."

Tanner bared his teeth at her, causing her to pull her hand back.

"Oh, he won't bite you, but he does that all the time. I don't know why."

"Would you please be a dear and brush me teeth? They are utterly filthy," Tanner asked, baring his teeth again.

Alanna smiled. "Would you mind if I took him in the house for a while?"

"No, go ahead. Just know that he likes to chew on things."

"Ok." Alanna started to walk away when she stopped to look back at Fintan. "Dad, did you hear that Cecilia Collins died?"

Fintan rose up from under the hood. "How?" His eyes narrowed.

"They said it was an allergic reaction. Paramedics tried to save her but couldn't."

"When did this happen?" He reached over and took a drag of his cigarette.

"Last night. I think it's weird though because she was only allergic to Benadryl and Epinephrine, which is what the paramedics gave her to try and save her."

"Didn't she have some kind of allergy alert system?"

"Yes, she always wore a bracelet, but for some reason she wasn't wearing it. They couldn't find it anywhere."

"Do her family suspect anything?"

"No, not that I know of, but something just doesn't seem right to me."

"Want me to have someone look into it?" He flicked ashes into the ashtray on the top of the car.

"I don't want to upset anyone, especially Zara. She just lost her mother."

Fintan only had to take one look into her eyes to see what she meant.

"I'll just find out what the paramedics and the M.E. have to say about it. Ok?"

"Ok." She turned and walked across the yard. "Come on, Tanner." She patted her leg.

They all walked into the kitchen.

"Very posh, and sooo spacious." Tanner looked and sniffed around. Alanna refilled her coffee cup, leaning her back against the counter. Abbey was pawing at Tanner's curly tail.

"His tail is funny."

"So, Tanner, you want me to brush your teeth for you?"

He looked up at her from the water bowl he was drinking from, completely astonished. *"Blimey! Did you understand me?"*

"Yes, I understood you."

"Told you," Jet said, lying down on the kitchen floor.

"Brilliant!" He came over and sat down in front of her. *"You are the first 'uman I've met that could understand me. I must admit when Jet said that 'er master could ear 'er and understand 'er, I thought she was a little daft."*

"That doesn't surprise me."

"Yes, please. Me old master used to brush me teeth every day and it's been sooo long. They feel 'orrid." He licked his teeth.

"Let's go upstairs. I think I have an extra toothbrush up there."

They all went upstairs to her bedroom.

"All of your rooms are so large." He sniffed around the room. *"Our flat is rather small."*

"Ok, come in here and let's see what we can do." He followed her into the bathroom connected to the bedroom. She opened a cabinet, getting out a small child-sized toothbrush that was still in the package, and opened it. She laid a towel down on the floor and had him sit on it. Then she got the toothpaste that Dr. Stuckey, the vet, had sold her for Jet. She wet the brush and added the paste, kneeling down in front of him. He bared his teeth as she slowly and gently brushed. He licked and then opened his mouth for her to do the inside.

"Thank the maker." He licked again. *"Umm, tastes like pâté."*

"Tastes like liver to me," Jet said, sitting by the overly large bathtub.

"Pâté is liver."

Abbey sat on the counter and played with the cap of the toothpaste tube, pushing it into the sink.

"Ok. How's that?"

Tanner licked and licked, flicking his tongue in and out of his mouth. *"Fabulous! Thank you so much."*

"You might need to get your teeth cleaned professionally; there is a little tartar."

"I thought me master was taking me to get me teeth cleaned a few months ago. Doctor made me go to sleep and then 'e took me bollocks! The wanker! I want 'em back!"

Alanna laughed. "Ah, I don't think he can give them back. Ok Jet, your turn."

Jet took her place on the towel as Alanna got Jet's toothbrush and brushed her teeth.

While this was going on, Tanner walked into the bedroom and Abbey followed him. He sat down and licked his paw, then pulled his paw over his head and ears, cleaning himself like a cat would. Abbey sat across from him and began to clean herself the same way. The licking caused Juneau to peek one eye over the edge of her cat bed. When she saw a dog cleaning itself like a cat she raised her head up and stared. Was she seeing this right? What kind of dog was this? It continued to lick and clean its entire body. It had a very strange tail. Tanner stopped in mid-lick, looking up at her. His brow furrowed, resulting in lots of wrinkles. He sniffed the air towards her. Alanna and Jet walked in at that point.

"Ok, who's up for a good brushing?"

Abbey and Jet both jumped towards her.

"Me!"

"No. Me!"

"Me!"

"No. Me!"

"How about everyone?" Alanna reached into the nightstand and retrieved a brush. Abbey wound herself in and out of Alanna's legs.

"Me first. Me first."

"Guest first," Alanna said, sitting cross-legged down next to Tanner. He closed his eyes and leaned his head to the side as she brushed his silky coat. "You're a very clean dog."

"It is the only way to be."

"How did you end up with Derek?" She kept brushing.

"Me old master was an ambassador from London. We spent a bit of our time in Washington. 'E 'ad me taken to a few shows, then 'e wanted me to stay with 'im all the time. We were visiting a cousin of 'is when 'e died. Then she took me to the pound. She's a prat she is . . . didn't like me. She was mad at me for cleaning me teeth on 'er snakeskin pumps. They didn't taste like snakeskin. I've tasted real snakeskin and those were not real snakeskin. So, I don't know why she was so upset. Then a lady with a lot of Basenjis came and got me. I was with 'er for a few weeks and then she gave me to me new master. 'E's good to me. Treats me well; just doesn't listen to me."

"He can't hear you."

"'E don't 'ave to. If I get the clicker, I want the telly on. If I get the lead, I want to go to the park. If I get into the cupboard, I want some crisps. It's not that 'ard."

"He just doesn't understand, but maybe I can help. Give me a little time, ok?"

"Right then." He didn't seem too hopeful.

"My turn!" Abbey pushed herself under the brush. *"Now!"*

"Ok, stay still." Alanna brushed Abbey, who fell on her side and pulled herself along the carpet with her claws. Alanna had to get on her hands and knees to keep up with her.

"Ok, now Jet."

"Not done!" Abbey ran over pushing into Alanna's knee. *"Me. Still me!"*

"It's Jet's turn." She started to brush Jet as Abbey tried to walk under Jet who promptly sat down on her.

"Ouch!" Abbey wiggled under Jet's hindquarters. *"Off! Off!"*

Alanna finished brushing Jet and moved over to Juneau's bed.

"Your turn, Miss Sleepyhead." She began to brush her. Juneau rolled over in her bed to expose her other side.

"What kind of dog is that?" She eyed Tanner.

"He's a Basenji."

"He doesn't act like a normal dog."

"He doesn't bark either."

"A dog that doesn't bark? What on earth does he do?" She laughed, sitting up and looking down at Tanner.

"I yodel, howl, laugh, and growl." He came over, grumbling audibly, sounding kind of like a mixture of a growl and yodel.

"Fascinating." Juneau leaned over the edge of the dresser.

"Juneau, this is Tanner. Tanner, this is Juneau."

"'Ello."

"So you really can't bark?"

"No, but I can make meself 'eard if need be."

Juneau stood up and jumped on the bed. Her largeness caused Tanner to raise an eyebrow.

She got down and they sniffed each other.

"You don't smell like any dog I've ever met."

"I keep clean. Most dogs I've met don't clean themselves very well."

"Hey!" Jet took offense.

"Nothing personal. It's just me kind . . . we clean ourselves constantly."

"It's tough staying clean. Isn't it?" Juneau headed for the door as Tanner fell into step beside her.

"Dirt everywhere, and me toes are always filthy."

"I know. I have so much trouble with my tail. It is always getting dusty."

They walked out of the room like two old friends chatting away. Alanna and Jet looked at each other in shock.

"What do you make of that?"

"Did you call a priest and have an exorcism done, or something else I don't know about?"

"Don't be catty."

"I'm serious. She usually doesn't like anyone. Especially a dog."

"Oh, she's just little standoffish."

"Stand on you-ish is more like it."

"She likes me!" Abbey sat on the bed.

"She tolerates you just like she tolerates me."

"She likes me! She said so. Once."

"Once." Jet stretched. *"When you let her have some of your tuna she said 'you're ok'. I remember."*

"See? She likes me."

Chapter 13

Alanna walked outside to the backyard. The cleaning crew was working on the east side of the house. She saw one of them at a downstairs window. She had completed her inside chores of food dishes, water bowls and litter boxes. Now she was filling the squirrel, bird feeders and water sources all over the yard. Juneau was following Tanner around the back yard as he sniffed and investigated everything. Jet was sunning herself on the patio and Abbey was chasing a bug. A squirrel ran up a tree as Alanna approached it.

"Chick, chick, chickahhak!" the squirrel above her yelled. *"Leave, leave, go away!"*

"Hold your horses." She lifted the lid, filling the feeder. "You little ones eat this faster than I can fill it."

"Chick, chick." He leaned over the branch. *"You give me more?"*

Alanna had found, as most Aurums had discovered over the years, that it was better to feed the hordes of squirrel than to have them raid all possible food sources, and she really liked having all the squirrels around. They did get into lots of mischief but they were very comical. She'd explained to Tanner the rules of yard and house, so he knew he could playfully chase the squirrels but was not allowed to touch or hurt them. He took off after one and it scurried up a tree.

"He almost got you," the squirrel above Alanna yelled across to the other squirrel.

"That was close."

"He seems faster than the black one."

"He is." The squirrel breathed easier. *"Quiet too."*

"You should give him a run."

"You do it."

"You're quicker."

"Yes, I am." The squirrel jumped to a lower branch and yelled down at Tanner. *"Hey, Pig Tail! Bet you can't catch me."*

Tanner looked up from the patch of grass he was sniffing. *"Are you addressing me?"*

"Yeah! Pig Tail! Pig Tail! Pig Tail!" The squirrel hopped up and down on the branch, chattering.

Tanner looked over at Juneau. *"What does 'e mean by Pig Tail?"*

"I think he is comparing your tail to that of a filthy common swine."

"'ow rude!" Tanner walked over to the squirrel's tree and looked up at him. *"I'll box your ears if you talk to me that way again."*

"Oink, oink!" the squirrel chattered as he jumped from one branch to another, moving three trees over. Tanner followed on the ground until he got to the tree which had a lower branch. He jumped up, climbed onto the branch, and with his paws splayed and toenails digging in he climbed, pulling himself up to the next branch.

"Fascinating," Juneau murmured.

The squirrel ran to the end of the branch above him. *"What are you, man?"* the squirrel yelled. *"I've never seen a dog that climbs trees!"*

"You are evil and evil must be destroyed." Tanner quoted a line he'd heard on the television. He pulled himself up one more branch, moving closer to the squirrel, who moved further out onto the limb. All the commotion had gotten Alanna's attention as she walked over to Juneau and looked down at her.

"What's going on?"

"Tanner is chasing a rude squirrel."

"Which way did he go?" Alanna looked around the yard and bases of the trees.

"Up."

"What do you mean up?" Alanna shielded her eyes from the sun, looking up into the branches. "Holy cow! How'd he get up there?" She saw Tanner sitting on the branch, close to the trunk of the tree, with the squirrel at the end of the same branch chattering away and twitching its tail angrily.

"Get out of here you crazy dog! Dogs don't climb trees! Get out of my tree!"

"You're really out on a limb now, aren't you?" Tanner curved his lips up in a smile as he secured his footing.

"Tanner! Come down from there." Alanna shouted up. "Right now."

"'E called me a Pig Tail, 'e did."

"He's just a squirrel. You're going to get hurt. Please come down." She contemplated how she would get him down.

"'E deserves a good boxing."

"I'm sure he does, but I need you to come down. Now, please?"

"You're a lucky bugger," Tanner said to the squirrel as he turned

himself around and lowered his body backwards down to the branch below. He held on with his front paws and splayed his back paws, gripping the branch below. Alanna held her arms up to catch him just in case. He moved slowly but steadily down to the next branch. She reached up and retrieved him from the lowest branch.

She sat him gently on the ground. "I think that's one of the strangest things I've ever seen. You're an amazing dog."

"Yes, I know." He began to clean his paws and ears.

"Please stay on the ground." She patted him on the head.

"If you insist." He trotted over to investigate the bushes along the inside of the large cement wall. Juneau followed him.

Alanna looked around the yard for Abbey, not seeing her. Jet was sunning herself on the patio.

She called out. "Abbey?" She walked into the house. "Abbey?" No answer. She heard a noise out in the garage so she walked through the laundry room and out to the garage. The large door to her stall was still open.

She saw Abbey inside the SUV, pawing at her cat bed. She opened the door to the backseat.

"Abbey, what're you doing?"

"Looking for my treasure."

"What treasure?" She pulled the cushion out of the cat bed, and a small, dirty object fell down into the middle of the outer shell as Abbey pounced on it.

"Mine!" She grabbed it in her mouth and jumped out the door. Alanna put the cushion back and closed the door, following her into the kitchen.

"What is that, and where did you get it?"

"Mine!" Abbey raced up the stairs around the hallway corner with it in her mouth. She almost ran into a cleaning crew worker, causing the worker to clutch the tray of cleaning supplies she had in her hands. Alanna came around the corner.

"Hello. Did you see a cat run by here?"

"Yes, it went in there." The lady pointed towards Alanna's bedroom door.

"Thank you." Alanna went into her room and closed the door.

"Abbey?" She looked around the room and then got on her hands and knees. She lifted up the bed skirt and looked under the bed.

"My treasure." Abbey held the dirty object between her paws and pulled it close to her chest.

"Let me see it." Alanna reached for it, but Abbey was just out of reach.

"I found it. It's mine!" She scooted back a few more inches.

"I just want to see it."

"You'll take it. You always take my treasures."

"Not always." Alanna flattened herself down onto the floor and reached further under the bed. "Just let me see what it is."

"No." She scooted back a little more.

"Fine. I was going to give you a treat for it but that's ok. I'll go back outside." Alanna got out from under the bed and sat on the floor, waiting.

"What kind of treat?"

She smiled playing to Abbey's weakness. "How about some shrimp?"

"Really?" Abbey poked her head out from under the bed skirt a little.

"Yes, really. I'll open a can of those little ones you like, but you can't have the whole can because you'll get sick, so just a few."

"K." Abbey ran out from under the bed leaving the object behind. She jumped up at the closed door. *"Shrimp!"*

Alanna lay back down on the floor and reached as far as she could under the bed. Her fingertips just barely touched the object. She finally came out from under the bed. In her hand was a dirt-encrusted medical alert bracelet. She rubbed her thumb over the top of it, removing a layer of dirt. Embedded with dirt, the engraving read "Cecilia Collins".

"Abbey! Where did you get this?"

"Shrimp. Shrimp now!" She pawed towards the doorknob.

"Abbey this is important." Alanna moved closer to her, thinking about earlier when they had been at Cecilia's house. "Very important, baby. When you got out of the truck to go to potty, where did you find this?" She held out the bracelet.

"You promised shrimp." Abbey sat down in front of the door with a pout, backing her ears a little.

"Yes, and I'll get it for you, but just tell me where you found this. Please?"

"Under the pokey flower bush by the fence. Shrimp now?"

She looked at the clasp on the bracelet; it wasn't broken. The wheels in her mind were turning as she opened the door and Abbey ran as fast as she could down the stairs to the kitchen. *"Yay, shrimp!"*

Alanna slowly descended the stairs, setting the bracelet down on the counter as she got a can of shrimp and placed some of the contents on a small plate. She sat the plate on the floor and Abbey began devouring the shrimp.

"Shrimp good."

Alanna put the rest of the shrimp in the fridge. She rinsed the can and put it in the recycling container under the sink. As she leaned against the counter drying her hands, she wondered why the bracelet had fallen off if the clasp wasn't broken. What should she do with it? Take it back to Zara? Give it to her dad? Try to find which bush it had been under? If she could just remember . . . did Cecilia have it on last night? The phone rang.

"Hello."

"Hey, Al. I was thinking about running up to Pavo Inn. I'm going to check out their honeymoon suite. Wanna come?"

"Isn't it a little soon to be doing that?"

"Al, if I don't book a suite now we'll never get one."

"I thought you were doing laundry?"

"I can do it tomorrow. So, you wanna come?"

"Yeah, sure."

"I'll pick you up in a few."

She replaced the receiver then she put the bracelet into a plastic zip bag.

Abbey licked her whiskers. *"More shrimp?"*

"No. You've had enough."

"Want more."

"Abbey." She reached down, picking her up, cuddling and petting her. "No more, and thank you for finding the bracelet." She kissed the top of Abbey's head.

"Can I have it back?"

"No, it belongs to someone else, but I can get you something to play with if you want."

"What?"

She went to a drawer and pulled out a small, fuzzy fake mouse.

"Here. Play with this." She sat her down and threw the mouse down the hall. Abbey ran after it. She could hear her batting it around the floor. She picked up the bag with the bracelet in it as she went outside to Man Land.

"Dad, can I talk to you a minute?" She saw him by his toolbox. Derek was under the open hood of the car, making a lot of noise with a socket wrench.

"Yeah, what's up?"

"Abbey found this under a rose bush at Cecilia's when we were there earlier." She showed him the bag. "What should I do?"

Fintan looked at the bracelet without touching the bag. His hands were covered in grease and oil. "Is it damaged?"

"No, not that I can tell, and the clasp isn't bent or broken in any way."

"Put it in my desk drawer. I already put a call in. Don't tell anyone you found it. Let's wait to hear back and see what they find."

"Ok, I understand." She stepped away. "I'm going with Sam up to Pavo Inn to check out their honeymoon suite so I'll be gone for a while."

"Honeymoon suite?"

"Yeah, she says she needs to reserve one now."

"Just be careful. Those roads are dangerous."

Chapter 14

Sam and Alanna drove to the end of Treasure Grove Way then turned right, passing the windmill house, which was where Roger Atherton and his wife lived, then ten miles later they turned onto Red-Tailed Hawk Ridge Road. This road ran along the east side of Lake Oro. At one point, the road started to climb up the side of the adjacent mountain. Sharp turns along the side of the mountain carved out a huge section of tall trees next to the lake shore. A large number of red-tailed hawks nested in those trees. Bird watchers from all over came to watch and study them. Alanna stared out the windshield at the trees as they went by. They towered overhead and blocked a lot of the afternoon sun.

"You're thinking about it aren't you?" Sam glanced over.

Alanna's brow furrowed as the bracelet crossed her mind. Had she said something, not realizing it? No. She'd been careful not to say anything. She looked cautiously at Sam.

"About what?"

"Your date."

Alanna sighed. "Oh, a little."

"Don't worry. It's like riding a bike. Just don't overthink it. Try to relax and just be yourself."

"Be myself, huh? You don't think the whole I-hate-dating thing will show?"

"Well, it will if you want it to. You two got along great the other night. You also have a lot in common."

"I don't know. I'm starting to have second thoughts. I really like being single, no one to answer to or worry about. No stress. No hassles."

"No fun. No passion. No adventure."

"No pain. No sorrow. No devastation."

"Do you have to be so negative?"

"Yeah, well, I don't have a very good track record with men."

"So? That doesn't mean anything. You still have to get out there and try."

"Says who? Actually, now that you mention it, maybe I should call and cancel?" Alanna pulled her phone out of her purse.

"Woman! You put that phone away. You're going! If I have to dress you and push you out the front door myself, I swear you're going."

"Ok, ok. Calm down and watch the road." Alanna put her phone away.

Sam slowed down as they came to a really sharp turn. Alanna glanced over her left shoulder as they turned. She saw a white cross with a ring of flowers looped around the top on the side of the road by the drop-off.

"Sam, stop!"

"I can't stop here, it's a sheer rock wall." Sam looked in her rearview mirror. "What's wrong? What did you see?"

Alanna continued to look at the road behind them. "This is it! This is the section of the road from my dream." They passed the sign with the flashing yellow light.

"Well, I can't stop. Sorry. Maybe on the way back we can pull off, but I didn't see any room on that side either."

"Maybe there's a turn close by."

Sam saw a small patch on the opposite side of the road just barely big enough for a car to pull into; however, the passenger would be opening their door to a drop off.

"Do you want me to pull in there?"

"No, it's too dangerous. Just keep going." She sat back in the seat.

"Sorry."

"It's ok . . . maybe on the way back."

They kept driving. Fifteen minutes later they turned onto Kome Road which led to the large casino and resort on the east side of the lake. They passed the entrance to the casino and went further up the road. There, nestled among the large trees on the bank of the lake was a very attractive bed and breakfast: The Pavo Inn. It was a very old Victorian home that the owners had converted.

They pulled into the long driveway, crossing a type of cattle guard. The inn was very beautiful and tranquil. The sounds of the lake lapping at the shore could be heard, along with the calls of a peacock. They went to the front double doors; the inn still looked like someone's home. A small sign above the doorbell said *Ring If Locked*. They tried the doorknob; it was open. Inside, the Greek theme was very apparent. In the entryway they found a small marble table with a bell. They rang the bell.

"Hello." A young woman with an apron approached them from a

doorway down the hall. "Welcome to the Pavo Inn. How can I help you?"

"Hi, I'm Sam, and this is my best friend Alanna. I called earlier about the bridal suite."

"Oh, yes. I'm Selena, nice to meet you. My husband, Richard, and I are the owners and managers. Thank you for considering our inn. We have one suite we consider the bridal suite. There's nobody in it today, so go on in. It's unlocked. It's the first door at the end of hall to the left. Number 1. I'll be in the kitchen when you're done."

"Thank you." Sam started down the hall.

Alanna glanced back at Selena, having noticed her matching peacock feather earrings and necklace. She was also taking in the artwork as they walked. Rich, dark wood and marble were everywhere.

They found the door, which was decorated with a ceramic peacock plume with a gold 1 in the eye. The Greek gods would have been proud of the lavishness. The walls were draped in cream-colored silk. Marble pillars surrounded the marble oval bath with steps going up to it. The bed was large and covered with black, cream and gold silks and satins. The floors were also of marble, with black fur rugs scattered here and there.

Alanna walked to the balcony doors, opened them and stepped outside. The view of the lake was beautiful. There were three peacocks in the yard. The male didn't have his tail up; it dragged behind him as he walked across the stone path to the lake.

"So, what do you think?" Sam asked, coming out of the bathroom. "The shower has three shower heads." She giggled.

"It's not my wedding night, it's yours. What will Nick think?"

"He'll think it's fun. It was his idea."

"Guess you'll have to get him a toga or a loincloth."

"Oh, I am so doing that. Do you think Aphrodite wore lingerie?"

"I think she may have invented it. Well, the goddess version anyway."

"We'll be here one night, then we'll leave the next day to go on our honeymoon."

"Where did you guys decide to go?" Alanna lay down on the bed and looked up at herself in the mirror on the ceiling. Sam closed the balcony doors, walked over and lay on the opposite side of the bed. As the tops of their heads touched, they stared up at each other's reflections. Alanna reached above her head and touched Sam's head and then poked her in the ear.

"We were thinking about an Alaskan cruise but we're not sure yet." Sam reached up and squeezed Alanna's nose. "Nick wants to go on a cruise. Ever since we all took that one last year, he's wanted to take another one. Besides, we've lived together for two years. So, it's not going to be a stay-in-bed honeymoon." She held Alanna's nose closed as Alanna answered.

"It could be if you want it to be." Alanna roughed up Sam's eyebrows and patted her cheeks. Sam let go of her nose.

"Nah, we like doing things outdoors together. I've been looking into it. There are lots of excursions and activities: helicopter rides to glaciers, treks through the rainforest, and dog-sledding if it's the right time of year. But a cruise to some place tropical might be nice also."

They both got up from the bed and smoothed the bedspread.

"This would be a nice start to a honeymoon." Alanna pointed to the oversize jetted tub.

"We were looking at the calendar when I got home and we narrowed it down to two dates. So he asked if I could check this place out and see if one of those dates was available."

They left the room and walked down the hall toward the dining room and kitchen. They passed a door that had a sign on it that read *Manager*, and under that sign there was another with a peacock feather swinging arrow that read that *Dick* was *In* or *Out*, depending which way the arrow was pointing. Sam pointed to it and giggled. It indicated *Dick* was *In*. They found Selena in the kitchen, chopping celery.

"So, did you like the suite?" She put the knife down and wiped her hands.

"Yes, yes I did. We were hoping it was available for the tenth of May next year?"

"Let me see." She went to a table in the corner and leafed through the pages of a leather binder. "Yes, that day is open."

"Great. We'd like to book it."

"There is a deposit that is refundable with at least seventy two hours' notice."

"Ok." Sam dug in her purse, retrieved her credit card, and handed it to Selena.

"I'll be right back." She left the kitchen and went down the hall to the office.

"Well, we're getting married on the tenth," Sam said with a deep breath.

"Are you ok with that day?"

"Yeah, I'm just glad we have a date set. It's so hard to really start planning without it. So now, we have a date. Next, I need to choose a dress."

"Why the dress?"

"They say the dress sets the tone for everything, it's kind of the focal point. It determines what kind of wedding you're having. I want a traditional wedding. Nick and I are old fashioned in that way. I loved the dress we saw in Lodi, I mean totally loved that dress, but it's way out of our budget. We don't believe in starting our married life in debt. If it was a mortgage that would be different, but not for the wedding."

"I think that's smart. Some people don't get the wedding paid off before they have to start paying the divorce attorneys."

Sam shot her a look. "Negativity!"

"Sorry." Alanna sighed, looking around the large gourmet kitchen to avoid Sam's irritated eyes.

Selena came back into the kitchen handing Sam a receipt and pen. Sam signed then put her copy and credit card back in her purse.

"Here's a brochure on the inn and our amenities."

"Thank you."

"If there are any special needs or requests you have for your stay, don't hesitate to call. The number is on the brochure."

They said goodbye and left. As they drove Alanna thought about Sam and Nick; how they'd finally got together, dated and fallen in love. They were good together. She'd seen them argue, but for the most part they were happy to compromise. It seemed effortless for them. Alanna envied that a little. Relationships were always hard work to her. Sam was right. She needed to stop being so negative and pessimistic about men.

There was something about Derek that intrigued her, she was drawn to him in a way, and that's why she'd agreed to go out with him; just what it was that drew her she couldn't yet put her finger on. She noticed they were coming close to the spot where she wanted to stop.

"Do you see a turn off?" She rolled down her window and looked out a little.

"There's a dirt road by that tree." Sam flipped on her blinker.

"That's about as close as we can get, huh?"

"Yeah." Sam turned onto the small dirt road and followed it a short way and then stopped. "Do you want to get out?"

"Follow this road a little. It looks like it turns up there." She pointed.

The road did turn, then went down to the bottom of the mountain. They stopped at the spot they thought would align with the cross on the road above. Alanna got out and walked to the edge of the tree-line by the road. Grass, weeds and saplings were growing up over small pieces of metal, glass and what looked like tail-light plastic. She bent down and came up with a piece of metal. It was painted red on one side. Had Lori's car been red? Yes, it had been.

She looked up the side of the mountain. This was the place where the car had come to rest. Some of the tree trunks and branches still showed signs of trauma, but you had to look for it. Time and nature had a way of healing and covering things up. In the dark of night and the pouring rain she wondered how long it had taken for someone to find the wreck, and Lori. She remembered that Lori had been coming from the casino. Something occurred to Alanna. What had scared Lori? Alanna had felt her fear and her tears. It had felt like she was trying to flee from something savage. She remembered the beating of her terror-gripped heart.

"Hey, Al. Are you going to stare at those trees all day?"

"No." She got back in the car.

"So?"

"This is the place." She fastened her seat belt. "This is where she died."

"Creepy." Sam put the car in reverse. "Are you still dreaming about her?"

"Yeah, kind of." Alanna sat back. "Actually, my last dream ended with . . ."

"With what?"

Alanna hesitated. "Nothing."

"Oh, come on. I hate it when you do that. What was it? You can tell me. I won't judge." Sam pulled on to the main road and shortly passed the white cross and flowers.

Alanna watched it go by. "Derek. It ended with Derek."

Sam glanced over smiling. "Was he naked?"

"No! He was not!" Alanna rolled her eyes, shaking her head.

Sam laughed. "Too bad."

Chapter 15

Alanna sat in the passenger's side of Derek's pickup as he drove to the southwest side of town. They were going to his house so he could shower and change before they went on their date. Working on the car had taken longer than he'd anticipated. He'd washed his hands but his arms and clothes were still covered and smelled of grease, gasoline, and sweat. He wanted to go home, shower, change, then come back and escort her properly, but she'd insisted on not wasting the gas going back and forth. Tanner sat between them on the bench seat. Sam had helped pick out Alanna's outfit. She had wanted to wear jeans and a nice shirt, but Sam insisted she wear a dress. She owned a lot of nice dresses; she just never really had occasion to wear them. The one Sam wanted her to wear was too low-cut, especially for a first date, so she chose one she felt was flattering, not too revealing, but still a little sexy. She was glad he was tall so she was at least able to wear heels. Still, being 5'9" and wearing heels barely brought her eye-level to him. She guessed he must be 6'4" or taller. She'd enjoyed the look on his face when she came down the stairs all dressed up, hair and makeup perfect. "You're absolutely gorgeous," he'd said. She could tell by the way he looked her over from head to toe that he was sincere about the comment. She smoothed her dress and glanced over at him.

"How are things going with the Mustang?" She tried to make casual conversation.

"It's a great car. The body's in excellent condition and it needs a new paint job, but we got the engine pulled. Now your dad has to decide if he wants to rebuild this one or get a new one. I know a shop in Stockton that will bore out his old one. Doing a long block is a lot of work, but honestly the cost is about the same. He might be better off getting a new one . . . it's up to him. If the numbers match, he should keep it all original. He said he's had that car since he was seventeen, that his father bought it new in 1967."

"Grandpa gave him that car when he got his license. All of my uncles wanted it but Grandpa gave it to Dad because he was the most cautious and careful driver, and he truly loved the car. It's been sitting under that tarp since I was little."

He turned the truck onto Birch Street. "I can tell it means a lot to him."

She petted Tanner. "So, you do realize I didn't understand a thing you just said about all that long block and engine number stuff."

He glanced over. "Sorry. Do you want me to explain?"

"Maybe later. But, if you start naming parts I'll need visual aids." She smiled.

He chuckled. "Ok, I'll get my powerpoint while I'm home." He pulled into the driveway of 710 Birch Street next to his work truck. He shut the engine off and grabbed Tanner's leash. It was small, tan house with green trim. He had a nice yard and tree, but no flowers or gardener touches. She did notice the welcome mat as he held the door open for her. It was a picture of a pirate ship with a sail reading *AVAST*. Not very welcoming.

"Come on in," he said, showing her into the living room. Alanna looked around the room. It was a bachelor's pad, no doubt about that. To her surprise, it was neat and clean. And it smelled of . . . jasmine. Yes, definitely jasmine. There was nothing on the walls. No art. No pictures. Just bare white walls. Bookshelves covered two entire walls. A large black leather sectional sofa was between the dining room and living room and there the crowning jewel was an overly large, flat screen television that dominated one wall. She noticed not one or two gaming systems, but eight different ones.

"There are drinks in the fridge if you want anything. I'll be out in a few minutes." He unhooked Tanner's leash, hanging it on a hook by the front door.

"Ok, thanks." She crossed to the bookshelves, perusing the titles.

"Damn it, Tanner!" He rushed over and retrieved the mangled remote from Tanner who had it on the couch, chewing on it.

"Turn the telly on."

Tanner watched as Derek wiped the remote off then turned on the television.

"He loves to watch TV, but he keeps chewing up the remote." Derek picked an animal channel then placed the remote on one of upper shelves of the bookcases.

"Just make yourself at home." Derek left the room, going down the hall toward the bathroom. A few minutes later she heard the shower running.

"I was wondering why 'e tarted up the place a bit before we left,"

Tanner said with a yawn as he stretched out on the sofa. *"I wish 'e ad a clicker like yours . . . large buttons and all. Juneau showed me. I bet I could work one like that."* He sniffed the air. *"Smells like a bloody garden blew off in 'ere, 'im and that spray!"* He laid his head down on his paws, staring at the TV.

Alanna noticed that Derek's favorite author must be Stephen King. He had three shelves of his books, all in hardback. The rest were by a variety of authors, mostly paperbacks, but to her surprise they were all alphabetized by author. Then she moved to another bookshelf that housed only movies and video games. She liked a lot of these movies, but there were some she had never heard of. Lots of music, manga and comic books were on another bookshelf.

She spent the next few minutes walking around, glancing in the kitchen, dining room and out the sliding glass door to the back yard. She noticed that the only thing hanging on the wall was a calendar by the phone in the kitchen. She walked over to it. It didn't have scantily clad women or cars like she expected. Instead it had black and white photos taken by Ansel Adams. There was only one date circled: Saturday, April 29th. In the square it read *Mom's B day.* She sat down on the sofa next to Tanner, glancing at the paperback on the coffee table. It was by one of her favorite authors and had a bookmark halfway through it. She had read this one. She heard a door down the hall open and. Derek came in with bare feet and no shirt, just jeans, rubbing his wet hair with a towel.

"Doing ok?" he asked.

Her breath caught in her throat, and a weird, quivering feeling went through her, as she allowed her eyes to roam over his well-muscled body. God, he was gorgeous. So tall and tanned, with a rock hard body that included great biceps and really broad shoulders. There wasn't much hair on his incredible chest. His muscles glistened as drops rained down from his wet hair, running down his taut eight-pack abs to the waistband of his jeans. Her eyes followed them as they rolled down. There was a stirring deep inside of her and suddenly she became very self-conscious. One side of his mouth raised in a grin as he watched her stare at him.

"Ah . . . yeah, fine," she stammered snapping out of her intense gaze. "We like some of the same authors." She motioned to the bookcase, averting her eyes and trying to ignore the thoughts running through her mind.

He leaned against the door frame. "I like to read. My mom always made us kids read an hour every day. When I was little I thought it was a punishment, but then I discovered a series of books where kids turn into animals and could talk to them and I was hooked. Mom couldn't get me to stop reading."

Alanna froze. *Did he say talk to animals?* Yes he did. He wasn't referring to her. Books. He was referring to books. Books he liked. She was becoming increasingly nervous. She took a deep breath, trying to steady her nerves.

"I'm the same way. I love to read. My mom was a teacher. We used to read to each other all the time when I was little."

"I had your mom for English when I was in the eighth grade."

"Really?"

"Yeah. Even though she tried, I was never very good at diagramming sentences."

"Me neither."

"I'll be ready in a few minutes." He turned to go back down the hall when she noticed a mark on his right shoulder blade. It wasn't a tattoo, it was more like a birthmark. It looked like a backwards K next to an F, but they weren't shaped right, and there were other lines connecting them, with arrows and triangles in between them. It was a pretty complicated looking design. The mark was a good two and a half inches high. It looked like a brand, but it wasn't burned in.

She heard a hairdryer start.

She shifted, uncrossing and then crossing her legs again. Thoughts ran through her mind. She hardly knew him, yet she was drawn to him. Maybe she should have worn the low-cut dress. Her mouth was very dry. She was so out of practice at dating. She drummed her fingers on the arm of the sofa and looked at her watch.

"You want to mate 'im?" Tanner looked up at her.

"No, I do not." She crossed her arms. "What on earth makes you say that?"

"Your scent changed."

She stood up, walking around the room. "Well, just keep that to yourself, thank you very much."

He snorted and laid his head back down. *"Females."*

Then she sat back down by him lowering her voice. "Tanner, does Derek have a lot of females come over?"

He yawned and stretched. *"Nah, 'e 'asn't 'ad any since I been 'ere. Just 'is mom and 'is sister and they're on at 'im to get a mate. 'E just works, works out, plays ball, rides 'is bike, watches telly, plays telly games and reads. 'E likes to read a lot."* He cocked his head. *"E's talked to me about females though, tells me not to trust 'em. That they aren't worth me time. 'E likes it being just 'im and me."* He moved onto his side.

"Hum." She sat back. "So why me?" Her wealth crossed her mind, as it always did in these situations.

"'E likes your eyes. 'E said 'e could live in your eyes, whatever that means." He licked his paw. *"But 'e didn't think you'd spend time with 'im. 'E was very 'appy when you said you would."*

"Did you say something?" Derek entered the room dressed in a black dress shirt with his jeans and black biker boots. His hair was loose and swung lightly by his shoulders, setting off his eyes. She breathed deeply, taking in the sensual smell of his cologne.

"Oh, I was just talking to Tanner. He's a good dog." She rubbed Tanner's back.

"When he's not chewing up everything." He grabbed his keys. "I buy him chew toys but he goes through them like they were nothing."

"Love to get me teeth into a nice fresh 'am bone."

"Maybe you could get him a nice bone from the butcher. It might keep him busy." She smiled as she scratched his ears. He tilted his head, leaning into her hand.

"I thought raw bones were dangerous for dogs."

"Some can be, but a nice knuckle bone wouldn't be bad. He could scrape his teeth on it and clean them."

"I'll do that. So I thought we might have dinner at Mulligan's."

"I love Mulligan's." She stood up, putting her purse over her shoulder.

"Great." He walked into the kitchen and opened the fridge door. He reached in and retrieved a single red rose. He walked over and handed it to her. "Then may the evening commence."

"Thank you." She smiled, sniffing the rose as they walked to the front door.

"Tanner, you be a good boy." Derek closed and locked the door behind them.

Tanner raised his head. *"Ta."*

As they drove through town, they discussed books and their favorite authors. When they arrived at Mulligan's Pub and Grill, he opened the truck door for her; he was a perfect gentleman. Mulligan's was a casual place next to the lake. You could eat inside or out on the dock at a table with an umbrella. Two pool tables took up one corner of the establishment and you had to seat yourself. The music was a little loud, and it was very busy since it was a Saturday night. They chose to sit closer to the pool tables so they could have a little more quiet conversation. Alanna laid her rose on the table next to her plate. They picked up menus and began looking them over. A few minutes later a waitress with a long red ponytail came over. She put a glass of soda with two cherries in it down in front of Alanna.

"Hey, sweetie. You want your usual?" She smiled at Alanna.

"Yes, I would. Thanks, Lin. But tell Eric no onions please."

"Oh, I get it." Lin winked at Derek, glancing down at the rose on the table. "So, Derek what can I getcha?"

"Burger and fries." He smiled. "No pickles or onions."

"And to drink?"

"Dr. Pepper."

"Ok, I'll have this up shortly." She turned and left. A few minutes later she brought Derek his drink. He noticed that the bartender had been staring at them since he'd handed Lin the drink. The bartender, Kelton MacLachlin, was a tall, burly man with a long, thick, black pony tail down to his waist, a full beard neatly trimmed and lots of tattoos. He had a toothpick in his mouth. He flicked it with his tongue as it sat in a hole where he was missing a bottom tooth.

"Your uncle is staring at us."

She looked towards the bar, and waved. "Hi, Uncle Kel."

He nodded, tossing his bar towel over his shoulder as he poured a beer. Kelton owned and operated Mulligan's. His wife, Linette, was the bookkeeper, waitress and part-time cook when necessary.

"I love this place." Alanna sipped her drink. "When I was little, Uncle Kel would lift me up each month to change the moose's hat." She pointed to the large stuffed moose- head at the end of the room above the jukebox. It had pink and white bunny ears balanced on its head. The moose had a hat for every month. At times, overly intoxicated customers took great pleasure in changing its head attire with their own. Then Kelton would have to retrieve it as peacefully as possible. The green satin top hat that it wore in March was said to be very lucky, and many people tried to abscond with it.

"I like the Viking horns it wears in September," Derek said as he leaned forward a little to hear her better.

"Uncle Kel was wearing those when he met Aunt Lin." She looked toward the ceiling and her brow wrinkled in thought. "I think it had something to do with a football game.”

“You have a lot of uncles, don’t you?”

“My dad has five brothers, but if you also count the adopted ones like Uncle Buck and Uncle Andy, then I have ten in total.” She smiled. “Twelve aunts, thirty two cousins, and thirteen second cousins.”

“At least you can keep track.” He took a drink.

“I bet your family gatherings are huge with all your siblings.”

“I do have a large family. Most people stop at two or three kids, but twins run in my family so my mother and grandmother got more than they bargained most of the time.” Most women gave him a funny look when he told them that, but Alanna didn’t even bat an eyelid.

“How many uncles do you have?”

“My dad has six brothers, but I have a lot of uncle-in-laws also.” he said as he watched her touch the rose, playing with a leaf.

“Cousins?”

“Too many to count. My family tree sprouts new branches all the time.”

“I bet it was fun growing up with all those brothers.”

“Painfully so,” he mused. “Brothers tend to point out all your flaws all the time.”

“Well, everyone has flaws.”

“You don’t seem to have any.” His gaze became a little more intense.

She raised an eyebrow at his compliment. “I have lots of flaws.”

“I don’t see any.”

She was flattered, feeling her cheeks blush.

Lin walked up, placing plates of food in front of them. Derek looked at the large plate of fries covered in melted shredded cheddar cheese, sour cream and chili sitting in front of her.

“They have the best smothered fries here,” Alanna smiled.

He was glad she wasn’t one of those women who are afraid to really eat.

Lin glanced at their drinks. “Need anything else?”

“I’m fine.” Alanna looked over.

“No, I’m good. Thank you.” Derek noticed Kel still watching them.

Usually on Wednesday or Thursday nights when she and Fintan came here to eat she would pull out the fries around the edges of the plate with her fingers and eat them. Tonight though, she pulled her fork and knife out of the paper napkin, cutting bite-sized-pieces and remembering her table manners. Derek was trying to put ketchup on his plate but it was a new bottle and was being stubborn. He popped it on the bottom a couple of times and almost half the bottle shot out, covering his burger and fries.

"Oh well, I'm glad I like ketchup."

They had taken a few bites when two men at the pool table closest to their booth started to raise their voices.

"You're cheating!" one yelled at the other. "I saw you move the ball!"

Lots of people stopped talking, turning to look at the men. Kel moved out from behind the bar.

"I don't need to cheat. You suck at pool!"

"Why, you son of a bitch! I'm gonna kick your ass!"

The man took a swing but his fist was caught by Kel's massive hand. The man was no match for Kel's strength as he pulled his arm behind his back and said, "You boys need to take this outside . . . now!"

Derek murmured, "Your uncle is one dude I would not mess with."

What happened next was very fast. The other man picked up his pool cue, swinging it hard at the man Kel was holding. Kel and the man ducked as the cue came flying toward Derek and Alanna.

"Duck!" Alanna yelled as she pulled her head down sideways into the booth. She saw the cue hit Derek on the back of the head, breaking upon impact and catapulting his face into his plate and knocking him unconscious.

"Derek!" she shouted as she came up from the booth seat, concern flooding her.

Kel had both men pinned down on the floor in a matter of seconds. Eric came from the back and another employee helped hold the men down while Lin called the cops. Kel stood up and grabbed Derek by the hair, lifting his face out of his plate. Covered in food and ketchup, his head hung limp in Kel's grip. Kel moved the plate and rested Derek's head on the table.

"Don't want the boy to drown." Only then did Kel notice the blood on his hand from Derek's head.

"Oh, my God! He's bleeding!" Alanna exclaimed, grabbing a handful of napkins and holding them to the wound.

"He's not coming round." Kel said, slapping Derek's cheek a little.

"Uncle Kel! Stop that!" She brushed the ketchup-coated hair away from Derek's face.

"The boy needs to learn to take a hit." Kel stepped back as Lin came forward with a towel to replace the napkins.

"Don't be so callous—he didn't see it coming. An ambulance is on the way."

Kel crossed his arms over his chest. "I'm just sayin' . . ."

Alanna shot him an angry glare, making him rethink finishing his sentence.

Derek opened his eyes. His head hurt like hell and his eyes wouldn't focus very well. He was in a hospital bed with an IV line in his arm. His eyelashes, eyebrows and hair were caked with dried ketchup.

"What the hell happened?" he said in almost a whisper, looking around to find Buck sitting by his bed.

"Told you she was dangerous." Buck tried to sound serious but chuckled. "But you wouldn't listen. Luckily you're hard-headed."

Derek ran his hand over his head. They'd shaved a small patch at the back of his head and he now had ten stitches on his scalp. "Shit!"

Buck put down the magazine he was reading as Alanna came into the room with Fintan.

"Thank goodness you're awake. They gave you something for pain and you fell asleep again." The worry on her face showed as she stood by the side of the bed and without realizing it she reached down, taking Derek's hand in hers and touching his arm. "The doctor says you may have a concussion and they want to keep you for observation."

"What happened? All I remember is having dinner, and then nothing."

"You got hit on the back of your head with a pool cue." Her eyes conveyed her concern.

"She's sneaky like that." Buck winked. "You never see it coming." He laughed.

"Buck, thank you for watching him but I'm sure you need to get back to your mother," Alanna said, not finding Buck's humor amusing at this particular moment.

Buck stood up, tossing the magazine on the table. "Yeah, Mom goes in for surgery tomorrow, so I'm taking the day off. You two should hold off dating for a day or two until I can make sure all emergency services are at full force. This makes what two for two?" He laughed.

Alanna shot him an annoyed look.

"Buck, give your mom our best," Fintan said, walking him to the door with a pat on the back.

"Will do. You two try to stay out of trouble." He laughed as he left.

"We have the man that hit you downtown." Fintan took Buck's empty seat. "When you're ready to press charges, we'll take your statement."

"Statement? I don't remember anything. I don't even remember coming to the hospital. All I remember is being at the bar then waking up just now." He looked at the clock on the wall.

"We have him on disturbing the peace, assault and battery, public intoxication, and a few others."

Derek leaned his head toward Fintan. "I don't know if I want him to go to jail but he sure as hell better pay for my medical expenses. Who was it? Anybody I know?"

"Some guy from Stockton who was in town with some friends. He said he didn't know you and he didn't mean to do it. He thought Kel was going to break his friend's arm."

"Well, he can be intimidating." Derek glanced down at his hand in Alanna's. It felt so soft and warm. He tried to remember what they'd been talking about over dinner. All he remembered was that when she smiled, her green eyes seemed to glimmer with little sparkles of gold.

A middle-aged woman shorter than Alanna came rushing into the room. "Derek! My baby! Are you all right? Is that blood?"

Fintan stood as Elsa Atherton came rushing into the room. Alanna let go of Derek's hand and stepped back, realizing who Elsa was as she rushed past Alanna to Derek's side.

"I'm ok, Mom." Derek closed his eyes, letting out a sigh of mild annoyance.

He didn't like being called her baby. She clung to him because he was the youngest.

"What happened?" She touched his face, grabbing a tissue from box on the table to clean his ketchup-caked eyebrows. He tried to pull away.

"I got hit on the head, Mom. It's nothing. I'm gonna be fine."

Elsa turned to Fintan. "Did you arrest the man that did this to my baby?"

Derek seemed to flinch when she said it again.

"Yes, ma'am. He is in custody at this time."

"Well, good. You throw the book at him, you hear me? The whole book!" Her motherly instincts were in full swing. She turned, extending her hand to Alanna. "You must be Alanna."

"Yes, ma'am." Alanna shook her hand.

"Sorry to meet you this way. Emma has mentioned you a lot. She and I go to the same church."

The doctor came into the room, so Fintan and Alanna stepped out into the hall to give them some privacy.

"You doin' all right?" He placed a hand on her shoulder.

"Yeah, Dad. I'm fine . . . just concerned for Derek."

A tall man, who was definitely a serious body builder in his spare time, came around the corner pushing a wheelchair.

"Hey, Alanna." He stopped beside them. "How's Stitches?" He indicated his head toward the room Derek was in.

"The doctor's in with him now."

"Chief." Tommy inclined his head in greeting.

"Tommy."

"He'll be fine. We played football together. He can take a hit or two and survive. How's things at Bizmart without Brian?" There was a note of interest in Tommy's voice. He had been the in-store security guard for two years until he'd gotten a better paying job at the casino. He was putting himself through radiology school.

"It's not the same. We have a temporary manager. Did you hear about Cecilia?"

He let out a heavy sigh. "Yeah, I was here when they brought her in. They did everything they could for her but she crashed and just never came out of it."

The doctor left the room to continue his rounds.

"Well, I gotta get back to work. I'll see you later." Tommy headed off down the hall.

"Bye." Alanna turned to go back into the room.

As they entered, Elsa was still trying to clean Derek's hair with a washcloth.

"Mom, please. Leave it be."

"It's filthy, Derek. I wish you'd cut it all off."

"I like my hair long, Mom. I always have." He sighed and looked up as Alanna and Fintan came in.

"Doctor says I can go home tomorrow morning."

Alanna moved to the end of his bed and Fintan stayed by the door. "Good. Your truck is parked downstairs. I drove it over, and your keys are over there." She indicated toward the night stand. "Do you want me to do anything, like check on Tanner?"

"Oh, I'll do that. Don't you worry," Elsa jumped in.

Derek looked over at his mother. "Mom, could ya give us a minute please?"

It took a moment for her to register what he was asking. "Ooh . . . yes, of course." Elsa stepped away, going into the bathroom to rinse the washcloth.

Derek sat forward a little, reaching out his hand to her. Alanna came around the side of the bed and took it as she sat.

"Tonight didn't go like I had planned." He frowned slightly.

"Really? It's been one of the most interesting dates I've ever been on; I won't ever forget it, that's for sure."

"Yeah, me neither." He rubbed his head with his other hand. "At least they left some hair."

"I asked them to cut as little as possible so your ponytail will cover it while it grows back in."

His smile showed also in his eyes. "Thank you. I know it's stupid to care so much about my hair."

She grinned a devilish grin, leaning in to whisper in his ear. "I like your hair. I think it's sexy."

Her breath on his cheek sent a sensual shiver through him as did her words. Those few words gave him just the glimmer of hope he was looking for, causing him to grin. Fintan cleared his throat and Alanna pulled back, rising to her feet. A slight pinkness came into her cheeks. "Well, I better go. I'll call you tomorrow, ok?"

"Yeah, that'd be great." He pulled her hand to his lips, giving it a gentle kiss. "I promise if you agree to go out with me again I won't spend the majority of our time together asleep."

"Ok. Get some rest and I'll talk to you tomorrow." She let go of his hand. "It was nice to meet you Mrs. Atherton."

"Nice to meet you too, dear." Elsa walked back over to Derek, resuming her task of cleaning his hair. He did not seem to notice her; he was too busy watching Alanna.

"I'll have one of my officers come in and talk to you, Derek," Fintan stated. "Right now, get some rest."

Fintan walked out of the room, but Alanna hesitated at the doorway and looked back over her shoulder at Derek. She felt compelled to stay. She didn't know why, but when he'd gotten hurt, the amount of fear and concern she'd felt for him had been a lot more than she'd expected. More than she could explain at this point.

Derek saw her standing in the doorway as if she didn't want to leave. That touched him. He so wanted to kick his mom out of the room and have Alanna stay instead, but he could only imagine how awful he looked right now. He sighed deeply, thinking the powers-that-be must truly hate him. Their first date had gone so wrong, which solidified that belief for him. His stomach clenched as their eyes locked across the room. Seeing her standing there he damned the Fates. Perseverance and fortitude, that was the key, but she would be worth whatever he had to go through.

"I'll call you," she said softly, giving him a wink and a wave. "Bye."

"Ok, bye." He leaned back, ignoring his mother, and closed his eyes, lingering on the thought of Alanna's eyes, touch, and words. He had so been looking forward to their first kiss this evening. Deep down he was a true romantic, hoping that in that one kiss she would start falling for him . . . like he was falling for her. His mind went to work on how to make up for tonight and impress her on their next date. If she would give him a next date after tonight's disaster.

Chapter 16

Alanna felt the rain coming down on her. Everything was pitch black. Slowly her eyes adjusted. She was standing at the base of the hill where Lori's car had come to rest. It was lying just in front of her in a dark, motionless heap. There was a faint buzzing sound. It was getting louder and louder. A single light blinded her as she turned to see a motorcycle approach. The rider stopped the bike and got off, leaving the engine running. Not raising the darkened visor of the helmet the rider walked over to the wrecked car, looking down into what was left of the driver's side. With one hand, the rider reached in through the broken windshield and removed something, pausing only briefly to look down at Lori's lifeless body before getting back onto the motorcycle.

Alanna stood cold, wet, shivering and watching. She couldn't move. She tried to move toward the wreck, but couldn't, as everything went black again. The rain still fell heavily on her.

A flash of lightning streaked across the black sky. She was not at the base of the hill anymore, but in a forest of thick trees. She looked around, letting her eyes adjust. Another flash of lightning lit up the sky. She hugged herself for warmth and looked down, seeing the huge distended belly in front of her.

Holy crap! She was pregnant! And not just a little, but a lot. Her back hurt like hell and she needed to pee. She was clothed in a long dress of thick, itchy material. She tried to get her bearings. She was on a mountain side, judging by the angle and slope of the terrain, in a dense forest. She started walking, leaning her hand on tree trunks as she passed them. The baby kicked.

"Oh, my ribs!" She moved around the side of a tree and slipped as the ground gave way beneath her. She reached out with her hands and was able to grab a branch with her left hand. A flash of lightning illuminated the silver band on her ring finger as her hand slipped to the end of the breaking branch. She fell back into a large hole. The pain was excruciating when she hit the bottom. Her arm was broken and so was her ankle. She cried out as tears mixed with the mud on her face. The hole was dark and very deep. Even the

lightning could only be seen above faintly as if at the end of a long tunnel. The baby kicked again. The pain was more than she could bear. She closed her eyes and cried. All of a sudden she felt a heavy weight on her chest. Something sharp started cutting into the soft flesh above her breast. In the distance she heard a voice.

"Mother!"

"I'm here!" she called as loud as she could, but the thunder drowned her out.

"Mother!"

She felt the weight on her chest constricting it. She gasped for the air to yell.

Everything went black.

The weight was still on her as something touched her cheek. Alanna slowly opened her eyes.

"Mother!" Juneau meowed as loud as she could. Alanna raised her eyelids to find Juneau sitting on her chest, claws on one paw slightly dug in.

"Abbey's in trouble!"

"What?" Alanna sat up launching Juneau to the side. She rubbed her body where the cat's claws had dug in.

"Abbey! She's been treed by a coyote!" Juneau jumped off the bed and stood by the bed.

"What are you talking about? A coyote can't get over the wall."

"Abbey was playing chase with Danny when he jumped to a tree outside the wall and she followed. A coyote saw them and is trying to get them. Get up! Now!"

Alanna jumped up out of bed and grabbed her robe and slippers. Flying down the stairs she rushed into Fintan's office. She threw open the door to the closet, and punched in the code to unlock the gun safe as fast as she could. She opened the door, grabbed a rifle she had used before, loaded it and ran towards the back door.

Fintan and Ronan pulled up Treasure Grove Way with Fintan's wet fishing boat hooked to the truck when he noticed the gate closing before he got to it as if someone had just left the house, but he had not seen anyone leave or passed anyone on the road.

"Let me out! Let me out!" Jet whined as she tried to get past Fintan and out the open window. She'd been sitting calmly on the truck seat between them, but suddenly became very agitated. Fintan stopped the truck and opened the truck door to let her out.

Jet took off running as fast as she could around the outside corner of the wall and raced past Alanna, her hackles raised, baring her teeth and growling as ferociously as she could.

"Get away from here you filthy coyote!" The skinny coyote was baring its teeth and slowly circling, head low. *"Get away now!"*

"I'll have you for lunch too, you overgrown pup." The coyote's eyes narrowed as he prepared to leap at Jet. Just then a pinecone hit the coyote on the head.

"Go away! You big bully! Go away!" Danny chattered in his squirrel warning. He was one branch higher than Abbey, looking for something else to throw. Abbey was crouched in a tight ball on a limb holding on for all she was worth, shaking from fear.

Noise from a gunshot startled the coyote. He jumped back and saw Alanna running toward him with the gun trained on him.

"I'll get you. You wait and see." He turned tail and ran, Jet following him for a short distance to make sure he was gone. She scraped her hind feet back and forth kicking up the dirt and leaves, snorting and barking.

"And don't come back! I have a human and I'm not afraid to use it!"

She went back to the tree to find that Alanna had slung the rifle over her shoulder and was trying to figure out how to get Abbey down. She was pretty high up, clinging to the branch and not moving except for her shaking. Danny came over to her and tried to lift her backside. She hissed at him.

"Come on. We get down now," Danny said, trying to pull her claws out of the branch.

"Abbey? Abbey, come down baby," Alanna called. "It's ok. He's gone now."

"You have to go back now." Danny crawled over to the other side and pushed with his little squirrel hands. *"You go back to the wall."* He turned and put his back to her and pushed with his back feet.

Abbey looked down at Alanna. *"I'm scared, Mommy."*

"I know, just come down. We need to get inside the wall."

Abbey pulled one shaky paw from the branch and moved toward the trunk. Danny pushed at the same time. Abbey slipped and fell. Alanna gasped as she saw Abbey hanging by one paw from the branch but was relieved to see her scramble to regain her hold and pull herself up.

"Danny! Stop helping," Alanna yelled. "She'll get it."

"You go now. Down tree. Go. Go."

"Just let me do it!" Abbey hissed. She slowly backed down the trunk until Alanna reached up and grabbed her. Alanna held her tight as Abbey buried her head in the crook of her mother's arm.

"It's ok, baby, I've got you."

Abbey's fur was bushed up twice its size and she was shaking and shedding profusely. She continued to shake as Alanna carried her back to the house. She saw Juneau on the top of the wall, watching the events which had just occurred. Juneau turned and went back to the tree she'd climbed up in the yard to get to the top of the wall.

Alanna carried Abbey around to the gate and up the long driveway to the house. Jet followed, looking behind them to make sure the coyote wasn't coming back. They made their way to the back door and into the kitchen where Alanna leaned the rifle by the door and sat down to examine Abbey.

"Are you ok, baby?" She held Abbey close, petting her. She wasn't shaking as badly, but she still didn't want to let go of Alanna.

Fintan and Ronan came into the kitchen from the garage. "What's going on? I heard a gunshot," Fintan asked, crossing the large kitchen quickly.

"A coyote had Abbey up a tree."

"She knows better than to go outside the wall without you."

"Kids will be kids," Ronan said, taking a seat. Fintan poured three cups of coffee and set them down on the table.

"She's so scared." Alanna made sure Abbey was ok and then put her down, watching her run upstairs. She ran her hands together, gathering cat hair from her arms and hands.

"So, did you shoot it?" Ronan picked up his coffee.

"Of course not."

"It'll probably be back then."

"Maybe." She yawned and took a drink of coffee.

"Rough night?" Ronan asked with a raised eyebrow.

"Between worrying about Derek, not getting to sleep until three, and my nerve racking dreams, I'd say, yes." She rested her head down on the table on top of her arms.

"Was it the same dream?" Fintan asked.

"No." She didn't raise her head. "It was different. I was out in the forest in the rain and very pregnant and I fell down the air shaft again."

Fintan and Ronan exchanged looks. One thought ran through Fintan's mind. He should call the hospital and schedule Derek for castration.

"Just how long have you been seeing this boy?" her grandfather asked in a stern tone.

She raised her head rubbing her eyes. "Last night was our first date."

"And it ended with him in the hospital?" Ronan asked with a slight chuckle.

"Yup." She took a drink, then laid her head back down. "Par for the course."

"Oh, come on, Pumpkin." Ronan reached over, patting her head. "I'm sure it'll all be just fine. If this boy likes you he won't be scared off by a few stitches or your daddy."

"He didn't file any charges." Fintan talked to the back of her lowered head. "He told the officer as long as his medical expenses were covered he'd just let it go. He knows the guy didn't mean to do it."

"There, that right there . . . says a lot about the boy's character." Ronan sat back, holding his cup.

She raised her head, giving Fintan a questioning look. "Did you talk to him?" She glanced over at the clock. It said 9:45.

"No, I talked to the officer we sent to take his statement."

"I should call him and see how he's doing."

"So, in this dream of yours, you were pregnant, out in the rain and you fell down the air shaft again?" Fintan raised an eyebrow.

She took a long drink of coffee. "Yeah, but I don't think it was me because I was in this really old-time looking long dress that itched real bad and I had a silver wedding band on." She rose to go to the phone. "It was probably just all the coffee I drank at the hospital affecting me."

She picked her cellphone up off the counter where she had left it the night before, after calling Sam to let her know just how badly the date had gone. Sam's suggestion had been for her to show Derek her very best bedside manner. Then she had laughed and asked if Al wanted to borrow her stethoscope.

She brought up Derek's contact on her phone and called him. He answered on the first ring.

"Hey, Alanna, so do I get to make up for last night?"

She smiled. "Hey, Derek. How are you feeling?" She picked up her cup, taking a drink as she leaned against the counter closest to her.

"Fine. Doctor says no concussion and the stitches can come out in a four or five days."

"Are you home?"

"Yeah, they let me go about eight this morning. I hate hospital food though . . . it's so bland."

An idea came to her as she looked at the clock again.

"How would you like it if I brought you some lunch?"

There was no hesitation in his voice. "I'd love it, but the next meal is on me. Ok?"

"Ah, Derek."

"Yeah?"

"The last meal *was* on you."

"So it was." He laughed. "What time will I see you?"

"Give me about an hour and a half, ok?"

"Ok."

They said goodbye and she hung up, refilled her cup and headed upstairs to shower and dress.

Ronan looked over at Fintan. "It's amazing what will bring you up from a bad night." Fintan's jaw clicked, his eyes cutting to his father's. Ronan drank his coffee as a faint smile played at the corner of his lips. He liked pushing his son's buttons.

Alanna was in the shower when the first part of her dream came back to her. There had been someone at the scene of Lori's accident and they had taken something. She closed her eyes and let the hot water run over her as she tried to remember. Something her Aunt Vi had asked came to her mind. "Are you seeing everything that the dream has to offer?"

"What am I missing?"

"Are you missing something, Mom?" Jet's voice came from the other side of the shower stall door as she lay on the floor waiting for Alanna to finish her shower.

"I'm ok, Jet, just thinking out loud."

"About what?"

"About the car accident I keep dreaming about."

"How do you know it was an accident?"

Good question. Alanna finished shaving her legs. What if it wasn't an accident? In her dream Lori had been crying. She remembered she'd felt afraid, terrified even. That's why she had been driving so fast. She was trying to get away from something. Or someone. Alanna finished her shower and stepped out. As she toweled herself off, Jet licked her newly-shaven legs.

"Must you do that?"

"*Yes.*"

"Why?"

"*It's tasty, salty yet sweet.*"

"Doesn't it taste like soap?"

"No. Oatmeal."

"Oh. My shaving cream does have oatmeal in it."

She put on her robe, grabbed her cellphone and made a couple of calls while she toweled her hair, then she checked on Abbey again who was asleep under the bed. She blow-dried her hair and went to her closet to choose a pair of jeans that showed off her long legs, along with a lightweight black scoop neck sweater with a lace camisole underneath. She put her hair up in a large clip in the back with a few ringlets falling down, taking a little more time than usual with her makeup and curling iron.

She used her really good perfume and selected a pair of black, slip-on high heels. She looked down at her feet: time for another pedicure. She looked at herself in her full-length mirror and was inspecting the back of her hair with a hand mirror when Sam burst into her room.

"Whoa!" Sam stopped in the doorway, looking her over. "I approve. You are sending that message loud and clear." Sam grinned as her eyebrows shot up.

"Really?" Alanna looked at herself again. That wasn't what she'd intended. Was it? She just wanted to look nice for Derek, but she didn't want him to lose any respect for her.

"Oh yeah, honey. No man is going to resist you in those jeans and high heels. And that sweater is even lower than the dress I picked out."

Alanna sighed. Sam was right. She went into the closet, taking off the shoes.

"Hey, wait! What're you doing? You look awesome! Don't change!"

"I don't want him to think that I'm easy or out to jump his bones."

"Oh believe me, he doesn't think that at all." She bent down, putting Alanna's foot back into the high heel. "Trust me. He needs to know you're interested and not a prude."

"He knows that already."

"How?" Sam put her hand on her hips. "I know you, Al, and you emanate prude."

"I told him last night that I thought his hair was sexy."

Sam pulled her head back a little in shock. "*You,* told a *man,* that something was *sexy* about him?"

Alanna sat down on the bench at the end of her bed, looking baffled. "Yeah, it just kinda came out. I don't know why. Why would I say that to someone I barely know?"

Sam sat down beside her and put an arm around her shoulders. "Because it's how you feel. Al, it's ok to have wants, needs and feelings like other women. Trust me, it's totally normal." Sam curled one of the ringlets around her finger. "I know you've kept that part of yourself closed off for a long time, because Chris was such an oversexed groping jerk, and it really pisses me off that he treated you the way he did, putting you off men for so long. But I don't think Derek's like that. He seems sincere and respectful and I don't think he's the type to pressure you."

Alanna sighed. "He is very respectful."

Sam leaned forward so she could see Alanna's face. "And you find him attractive, right?"

"Yes." The image of him shirtless ran through her mind. "Very much so."

"Ok. Now if you want him to know that, then you're dressed just fine. You look sexy but elegant."

Alanna was still not sure. "You sure I don't look slutty?"

"No, just hot. If you want to look slutty, put on a push up bra and take off the camisole."

"I have on a push-up bra."

"Oh." Sam laughed a little. "Well, the camisole makes all the difference in the world."

"Sure it does."

They both laughed.

"So, what else is bothering you?" Sam nudged her with her shoulder.

"Nothing."

"I know you, Al." She bumped her with her shoulder again. "Come on, spill it."

"I just . . ."

"Just what?"

Alanna took a deep breath. "I feel so naïve and dense when it comes to relationships and men. It's like being an apprehensive teenager all over again. All awkward and uncomfortable." She looked at Sam. "I'm so lacking, and what little experience I do have is really bad."

"You're overthinking things. Just relax and enjoy your time with him. Don't think of it as anything but hanging out with a friend." Sam grinned. "A friend you find really sexy. And then, if things progress let him take the reins and make all the moves."

"Moves?" Alanna's eyebrows shot up.

"When you're ready, of course."

"And if I'm never ready?"

"I get the feeling he'll wait, and if you explain to him how you feel about the issue I bet he'll be a gentleman about it. And if he's not, then he's not the one for you." She gave Alanna a serious look. "If he truly cares for you and respects you he'll wait for as long as he has too."

"Isn't that expecting a lot?"

"No. Not if he's the right one."

"You and Nick didn't wait."

Sam laughed. "Like I could wait, be real. Have you seen my man?"

Alanna smiled, knowing her best friend wasn't one for patience.

Sam smiled. "Hey, when you know it's right, it's right. And who knows, you might surprise yourself and be the one taking the lead in all this." She raised an eyebrow. "Are you overly anxious and nervous around him when he gets really close to you?"

"Yes.

"And you've thought about . . . well, him in a state of undress?"

"Yes," she admitted sheepishly. "It's hard not to."

"Ok, so just let nature take its course and don't think, just go with your gut and your heart. Act on instinct. The rest will happen if it's meant to happen. Just respect him and his body, like you expect him to respect you and yours. Trust me, if something's going to happen, it won't be until you know him well enough to know if he's Mr. Right or not. Al, you're one of the most cautious people I know, nothing's going to happen unless you want it to."

"I hope you're right." Alanna sighed loudly.

"I'm always right. So, where you goin' with him?"

"I'm going to take him lunch at his house."

"Good. Maybe some wine."

"He just got out of the hospital, Sam. I'm not gonna give him wine." She stood up, and went to her jewelry box to look for a necklace.

"Ok. Take it slow, tend to his wounds. Let him know what he has to look forward to when he does feel better." She wiggled her eyebrow.

"Your mind is always in the gutter."

"Most of the time. I like it there. It feels at home."

"I've seen some pretty nasty things growing in gutters."

"Speaking of which . . ." Sam reached into her purse, pulling out a paperback novel. "Laura in Lawn and Garden at work told me to give this back to you. She said she really enjoyed it. She wants to read more of them."

"I'm glad she liked it."

"That's one of the books your cousin writes isn't it?"

"Yeah, she writes a lot of romance, but this series is a little darker. Lots of myth, lore and supernatural stuff. You should give it a try." Alanna tried to hand the book back to Sam who pushed it away.

"No thanks. You know it takes me months to read a book. Besides, maybe you should read some more of her romance ones. You could use a little heat in the romance department." She gestured toward Alanna's outfit.

"I've read all her books, but some of them are a little too . . . descriptive for my taste."

Sam seemed intrigued. "Really, give me one of those. I like descriptive."

Alanna crossed to a bookshelf, pulled out a paperback and handed it to Sam.

"Here, start with this one."

"Cool." She turned it over, reading the back cover. "Sounds interesting."

"It is." She looked down at the book in her hand that Sam had returned to her. It had a lot of romance in it also, but it had a great plot with lots of mythology and supernatural stuff. She set the paperback on her nightstand on top of the book she'd just finished.

Sam flipped open the book in her hands reading a passage to herself. "Oh yeah, I like this . . . very descriptive."

Alanna shook her head as she fastened the silver Celtic necklace around her neck.

"Figured you'd like those and not the mythological ones." Alanna found all ancient tales and folklore fascinating.

"Well, I gotta scoot. Nicky's taking me to his mom's for Sunday brunch. I just wanted to stop and check on you after last night."

"Thanks."

They walked downstairs to the kitchen to find Fintan and Ronan were still at the table reading the newspaper.

"Call me later, k?" Sam asked.

"K. See ya."

"Bye," Sam said to all of them as she headed out the door.

"Bye, Sammy," Ronan said. Fintan was preoccupied with looking at his daughter's attire.

"Ok, I'm gonna head out. I have my phone if you need me. I'm gonna take Mom's car, ok?"

Ronan let out a low whistle after she left. "My granddaughter is a major heartbreaker that's for sure. Reminds me of your mother." He lifted the paper to cover the smile on his face as he noticed Fintan's jaw tighten. Alanna pushed the button to open the last garage stall door. Walking around the car she lifted the tarp off of her mother's car: a metallic midnight blue 911 Porsche Carrera Turbo convertible. She put the key in the ignition, started it and put the top down. She pulled out slowly and drove toward town, making a stop at Mulligan's.

"Hey sweetie. How's Derek?" Lin asked from behind the bar when Alanna walked up.

"He's good. No concussion."

"I guess you're taking him lunch?" She stepped to the side to get Alanna's to-go bag on the counter.

"Yes, I thought it'd be the right thing to do." She took the filled bag and handed Lin her bank card. Lin shooed it away.

"Put that away." Lin went over to the cash register. There, sitting beside it was a Jack Daniels bottle filled with water and a single rose. She lifted it out, handing it to Alanna. "You forgot this last night in all the commotion."

"Thank you, Auntie. It means a lot to me. I didn't realize I'd left it."

"Now, you get that to him while it's hot."

"Ok. Thanks." She picked up the bag and left.

She rang the doorbell and Derek opened the door. He was dressed in a plain white T-shirt that was tight across his broad shoulders and chest and hugged his abs, jeans and no socks, his clean hair down loose around his shoulders.

"Hi!" he said with a big smile on his face as he held the door open. He seemed very happy to see her.

"Hi," she said, walking past him into the house. She took in a long breath then let it out slowly, her nerves kicking into high gear as she brushed past him, touching his arm on the way to the dining table. She had been anxious to see him again, but didn't know what to say or do around him. What was wrong with her? She had been fine driving over, but the moment she saw him her whole body had turned against her. She looked up and noticed he was watching her. "So, how are you feeling?" she asked quickly.

"Great, especially now that you're here." He moved a little closer to her. "I have to say, you get prettier and prettier every time I see you."

"Oh, stop." She waved a hand at him, turning back toward the bag. He moved in front of her.

"I mean it." He gently lifted her chin to look at him. "You take my breath away."

"What type of drugs do they have you on?" She raised an eyebrow. "Because they are making you totally delusional."

He took her hand and gently kissed it. "I'm not delusional, I'm in awe." He reached up, touching one of her ringlets.

She cocked her head, looking up at the ceiling. "Note to self: Blow to the head causes Derek to hallucinate."

"You don't take compliments well, do you?"

"Sure I do." She avoided his gaze. "I'm just a little embarrassed by what you're saying."

"I'm just being honest with you." He pulled her hand up to his chest and placed it there, holding it against him. Part of her felt she should pull away as his gaze caught hers, but another part of her really liked the feel of him under her hand.

"Honesty is good." She cleared her throat. "I just embarrass easily, that's all." She could feel the warmth of him through his shirt and feel his heartbeat in his firm chest.

"I didn't mean to embarrass you."

"Are you hungry?" She averted her eyes, feeling his gaze down to her toes.

"Starving." He let her hand go as he helped her open the containers. He realized she had gotten exactly what they'd been having for dinner the night before.

"Got any ketchup?" she asked with a grin.

"As a matter of fact I do." He went to the fridge, retrieved the bottle and brought it back to the table. "What would you like to drink?" He went to the fridge again.

"A diet soda would be fine, if you have it." She sat down at the table and saw Tanner through the sliding glass door, asleep outside on the patio in the backyard.

Derek put a bottle of diet soda and a glass of ice in front of her as he sat down. They had started to eat when his phone rang.

"Sorry, please excuse me." He stood up, wiping his mouth on a napkin as he picked up the cordless phone and pushed a button. "Hello. Oh hey, Mom. No. I'm eating right now. Alanna brought me lunch. No. Mom really. I'm good." He turned to face her. He smiled as he covered the mouthpiece. "What are you doing this afternoon?"

She thought about it for a second. There was something she wanted to check out. "I'm going to drive over to the casino to pick something up." She smiled. "Want to go with me?"

He nodded his head. "No, Mom, we already have plans for today. Yeah, I will. Ok. Love you too. Bye." He hung up the phone, and sat back down. "I love my mom, but sometimes she can be a little much."

Alanna took a bite as thoughts of her own mother hit her. "At least you have her."

He heard the sadness in her voice. "I'm so sorry about your mom. I don't know what I'd do if I lost mine. She drives me nuts, but I wouldn't want to be without her."

"It's hard, but you just go on. That's all you can do."

Wanting to change the subject, not liking to see her sad, he said, "So, do you gamble a lot?"

"No. Why?"

"Well, if you're going out to the casino I figured you gambled."

"No, I don't like to gamble." She took a drink. "I have a friend there that's getting some information for me."

"What kind of information, if you don't mind me asking?" He took a bite.

"If I tell, you'll think I'm crazy." She lowered her gaze.

"I already think you're crazy so it's no big deal." He smiled.

She gasped playfully. "And what makes you think I'm crazy?"

"Because you're going out with me," he teased.

"You have a point there. Well, my father is working on a case and he needs some security footage from the casino."

He raised an eyebrow. "And he's sending you to get it? That doesn't sound right."

"Well, maybe he doesn't know I'm going to get it, but he'll need it . . . if I'm right anyway."

"Right about what?"

She let out a long loud sigh.

"Come on," he smiled, "Tell me what you're up to."

"Ok, but just hear me out before you think I really am crazy."

"Ok." He took another bite.

"In the last nine months, three employees from the company I work for have died, two of them managers, and all of them right here in our area. I knew two of them and think that all three deaths may be linked to each other."

"So, you're doing some amateur sleuthing without your dad knowing."

"Yup."

"What makes you think that these deaths are linked to one another?"

"Just a gut feeling I guess."

"Would your dad be mad if he found out you were snooping around?"

"I don't know, maybe." She shrugged.

"Well, if you make him mad at me you have to bail me out." He took a drink. "I don't want him to tell me I can't see you."

"He wouldn't do that. I'm an adult."

"Yeah, that's why he grilled me the whole time we were working on his car after I asked his permission to date you."

"You asked him if you could date me? When?" That struck her as a little odd.

"The day after we went to dinner with Nick and Sam. I felt it was the right thing to do. I've got a little history with your dad, so I wanted to know where I stood with him. He said he was ok with it. That's when I sent you the flowers."

"What history?" This must be what Mark had mentioned.

He glanced at her, then back down at his food. "He got me out of a bind once."

Her eyes narrowed a little. "What kind of bind?"

He sat back and sighed. "It was stupid really, but a couple of years ago some friends of mine and I went to Mulligan's. I was designated driver for them. They got a little out of hand and stole a couple pitchers of beer and a napkin holder. I didn't know they had them in the back of the truck but I found out when I got them home. I tried to take the pitchers and napkin holder back but your uncle had called the cops by then. So, I wound up in a cell and your dad convinced your uncle to let me off. I paid for the beer, but your uncle still looks at me strangely when he sees me."

She looked at him for a second, then she burst out laughing.

"You got arrested for stealing beer, napkins, and trying to do the right thing?"

He crossed his arms over his chest. "Your dad never arrested me, he kinda missed that step, on purpose."

"No wonder you asked him if you could date me, you being a hardened criminal and all." She giggled.

He leaned forward, looking deep into her eyes. "I respect you, and your father, and felt it was the proper thing to do." His look was so insistent she was somewhat taken aback.

"Derek, I think it was sweet that you asked him."

"Not embarrassing you, am I?"

"No." She felt a little bad. "I'm sorry if I overreacted before about being embarrassed."

He looked down at his food. "It's hard for me to have the nerve to open up to you and tell you what I'm thinking, so cut me a little slack. Please?"

"Ok." She tilted her head, softening her tone. "Why is it so hard for you?"

He met her gaze. "I take it you haven't been talking to Nick?"

"No, why?"

"Never mind." His eyes went down to his food.

"No, what is it?" She reached over, lifting his chin so she could see his eyes. "Please, tell me. I'd like to know."

He took a deep breath. "Alanna, I don't do well at relationships. I've been burned really bad, so opening up to someone is, well, beyond hard." He leaned back. "I'm trying to not let the past affect me and I'm trying to not be closed off. It's my first instinct to close myself off and not let anyone near."

Well, that hit home. She, of all people, could understand that feeling.

"I understand that more than you know, but what does Nick have to do with anything?"

"Well, I kind of talked to him about whether or not you would even consider going out with me."

"Why would you think I wouldn't go out with you?"

"Well, you really are way out of my league."

She smiled. "I think that's the sweetest thing anyone has ever said to me." She reached over, touching his arm. "So, what'd Nick say?"

He looked down at her hand on his arm. "Nick said the best thing to do was just be myself, speak my mind, and don't hold anything back. To accept you for exactly who you are if I expect you to accept me for who I am." He looked up, smiling sheepishly. "And he agreed that you are totally out of my league, but he said what the hell, you only live once." He reached up and gently touched her cheek.

She leaned into his hand a little. "I want you to be yourself and let me get to know you, but you have to cut me some slack too."

"So, I cut you slack and you cut me slack?"

"Deal."

"And will you accept a compliment for heaven's sake?"

"One a day is all I can take." She smiled feeling a little more comfortable knowing he was nervous too, and didn't like opening up. She couldn't explain it, but a little voice deep down told her she could trust him. She had never felt that way, especially around someone she didn't know that well. She began to relax and saw him loosening up a little too. They ate, talked and laughed and then when they were done she helped him clean up.

"Let me grab a shirt and get my boots on." She watched him go down the hall. He came back with an open, light blue shirt on. He sat down on the couch to put his socks and black biker boots on. Then he stood up and buttoned his shirt, tucking it into his jeans. He grabbed his belt, put it on, then reached for a hair tie to pull his hair into a low ponytail.

She watched him as she leaned against the doorway to the kitchen. Watching him move around the living room she said, "You are so handsome. Are all your brothers as good-looking as you are?"

"Well, thank you," he murmured as he walked past her, leaning in a little "I'm glad you think so." She could smell his cologne, breathing him in as he went past her to the sliding glass door. "But, yes, good looks do run in our family. I even have a cousin that's a male model." He looked out the door, tapping on the glass to get Tanner's attention. "Tanner, boy, we'll be back soon."

Tanner opened one eye and lifted his head then went back to sleep. Derek made sure Tanner had water and food, then grabbed a leather jacket off the rack and checked his back pocket for his wallet.

"Ok. Let's go." He held the door for her, closing and locking it behind him.

He stopped when he saw her mother's car in the driveway.

"Nice." He walked around it, admiring the car. "I thought you only drove an SUV."

"I do. This was my mom's. Dad and I don't have the heart to part with it so I take it out every now and then."

"I hear they handle like a dream." He opened the passenger door.

"They do." Then she did something totally out of character. She dangled the keys in front of him. "Wanna drive?" She never let anyone drive this car, not even Sam, and she had begged many times to drive it.

"Absolutely, and I promise my insurance is good for this." He held the door for her as she got into the passenger side. He went around and slowly got in, pushing back the seat to accommodate his long legs. He adjusted the mirrors and then started the engine, grinning as it roared into life. He reached down into his jacket and pulled out his sunglasses as Alanna removed hers from the dash. At the push of a button the Bose system came to life with a rock song and he nodded in approval. Resisting the urge to peel out, he took off with the careful ease of an expert.

She watched him thoroughly enjoy himself driving the winding roads to the casino. They didn't talk, the music was too loud to do so, and she wanted him to concentrate on the road. On a couple of straight spots he looked over at her, raising an eyebrow. She just smiled and nodded as he pushed the accelerator just to see what it would do. As they came close to the casino, she noticed the white cross as they drove by. When they pulled into the driveway to the casino, she turned down the stereo and then pointed to the valet. Derek pulled up and put it in park before getting out. Another attendant opened Alanna's door. She hooked her arm in Derek's as they walked inside.

"I take it you enjoyed the drive." She saw his smile.

"Totally." He pulled his sunglasses off and put them in his jacket pocket. "I know that car must mean a lot to you."

"It does."

"Thank you for letting me drive."

"You're welcome."

She went to the front desk and asked to see Tommy while Derek looked around at the list of upcoming concerts and shows.

"Hey, look." He pointed to a flyer of a comedian coming to the casino soon. "Do you like him?"

She moved up beside him. "Yeah, he's really funny. I've seen him on TV."

"Would you want to go with me?" He pointed to the date on the flyer.

She smiled. "Yes, I would."

"Great! Let me go get us some tickets." He went over to the ticket booth, ecstatic that they now had made plans together that were over a month away.

She saw Tommy coming down the stairs.

"Hey, girl, here's what you asked for." He handed her a DVD. "When you called this morning I was surprised. The sheriff has a copy of this also. I'm not sure what you're looking for, but good luck. It was a very boring night that night."

"Thank you, Tommy. I really appreciate it."

"You're welcome, but I gotta get back to work." He looked up to see Derek coming toward them. "Hey, Derek."

"Hey, Tommy."

Tommy went back upstairs as Derek walked up with four tickets in his hand.

"I got us some good seats and went ahead and got two extra in case Nick and Sam want to join us."

"How thoughtful. That was so nice of you to think of them."

He paused for a second. "Would your dad wanna come?"

"I doubt it. He's more into sports than shows and concerts but it was a nice thought."

"You want to get something to drink?" He motioned to the dimly lit, almost deserted bar to the left of them.

"Sure."

They went in and sat at one of the many unoccupied booths. Derek laid his jacket down and glanced around. There was one couple in the back corner booth giggling and an older man at the bar that looked like he was having a bad day. The bartender was behind the bar and waitresses came in every so often to get drinks and take them out. Derek stood by her. "What would you like?"

"Diet soda."

He walked to the bar and a few minutes later returned with their sodas. "I'll be right back." He smiled as he crossed the bar to the jukebox and took a few minutes making some selections. She watched him glance back at her every so often. The music started and it was a song she recognized. He came over and sat down.

"Do you like them?" He indicated towards the music.

"Yes, I have a lot of their stuff." She sipped her drink as he reached over and held her hand.

"I'm glad you came over today. I'm supposed to go over tomorrow and help your dad with his car again in the afternoon. What time do you get off work?"

"Four." She rubbed her finger over his. "Do you want to stay for dinner tomorrow?"

"I told you the next meal was on me." He grinned.

She looked at him wanting to say don't tempt me, but thought otherwise. The song ended and the next song came on. Derek stood up and pulled her gently to her feet. He led her to the dance floor not far from them then pulled her close and they began to dance. She seemed to melt into him, wrapping her arms around his neck as he slipped his arms around her waist. She laid her head against his chest and shoulder as he pressed his cheek against her head. They moved slowly as the music played; they were in their own world, just the two of them as the music slowed and ended. She pulled back a little and he whispered in her ear. "Don't stop, not yet."

The next song started and they continued to dance. He breathed her in; her smell was sweet like fresh flowers. He closed his eyes as he held her close. The song changed again as they danced, feeling so close and warm to each other. Alanna felt very relaxed and happy. As the song was about to end, Derek pulled back, looking down at her and whispered the words of the song to her as it played. They stopped dancing as he leaned down and kissed her. At first it was soft and gentle, but then turned deep and passionate. She'd never been kissed this way before. She began to return his passion, feeling more alive than she had in a long time. The music completely stopped as they stood there kissing until the old man at the bar yelled, "Get a room."

They both started laughing as they left the dance floor. He held her close as they stood waiting for the car. She leaned against him as they drove back to Aurum. They pulled into his driveway at a little past five.

"Wanna come in for a bit?" he asked as he opened her door.

"Sure." She followed him into the house. He hung up his jacket as she put down her purse.

"Mind if I use your bathroom?" She gave him a shy smile.

"First door on the left." He motioned toward the hallway.

While she was gone, he turned on his stereo and changed the radio stations. When she came out, she heard a song by the same band that they had just been dancing to on the stereo. He was standing by the bookcase when she came through the door.

"Thank you for today," he said. "I haven't had fun like that in a long time."

"Me too, I'm really enjoying spending time with you."

"I enjoy spending time with you too. I'll get to see you tomorrow, right?"

"Yeah, I'll be home a little after four." She moved to pick up her purse and he turned, reaching up and brushing her cheek softly with his hand. She closed her eyes at his touch. The next thing she knew his lips were on hers.

He reached up and removed the clip from her hair, letting it spill down around her shoulders. He ran his hand thorough her hair, pulling her closer as they kissed. His hands running down her back sent shivers through her. She was trembling in his arms and he treasured that feeling.

She fisted her hands in the back of his shirt and started to tug, pulling it out of his jeans. He started to help her pull his shirt out when a knock came at the front door. They stopped kissing and she laid her forehead against his chest, biting her lower lip, her hands still clenched in the fabric of his shirt. She breathed deeply as he placed a kiss on the top of her head. There was another knock at the door and then the sound of a key in the lock.

"Crap!" Derek whispered. She stepped away, stopping to pick up her hair clip off the floor, then her purse just as a tall man with a grocery bag came in the door. He looked around and saw Derek and then Alanna.

"Hey, bro. Why didn't you answer the door? Mom told me to bring this to you. She's worried about you." He stepped into the living room.

"I'll see you tomorrow, Derek," Alanna said, her cheeks flushed with embarrassment as she walked to the door.

"Alanna, this is my brother Adrian, Adrian this is Alanna."

"Nice to meet you." She smiled, opening the screen door and trying to get out of there quickly.

"You too," Adrian said, setting the bag down on the coffee table.

Derek leaned on the door as he held it for her. "Do you want me to walk you out?"

"No, it's ok." She reached up, giving him a quick kiss goodbye. "Bye."

He watched her get in her car and leave before he closed the door. Then he turned to his brother and said, "You didn't think the Porsche was mine did you?" with a playful tap on Adrian's head.

***

Alanna drove through town, thinking, with whatever it was that he did to her still making her shake. At a stop light she picked up her phone and pushed the button.

"Hey, Al." Sam answered with something in her mouth.

"Sam. I need to talk."

"I'm on my way." Click.

Chapter 17

Jet came running up to the car as Alanna parked in the garage stall.

"How was your date, Mom?"

She petted the dog's head as she retrieved her purse and rose from the car. "It was good." She put the car's top up and covered it with the tarp.

Jet followed her into the house, hearing the TV in the den. Abbey came running into the kitchen. *"Juneau has plan."*

"A plan to do what?" She put her keys and purse down, getting a small vase out for the rose.

"To kill the mean coyote." She rubbed her body against Alanna's legs.

"She's not going to kill the coyote."

"Yes she is. She said all she needs is humper cables, and a metal dog dish."

Alanna laughed. "Jumper cables."

Juneau sauntered into the room from the hall. *"Actually, lamp wire might be better."* She stopped to lick her paw as she ran her evil plan over in her diabolical mind.

"You're not going to do anything." Alanna wagged a finger at her. "Do you hear me?"

"What's one dead coyote? A throw rug?" Juneau called after her as she walked down the hall to the den. Fintan was there cleaning the rifle she'd used and watching a baseball game. Jet trotted in and curled herself up on the rug by the fireplace, getting ready for a nice nap now that everyone was home safe and sound.

"Hey, Dad."

"Hi. How's Derek?" he said as he ran the steel cleaning rod up and down in the barrel.

"He's good," she said with a sigh, collapsing on the couch. She kicked off her shoes and pulled her feet up. "Sorry, I didn't clean the rifle after I used it. I know the rules."

"It's ok. You seemed to have a lot on your mind. I'll let it slide this time."

"Thanks." She sat back, hugging a throw pillow.

They sat in silence for a while. She let out a long sigh. She was close to her dad, but did she really want to ask him what was on her mind? He looked over at her, giving her a knowing look.

"Dad, can I ask you something?"

"Does it have to do with Derek?"

"Yes."

He took a long deep breath, letting it out loudly. "Ok. Go ahead."

"How did you feel when you realized you wanted to be with Mom?" She stared down at the pillow. Fintan had told her for years how he had waited for that one special person, and hoped that she would do the same thing. She needed to talk about this. It was so confusing to her, but she didn't know if her dad was the right person to talk to.

He swallowed, clearing his throat. He knew her issues with men and as an overprotective father, he was glad she didn't want a man around, but he loved her and wanted her to be happy. She must be starting to have feelings for Derek, or she would not be asking about this. He wanted to be open-minded, but she was his baby girl, and he did not want anyone touching her, ever, but that was unrealistic. He needed to be honest with her and help her, like Eva would have done.

"Like a fish out of water." A small smile crossed his lips, tipping his mustache a little as he remembered Eva. "I wasn't sure what to say or how to act. She actually intimidated me at first and I was the one with the gun." He laid the rifle across his lap, looking over at her. "We knew each other all through school, but something just changed when she came back from college. We'd both matured a little I guess." He frowned. "I know you wish she was here to talk to right now."

"Yeah, I do."

"Not too comfortable talking to the old man about this kind of stuff?"

She laid her head over on the couch and gave him a strange look. "You're holding a gun. Talking to you about my love life is probably not a good idea right now."

He lifted it and slid the bolt forward to check the sights. "Oh, I don't know. I think this is the perfect time." A grin tugged at his mustache.

"Derek said he asked your permission to date me." She steered the conversation off that course a little.

"Yes, he did."

"What did you think about that?" She had found it romantically old-fashioned in a way. Others her age wouldn't see it that way. She was curious how he'd answer.

"I've known Derek awhile. I think he is an honorable young man. It was a refreshing change in today's society. Are you aware that he's wanted to ask you out for over a year, but he's a contractor and thinks he's not up to your social status?"

"No way!" She sat forward a little. "Over a year? Seriously?"

"Seriously." He leaned the gun against the table. "He said every time he saw you he wanted to go up and talk to you, but he didn't feel . . . well, worthy. I think you intimidate him a little." Fintan picked up his beer and took a drink. "I can understand how he feels. Eva and I had been friends in school, but I didn't think she'd date a cop. Men tend to shy away from women who have more power or financial influence than themselves. I know you don't think of yourself as influential, but you know how much pull families have in this county."

They heard the front door open and a few minutes later Sam appeared in the doorway with two pints of ice cream and two spoons.

Fintan shook his head. "And all my fatherly advice goes out the window."

She stood up, kissing him on the cheek as she passed by his chair. "I heard what you said, Daddy. Thanks." She left the room with Sam and they headed upstairs to her room.

Alanna got upstairs, tossing her shoes on the floor and falling across the bed face up.

"So, spill it. What happened? I take it the outfit worked?" Sam said, sitting in a chair not far from the bed and removing the lid of her ice cream.

Alanna pulled a pillow across her face gripping it tight. She screamed into it then answered her. Her muffled voice came from under the pillow. "Yes."

"Good so tell me how you feel about him now that you've had some time alone with him."

Alanna pulled the pillow away from her face, rolling onto her side. "I don't understand what I'm feeling. It's doesn't make sense. It's overwhelming. It's . . . I'm just all mixed up." She rolled over, lying face down on the bed.

"Did he kiss you?"

"Yes." Her muffled voice came slowly.

"And? How was it?"

She rolled over on her back again. "It was amazing. It was like electricity coursed through my veins. All I wanted to do was to get his shirt off and feel his chest and arms."

Sam stood up quickly, moving to the bed. "Ok, now we're getting to the good stuff." She handed her a spoon as Alanna took a bite. "So you got his shirt off, then what?"

"I didn't get his shirt off." She sighed deeply. "His brother showed up and I left."

Sam raised an eyebrow, tapping the spoon against her lips in thought. "Ok, did you feel relief or disappointment when his brother showed up?"

Alanna thought about it. "Both." She took another bite.

"Was it one more than the other?"

"Disappointment. I think."

"Ok. Now what was going on right before his brother showed up?"

"We were kissing. Then I started tugging his shirt out of his jeans and that was it." She grabbed the other ice cream container and opened it.

"You started to undress the man?" Sam raised a well-shaped eyebrow.

"Well, yeah. I guess so. I'm not sure what possessed me to do that!"

"You go, girl." Sam grinned. "I'm proud of you. We'll get you to loosen that concrete from between your knees yet."

Alanna frowned. "Don't be crude."

"Sorry, I'm just excited and happy for you. For years you've kept guys away with a ten foot cattle prod. I'm glad you're finally letting one get close."

"Derek said he had been talking to Nick."

"Yeah, he came over a couple of days ago and they hung out on the terrace, drank a few beers, and talked. I knew they were talking about women, because I heard Nick say, 'She drives me nuts, but it's worth it. I couldn't imagine life without her'. I know my Nick is not the best one to give advice, but he understands that a little lust is good for a relationship."

"Lust? Do you think that's what's going on with me?"

"Oh yeah, honey. . . no doubt. Ain't it grand?" Sam said with a big smile. "I know you never felt that way about Chris, so Derek has something that's trippin' your trigger."

"Chris said the reason he cheated on me was because I wouldn't sleep with him."

"He was an asshole, plain and simple. He always had you pay for everything and he was always calling you 'baby cakes' like he owned you."

"Yeah, I remember. Derek said he'd been hurt real bad also."

"I'll say. Gina left him for his cousin that she'd met over at his parents' house during a family barbecue. I heard he came home and found them in his house, and in his bed! He burnt the bed, by the way."

"That explains a lot." Alanna licked her spoon. "I guess we both have trust issues."

"Well, you never trusted Chris, or confided in him. That says it was just wrong to begin with. You have to be able to trust who you're with completely. Do you feel you can trust Derek?" She looked at Al's furrowed brow. "What's your gut say? Think you can trust him?"

"Funny you ask that. We haven't known each other long, but when I was with him this afternoon I actually felt very comfortable and relaxed, so yes, I feel I can trust him." She gave Sam a puzzled look. "I never feel that way about people, especially right away."

"I know. People have to earn your trust. That's just how you are. So, what did you two do besides kiss?"

"We took a drive up to the casino and we danced. He really enjoyed driving the . . ." Alanna stopped abruptly, looking up at Sam whose eyes had narrowed.

"You let him drive the Porsche, didn't you?"

"Yes." Alanna lowered her eyes.

"Well, if that don't beat all! I've known you almost all of your life, but Mister Hard Body walks in and you just hand over the keys!" Sam stood up dramatically and stomped out of the room.

"Ah, come on Sammy. Don't be that way. I still haven't told you about the drunk that told us to get a room."

Sam leaned around the door frame from the hall. "But you didn't."

"No, but I wanted to."

Sam slowly came back into the room, sat down and picked up her spoon. "Why don't you tell me tomorrow while I drive the Porsche?"

"Sam, you know you don't drive that well."

"I'll be careful. I promise." She was quiet for a second. "I know I'll get Derek to ask you if I can. I bet you won't tell him no!"

Alanna let out a long breath. "That's just it—I don't think I can tell him no."

Sam smiled, knowing what she meant. "You do have protection, don't you?"

"Yes, Mom."

"Does he know you're still a virgin?"

"Which makes me a freak of nature."

"Not really. More women are making those kinds of choices these days, but does he know that about you?"

"No. He doesn't know. How do you tell someone that?"

"Well, it's not something you open a conversation with, but you should be proud. Most people can't hold out this long. I know I couldn't. I met Nick and you couldn't keep us apart for weeks."

"I remember."

"So, what happened at the casino? Why'd you go there anyway?"

"Tommy got me the security footage of the night Lori died."

"And you want that because . . ."

"I think she was being chased that night." Alanna sat back against the pillows.

"You think the footage will show you who was chasing her?"

"Maybe. Let's find out." Alanna went downstairs then came back with the DVD and put it into the player under the TV across from her bed. She picked up the remote and fast-forwarded to the time indicator Tommy had written on a post-it note attached to the cover of the DVD. They watched as people went in and out the doors and out to the parking lot. It showed four blocks on the screen, each on a different camera.

"So. What are we looking for?"

"I don't know. I guess we'll know it when we see it." They lay there watching the footage for a few minutes, eating their ice cream.

Juneau walked into the room. *"Ice cream?"*

"Yes, here." Alanna gave her some as she jumped up on the bed.

"Makes my whiskers tingle. What are you watching . . . a cop show?"

"No. It's security footage from the casino the night the lady I dream about died."

Juneau sat down beside them and cleaned her whiskers.

"That's her!" Alanna got up, jostling Juneau as she pointed to Lori walking out of the front door toward the parking lot. They continued to watch. It seemed to take a long time for her to show up on the parking lot camera, but then she came into view. She was walking very fast, got in her car and took off. That's when Alanna saw the single headlight follow her. A chill went through her. So, she was being followed but by whom, and why?

"Isn't that the man that was killed? I saw his picture in the paper." Juneau was looking at the bottom square.

"Where?"

"Right there next to the man in the hat."

"What's she saying?" Sam asked.

"She said she saw Brian." Alanna looked closer . . . it *was* Brian. "Look! There he is." She pointed to the screen. He was there at the same time Lori had been. They watched him play a slot machine for about fifteen minutes. Then he headed for the front doors. Unlike Lori, it only took a few seconds for him to show up in the next camera angle for the parking lot. He got in his car and left.

"Why did it take Lori so long to get to her car?" Alanna said, backing the footage up and watching it all again.

"Maybe she stopped to talk to someone, or maybe she went to the restroom."

"We should back it up and see if they were together before she left."

They backed up the footage and watched. They had both come down the same set of stairs a few minutes apart. Then she left and he went to the slot machines. The staircase had led to the upper level of rooms.

"So, what do ya think?" Alanna asked, backing up the footage to watch it again.

"I think Brian was getting a little on the side." Sam shook her spoon at the TV.

Alanna's cellphone rang. She walked over and picked it up off the nightstand, and smiled: It was Derek calling.

"Hey," she said as she sat down on the bed, leaning back against the pillows and pushing Sam to the other side of the bed.

"Hey, so what're you doin'?" His voice sounded even deeper on the phone.

"I'm watching the security footage Tommy gave me."

"So did you find out what you were hoping to?"

"Yeah, but I still don't know if it's enough to convince my dad."

"You should tell him. Give him a chance. I'm sure he'll listen to you."

"Maybe . . . what're you doin'?"

"I'm lying here thinking of you." His voice softened a little.

"Awww, that's so sweet."

Sam looked over and whispered. "What'd he say?"

Alanna covered the mouthpiece, and whispered. "He's thinking about me."

Juneau gave Alanna a look of disgust as she jumped up into her cat bed. *"Yuck, the dog lover."*

"I'm sorry my brother showed up. I was hoping you could've stayed a little longer," Derek said, disappointment lacing his words.

"Yeah, but I had to get home."

Sam slapped Alanna's foot and whispered. "Ask him what he's wearing." Alanna frowned shaking her head. Sam nodded her head. No! Yes! No! Yes!

"Well, the reason I called was I was wondering if you like Italian food?" He was leading up to something.

"I love Italian food. Why?" Alanna tried to ignore Sam who kept nodding her head. Sam made a face and whispered again pulling on her shirt to indicate clothing. "Ask him."

"Would you like to have dinner with me tomorrow night?" Derek asked.

"Yes, I'd like that a lot." She tried to ignore Sam.

"Good, I look forward to it."

"Me too."

There was a long moment of silence. Sam nodded her head yes; Alanna shook her head no.

"Well, I guess I'll see you tomorrow then." He hesitated, not wanting to end the conversation.

"Yeah." Alanna bit her lip as her curiosity got the better of her now that Sam had mentioned it. "Ah, Derek?"

"Yeah?"

"Can I ask you a personal question?" She couldn't believe she was about to do this.

"Sure," he said casually. "What'd ya wanna know?"

She closed her eyes tight, getting her nerve up. "What are you wearing right now?"

He laughed a deep, mock-sinister laugh. "A bed sheet."

She opened her eyes as her cheeks flushed a little with that thought. "And?"

"That's it. I like to sleep naked and after Adrian left, I lay down to take a nap, but I couldn't sleep. I kept thinking of you."

She said with a dry throat. "Good to know."

"Now, can I ask you something personal?" He smiled to himself.

"Yes," she said, swallowing hard.

"Are you still wearing those black high heels?"

"No."

"What else are you not wearing?"

She covered her eyes with her other hand, feeing her cheeks get hot. "I haven't changed yet."

"Go ahead . . . I'll wait," he said seductively.

She laughed. "Sam's here. Can I call you later?"

"You, my lady, can call me anytime. Day or night."

"Ok. I gotta go."

"Ok. Bye."

"Bye." She hung up the phone and pulled a pillow over her face to hide her embarrassment.

Sam lifted the pillow off her face. "So, what'd he say?"

"He's not wearing anything at all. He's in bed naked."

Sam grabbed her by the hand and pulled. "Well, come on! What're you waiting for? Grab your keys! Better yet, I'll drive you so you don't chicken out." She tried to stand and kept pulling on her.

"Stop it. I'm not going over there."

Sam sat down on the edge of the bed. "But you want to, don't you?"

"With every fiber of my being. Yes, but I can't . . . not yet. This is just all too much, way too fast and I don't know why it's happening, or what to do."

Fintan knocked on the door frame and stuck his head in the door. "I'm getting ready to grill myself a burger. Do you girls want one?"

"I do," Alanna said, hoping he hadn't heard what they'd been talking about.

"Not me. I gotta get home to Nick." Sam stood up, knowing it was the cue to end their conversation. "Al, I'll see you tomorrow at work." She grabbed her ice cream carton and headed out the door past Fintan.

"Hey, Sam," Alanna smiled, "thanks."

"No prob. I'm always here for ya, you know that."

"You get to cut up the vegetables," Fintan said to Alanna. As he turned to leave he noticed the frozen scene on the TV. "What is that?"

"Ah, I just was curious about something." Alanna tried to grab the remote but didn't make it. He unfroze the scene and watched the footage, running it back and forward again.

"Where did you get this and why do you have it?" He gave her a stern look.

Juneau laughed from her cat bed. *"Busted!"*

Alanna shot her a glare as Derek's words, "Tell him!" rang in her head. She looked him in the eye. "Dad, I need to tell you about the woman in my dreams." She sat down on the bench at the end of the bed. "I don't think her death was an accident."

Chapter 18

Later Alanna was in her pajamas and lying in bed, reading the paperback novel Sam had returned to her. Abbey was sleeping beside her, Jet was downstairs with Fintan and Juneau was in her cat bed, snoring.

Alanna had read a few chapters but her mind kept wandering to Derek. She looked over at the clock: It was almost nine. She read a paragraph, her thoughts drifting once again. She read the same paragraph over. She glanced at her phone on the nightstand then tried to concentrate on the book and read the same paragraph yet again. She reached over, picking up her cellphone. She typed in the words *Are you still awake?* and sent Derek the text.

A few seconds later her phone rang. She pushed the button and held it to her ear.

"Yes, I am." Derek's voice was sensually deep and soothing.

"I'm not disturbing you, am I?" she asked.

"No. I'm lying here trying to read, but I've read the same paragraph over and over because my mind won't focus."

"Really? Me too." She smiled.

"So, what're you reading?" He was curious.

She hesitated then answered in a bashful tone. "Lustful Spells."

"Umm, I like the title." He took a deep breath. "So, read me the paragraph you're on."

"Why?" She thought it was a strange request.

"Just curious." His tone changed a little. "Come on. Read it to me, please?"

"I don't know."

"Please?"

"Oh, ok," she said reluctantly, opening her book and finding her place. She took a deep breath, clearing her throat a little. *"Ulric's thin, damp shirt pulled tightly across his broad shoulders as he brought the axe down with a forceful blow, splitting the log in front of him. His biceps swelled, threatening to tear through the thin, worn fabric around them with each swing. Amber stood in the doorway watching him. She clenched her fists as her nails itched to help the straining fabric give way. She had to resist; she could not give in to these urges. By the next full moon he would be her sister's husband, and if Clare did still live, by village law he was hers. But the chances that Clare had survived the night were slim. Still, she was a strong, cunning sorceress and if anyone could have survived, it would be Clare. Ulric bent to lift another log onto the stump, causing the faded denim to hug his firm backside. Amber let a soft moan escape from between her lips and he turned, catching her fiery gaze."* Alanna stopped at the end of the paragraph.

"Don't stop, keep going." Derek's voice was soft and low.

"I think I should stop there."

"But now I'll never know if her sister is alive."

"I'll let you borrow it sometime and you can find out."

"Or, you could just keep reading."

"Or you could just ask your sister-in-law how it ends."

"Which one? I've got a lot of sister-in-laws."

"Laura."

"That's right. You work together. Are you friends?"

"Yeah, and we exchange books a lot."

"My brother Adrian says she reads a lot of romance novels. Are you the romance novel type?"

"Yeah, sort of, but my cousin writes this series and it's got a lot of supernatural and mythological stuff mixed in." She heard him moving around.

"You like mythology?" he asked, liking the fact that they had that in common.

"I love mythology. If I ever get the chance to go back to school, I'd like to get my Masters and Doctorate in Mythological Studies."

"I like mythology too."

"I noticed you like a lot of the authors that lean toward the supernatural. You really like that dark off-beat stuff don't you?"

"Yeah." He took a drink of something. "I like things that are out of the ordinary or unusual."

"So that's why you're dating me?"

"Well of course." He laughed. "Why are you dating me?"

"Oh, just taking a walk on the dark side."

He laughed, covering his hand over his mouth and the phone, breathing heavy into it. "Come to the dark side, Alanna, we have cookies."

She laughed as he pulled his hand away.

"Ok, let me ask you this. You're into mythology," he said, settling back against his pillow. "Who's your favorite god?"

"Celtic, Egyptian, Norse, Greek? Narrow it down a little. I have a lot of favorites," she said, closing the book and laying it on the nightstand.

"Ok, Norse."

"Loki."

"Really? Do I detect a bit of a mischief maker in you?"

"Maybe a little. Who's yours?"

"Thor."

"That doesn't surprise me."

"Why's that?"

"You're a guy. Just whack it with a hammer and it's all good."

"Pretty much." He laughed. "Actually I have a thing for all the Norse gods. My grandfather use to tell me all kinds of stories about how my family is descended from Odin himself. He would go on for hours about it. He's the one that made me aware of my attraction for the strange and unusual. I love the old lore and tales of ancient times he used to tell me. He made it sound so exciting and dangerous. He said I was living proof that we were descended from the gods because I was born with the mark of a curse for the 'chosen one'."

"Is that the mark on your shoulder?"

"Saw that, did you? What else did you see?" His tone was masculine and smooth, like warm fingers down her spine.

She could have gone into a long list but chose not to. "What does 'chosen one' mean?"

"He wouldn't really tell me. Just that he hoped I would never find out because it would be dangerous for me. He always made things sound really dramatic. I know the mark really bothers my mother, and being the seventh son of a seventh son doesn't help."

Alanna was quiet for a moment while that piece of information sunk in. "You're the seventh son of a seventh son?"

"Yeah, yeah, I know. Evil incarnate. Believe me I heard it all growing up."

"Derek, that's only one version of a religion-based myth. There are many other theories about seventh sons, some of which are of Norse origin. Others say you should have things like the power of healing or second sight. Who was the last one in your family born with the mark before you, and were they a seventh son?"

"My great-great-grandfather was the last one born with this

birthmark, and while he was a seventh son of a seventh son, he died a horrific death due to the curse, according to my grandfather. My family won't talk about it or my mark. I used to talk to Uncle Roger about it, but then my father told him to stop filling my head with stupid superstitions, so he hasn't talked about it since I was a kid, but he remembers all the tales my grandfather used to tell."

"All myth and legend is based on a grain of truth," the scholar in her stated. "And some superstitions aren't stupid. Buuut . . . in Latin America a seventh son, according to superstition, would be considered a werewolf. You don't get furry during a full moon do you?"

He laughed. "Not yet, but my grandfather got pretty hairy as he got older."

She laughed. At least she wasn't the only one with family heritage issues. "Well, I understand your love of ancient times. My grandmother exposed me to myth and lore when I was young also and, just so you know sir, you're not the only one descended from the gods. My grandmother insisted that our line is from Epona, Celtic Goddess of the Horse and that's where we get our . . ." She stopped, realizing she'd almost said too much.

"Get your what?"

She was silent, her pulse quickening and a lump in her throat. She'd almost exposed herself and her family.

"Alanna?" A note of concern was in his voice.

"Our love of animals," she said quickly.

"Oh, I thought you were going to say your looks because you look like a goddess to me."

Her fear lessened as his words touched her, but her ease in opening up to him about herself scared her a little. She'd have to be more careful. "You've already used up your compliment for today, remember?"

"We may have to alter that deal. I don't think one's gonna cut it."

They talked and laughed for the next two and a half hours: books, movies, music and favorite places to travel. They talked about any and everything. One subject led to another. There were no lulls in the conversation, not even when she went downstairs to get something to drink. She glanced over at the clock; she couldn't believe that it was after eleven thirty. She yawned.

"I guess I should let you get to sleep," he said, sounding a little disappointed.

"Well, I need to sleep, but lately my nightmares don't let me get much rest."

"What're your nightmares about?"

She hesitated. "If I tell you, you'll think I really am strange."

"Ah, you forget how much I love the strange and unusual."

"I don't know. It might change the way you think of me."

"I promise to be open-minded; besides, it was foretold."

"What was?"

"About six weeks ago I was coming out of my uncle's bookstore and I heard this voice say, "Mister Atherton." It sounded like something out of *The Matrix*. I turned around and your Aunt Vivian was sitting at a table by the café next door. She looked up at me from her newspaper and said, and I quote, "True open-mindedness sometimes comes from listening with an open heart and not only in breaking down your own barriers but in helping others break down theirs as well." I'll never forget it. She raised her paper back up, and that was it. I thought about what she said a lot, trying to understand what she'd meant by it."

"She didn't freak you out?"

"No, I thought it was cool."

"She makes a lot of people uncomfortable."

"I like her. She's a woman who doesn't care what people think and she has this, like air of mystery about her." He took a deep breath. Imitating Sigmund Freud, he said, "So, tell me about your dreams, my dear."

She laughed. "Well, ok, but don't say I didn't warn you."

She began by telling him about the first time she'd had the dream about Lori, the crash, and how over time the dream had changed to show her more. She went into every detail about it and he listened, not saying much. She told him how intense and real her feelings were while she was dreaming.

After she was done he surprised her when he asked, "So do you believe that's what really happened and she's trying to get you to help solve her death?"

"You're starting to sound like Sam."

"No seriously, Alanna. I believe there are people out there that are more in tune with these types of things, and you might be one of them. Is that why you've been digging into what happened that night?"

"Yes that, and my curiosity gets the better of me. I get that from my dad."

"Have you had dreams before like this?"

"All my life, but they don't usually involve death or strangers. It's more like déjà vu; I'll dream about something and it will happen later that week, or so."

"You should really tell your dad about your dreams."

"I have, and I also showed him the security footage and told him my suspicions."

"And what did he say?"

"He said he'd look into it."

"See, I told you he'd understand."

"Yeah, but he was still a little perturbed that I've been digging around."

"That's understandable; he's a cop."

"If these dreams would stop, then I wouldn't have to worry about it."

"Your dreams are amazing, and kind of disturbing."

"Yeah, I know."

His voice softened. "I wish I could hold you and make all your nightmares go away."

"That would be nice."

"Sure you don't want to read to me from your book some more?" A hint of devilishness tinged his voice.

She laughed. "Not tonight. I need to get some sleep. I have to be up early for work."

"Yeah, me too."

"You know, you're very easy to talk to." She sighed.

"Well, you make me that way and you also seem to bring out the chatterbox in me."

"I really like your voice. It's very masculine and you do impressions really well."

"Thank you, thank you very much," he said in an Elvis tone. Then his voice softened. "I can honestly say I like everything about you and the more I get to know you, the more I find to like."

"You already used up your one compliment for today."

"Look at the clock."

She did . . . it was one minute after midnight.

"Ok." She yawned again. "I thank you for the compliment."

"I'm going to let you sleep. I'll see you later today. Ok?"

"Ok." She smiled. "Goodnight, Derek."

"Good night, Alanna. Sweet dreams."

She ended the call, putting the phone down on the night stand.

***

A few hours later the dream did come, but this time it was different. The rain was not as heavy and as she stood watching the motorcycle rider dismount the bike he didn't walk towards the wrecked car. Instead, the rider approached her slowly, unbuckling his helmet. He stopped in front of her and with one motion of his arm removed the helmet, tossing it to the side. It was Derek. She tilted her head up at him as the rain fell upon his mussed, loose hair. She slid her hand up the front of his wet leather jacket and slowly unzipped it. He wasn't wearing anything underneath. She slipped her hand inside, caressing his warm, well-muscled chest. She pushed the jacket off his shoulder as he bent down, kissing her passionately. Then the car beside her was no longer the wrecked one, but it became the Porsche. He gently pushed her down onto the hood of the car, kissing his way down her neck as . . . Her alarm clock went off.

She opened one eye to sunlight streaming into her bedroom. She reached over and slapped her alarm clock, then rolled over, hugging her pillow and not wanting the dream to end.

Alanna and Fintan sat at the kitchen table eating breakfast. All three animals were out in the backyard. Fintan folded his newspaper, set it down on the table and took a drink of coffee.

"So, you were up late last night."

"Yeah, I was talking to Derek. We talked for almost three hours."

"You seem to really like him."

"I do. He's a really nice guy and we seem to have so much in common. And he makes me laugh." She pushed her food around her plate. "Dad, can I ask you a question?"

"Does it have to do with Derek?"

She turned her head sideways. "Why do you always ask me that?"

He cleared his throat. "Alanna, as your father there are certain questions I know you will ask someday and I have to prepare myself for them, but I don't know if I'll ever really be ready for them."

"Ok." She wasn't quite sure what he meant by that, and she wasn't sure how to broach the question she wanted to ask since he was so overprotective. "Dad, I'm twenty four years old and I know you respect me as an adult, but out of respect for you and our home, I would like to know how you'd feel if I asked Derek to stay the night."

He closed his eyes for a long moment as he said. "And that would be one of those questions."

She gave him a quick glance to try to read his face.

"You know, I promised your mother several years ago that when you made decisions like this, I would be open-minded and remember that you're not a little girl anymore." He leaned forward, drumming his fingers on his coffee cup. "I know you don't make big decisions easily, and three years ago when you were dating that weasel Chris, I had a speech all prepared if you were to ask me something like this. I had all kinds of valid points why not to do it. I didn't trust him, not as far as I could throw him, but you seemed to care for him, so I didn't interfere. He finally did show his true colors . . . I was just sorry you got hurt during the process. I would have shot that little S.O.B. in the ass if I could have. That being said, I don't have a speech prepared for the situation with Derek." He took a drink of coffee. "He seems like an honorable young man, and I believe his intentions are as such. Now, I may not like it, but if it's your choice to do so, I promise not to do or say anything to make him feel uncomfortable while he's here. And thank you for considering my feelings and warning me."

"Well, I just didn't want it to be a total shock if he came down to breakfast one morning."

Fintan raised an eyebrow. "He's not going to walk around in his underwear is he?"

She glanced down at his boxer shorts. "No, I don't think so. You're the only one who gets to do that."

"This is not my underwear, young lady. They're my comfy shorts." He picked up his fork. "And you know that." Emma came into the kitchen from the hall. He motioned with his head at her. "You get to tell Emma what you're intending to do."

"What are you going to do, Sweetie?" Emma smiled, reaching over to refill their cups.

She looked up into Emma's happy, smiling face. "I'm thinking about asking Derek to stay the night."

Emma turned and put the coffee pot back on the warmer. "Well." She cleared her throat, picked up her dishtowel and wiped the counter. Then she turned to them. "He's not going to walk around here in his underwear is he?"

Alanna leaned back. "What is it with you people and his underwear?" She waved her fork in the air. "No! He won't walk around in his underwear. He sleeps naked!" She continued to eat her breakfast as Fintan and Emma exchanged looks.

Chapter 19

Alanna clocked in for work and went behind the jewelry counter. She saw Sam over in her department, working on the new shoe freight that'd come in. She took a new shoe out of the box and made a disgusted face when she looked at it. She shook her head and put it back in the box. Alanna went about her morning duties. About fifteen minutes later Sam came over to the counter.

"I don't know what the shoe buyers at corporate are thinking. Those new shoes are so ugly. I don't think I'll be able to give them away."

Alanna looked over the reports in front of her. "Last year you said they were on crack."

"Well, they are." She leaned against the counter. "I swear they don't look at this stuff before they order it. They just hang up a bunch of descriptions on a bulletin board and throw darts at them. If they hit one they order thousands of them."

A tall, thin attractive-looking woman with a short ponytail and small glasses walked up to them carrying a clipboard.

"Hey, Sam. Hey, Alanna."

"Hey, Laura," Sam said.

"It's so sad what happened to Cecilia, isn't it?" Laura asked.

"Yes, we were just with her on Friday night."

"I really feel for Zara," Alanna said.

"Me too." They were all quiet for a moment.

Laura tried to change the subject. "Thank you for the book. I really enjoyed it. Can I get the next one in the series from you?"

Alanna smiled. "Absolutely. I knew you'd like it. Once you're a few books in, we can talk about all the characters and stuff."

"Hey, speaking of characters, my husband tells me that you're dating my brother-in-law."

Sam raised an eyebrow. "That's right, Derek's your brother-in-law isn't he?"

"Yeah, I'm glad to hear you two are going out. He's such a great guy. He deserves some happiness in his life."

Alanna smiled. "He and I talked on the phone for almost three hours last night."

"Really? He's got a bit of a strange sense of humor and can be a little off the beaten path sometimes." Laura leaned in a little. "Just F.Y.I., his mother treats him like he's five years old though. He's the youngest and she just can't handle cutting those apron strings."

"He says she drives him nuts, but he loves her and just lets it go."

"His dad is grooming him to take over one of their stores one day. They have four stores in different towns. Derek is one of the boys who followed in his father's footsteps and went into the flooring trade. Adrian tried it for a while and didn't like it, but Derek seems to."

"He says he likes to work with his hands," Alanna said.

Sam giggled. "I bet he does."

"I will commend his mother on one thing though," Laura smiled. "She raised her boys to respect women. She makes sure they treat women right. They better never degrade or talk down to them or she'll have their hides. Their father is the same way."

"He does seem pretty old fashioned."

"He is. All the boys believe in treating a woman like a lady. That's one of the reasons I fell in love with Adrian; he treats me very well. Well, we treat each other really good."

Alanna smiled. "I like Derek's sense of humor, he makes me laugh a lot."

"Well, his sense of humor is better than Adrian's. Adrian's is much drier. Sometimes I'll make a joke and he just looks at me like I'm nuts."

"Derek already knows I'm nuts."

Laura laughed. "He might think you're nuts, but he must really like you or he wouldn't be dating you. He's not one to date much, he's kind of a loner. He spends a lot of his time reading or playing video games."

"I noticed he and I like some of the same authors."

"You get into those dark authors like he does?"

"Not the darker ones, but there are a few we have in common."

"He reads some strange stuff but actually his reading is quite eclectic. He can be quite deep when he wants to be." Laura rolled her eyes. "Not like Adrian . . . he never reads. He says he reads the newspaper and that counts, with it being current events and all, but what am I to do? He watches TV while I read. The kids like to read, so I'm glad they take after me in that respect." She turned to leave. "Well, I gotta get back to work. Maybe I'll see you at break."

"Later."

She went on down the aisle as Sam turned to look at Alanna, surprise and confusion etching her face. "You talked to him for three hours last night?"

"Yeah, it didn't seem that long though."

"What did you talk about?"

"Everything." Alanna shrugged.

"I remember those days. Nick and I talked on the phone a lot when we first met. Now we don't seem to talk that much."

"You guys talk."

"Not like we used to. I wonder why?"

"Because you know each other. Derek and I are only just getting to know one another. The only way to do that is by talking."

Sam raised her eyebrows up and down. "That's not the only way."

"Sam . . . I swear. Your mind is always on sex."

"I know." She shrugged her shoulders. "But what was he wearing when you talked last night?" She gave Alanna a knowing smile, wiggling her eyebrows.

Mr. Beckman turned the corner at that moment.

"Good morning, ladies."

"Morning, Mr. Beckman." They both blushed as he looked over at Alanna.

"Alanna, could I see you in my office for a few minutes?"

"Sure." Alanna passed her keys to Sam. "Would you cover the counter for a little while?"

Sam shrugged her shoulders. "Yeah."

Alanna followed him into the Managers Office, where he pulled a chair out, offering it to her.

"Have a seat." He sat down in his chair by the desk and opened a folder.

"Is something wrong?" Alanna asked, sitting down. She looked over at the long desk next to her. There was a cardboard box with all of Cecilia's personal things in it. On top was a well-worn paperback copy of *Best Loved Plays of William Shakespeare*.

"No, not at all." He gave her a half smile. "I was looking over your file and was wondering if you'd ever thought about going into the management training program? I noticed that you have your Bachelors in History, and from what I understand you are an exemplary employee and you show true leadership skills."

"Well thank you." She smiled a little; she'd never even considered moving up in the company. She just came to work and did her job, waiting until her trust fund obligations were fulfilled; she hadn't really thought about what she was going to do afterwards.

"So, we have an opening coming up in the management training program. I would like you to consider applying for it."

"Really?" She was shocked by this turn of events.

"Yes. You'd have to go through the interview process with the other applicants, but I want you to take some time to think about it and if you have any questions I'd be happy to answer them. You have true potential and I think you could go far in our company if you want to." He put the folder down. "I would need an answer by next Monday, but I really think you should consider it. I think you'd do really well at it."

"Thank you, Mr. Beckman." She wasn't sure what else to say. "I hadn't ever thought about it."

"Like I said, I'm here if you have any questions."

One thing did cross her mind. "I do have one question."

"Certainly. What is it?"

"It might be a bit inappropriate, but I have some vacation time and since this is a lot to think about is there any way I could take a couple of days off?"

"Well, as you know, we usually like at least a couple of weeks' notice to take vacation time, but under the circumstances with everything that has happened, I don't see why not. Just get in touch with H.R. and put in for the time, I'll approve it and get your assistant manager to find someone to cover your shifts." He stood up and shook her hand. "Just remember I need an answer by Monday."

"Ok." She turned to leave. "Thank you, Mr. Beckman. I will give it a lot of thought."

She stood up and turned to leave but paused to pick up the tattered paperback. "She really loved Shakespeare. I gave this to her for her birthday two years ago."

"Yes, she did from what I understand, that's one of many books that was in her locker. You seemed to have had an amicable relationship with her. I'm sure she wouldn't mind you having a reminder of her."

Alanna smiled a sad smile. "It would definitely remind me of her, but I don't think I should."

"It's up to you. I'm sure her family wouldn't mind. You gave it to her, and it would be one less thing they'd have to deal with."

"Ok." She took the book and reached for the door. "Thank you again, Mr. Beckman."

"Just think about what I said and have a good day."

"You too."

She left his office with the book and went back out to the sales floor. Sam was standing behind the jewelry counter, swinging the keys and looking down into a showcase.

"Don't swing the keys, the cord could break." Alanna said as she came up to her, setting the book on the counter.

"So, what'd he want?" she asked curiously as she handed the keys over.

"He wants me to think about going into the management training program."

Sam laughed. "Does he know that in two months you'll be able to buy and sell this place like ten times over?"

"No, I don't think he's aware of my family, which is kind of cool."

"You're not really going to do it are you? I mean, I think you'd do a good job. Don't get me wrong, but I don't think you want to be tied down to a retail store, do you?"

"I don't know what I want."

"You should take up your painting again. That's what you're really good at."

Alanna sighed. She did love to paint. Her mother had been a very talented artist, and had taught Alanna to paint. She just didn't know what she wanted to do. "How is it that some people know what they want to do with their lives from the beginning and for others it takes forever to figure it out?"

"Don't look at me. I wanted to be a doctor. I just didn't realize that I'd actually have to be good at all that science stuff."

"I did ask for a few days off to think about it." She unlocked a case and straightened a necklace.

"You going to go away somewhere?"

"No, just going to look into my options."

"At least you have options." Sam turned to go back to her department. "Some of us will always be stuck in retail hell."

"You have options." Alanna smiled. "You just think they're limited to the vending machine."

"Yeah, yeah. I'll see you at break."

Alanna went about her day. She talked to H.R. and put in to take the rest of the week off. She didn't know why all of a sudden she felt like she was trapped in this building. The sooner she could get off work and go home the better. Just as she was going to lunch a woman came walking down the aisle with a large bouquet of balloons. She stopped at the counter.

"Alanna MacLachlin?"

"Yes."

She handed them over to her. They were attached and anchored down to a very large bottle of ketchup. "These are for you. Have a nice day."

Sam strolled over as Alanna looked for a card. She finally found it.

"So, what's it say?" Sam poked a balloon with her finger, making it bounce.

"It says, *You know I like ketchup but do you like balloons? Derek.*"

"What does that mean?" Sam leaned over and bounced a balloon on Alanna's head.

"I'm not sure." She read the card again. "He likes metaphors but I'm not sure what he means by this."

"Hey, don't knock it. You've got a very hot guy giving you gifts. Just enjoy it."

"Yeah, I guess you're right." She looked up at the balloons, and smiled.

Dave walked around the corner carrying long fluorescent light tubes. He looked at Alanna and then the balloons. "I wouldn't breathe around those if I were you. They're leaking nerve gas. . . I can smell it," he said to her in a hushed tone as he walked by, glancing back over his shoulder as he continued to the front of the store.

Sam looked over at her and mouthed the word crazy.

They went to lunch and were coming back into the building when they ran into Zara and Kristina. Kristina was carrying the cardboard box that had all of Cecilia's stuff from her office and locker in it.

"Hey, Zara. Hey, Kristina."

"Hello," Kristina said. Zara looked on the verge of tears. Alanna reached out and touched Zara's arm.

"I know what you're going through and I know how difficult it is. If there's anything I can do."

Zara sniffled a little. "Thank you. I want you to know how much that means to me. We will be having a memorial service for Mom soon. She didn't want to be buried. My aunt is planning everything. I'll let you know when it is."

"I will definitely be there." Alanna noticed the rings on Kristina's hands, which were holding the cardboard box.

"We came and got Mom's stuff from her office. My aunt says it's better to face things now rather than to wait."

"By the way, I have one of your mother's paperbacks. Do you want me to get it?"

Zara shook her head. "No. You keep it. She had so many books and I have no idea what to do with them all."

"Ok, thank you. Remember, if there is anything I can do just let me know."

Zara gave Alanna a quick hug and then turned to leave.

"We'll let you know about the service."

They left and Alanna was quiet all the way back to her department. Sam knew she was thinking about her own mother. She gave her shoulders a quick hug before she headed off to the shoe section. As she walked up to her counter, the balloons caught her eye. She smiled a faint smile. Her mother would have liked Derek.

She tossed Cecilia's paperback in her purse as she was leaving work and carried the balloons to her SUV, putting them in the back. She turned to get in when she heard a voice calling.

"Yooo hooo! Human!" Beth called from the fence. *"Helloooo."*

Alanna smiled, walking toward the fence. "Hello, Beth. How are you today?" She leaned over and plucked a bunch of dandelions as she walked to the fence.

"Lovely, just lovely." Beth took the dandelions on her long tongue. *"Thank you. You're so sweet. What was your name?"*

"Alanna."

Lois walked up beside Beth. *"Oh, I'm not walking behind you to the water trough today."* She giggled.

"You don't have to. I'll take the back of the line . . . it's worth it." She raised her head. *"More please."*

Alanna gathered more and gave them to her. She offered Lois one.

"No, thank you. They say it makes milk bitter." She rolled her eyes at Beth. *"She doesn't care. She's addicted to the things."*

Beth sighed in pure bliss as she chewed. *"So, I see you keep bringing flowers and stuff to your vehicle. Is there a burly bull . . . I mean human male interested? That is how you humans court isn't it? The male makes a fool of himself and the female ignores or enjoys it. The bigger the fool, the more she feels he's worthy."*

Alanna laughed. "Yes, kind of."

Lois interjected. *"Remember that human male that was here two seasons ago and put those balloon things all over a female's vehicle? She thought he was foolish enough."*

Alanna smiled. "That was my friend, Sam. She's going to marry him."

All of a sudden behind them a motorcycle kicked to life and raced out of the parking lot. Lois jumped, startled. *"Bee! Beeeeee!"* She ran away from the fence as fast as she could.

"It's not a bee, Lois!" Beth yelled shaking her head. *"Hates bees. Really, really hates bees."*

Alanna watched the bike speed off and up the road. "It does have a high pitched whine. Like a bee."

"Some of them scare her more than others. It's a heiferhood fear she has. As a heifer she backed into a hive of bees and they attacked her. She's never been the same, although she does break up the monotony at times. She's what you humans would call comic relief." Beth took another handful of dandelions from her.

"Well, I have to get home. I'm going to see my foolish male."

"Good luck, honey. I say the bigger the fool they are for you the better." She flicked her ears. *"But the biggest bull isn't always better; it's just more weight on your back."*

Alanna got in her SUV and drove home. As she pulled up the driveway she saw Derek's truck. Her heart gave a small jump, and a large smile spread across her face. She pulled into the garage and got out as Jet came running up to her.

"Hi, Mom. I almost caught a gopher today. He was fast and got down his hole before I could catch him, but I'll get him next time."

She opened the back and took out the balloons. *"Oh, toys for Abbey and Juneau?"*

"No, these are not toys. These are from Derek." She carried them inside.

"Can I chase one?"

Abbey came running to the door. *"Toys! Love toys!"* She jumped at Alanna's legs.

"These aren't toys." She set them down in the middle of the table.

"Please? Just one?" Abbey and Jet both sat in front of her.

"Oh, ok." She reached into a drawer and got a pair of scissors to cut one of the balloons loose and then let it go, pushing it toward the hall. "Don't break anything."

They chased after it, both jumping trying to get the ribbon that was bobbing along as the balloon skidded along the ceiling of the hall. Alanna went upstairs and changed into nice jeans and a buttoned shirt with a tank top underneath. She stopped to look in the mirror. Normally it was her running clothes she would wear. She needed to go for a run. It might help her think, but first she wanted to see Derek. She walked downstairs and could hear Jet and Abbey.

"Let me try."

"You had your chance."

"Get your tail out of the way."

"Oh, I think we have it cornered."

"Quick, get over there."

"You go over there."

Alanna made herself a glass of iced tea then walked out onto the patio. Emma was there, reading on a chaise lounge.

"Hey, sweetie." She started to get up.

"Don't get up, Emma. Just relax, I'm fine." Alanna sat down on another lounge chair next to her. The sun was hot, but here in the shade of the patio it was really nice.

Derek walked out of the small barn door and used a water hose to wash a car part off, then he went back inside.

"So, I think you've got a real keeper there." Emma motioned towards Derek.

"What makes you say that?" Alanna looked over at her.

"He called me this morning, wanting to let me know he was making you dinner and he wanted to know what your favorite wine and flowers were. Oh, and your favorite dessert." She sipped her tea.

Alanna smiled. "And that makes him a keeper?"

"Any man willing to do the research to make you happy is definitely worth considering keeping. I see he sent you balloons." She motioned her head toward the kitchen.

"Yes, he did."

"He's thoughtful, kind, considerate, handsome, and built."

"You didn't say this much about him this morning," Alanna pointed out.

"Your father was sitting there." Emma looked over and grinned. "It's fine with me if Derek walks around in his underwear . . . I won't object."

"Emma, stop! You're making me feel uncomfortable."

"I'm—"

Alanna cut her off. "I know, old not dead."

"I'm just giving you a hard time." She reached over, patting her hand. "It wouldn't be appropriate for him to do that. Now if you were to buy him some boxers like Fintan's, I don't think we'd object too strongly."

"Dad wears briefs under his comfy shorts, as he calls them."

"Then tell Derek he has to do the same." She took a drink. "Is he a boxers or briefs man?"

"I don't know!"

"You know he sleeps naked but you don't know what unders he wears?"

"Yeah, well the underwear thing didn't come up in conversation."

"I see."

Derek walked out of the door again and started the water hose. He washed off another part, then he put the hose to the back of his neck and wet his head and ponytail. Alanna watched him as he raised up and shook his head. He seemed to move in slow motion. He went back inside. She sighed deeply.

Emma smiled as she looked over at her and asked. "Does he like sausage or bacon?"

"What?" She snapped back from her daydream.

"You and Fintan like bacon, but if he likes sausage I think I need to stock up."

Alanna laughed. "I don't know, but I'll find out for you. Ok?"

"Ok, you do that."

Alanna heard wings flapping as Nemesis came into sight and landed on the back of the chair.

"Your aunt wants to speak to you." He preened a feather. *"She's waiting."*

"Ok, I'll be there in a minute."

"I shall convey your response." He flew off.

"Does Vi want something?" Emma asked.

"Yeah, me."

"Well, you be careful. Don't let her give you any more drugs."

She shook her head. "They weren't drugs."

"They made you not right. . . I don't care what she calls them. They messed you up."

"Ok, I'll be careful." She stood up and walked toward the barn. She entered through the small door. Derek was leaning over the engine that was on a stand and Fintan was holding something in place while Derek loosened it. Derek looked up and smiled when he saw her.

"Hi."

"Hi." She walked over and stood by him, looking down at the engine they were disassembling. "So, how's it going?"

Fintan let go to grab a cigarette and light it.

"Good." Derek straightened up. "I should be done here in a few minutes and then I'm going to run home and take a shower. If it's ok with you, I'll be back here by six to pick you up."

"Ok. I'm going to walk over and visit my aunt for a little while." She looked into his eyes. "Thank you for the balloons."

"So, you do like balloons?" He grinned.

"Yeah, why?"

"Just checking." He winked.

"Ok." She furrowed her brow a little. "Well, I'll be back in a little bit. Should I change for dinner?"

He looked her up and down, noticing the athletic shoes she was wearing. He leaned forward and whispered, "I liked the shoes you had on yesterday," then he pulled back. "But, for what I have planned tonight, you're dressed fine."

"And just what do you have planned?"

"It's a surprise."

"Not even a hint?" She gave him a sideways glance.

"I gave you a hint." He picked up his wrench and went back to what he was doing.

"Ok then." She turned to leave. "I'll be back in a bit."

Fintan winked at her as she left. She walked the short distance to Bob and Vivian's.

As she entered the house, the black and white ferret, Artemis, ran up to her. *"Lana, you come to play?"*

She picked the ferret up, carrying it into the kitchen. "No."

"Awww, want to play later?"

"Not today."

She sat Artemis down as she entered the kitchen, finding Vi at the stove, stirring a large pot of what smelled of citrus. She had her back to Alanna. "Hello, love. Have a seat. Want some juice or tea?"

"Tea would be great."

Vi went to the refrigerator, placed a glass of iced tea in front of her, then took a seat opposite and began sipping her cup of tea.

"So, tell me of Derek Atherton."

Alanna shook her head; she should have known. "I'm sure you already know more than me. You could probably tell me a thing or two."

"Don't be disrespectful. You know it doesn't work that way." She set her cup down.

Alanna let out a long sigh. "I know, sorry. I'm just a little confused."

Vi tilted her head, saying, "And that's why you are here. You have feelings for him. I can sense it, yet you pull back on the reins afraid of going too fast and allowing the horse to have its head."

"It's happening way too fast. We just met, and yet I feel like I've known him forever."

"I understand what you're saying." Vi picked up her cup. "The same thing happened when I met Bobby. I was so bowled over by him I almost threw him down on the lawn at the University of Edinburgh and had my way with him." A whimsical smile crossed her lips. "And I had never been with a man, but umm, umm, umm, my Bobby. He captivated me. He had the most beautiful aura."

"So you knew right away he was the one?" Alanna knitted her eyebrows together.

"Well, no. I just knew I was drawn to him, and that he was supposed to be a part of my life. I had no idea at that time he was 'the one'. But I fell in love with him quickly. At first it was a purely physical attraction." Vi smiled, remembering that time of her life.

"How do you know if it can be more than just physical? That seems . . . I don't know . . . shallow?" Alanna said.

"We have to wade in and see just how deep it goes." Vi looked into her cup. "No one knows how deep a loch is until they take time to explore its depths."

"I am very attracted to him." Alanna hesitated in taking a drink of her tea as she tried to sort out her feelings. "I'm just . . . scared."

Vi nodded her head slowly. "Fear is the one thing that can make you weak or strong. Only you can decide how to use it."

"How do you know the difference between love and lust?" Alanna asked this question sincerely.

Vi leaned forward a little. "Ahh, lust can be fleeting, but love is something that grabs you and takes your breath away. It takes hold of you, totally consuming you. But you can have both. It's absolute bliss when you have both . . . take my word for it."

Alanna took a deep breath. "I'm not sure what I feel, or think for that matter."

"You're a lot like Eva, she always tried to categorize and compartmentalize everything. And she overthought everything. Try not to be that way. Don't worry about all the what ifs. Don't try to decide what it is or isn't at this early stage. Just go with it and try not to label it. As long as it gives you joy, it doesn't matter what it is. Enjoy the moment and don't try to read too much into it. All will reveal itself in time." Vi winked.

"Your riddles aren't really helping."

"Yes they are."

Alanna gave her a puzzled look. "Derek said about six weeks ago he came out of the bookstore and you told him something about being open-minded."

Vi tapped her finger to her chin. "Ah, yes. His horoscope was rather insightful that day."

"His horoscope?"

"Well, that's my story and I'm sticking to it." Vi gave a coy look as she sipped her tea. "Now, Mister Atherton is not the only thing on your mind. I sense you have a conflict about your future."

"Yeah, my boss wants me to go into the management training program, but I'm just not sure what I want to do with my life. I feel so . . . lost."

"You've completed your obligations for the trust fund, have you not?"

"Yeah, I just have to wait for my next birthday." Alanna glanced at the calendar.

Vi looked her in the eye. "I chose a retail store to keep myself busy and to annoy the townspeople with what I sold. You, on the other hand, take after your mother. You have true talent, Alanna. You should not trap yourself in a cold, sterile environment. You should explore your true passions. Only then will you find the answers you seek. Your true path will reveal itself but you must be willing to take a chance on yourself."

"You're a walking fortune cookie aren't you?"

"Not really." Vi played with her necklace. "I just tell people what I see." She motioned toward the blue velvet cloth bundle on the counter. "I can do a reading for you if you like. It might give you insight." Vi liked to do tarot readings.

"No, I have a date and should get home." Alanna took a drink.

"You have to look within to discover what you truly want. Worldly things are just that, things. You, my dear, have something untapped that is waiting and wanting to get out."

"I don't know if I like the sound of that."

"Don't be afraid. Just relax, breathe and embrace."

"Are you talking life, or sex?"

Vi laughed. "Both."

Alanna stood up, giving Vi a hug and a kiss on the cheek.

"Thanks, Auntie."

"You're welcome, love." Vi picked up her cup. "Oh, and Alanna?"

She stopped in the doorway. "Yes?"

"Don't be afraid that he'll hurt or destroy you." She looked past the steam from the cup. "His intentions are pure, but trust is a two-way street." She began to sip.

Alanna smiled. "Thanks, and here I was worried because he's the seventh son of a seventh son with an ancient curse marked on his back." She left while Vi choked loudly on her tea and almost dropped her cup when she realized what had just been said.

Alanna thought about all that Vi had said as she walked home. She got to the patio door just in time to hear a balloon pop.

Jet came walking into the kitchen with the deflated balloon in her mouth. Abbey was chasing the ribbon that trailed behind.

"Ha, I killed it." Jet laid it at Alanna's feet. *"Can we have another?"*

"No. One's enough."

"Please?"

"No." She picked up the mangled balloon and tossed it in the trash. Then walked down the hall to a closed door that she hadn't opened in about four months. She turned the knob and pushed open the door to the studio. Her great-grandmother had built this room specifically as an art studio. She had liked to paint sunsets and sunrises. Her grandmother had painted mostly landscapes, rivers, lakes and streams. Her mother had preferred birds and flowers. Alanna, however, liked to paint animals; any and all animals. She walked into the room and looked around. The sunlight spilled in through the large floor-to-ceiling windows. It was a large room with tall ceilings and totally open and airy. The walls were covered with art pieces from her female relatives. All along the walls were stacks of paintings and on one side a wall of cabinets and two sinks. Around the room were a few easels folded up, some open and standing empty. She walked to the one by the window, pulled the sheet off and revealed her latest painting. She'd finished it months ago and had left it to dry. It was of three bears: A mother and two cubs cuddling in fall leaves. She stood and stared at it. It wasn't half bad.

"Alanna?" She heard Derek calling her as he got closer to the hallway.

"In here. At the end of the hall." He followed the sound of her voice and appeared in the doorway. He had on jeans, a dark red dress shirt and his biker boots.

"Whoa." He walked into the room, looking around in amazement. "This is amazing. I didn't know you painted."

"Yeah. It's a hobby." She pointed to the ones on the walls. "My great-grandmother, grandmother and mother painted all those."

"I saw the ones in your dad's room. I had no idea that your mother painted them. I especially liked the one of the eagle circling above the forest."

"That's my dad's favorite."

He walked over to the one of the bears on the easel. "Wow! This one is awesome! There's so much detail. It looks like it could be a photograph."

"Really?"

"Yeah. Did you paint this?" He was truly astonished by her talent.

"Uh huh."

"Oh my God, Alanna, you're so talented. This is one of the most amazing things I've ever seen." He looked closer at it to see the brush strokes.

"You're just saying that." She waved dismissively.

"No, I'm not. I'm no art critic but you have an amazing eye for detail. Have you ever taken them to a gallery or showed them to anyone in the art business?"

"No."

"Why not?"

"It's just a hobby. It's not my life's work."

"Well, it should be. I bet people would love to buy your art."

She shook her head. "I don't know about that. Besides, you don't have one thing hanging on your walls. If you like art, why are your walls bare?"

"My mother." He tilted his head. "I do it to annoy her. When she comes over she gripes about the bare walls instead of me."

"Would you like a painting to hang?" She smiled at the idea of her work hanging on his wall.

"Oh, I couldn't." He smiled. "Really?"

"Yeah, really." She gestured over to stacks of her paintings leaning against the wall.

He walked over with her and looked through them. They all appealed to him. "I feel bad taking one. They must be worth a fortune."

She gave a slight laugh. "It's just paint and canvas."

"No, it's not. It's your heart and soul. I can see it in every one of them."

That struck her. She had never thought about them in that way, but yet as she looked around, that was what she saw in the others' paintings. Their hearts and souls.

"So, which one would you like?"

"I think I'll take this one." He pulled one out that had Abbey curled up asleep on the seat of a black Harley Davidson motorcycle. She had painted that last year when Uncle Kel had come to visit and Abbey had taken a nap on his bike. "If you're sure, and if it's ok?"

"Sure. If you leave it I'll take it and get it framed."

"Oh, I'll do that." He held it out looking at it. "It will go great in my bedroom."

"I'd like to frame it for you. Please?" She touched his hand. "It will complete it."

"Ok, if you insist." He handed it to her and she leaned it against the others. "So, are you ready to go?"

"Yeah, we better get going." She closed the door behind them. She told Fintan they were leaving and he waved from his chair in the den.

As they walked toward the front door Derek said, "You might want to bring a jacket."

"It's ninety degrees outside."

"I know. I just think you might need it." He grinned.

"Ok." She opened the closet door, grabbing a light jacket. She put her purse over her shoulder as he held the truck door open for her. They drove to the edge of town and pulled up to a field. Derek stopped the truck, got out and opened the door for Alanna. She exited and they walked over the field, where a man awaited them with transport.

"Hey, Henry." Derek shook the man's hand. "This is Alanna."

"Hello," Henry said to them.

"Hello." She shook his hand.

"So, are you ready?" He opened his truck door for them.

"Yes," Derek said, letting Alanna get into the truck. They sat in the back seat while Henry got in the front. Alanna didn't ask any questions as it was apparent to her that Derek wanted it to be a surprise. Henry drove through town and over to the other side of the lake. They drove for almost twenty minutes. Derek reached over, holding her hand. They came to a dirt road and he drove onto the fields. That was when she saw his surprise. It was a red and white checkered hot air balloon. It was up and ready to go.

"You're not scared of heights are you?"

She shook her head.

"Good." He smiled, squeezing her hand gently.

They stopped and got out as Henry checked some of the lines holding the balloon down. There was a lady in the basket checking some gauges.

"Hey, Derek," the lady greeted him.

"Hey, Mary."

"So, you must be Alanna." She leaned down and proffered her hand. "You two should get aboard now, the wind is picking up."

Derek helped Alanna into the basket and then climbed in beside her. She'd never been up in a hot air balloon before.

"Ok. You two stand over there while we cast off." She called to Henry and he unhooked the lines one by one. She had her hand on a lever and pushed it, igniting the fuel. It made a loud noise as they started to lift off. Derek stood behind Alanna, moving her to the edge of the basket. He wrapped his arms around her waist, leaning his chin over her shoulder as they ascended quickly into the air. It was faster than she had expected. She was grateful for Derek's strong arms bracing her. She leaned back against his chest and held onto the basket. It was so quiet and peaceful as they floated across the sky. The only noise was the fuel being ignited every so often.

As they went across the lake, she asked if they could go over her house. With a lot of skill and maneuvering on Mary's part they floated over Treasure Grove. It was wonderful to see it from that point of view. She saw Vi and Bob's house also. Then they floated over the town and he pointed out his house and his family's numerous homes scattered throughout. She looked down at the park, Roger and Vi's shops, the police station and town square. She waved at some people and they waved back. The town looked so neat from this viewpoint: so many trees and so very serene. The sun was setting and it was absolutely gorgeous, so very enchanting. The pinks, oranges and purples were vivid in one of the most amazing sunsets she had ever seen. They came to the other side of town and started to descend.

They landed in the field where Derek had parked his truck. Henry was there, waiting, and as they landed he came over and secured the lines.

She turned to Mary and said, "Thank you so much. That was amazing!"

Mary smiled. "You're welcome. Anytime you want to go up just call. We try to get out at least twice a week and our club goes out every weekend, weather permitting."

Derek thanked them before climbing out of the basket, then he helped Alanna out by lifting her into his arms. He held the door of the truck open for her as she got in. She watched as they started to deflate the balloon.

Derek got in and started the truck, waving as they pulled out and headed back to town.

"That was so amazing." She beamed at him.

He smiled, reaching over to hold her hand. "I'm glad you enjoyed it. I was worried you might be afraid of heights or something."

"No, not at all." She leaned over, giving him a kiss on the cheek. "Thank you. That was very special."

"You're welcome." He pulled into his driveway, shutting the engine off. He walked around and opened her door, putting his arm around her waist as he led her to the front door. They went inside and she set her purse and jacket down. A wonderful aroma met her nose.

"Oh, that smells wonderful. What is it?"

"Lasagna." He smiled. "You said you liked Italian."

"I do." She walked into the living room, noticing that the dining room table was set for two, with candles and a single purple calla lily lying across her plate. It was beautiful.

"Want some wine?" He walked into the kitchen and pulled a bottle out of the fridge.

"Yes, I would. Thank you." She stood by the table.

He opened the bottle and poured two glasses. He handed her one then clinked her glass. "Here's to the beginning of a wonderful evening."

She smiled as she took a drink. "Here's to the beginning of something wonderful." He arched an eyebrow, smiling before walking over to the stereo to turn it on. "Is that a CD?"

"It's satellite radio. No commercials. You can pick the channel if you like."

She walked over and he showed her how to go through and listen to each channel. She was picking a channel of rock love songs when she heard Tanner enter the room, his nails clicking on the wood floor.

"'*ello.*" He sat down beside them.

"Hello, boy." Derek reached down and scratched him behind the ears.

Alanna took a drink of wine just as she heard Tanner say *"Last night when 'e got off the phone 'e said 'e was fallin' in love with you."*

Alanna spit wine all over Derek and Tanner, choking and trying to regain control.

Derek stood there with his arms out and his eyes closed for a second. Tanner started cleaning himself, muttering nonstop about the quality of the wine. She covered her mouth with her hand as she continued to sputter and cough.

"Oh, Derek! I'm so sorry!" She felt her cheeks flush from embarrassment. "I didn't mean to do that."

He opened his eyes and shook his arms. "I'm glad it was white wine. Are you ok?"

"Yeah, I'm sorry. I just got choked."

"Let me get a towel." He went into the kitchen and came back with a small towel.

"I really am sorry." She used the cloth to wipe the mess.

"It's not so bad but I should change my shirt." He looked down at it and she saw his shirt had had the brunt of it. He left the room and went down the hall.

She looked down at Tanner and whispered, "Are you sure he said that?"

"Yes, but you didn't 'ave to 'ave a fit." He licked his paw, pulling it over his ear.

"Sorry." She bent down and used the cloth to wipe him down a little. "You caught me off guard. I'm just shocked he'd say something like that."

"Why? 'E's liked you for a while . . . you just didn't know it." Tanner continued to lick himself clean.

Derek came back into the room with a dark blue dress shirt on. "There, all better."

"I'll have your shirt cleaned if you want."

He walked into the kitchen, returning with the wine bottle and refilled her glass.

"Don't worry about that. Here. Have some more ammo."

She laughed as she took a small sip, then followed him into the kitchen. He reached into the oven with mitts and retrieved a dish, setting it on top of the stove. It looked perfect.

"Ok, now that needs to rest." He pulled off the oven mitts, walking over to light the candles on the table and pulled her chair out. "If you'll have a seat, I'll get our salads."

She smiled as she sat down and he helped her scoot her chair in. He returned with individual Caesar salads. As they sat and ate they talked a little about the balloon ride. Then he got up and cleared the salad plates, returning with their entrée, plus a basket of fresh bread. They ate, talked, and laughed. It was delicious and she asked him if she could get his recipe to give to Emma. He said he would make it for her whenever she wanted. They finished dinner and she helped him clear the table by putting away the food. As he started the dishwasher, he opened another bottle of wine. It was her favorite. They sat on the couch talking. She pulled her shoes off, tucking her feet up underneath her.

"We probably shouldn't drink too much if you're going to drive me home."

He nodded his head, setting the bottle down on the coffee table. "What time do you get off work tomorrow?" he asked.

"I took some vacation time. I don't have to work the rest of the week."

"Really? My overprotective mother made my father give me the week off to recover from my bar fight." He smiled, touching the stitches under his hair.

She laughed. "Some fight."

"So, do you want to do something tomorrow?" he asked hopefully.

"Like what?" She looked over at Tanner asleep on a rug by the back door.

"I don't know, but I'm sure we can think of something fun to do." He reached over, touching her hand softly. "I just like spending time with you. I don't care what we do. Maybe I could watch you paint," he said.

She chuckled. "Oh, that would be really boring. Do you know how long it takes me to complete a painting?"

He sat his glass down, leaning toward her a little. "No, how long does it take?"

"Oh, it depends on the piece."

He lifted her glass out of her hand and placed it on the table. They stood up, Derek gently pulling her to her feet. He had taken his boots off so they were both in their socks. He led her around the coffee table, pulling her close to him.

They started to dance slowly and as she laid her head against his chest, he leaned his cheek against her head. They danced to three songs. He felt so good in her arms, making her seem so safe and warm. She couldn't help herself as she began to rub her hands over his muscular back. He stopped moving and leaned down as she tilted her head up to his. They kissed, long, deep and passionately. He was such a good kisser.

She hadn't noticed it but she was walking him backwards. She pushed him up against the bookcase. He returned her vigor by running his hands down her back. Then he reached down, lifted one of her legs up to his waist, and held it there as he ran his hand along her thigh. She let out a soft moan as his mouth left hers and began to move down her neck. She knew what this was going to lead to and she was both nervous and excited.

"Ah, Derek?" she said in a low voice not sure what to say.

"Yes?" he said in a whisper, not stopping his pursuit down her neck.

She lost her thought for a moment and kissed his neck, reaching her hand up and running it through his soft hair, then turning her head to give him access to the front of her neck.

"I ah . . ." She needed to say something but was lost in the feeling of his lips under her chin.

He pulled back slightly, his smoldering gaze piercing her. "Yes?" he whispered.

"I . . . ah... don't have much experience with this."

His attention and lips went back to her neck. "That's ok . . . wait." He pulled back, letting her leg down as he realized what she might be implying. "Not much or none?" He searched her eyes and he saw the fear haunting her eyes.

"Well, none, to be honest."

He stepped back as she looked up and reached for him, her hand falling on his chest. He held it there. He wasn't sure what to say. He wanted her more than any woman he had ever wanted before, but his respect for her just leapt to new heights. She was truly the most surprising woman he'd ever met. "Are you saying what I think you're saying?"

She nodded her head slowly. "Yes." She was mortified.

"Ok," he said, taking in what she'd just revealed and he tilted his head. "You're, what, twenty four?"

"I'll be twenty five in two months." She tried but she couldn't read his emotions.

He raised her hand, kissed her fingers, then let her hand fall as he walked over, taking a deep breath, to pick up his wine glass and take a big drink. "You're a truly astonishing woman, Alanna," His forehead furrowed when he looked down at his glass. "More astonishing than I ever realized." He had his back to her. She wanted him to look at her. She didn't hear disappointment in his voice but she wasn't sure. "Alanna, I don't want you to do anything you're not ready for."

She came up behind him, put her arms around him and lay her head against his back. "But I think I am ready."

His chest inhaled deeply then he turned to face her. "We can take things slow. But if I leave the room to go take a cold shower or start talking about baseball to get my mind somewhere else don't take it personal. Ok?" He smiled.

She laughed moving closer to him. "I appreciate that, Derek, I really do. But I want to be with you," she said with conviction, and once she had said it, it was out there and she not only told him with her words, but also with her eyes. Her hormones raged, sparking a fire within her she didn't think would ever go out. Her decision was made. And she felt it was the right one. She was eager and scared all at the same time. *Damned hormones. Damned brain. God he is sexy as hell. Why does he have to be so irresistible?*

He kissed her gently saying, "It's a big decision, one I'm sure you've thought about before."

She took a deep breath, trying not to let her words show her trepidation. "All of these feelings are new to me, Derek, but I think it's you I've been waiting for." She realized that sounded kind of corny and clichéd until she saw his reaction.

He closed his eyes for a moment as he felt her words flow through him to his very soul. Did she realize what her saying that meant to him? He pulled her close, looking very serious as he said, "You're in the driver's seat here, ok? If you say stop, we stop. I'm going to follow your lead in this dance. But, if you decide this is what you truly want, I will be as gentle as possible, I promise. I would never do anything to hurt you. Ever."

She leaned back. "Thank you. That means a lot to me." Then she stepped back, taking the wine glass from his hand and drinking down the last of it. She set it down on the coffee table and took him by the hand, leading him down the hall to his bedroom. He followed without a word.

Juneau woke up, raising her head up from her cat bed. She peered across the dark room at the clock on the nightstand. It read 9:45 p.m. She raised up, stretching.

"I overslept." She stood up, jumping from the chest of drawers to the bed. She walked downstairs into the kitchen and looked at the empty dish that said *Tuna Breath.*

"Where's my num num?" She looked around and up at the clock by the door. *"It's 9:45. Where is my num num?"* She walked into the den to find Fintan asleep in his easy chair, Abbey asleep on the couch, and Jet asleep by the fireplace. She jumped up on the couch and swatted Abbey on the butt. *"Hey, wake up."*

Abbey opened her eyes and meowed. *"It num num time?"*

"Yeah, you didn't eat mine did you?" Juneau narrowed her eyes.

"No." Abbey raised up yawning. *"Where Mommy?"*

Juneau jumped down and began a thorough search of the house. A few minutes later she was sitting in the kitchen with Abbey by her side.

"Her truck is here. She left hours ago with that dog lover didn't she?"

Abbey yawned. *"She be back soon. She always gives us num num at night."*

"She's not here and it's getting late." Juneau eyed the cabinet where the wet cat food and treats were kept. *"She should be here."* She walked back into the den and over to Jet who was clearly dreaming, her paws twitching. Juneau swatted Jet's ear. *"Hey, wake up!"*

Jet twitched her ear but didn't wake up. Juneau swatted again extending her claws a little. Jet opened her eyes, raising her head. *"Hey, that hurt! Cut it out!"*

"Do you know what time it is?" She sat down by Jet.

"Nighttime." Jet laid her head back down, closing her eyes.

"It's num num time, you dimwit."

"Oh!" Jet opened her eyes, raising her head instantly *"That's right. Let's go!"* She stood up and started to run into the kitchen.

"Mother is not here. The dishes are empty!" Juneau exclaimed.

"Where is she?" Jet's concern for food changed to concern for her mother's safety.

"I don't know. She went somewhere with that dog lover and he hasn't brought her back."

"Well, she should be back soon." Jet sat down with a yawn.

"That what I said." Abbey said from the back of the couch.

"She should've been back by now. Something's wrong. It's a work night. She's usually getting ready for bed by now."

"So, what do you want to do?" Jet looked up at Fintan. *"We could wake Dad. He could call her and make sure she's ok."*

"Ok, you wake him." Juneau looked over at Fintan.

"No, you wake him." Jet stretched.

"I'm not going to wake him, you do it."

"You do it!"

"No, you!"

Abbey crossed over the couch to Fintan's chair as they argued. She hopped down into his lap and began rubbing her back under his chin as her tail passed under his nose. It took a second but he snorted and raised his head up, rubbing his itchy nose with his hand.

"I wake him," she said proudly as they all looked up at Fintan, who was blinking and pushing her down toward his lap.

"Abbey, stop that." He snorted, coughing a little and sitting up straighter in the chair. He looked at his watch, rubbing his eyes. Abbey hopped off the chair and went to sit by the other two as he sat up, pushing the footrest down. "What do you all want?" he asked in a sleepy tone.

"Mother is not home," Juneau meowed loudly. *"And I want my num num! Now! Now I say! Now!"*

"Num num now!" Abbey meowed, coming over to rub over his shins. *"Num num now!"*

He looked down at them, leaning forward a little. "What's all the meowing about?"

"Mom's not home. It's late." Jet gave a slight woof.

Fintan looked around and then stood up, setting the remote down on the table. He walked into the kitchen, grabbing a cigarette out of the pack on the counter. He went out the back door and lit it. He stood smoking just outside the door.

When he finished he came back into the kitchen and all three animals were lined up by their empty treat dishes. Their dry food feeders were full next to them. "What? Did she forget to give you your treat?"

"Yes!" Juneau meowed. *"Yes, she did!"*

"Yes!" Jet woofed slightly again.

"Yes!" Abbey meowed, weaving in and out of his legs as he tried to walk into the kitchen.

"Ok, let me see what we've got." He walked over to the cabinet and opened it. He reached in, retrieving a can of wet cat food and looked at it.

"Is turkey and gravy ok?" He eyed the cats. Abbey rubbed his legs.

"Want shrimp," she meowed.

"Good." Then he got out a can of wet dog food. "And for Jet we have . . ." he narrowed his eyes moving the can back and forth trying to read it ". . . something and liver. Is that acceptable?" He looked over at Jet. She wagged her tail. "Good."

He opened the cans up and emptied the contents into their individual dishes, splitting one between the cats, then recycled the empty cans. All three animals began devouring their treats. He looked at the clock then went upstairs, looking into Alanna's empty room. He came back downstairs and checked his cellphone and then the home phone message machine. Derek had said he was taking her on a hot air balloon ride then he was making her dinner at his place. Fintan had told him that sounded like something she would like. He checked the garage for her truck just because. He grabbed his pack of cigarettes, walked out the back door, sat at the table and smoked as he looked up at the stars.

"I know she's an adult, but I wish you were here, Evy," he said out loud with a sigh as he let out a breath of smoke. "You'd tell me she's grown and needs to have a nice young man in her life so you and I can have grandchildren." He took another drag, letting it out slowly. He looked up with a raised eyebrow. "That doesn't mean I have to be happy about it." He crushed his cigarette in the ashtray on the table and went inside. He looked down at all three animals. The cats were cleaning themselves as Jet was cleaning the cats' dishes.

"I don't think she's going to be coming home tonight, kids." He reached into the fridge to get a beer. They all looked up at him. "I think she's found a new bed to sleep in." He walked into the den.

Juneau looked up at the clock. *"Damned dog lover."*

Chapter 20

Alanna awoke to the early dawn light coming through the window of Derek's bedroom. The stereo was still playing and the music was coming through the speakers in the bedroom. She looked around the room, something she hadn't done the night before.

Now she knew why he'd picked the painting he had. The whole theme of the room was black and silver Harley Davidson. She was lying on Harley sheets with a Harley comforter over them. There were all kinds of Harley memorabilia all over the room. Even his lamps on the nightstands had Harley shades. She turned her head, looking over at Derek. He was asleep. One of his arms was draped over her. She reached up and brushed a lock of his hair away from his face. He stirred a little and smiled. He didn't open his eyes, but with his arm he pulled her close to him. His hand roamed over her body. Her cheek pressed into his neck and shoulder as he kissed her forehead then began to move his mouth down her face and neck. She giggled.

"Good morning," she said.

"Good is an understatement." He continued to trail kisses along her neck and shoulder.

"You need to hold that thought for a minute." She pulled away and reached over the side of the bed to the floor to retrieve his dark blue dress shirt. She sat up and slipped it on.

He watched her leave the room and go down the hall to the bathroom. He rolled over and stared at the ceiling. He heard her leave the bathroom and go into the kitchen. Then heard the fridge open, then the cabinet, the silverware drawer and then the fridge again. She came back into the bedroom with a glass of milk and a slice of cheesecake on a plate. She sat on the edge of the bed next to him.

"We didn't get a chance to have dessert last night." She fed him a bite of cheesecake.

"Oh, yes we did." He smiled and kissed her knee exposed from under the shirt.

She took a bite. "This is really good. Very tasty."

He came up under the plate she was holding, and kissed right above the button she'd fastened between her breasts. He undid the button. "Ummm, tasty indeed."

She giggled, waving the fork with a bite on it in front of him. He took the bite then took the plate from her hands, put it on the nightstand, and went back to undoing the buttons. "I know what I want for breakfast."

Two hours later they were lying in bed, holding each other as they talked.

"Do you have anything to do today?" he asked as he brushed the back of his fingers over her bare shoulder.

"Not really. I'd like to get that painting framed for you."

"That can wait." He just wanted to lie here with her for as long as possible.

"I suppose."

"Have you thought about your boss's offer?"

"Yeah, I just don't think that it's what I want to do."

"Alanna, I'm not prying, and I don't want details, but from what I hear you don't have to work if you don't want."

"It's true. I don't have to work, but my mom and dad taught me to work for what I want and not to be wasteful with my time or resources. But I just can't see myself stuck inside a building without windows for years of my life." A vision of the light-filled studio danced in her head.

"So, what do you want to do?" he asked, touching her arm.

She rolled over, running her fingers through his hair as it fell down framing his face. "To stay here in bed with you."

He laughed. "I like the sound of that."

She leaned forward, kissing his neck and chest.

At 11:30 there was the sound of a key in Derek's front door. Elsa Atherton opened the door and walked in carrying a grocery bag. She came out of the foyer, turning toward the kitchen and dining room. "Derek, I . . ." She stopped in mid-sentence and froze when she saw Derek in his black boxer briefs and Alanna in just his dress shirt, sitting at the dining room table feeding each other reheated lasagna. Derek took the bite off the fork Alanna was offering him. Neither of them even acknowledged his mother's presence as he kept his eyes on Alanna and chewed. Elsa's eyes widened as her face flushed deep red.

Elsa sat the bag down on the floor and left as quickly and quietly as possible.

"I really should put a chain lock on the inside of that door," he said as Alanna took a bite from his fork and they both started to chuckle. After they had finished, he picked her up in his arms and carried her over to the couch and began to make love to her.

"Derek, aren't you going to lock the door?"

He looked up. "Why? It doesn't do any good."

"Who else has a key?" She pushed him back a little.

"My sister, my six brothers, my father, Mr. and Mrs. Humphrey next door and my cousin Lenny."

"But!"

He let out a frustrated breath. "Ok." He got up and went to his desk with his computer. He pulled a blank piece of paper out of the printer, got a marker and wrote *Do Not Disturb, Upon Pain of Death!* on it. He held it up for her to read before he opened the door and attached the notice. He closed and locked the door then came back to the couch. "Better?"

"Yes." She pulled him to her. "Upon pain of death?"

"They have no idea." He kissed her.

At 5:15 Derek, Alanna and Tanner pulled up in front of her house. They went inside and were met by Jet, Juneau and Abbey. The three were lined up, sitting on the kitchen floor and staring at Alanna.

"Hello, ladies," Alanna said as she entered the kitchen.

"Hello? Hello! Is that all you have to say?" Juneau scolded her.

She bent down to pet them. "Sorry, I should've let you know I wasn't coming home last night."

Derek looked down at them. "Aw, look. They're all lined up to greet you."

"I missed you, Mommy," Abbey said, rubbing against her legs.

"Don't be nice to her! She abandoned us for that damn dog lover!" Juneau stood up and stalked out of the room.

"They just missed me." She reached into the cabinet, giving them all a crunchy treat.

"It's ok, Mom. Dad told us where you were." Jet went over to Tanner and sniffed him.

"'ello, all." Tanner ate Juneau's treat since she had left then he went after her into the den.

Emma came down the stairs. "There you are." She set a laundry basket down on the counter. "Dinner will be ready in about an hour. I took into consideration that Derek would probably be joining you so there is more than enough." She took her basket into the laundry room.

"I want to change my clothes." She gave him a quick kiss before she went upstairs.

He got a glass of iced tea and sat down at the kitchen table. Emma came back into the kitchen, lifted a lid on a pot on the stove and looked over the contents.

"How's your mother, Derek?"

Derek smiled, remembering his mother's intrusion, knowing she wouldn't do that again any time soon. "She's fine."

"She's so good at organizing." Emma started to remove dishes from the dishwasher and put them away. "Our church charity drives are such a success because of her."

"She does like telling people what to do," he said gently, sipping his tea as the door to the laundry room opened and Fintan came in dressed in his uniform.

"Evening," he said to Emma and Derek as he walked through the kitchen and headed upstairs.

"Hello, Fintan. Dinner will be ready in an hour."

"Evening, sir," Derek said.

Alanna came down the stairs with a little skip to her step. "Hi, Dad." She gave him a quick kiss on the cheek as she passed him on the stairs. He stopped and cleared his throat.

"Alanna."

"Yeah, Dad."

"I know you're an adult, but a modicum of consideration in the form of a phone call or text would be appreciated if you're not coming home at night. Is that too much to ask?" He looked at her, not seeing a woman of twenty plus years, but the small ten-year-old girl he'd given almost the exact speech to the time she stayed at Sam's one night and didn't call to check in.

"Oh, sorry, Dad. You're right. I'll call or text next time, promise." She hugged him and went downstairs.

He sighed as his hand rested on his gun. "Breathe deep," he told himself as he went upstairs to change. "Just breathe deep."

Alanna got a glass of iced tea and sat down at the table next to Derek. She noticed Jet was out in the back yard nosing through the bushes by the wall.

"You want a snack or something?" She smiled at him.

"No, I'm fine," Derek said, reaching over holding her hand. "I don't want to spoil my dinner." He motioned his head toward Emma.

Nemesis flew in through the open back doors, landing on one of the chair backs.

Derek jumped a little.

"It's ok, he's my aunt's pet."

"Pet! I'm no one's pet! I'll have you know that I'm a companion to my mistress. She's asked me to let you know she wishes for you to bring your young man to her house."

"That is so cool." Derek leaned forward as Nemesis got onto the table and walked toward them, eyeing Derek very skeptically.

"My aunt sends him over when she wants to see me."

"Doesn't she have a phone?"

"Yeah, but she likes this better." She looked down. "Nemesis, can Derek pet you?"

He walked over, took a drink out of Derek's glass, then made a curt nod of his head. *"Only for a moment."*

Derek reached forward, tentatively stroking Nemesis' neck and wing with his finger as he said, "You know, ravens are one of the most intelligent birds in the world. They're great puzzle solvers. They're such an amazing creatures." He ran his finger down the bird's back. "He's so tame."

"I'll peck your eye out if you cross me. I'm not as tame as you think. I'm finished here."

Alanna smiled. "He's not that tame, but he does put up with a lot."

Nemesis turned and flew out the open door.

"Want to go with me to visit my aunt?" She stood up.

"Sure." He followed her out the door and they walked hand in hand the short distance to Bob and Vi's house. They entered the open front door and as they did Derek felt an intense shock of static electricity as he entered after her. "Ouch." He looked back at the doorway. "Did you feel that?" he asked Alanna.

"No, what was it?"

"Nothing."

"Mister Atherton, so happy to see you." Vi was standing in her atrium, looking over a plant to check its soil moisture.

"Hello, Mrs. Dalton."

She wiped her hands on her apron and came forward into the kitchen. "Oh, you can call me Vi." She gave him a small hug. This was the first time she'd ever touched him. She felt the latent powers within him and it sent a strong shiver through her. She pulled back, eyeing him curiously at arm's length.

"Ok, as long as you call me Derek." He smiled, not thinking anything of her eyeing him like a newly discovered oddity.

"Well of course, Derek." Furrows creased her brow for a second and then she smiled warmly. She pulled out a chair for him. "Sit, sit."

They both took seats at the table and Vi placed glasses of juice in front of them. Then she took a seat, picking up her cup of tea. "So a little bird tells me you two are inseparable."

Alanna reached up to run her hand over her face, trying to hide her embarrassment. "Auntie Vi, please."

"Well, it's true is it not?"

"Yes, it's true. I don't want to let her out of my sight." Derek smiled and nudged Alanna with his elbow.

"Don't be embarrassed, my dear." Vi took a sip. "I'm very happy for the two of you."

"I know, it's just strange talking about this." Alanna fidgeted.

"So, talk to me about your decision then. I feel you've not only made one, but many. Hopefully, you've thought about what I said."

"Yes, I think I have."

"So, what've you decided?" Vi motioned in the air with her hand.

Alanna leaned back in the chair. "I want to paint. I just don't know if I can make a career out of it."

Vi reached over, retrieving her blue velvet bundle off the counter and unwrapping it. She handed the tarot deck to Alanna. "Shuffle." Vi smoothed out the cloth.

"But, I don't . . ."

Vi waved a finger at her, cutting her off. "Shuffle."

Alanna shuffled the cards a little and set them down.

Vi put her reading glasses on the tip of her nose and told her, "Now, hold them and ask them your question, then cut the deck."

Alanna picked them back up and sighed.

"Come on, a little insight never hurts."

Alanna closed her eyes while she held the deck between her palms and thought deeply about her question. Then she cut the cards and handed them back to Vi. She'd done this many times before to appease her aunt.

"Now let us see what the spirits have to say. Shall we?" Vi dealt nine cards off the top into three rows of three each and then set the rest of the deck to the side.

Something started tugging at Derek's jeans leg, then he felt it climbing up his leg.

"Ah, Alanna? The spirits have my leg." He leaned back as Apollo, a white albino ferret, pulled himself up into Derek's lap.

"It's ok," Alanna told him. "That's Apollo, he doesn't bite. His sister Artemis is around here somewhere, now she does bite."

Vi leaned forward, giving Derek a piece of cookie. "Give him this. He'll be your friend."

Derek fed Apollo the cookie and he curled up in Derek's lap, laying his head on his arm. "He's so soft and cute." Derek petted the ferret.

"He thinks he's a stud," Vi said, pushing her glasses to the bridge of her nose. "He's always humping my throw pillows."

Vi looked down at the cards. "My dear, it always amazes me the cards that are drawn to you, and not a one inverted. I love doing your readings because you have a true knack for getting right to the point, and look at all the pentacles."

Vi looked up at Derek as she explained each card. "Now the first three cards here represent her past." She waved her hand showing him the first row. She tapped the first card. "This first card, The Five of Pentacles, means significant loss. Probably Eva. Next, we have The High Priest. That's thirst for knowledge, education or a sense of strong tradition. Third we have The Four of Pentacles which is the building of one's wealth or security." She waved her hand over the middle row. "These three cards represent her present. Ah, The Fool." She lifted the first card.

"That figures," Alanna said.

"It does not mean you are a fool. It represents openness, new-found trust and freedom." The next card was The Lovers. She tapped it, smiling at Derek. "This card being here doesn't surprise me a bit. It represents love and fulfillment. The Moon means your dreams are awakening psychic abilities in you. No surprise there. Now the next three are about your future my dear."

She eyed the first card in the row. "The Strength card means you will be calling upon your courage and faith very soon. Don't forget that. Next we have The Fferyllt or Druid, which represents fluency between worlds, also that the creativity and magic within you will be harnessed. This usually means you have untapped powers lying in wait. That pleases me to see that."

She looked over her glasses at Alanna and smiled. "And last is The Ten of Pentacles. This, my dear," she held the card up to Alanna, "this is prosperity and legacy." Vi sighed, sitting back in her chair.

"So, there you have it. You cannot deny what the cards say. The spirits say you must paint like those before you and carry on the legacy and tradition." She smiled and picked up her tea, taking a sip.

Derek leaned over, took the next card from the top of the deck, and held it up. "What does this card mean?" he asked.

Vi looked over the top of her glasses at the card of an ominous man with a beard and mustache. He had hard, calculating eyes and was sitting on a stone throne. "The Lord." She smiled. "It means her father will have your hide and your testicles if you hurt her."

Derek flipped the card around to see. "It does kind of look like him."

Alanna and Vi laughed. Vi leaned forward, taking Alanna's hand in hers.

"Have faith in yourself, love. You have so much to offer the world through your eyes."

"I'll try." She stood up and gave Vi a hug. "We have to get back for dinner. I'll see you soon."

Derek handed Vi the furry bundle from his lap, which was Apollo. "Thank you for having us over." He stood up, pushing his chair back in.

"Anytime, come over anytime." Vi picked up her cup, pausing it before her.

"Oh, and Derek?" she called after them.

He reappeared in the doorway. She motioned for him to come stand beside her. He did and listened as she talked softly to him. Alanna leaned on the door frame, not able to hear what her aunt was saying.

"Ok, I will. I promise," he said to Vi as they left.

Vi sat back after they were out of the house and narrowed her eyes, saying softly to herself, "I must have a conversation with Roger and very soon. Very soon indeed."

They walked hand in hand back to Treasure Grove and Derek smiled as he looked around at the trees with the evening light coming through their top branches.

"Your aunt's a very interesting person."

"She's unique. She throws some people off sometimes, though. So, can I ask what she said to you?"

He squeezed her hand gently. "She told me that at some point you may confide family secrets in me and to please guard them as I'd guard my own."

"And you told her you would?"

"Of course." He stopped walking, pulling her other hand into his. "Alanna, I know we've only being going out for what? Not even a week? But I feel closer to you than anyone. I feel like we've known each other a lot longer than we have, and I know this sounds weird, but you totally get me. Some of my own family don't even get me, but I feel like I can tell you things and you wouldn't judge or ridicule me for my thoughts, feelings or opinions. I can't really explain how I'm feeling right now without looking like a fool and I know it's too soon for me to be saying all this, so, actually just ignore what I said. I'm just letting my mouth speak before I think and I should shut up now."

She laughed. "It's ok, and I understand what you're saying." She lifted her chin to look into his eyes as she said, "I feel the same way. Like we've known each other for ages, and I just want to say that last night was amazing for me, Derek. And I'm not going to ignore what you just said. You meant it, I can tell. I feel connected to you also, and not just physically."

He kissed her. "Well, I can honestly say last night was the most incredible night of my life." He gazed warmly at her, looking as if he wanted to say something else then changed his mind. Pulling her closer he kissed her gently, cupping her face in his hand. "Thank you."

"For what?" She gazed up at him.

"For being you."

"Well, that's not hard to do," she scoffed. "It comes so naturally for me."

He laughed. "And here I thought you'd taken lessons to become so wonderful."

"Nope, just born this way."

"Remind me to thank your father."

They got back to Treasure Grove and were walking across the lawn when they looked over at the wall past the barn to see Tanner and Juneau lying on the ground near to a bush. They got closer to them, noticing they were lying in front of a hole that went under the wall. Their backs were to the bush, on the other side of which was a gopher leaning around to observe them watching its home.

"Now that's funny," Derek said. "I wish I had a camera."

"I'm surprised Tanner doesn't smell it. It's so close to them."

They went into the house and Emma was setting the table. They helped as Fintan came in from the den. They all sat down and Emma served up an excellent chicken dish with dumplings.

"This is so good. Can I get the recipe for my mom?" Derek asked her.

"Sure." She smiled. "As long as you get her rum cake recipe for me?"

"I'll try. She's pretty protective of that one."

"I know. I've been trying to get it for a couple of years now."

Emma finished up and headed home as the three talked about sports and the weather over dinner. Then Fintan cleared his throat. "So, I presume you're taking some time off work?" He arched an eyebrow, knowing she hadn't been at work that day.

"Yeah, Mr. Beckman wants me to go into the management trainee program, so I took some vacation time to think about it."

Fintan leaned back in his chair. "What're your thoughts so far?"

"I don't want to be in retail anymore." She wiped her mouth with her napkin.

"So, what do you want to do?" He picked up his drink.

A small smile passed across Derek's lips as he remembered her response when he'd asked her that same question earlier in the day.

"I really want to paint, but I don't know if I can make a career out of it."

"Do you want a career?" Fintan asked.

"Well, Mom had a teaching career, and you're a cop."

"Yes, but your Grandmother Bermann was an artist, volunteer and socialite."

"She also ran her finances with an iron fist."

"True. She was excellent at investing, and she never loaned money without a written agreement, no matter how small the amount. She was a smart one." Fintan still respected his mother-in-law's ways of dealing with people and money.

"I think I'll go tomorrow and talk to Uncle Nevin. Since he's my financial advisor, he might be able to help me."

"Alanna, your mother was a very talented artist, there's no doubt about that. Your grandmothers were talented as well, but you are even better than all of them put together," he said with pride. "You should follow your dream if that's what you want to do. Don't worry about a career or anything else, just do what makes you happy. Your Uncle Nevin will make sure you're taken care of financially. He's even better at the investing and financial decisions than his mother was.

Just listen to him and don't go buying a jet or yacht thinking they'll give you pleasure . . . they're just things. You don't need things to be happy. That's what your mother and I always tried to teach you."

"And you did a fine job." She raised her arms out, presenting herself.

"Yes, we did." He smiled, picking up his plate to put it in the sink. He took his cigarettes as he went towards the patio. "Talk to Nevin, but do the right thing and give your boss the proper notice. I didn't raise you to just ditch your responsibilities."

"Ok, Dad." She stood up and put her and Derek's plates in the sink, and stared out the kitchen window for a moment.

Derek stood up and hugged her from behind while she stood at the sink. "He's a good dad. He just wants you to be happy."

She smiled and a thought occurred to her. "Hey, I have something to show you." She gently pulled him down the hall.

"Really? Right after dinner? Shouldn't we wait an hour or is that just swimming?"

"Not that, silly. Something I think you'll like."

"I'd like anything you show me," he said in a devilish tone, his expression matching his thoughts.

She took him past the den to two large, ornate wooden doors at the end of the hall. She opened them up to reveal a huge library. She turned on the lights. The ceiling was at least forty feet high and covered in large wooden beams that held the black, wrought-iron chandeliers. There were windows on one wall that were covered in heavy, dark burgundy drapes to keep the light from damaging the books. The bookshelves were from floor to ceiling. It looked like a library in a college or school. Everything was in deep red mahogany wood. Thousands of books lined the hundreds of shelves. He walked to the middle of the huge room, turning around. "Oh, wow! I've never seen such a large home library."

"My great-grandmother built this house just so she could have a large library, a ballroom and an art studio. The ballroom is the only room larger than this one."

He looked down at the floor. It was an intricately detailed mahogany parquet floor with beautiful rosewood and teak inlays throughout. "This floor is awesome! You don't see hand-laid floors like this anymore. It must have taken months to do this."

"It took them two years to do the floors here and in the ballroom."

He walked over to a glass case in the middle of the room. "Are those manuscripts?"

"Those are my great-grandfather's scientific findings." She laid a loving hand on the case. "He was an inventor and he used to write all his findings down. When he passed, my great-gram had this case made to keep his work."

"This is so cool." He looked around the room then noticed the large tapestry hanging on the wall and walked over to it. "Is this your family tree?"

"Yes, on my mother's side."

He noticed Alanna's name embroidered towards the bottom. "Your middle name is Skye?" He smiled as he read. "Which comes from your grandmother, Skye MacCool? And she had three sisters, Ember, River, and Terra." He liked those names.

"Yes, my mother loved the name Skye."

He looked up at the names of all the female descendants dating back to the early 1500s. "So why just the women? Where are all the men?"

She changed the subject quickly. "So what's your middle name?"

He hesitated as he looked to the very top of the tapestry. The wooden rod that held the tapestry looked like no other wood he'd ever seen before. It was very old and beautiful, seeming like a polished tree branch, and in this light it had a reddish-orange shimmer. He had an overwhelming desire to touch it, and was mesmerized by the swirls and knots in the wood. As he stared at it they seemed to move slightly, swimming slowly around the rod. He felt compelled to move his hands upwards. It would take a very tall telescoping ladder to reach it, but he wanted to touch it.

"Not going to tell me? Is it that bad?" Alanna asked.

"Huh?" he said, coming back to reality.

"Your middle name. Do you not want me to know what it is?" She was very curious now; had his parents named him something so bad?

"Oh, it's . . ." He glanced away from her. "Well, yeah, it's pretty bad. There were so many of us boys they let my grandfather name me."

"And?" She crossed her arms.

He shifted his gaze a little. "You're not gonna laugh are you?"

"No, I promise," she said sincerely.

"Theodoric Oddvar Atherton."

She raised an eyebrow. "Oddvar?" She smiled slightly.

"It was my great-great-grandfather's name." His eyes went to the tapestry rod again.

"I like Theodoric," she mused. "It sounds so worldly."

"Just don't call me Theo." He gave her a warning look. "I hate that."

"Ok, Theodoric." She said his name as sensuously as she could.

He smiled, looking back to all the books. Needing to change the subject he asked, "So have you read them all?"

She smiled, noticing that'd he changed the topic. "No, but I've read a lot of them. There's a whole science section that my great-grandfather collected. I have no interest in reading those, but my great-grandmother liked novels and plays."

He walked up the steps to the chairs by the windows. "This is like something out of a movie. It's so big." He reached to a shelf, pulled out a book, looked at it, then put it back.

"There are a lot of newer ones, but there're plenty of really old ones too. We have your Uncle Roger coming in to maintain the older ones, leather bindings and all that stuff."

"He never told me, probably because he knew I'd want to see this place."

"Hey, check this out." She walked over to what looked like an ancient key typewriter, reached into the card catalogue drawer in the cabinet next to it and thumbed through the cards until she found a number she liked. He walked over and stood beside her. She typed the numbers and letters onto the keys and hit the return bar. But instead of a roller at the top of the typewriter, there were a lot of thin wires running up the wall into a metal tube. He heard a bunch of clicking sounds. She pointed up to the next level of books on the shelves close to the ceiling. A metal accordion arm with four long, flat pincers on the end came out of a cabinet and ran along a rod. It stopped, and with a few jerky motions, it pulled a book from one of the very top shelves. It took the book back along the rod and placed it gently in a basket. The basket lowered on a wire to the top of the card catalogue.

"That's so cool." He picked the book up out of the basket. "Poe." He smiled. "How'd you know I liked Edgar Allan Poe?"

"Oh, a wild guess," she said sarcastically. "Strange and unusual, remember?"

"Right. So how do you send it back?" He was totally enthralled.

She put the book back in the basket and depressed the shift lock key then punched the numbers and letters in again. More clicking and the basket rose while the arm came out and returned the book to the shelf where it lived.

She shrugged. "My great-grandfather loved to invent things. He didn't want the ladies on the ladders so he invented this. If the books tilt or fall over you have to use the ladder and fix them, but for the most part it works great. Sometimes it puts them in upside down, but at least they are in the right spot."

They stayed in the library for a while, going up the curved wooden staircase to the second level, where they looked out the windows and he admired everything. Then she led him to the opposite end of the long hall and showed him the ballroom.

"Wow! This room is even bigger. I guess your great-grandmother really did like to entertain." He looked around and down at the exquisite wood floor.

"You have no idea." She flicked on all the lights. "Any reason to throw a party and she was all over it."

"I knew your house was huge, but I had no idea you had rooms like this."

She walked over, looking at the stereo equipment as he came up beside her. "See? You have satellite radio." He pointed to a small black box.

She nodded, not surprised by its appearance. "Dad likes any type of new technology."

He punched a button on the receiver and then another one on the small black box. Music started to come out of the speakers. He made a few adjustments, choosing a station, and then he raised the volume. "Nice system."

He took her hand, leading her to the middle of the room and they started to dance.

A few minutes later Fintan appeared in the doorway of the large double doors. He smiled and then went back down the hall to the den. Abbey came running into the room carrying a paperclip. She put it down and batted it around the smooth floor.

"Sam and Nick are going to have their wedding here."

Derek heard her, but instead of answering, he kissed her. They kissed for a while, forgetting to dance. He pulled back a little. "I'd better go before I try to convince you to come home with me."

"And if I asked you to stay?"

He tilted his head. "What about your dad? I don't want to wear out my welcome."

"Don't worry, I told him I might ask you to stay."

"You did?" He looked shocked. "And he's ok with that?"

"As long as you don't walk around in your underwear." She grinned.

"Ok. I hadn't planned on it, but if it's important, I'll make sure not to do that."

They walked over and turned off the stereo and the lights. She picked Abbey up, closing the doors behind them. She set Abbey down in the hallway and then took Derek by the hand and led him upstairs to her bedroom. She picked Juneau up from her cat bed. Tanner was on her bed taking a nap, so Derek picked him up and they placed both animals in the hall as they closed and locked the door.

"It's my bedroom too! It's a room with my bed in it!" Juneau meowed loudly.

Tanner yawned. *"Jet is downstairs in the den. Shall we go watch some telly?"*

"This is unacceptable! Dog lover walks in and I get booted out of my own bed?" Juneau complained the whole time as she followed Tanner down to the den. When they got there Tanner jumped up onto the couch, turned around a few times, then lay down and looked up at the TV.

Juneau got up on the couch and looked angrily over at Fintan. She meowed loudly. *"She kicked us out! Damned dog lover! This is unacceptable! What are you going to do about it?"* She stared at him, twitching her tail violently.

Fintan looked over at her. "Yeah, I'm not too happy about it either."

Chapter 21

Derek woke up, opened his eyes and looked over to where Alanna should have been. Instead, Juneau was sitting beside his pillow glaring down at him. Her eyes were cold and calculating. Her ears backed flat against her head.

"Hey, kitty." He reached out to her and she hissed.

"This is unacceptable! UNACCEPTABLE!"

He sat up looking around "Alanna?" he called, running his hand through his hair.

"She went for a run. You should follow . . . quickly, and don't come back!"

"She must be downstairs." He saw the door was partially open as he got out of bed naked and went into the bathroom.

"Put some clothes on!" Juneau demanded as she followed him, watching his every move. He came back into the room and put his clothes on as he looked down at her.

"You're a curious thing aren't you?" He walked past her to the door.

"Plotting your demise is not curiosity. It's learning your habits in order to strike at the precise time, which will be when you least expect it." She watched him leave then looked around. *"Damn. He didn't leave me anything to shred."*

Derek went downstairs to the kitchen. Fintan was sitting at the table and Emma was fixing breakfast. He stopped at the base of the stairs not sure of the reception he would receive without Alanna here. Emma looked over from the stove.

"Good morning. Would you like some coffee?" She smiled happily.

He walked toward the table. "Good morning, and yes, thank you."

Fintan didn't move behind his thin wall of newspaper.

Emma placed the cup down in front of Derek as he took a seat at the table. "Cream or sugar?"

"No, thank you, I like it black." He took a sip after he glanced around for Alanna.

"Alanna went for a run. She should be back in a little while," Emma said, returning to the stove. Fintan lowered his paper a little, then reached over and handed Derek the sports section.

"Thank you, sir." Derek took it as he sipped his coffee.

Fintan raised his paper back up and cleared his throat. "Didn't know my daughter could sing opera."

Derek choked loudly on his coffee coughing as Emma slammed down her spatula and then waved it at Fintan. "Fintan MacLachlin! This boy is nervous enough, and you promised Alanna you'd behave."

Fintan chuckled a little. "The boy can take a joke." He lowered his paper looking at Derek. "Can't you?"

Derek looked him in the eye, nodding his head. "Yes, sir."

Fintan raised his paper back up. "So, how about them Giants?"

Derek opened the sports section as he said, "That new rookie has one hell of an arm. He'll be worth the bonus."

"Yeah, he's looking good. I bet they start him next month." Fintan took a drink.

They continued to talk about baseball until Emma put their plates down in front of them. Then they talked about basketball as they ate. Fintan finished and got up from the table.

"Well, I have to get ready for work." He went upstairs as Derek picked up the plates, took them to the sink, rinsed them and put them in the dishwasher.

Emma refilled the coffee cup in his hand as she said, "Fintan is trying, he really is. He's just not used to Alanna spending . . . ah . . . time with a young man. Give him time." She patted him on the shoulder.

"Thanks, Emma."

Derek took his cup and went out onto the patio to sit down. The sun wasn't up over the trees yet and the light filtered through them as he took a deep breath. He looked back through the open patio doors, seeing Fintan come down the stairs in his uniform and leave through the laundry room door. Derek heard his car start and saw him drive down the long driveway. He honked as he passed Alanna coming in the gate. Jet, Tanner and Abbey were with her. She jogged up the drive and around to the back of the house. Tanner beat her to Derek.

"Ello. That was very invigorating. So much wildlife out there. Not allowed to chase it though. Not quite sure why not. Nasty tasting spray she put on me legs and feet."

Alanna came up to the table as she pulled her earbuds out of her ears then leaned over and kissed him.

"Good morning." She stretched and leaned over, touching the ground.

He looked over her backside in front of him. She was hanging upside down looking at him from between her legs. "From this angle it's very good." He sipped his coffee as his thoughts went to her wrapping those wonderful long legs around him.

She raised up smiling as Emma came over and put a plate of food, cutlery and a cup of coffee down on the table.

"Here, Sweetie. You probably worked up an appetite."

"Thank you, Emma, I did. I forgot how wonderful it is to run in the mornings."

She sat down and started to eat. She had needed to run. She was feeling guilty about neglecting her dreams and trying to help solve two, maybe three murders.

"I'm surprised Tanner didn't run off. I always have to keep him on a leash," Derek said.

"No, he's a good dog. He tried to chase a deer and a fox, but Jet brought him back." She took a drink of coffee. "So, what did my father say?"

"What do you mean?" he asked nonchalantly.

"I know my dad. If you came down and I wasn't here, he made a comment or two."

"Well, he did say he didn't know you could sing opera."

She coughed on her food. "I what?"

"He was just joking and Emma scolded him for it. But, I actually thought it was pretty funny."

"I told him to behave."

"And he did. That was really mild compared to what he could have said about us being together last night."

"Well, as long as he didn't offend you."

"Not at all." He leaned forward. "So what are you going to do today?"

"I wanted to take that painting down and have it framed for you. After that, nothing really. I called my Uncle Nevin to get an appointment, but he's out of town until Thursday and we have a truce meeting Thursday night anyway."

"A truce meeting?"

"That's when all the family members get together once a month to discuss our corporation's business."

"But a truce?"

"Yeah, we always call it that. Sometimes we don't all agree but at least we agree to disagree, so we call a truce. When an impasse is reached, we draw up a truce agreement."

"Sounds complicated."

"It can be sometimes, heated even. I understand most of it but some things I just don't get." She finished eating.

Emma stepped outside the doors. "I'm going to the store. I'll be back later."

"Ok."

Alanna stood up, leaned over and kissed him on the cheek. "I'm going to go take a shower." She took her empty plate and cup into the house.

Derek sat there for a minute, then he thought of her upstairs in the shower. Alanna had her head under the spray of hot water when she heard the shower door open.

"Can I wash your back?" Derek asked, standing naked in front of her.

She smiled. "Yes, please."

He stepped in and closed the door.

An hour later Abbey was pawing at the closed bedroom door.

"Mommy? Mommy?" she meowed.

Alanna pulled the door open a little. "What, Abbey?" She looked down at Abbey's cute, furry face.

"Mommy, the door's closed."

"Yes, it is," she whispered and went to close the door again.

"Mommy? Mommy?"

"What?"

"Don't want door closed." Abbey pushed her way into the opening.

She let Abbey into the room, then closed and locked the door. She got back into bed and snuggled up next to Derek. Abbey jumped up onto the bed, walking over him. She sat down on his hip.

"We have company."

He reached over, petting Abbey who began to purr.

"She wanted in."

"She's so little, what is she, six months old?"

"No, she's two and a half. She's just small."

"She looks like a teenage kitty." He rubbed her chin and ears.

"I'm fast. Very fast," Abbey boasted.

Alanna's cellphone rang. She scooted up in the bed, leaning against the pillows, and picked her cellphone up off the nightstand.

"Hey, Al. I'm on my break. You still chained to his bedpost?"

"Hey, Sam. No, now he's chained to mine."

"Awesome," Sam said with approval.

Derek set Abbey aside, leaning over. He began kissing Alanna's stomach as he raised his head up to the phone in her hand.

"Hey, Sam," he said before he went back to kissing her hip.

"Now that's my kind of vacation. You two drink lots of fluids, and some advice for you, Al."

"Yeah?"

"Let the man get some sleep." Click.

Alanna hung up, putting the phone back on the nightstand.

At a little after one, Derek and Alanna were dressed and downtown, carrying the painting in a large cardboard carrier as he helped her get through the door of the art gallery that did framing. Derek picked out a frame he liked and the owner said she'd have it ready by Monday. They left the gallery, deciding to walk down the street, looking in the shop windows and watching the tourists pass by.

Then they stopped at Atherton's Bookstore. Roger Atherton looked up from the book he was keying into the computer when they entered the store. "Hello Derek, Alanna."

"Hey, Uncle Roger." Derek closed the door behind them.

"Hello Mr. A. How are you?"

"Ahh, I see that my brother wasn't lying to me."

"About what?" Derek slipped his arm around her waist.

"About you dating a very beautiful woman."

"Yes, he was right." Derek gave Alanna a kiss on the temple. "I'm very pleased to say that she has agreed to date me."

She smiled. "Mr. A, do you by chance have any books on Nordic myths? Preferably ones about Grimhild or Freyja? I think Derek might like to learn about some female Norse deities."

He gave them a questioning look. "Yes, I do. Both of those women were known for their use of magic and control over men and gods. Right?"

"Yes, that's correct." She nodded her head.

He walked to the back of the store. As they followed, Derek pinched her butt a little. Roger reached up, retrieving two books. "Either of these should have the myths you are looking for."

"Thank you, I'll take both of them."

Roger smiled. "You're trying to teach him a lesson are you not?"

"Yes, but he's a quick learner."

"I try." Derek followed them back up front.

She paid for the books and took the bag from his hand.

"Thank you Mr. A, you've been a big help."

"Yes, thank you, Uncle Roger. I'm sure I'm going to love this lesson."

He smiled as he held the door for her. "You're welcome. I'm glad I could help." He waved as they closed the door.

Derek pulled her to him on the sidewalk. "Control me o' Goddess of the Norse." Then he kissed her. She raised her hand, using one finger to touch the center of his forehead.

"You will be my love slave for the next twenty four hours."

He bowed his head. "It is done. You have me under your spell o' beautiful one."

She laughed. "You're so silly." He kissed her hand as they walked down the street.

Vi watched from her store window as they walked off hand in hand down the street. Then she closed the shop and walked across the street and into the bookstore, closing the door behind her.

"Hello Vivian." Roger looked over from his computer.

"Roger. Any customers right now?"

"No, not at the moment."

"Good." She flipped the sign to *Closed* and locked the door. "Let's have a little chat."

Derek and Alanna stopped in front of a café. "Are you hungry?" he asked.

"A little."

"They have great sandwiches here, or would you prefer something else?"

She glanced around as something in the store window next door caught her eye then walked over and stared at it. A light of realization came on behind her eyes. Why hadn't she seen it before?

"Alanna?" Derek watched her, puzzled by her fascination, wondering what she was thinking.

"Derek, I need to go and see my father." There was an urgency in her voice.

He saw the intense look on her face. "Ok, I'll take you to him."

They walked back to his truck and he drove them to Police Headquarters. Officers in the outer office area watched as they made their way to the back to Fintan's office.

She knocked on his open door. "Dad, can I talk to you?"

He looked up from the papers in his hand. "Yeah, come on in."

Derek offered to stay outside the office, but she wanted him to stay so they stepped inside as Derek closed the door behind them. She spent the next twenty minutes explaining her theory. Fintan didn't say much, he just listened and made a few notes. Derek was amazed at how she was connecting the dots of her theory. When she was finished, Fintan leaned back in his chair and stroked his mustache.

"Ok, let me see what we can dig up."

She stood up. "Thank you, Daddy."

After they got back outside she said, "I'm hungry."

"Me too." Derek agreed, so they walked across the street to a diner to have lunch. Afterwards, they drove back to Treasure Grove and a very agitated Jet met them in the driveway.

"Mom, come quick! Abbey's in trouble!" Jet ran toward the backyard.

Alanna jumped out of the truck, running after Jet and leaving her door open.

"Hey, Alanna? What's going on?" Derek got out, shutting both truck doors, then running after Alanna and Jet to the backyard. All the animals were over by the wall near a deep gopher hole, where Tanner was digging frantically. Jet started digging again too. There was dirt thrown everywhere already.

Derek caught up with her. "What's going on?"

"Abbey crawled into that hole after the gopher. The hole collapsed in on her!" She held her hands up to the dogs. "Ok, stop digging!" They stopped and stood still. "Abbey! Abbey, baby? Can you hear me?" Alanna knelt down, yelling into the hole that went deep down and under the wall.

"Mommy?" Abbey's voice was faint as she meowed softly.

Alanna leaned further down to reach into the hole. With the tips of her fingers she could feel dirt blocking the tunnel. "Yes, baby, it's me."

"Mommy, I can't move! There's dirt all over me, I'm stuck and my leg's caught! My whiskers said I'd fit, but I don't. Mommy, I'm scared!"

"Hold on, baby, we'll get you out." Alanna looked around and down the hole.

Juneau walked out of the house and across the lawn, standing back a little watching the scene. *"Good, I was about to call you or 911 when you pulled in."* She sat down and watched.

Derek looked down into the hole. "Should we try to dig her out?"

"No, it's caved in around her and her leg is caught."

"How do you know that?" he asked her with narrowed eyes.

She waved a hand at him. "Trust me, I know. I can hear what she's saying. I'll tell you all about it later. Right now I have to get someone in there to help dig her out." She reached into her pocket and pulled out her cellphone.

Vi answered on the second ring. "I sense trouble. What do you need?" Vi said without a hello or other greeting.

"Abbey is stuck in a gopher hole. I need Apollo or Artemis."

"On the way." She hung up.

Alanna lay down and reached her arm into the hole as far as she could, barely feeling the tip of Abbey's tail. Hard dirt covered everything around her.

"Mommy, my tail, is that you?"

"Yes, that's me, baby. Don't worry. We're going to get you out. Just hold still."

"Mommy, I'm scared. Sing to me, please?"

Alanna let out a short laugh.

Derek knelt down. "What's so funny?"

"She's scared and wants me to sing to her."

"So, sing to her." He petted Tanner and Jet as he watched with fascination and confusion.

Alanna started singing *Do-Re-Mi*, one of Abbey's favorite songs. She was on the second chorus when Nemesis came into view with Vi's purple shawl bunched up in his claws. He swooped down and Derek caught the bundle as Nemesis let it go. Derek began to untie it as Apollo poked his head out.

"What's the emergency?" Apollo asked.

Derek set the ferret down on the ground and Apollo ran over to Alanna. *"What do you want me to do?"* he asked, putting his front paws on her leg.

She looked down at him as she pointed. "Over on the other side of that bush is another gopher hole. It connects with this one, so go in and see if you can get to Abbey from that side. The hole caved in on her and she's trapped."

"Ok, is it dark?" He looked down into the hole in front of her.

Alanna glared at Apollo. "Yes, it's dark! It's a hole. Why, are you afraid of the dark?"

"A little." He tilted his head.

"Apollo, you're a ferret. You're nocturnal! You see better in the dark than in the light."

"I know, I just don't like the dark." He twitched his nose.

"Oh, good heavens. Apollo just go, please?"

"Ok, ok . . . I'm going." He ran a few steps then looked back. *"Got a flashlight?"*

"You don't need a flashlight. Just go!"

"Ok, Geezze." He ran around the bush and down the other hole.

"Abbey, baby, Apollo is coming to help you out. Don't hiss at him, he'll be there soon. Close your eyes and try to relax. Can you breathe ok?"

"It's hard, Mommy. It hurts. There's something coming. I'm scared!"

"It's just Apollo. Don't be scared, he's there to help."

She listened as Apollo found the wall of dirt surrounding Abbey. He assessed the situation. *"She's in a burrowed-out sleeping area, and it appears both ends have collapsed around her. I'll go in and dig past her. There's a large, jagged rock here on my end. The tunnel on your end should be shorter. I'll dig through."*

Derek crouched down, continuing to pet Tanner and Jet while watching and listening.

"Hi hooo! Hi ho, hi ho, it's off to work I go," Apollo sang as he dug.

Alanna laughed, looking over at Derek. "He's singing the Seven Dwarves' work song while he's digging."

"I see him, Mommy!"

Alanna let out a big sigh. "She sees him." Leaning further down she said, "Ok, baby. Let him dig past you because you're going to have to back out."

"I feel it loosening!"

Dirt appeared in the hole, pushed up from underneath. Alanna grabbed the loose earth, pulling it out as Apollo pushed it to her. He poked his soil-covered head out then ducked back in and dug down past Abbey.

"You can get out now, baby kitty," he told Abbey. *"The way is clear."*

Alanna reached in, feeling for Abbey backing out and grabbing onto her hips. In a second Abbey was free of the hole but covered in dirt. Alanna hugged her as Abbey sneezed repeatedly. Apollo's dirty head reemerged from the hole.

"All's well, baby kitty safe."

Apollo walked out of the hole and Derek picked him up, brushing the debris from him as he said, "I guess you're our little hero."

Alanna brushed Abbey down, noticing a small cut on her shoulder, but it wasn't bad. "What were you thinking, young lady, going into that hole?"

"My whiskers said I would fit." Abbey sneezed again, shaking her head to get the dirt off her ears.

"I don't care what your whiskers told you. You don't go down into holes!"

"Well, you went into a hole."

"Yes I did, and it was very scary and I was rescued just like you had to be."

"It was scary. Stupid gopher!"

Alanna let out a long breath, giving Abbey one last hug then sat her down on the ground. Abbey shook herself and started to clean her cut.

"You're going to get a bath, young lady."

"No bath!"

"Yes, bath." Alanna stood up and brushed down her pants. "No arguing."

She looked up at Nemesis who was sitting on the wall above them.

"Thanks, Nem. Please go tell Auntie that we got her and that she's safe. We'll bring Apollo back. I know how he hates heights."

Nemesis took off in the direction of Vi's house, as Alanna turned to face Derek. He stood there petting Apollo, giving her a funny look. "So, is this later enough for you to tell me what's really going on?"

She took a deep breath, knowing the cat was out of the bag, so to speak. "Remember when Vi said I'd confide family secrets to you?" He nodded his head.

"Well, I'll tell you while we take Apollo back. Ok?"

"Ok."

She told all the animals to stay in the yard while she was gone and set Tanner and Jet the task of filling in the hole, which they happily agreed to do. As they walked the short distance to Vi's house, Alanna explained about her Celtic heritage and her gift being descended from Epona the Horse Goddess. Derek was quiet as they walked. He just listened and petted Apollo, who rode on his shoulder as they walked. When they reached the house, Vi appeared at the front door.

"Oh, my dear, I'm so glad Abbey is ok." Vi took Apollo from Derek as they followed her into the house. Derek noticed he didn't get a static shock this time when he entered. They stopped in the kitchen as Vi set Apollo down on the floor and gave him a snack. Nemesis was on his perch by the window.

"Yum, crunchy," Apollo said as he nibbled the cookie she gave him.

Alanna hung the purple shawl over the back of a chair. "Thank you, Auntie. I don't know what I would have done without Apollo, and thanks to Nemesis for getting him there so fast."

"Well, I'm just glad it all worked out and nobody was hurt. Nemesis has a tendency to drop things. That was what I was worried about." She reached down and stroked Apollo's back.

"Hummph." Nemesis was insulted by Vi's comment and turned his back to them.

Derek took a chair, staring down at the ferret. "You can hear them also?" he asked, looking over at Vi.

She nodded her head, realizing he knew the truth. "All of the females in our lineage have the gift."

Alanna took a chair across from him as Vi poured two glasses of ice tea, setting them down in front of them. "When Bob, my husband, first found out, he made me prove my ability. He had me talk to his dog and tell him things only his dog would know. When Eva told Fintan, he believed her because his cat wanted a special toy that had fallen down an air vent and he didn't understand what it wanted. When he got the toy for the cat, it showed him how happy it was. Plus it told her that it was the one taking his bullets out of his belt at night and hiding them around the house."

"Oh, I believe what she's telling me. I just saw her save her cat and the way she talked to Apollo. Did you know he's afraid of the dark?" Derek asked.

"Yes, we keep a night light on for him." Vi raised a hand to her lips. "Oh dear, I didn't think about it being dark down the hole. I just thought he'd be nicer to Abbey than Artemis in that situation. Well, it is why I named him Apollo."

"Can you hear all animals?" He looked at Alanna.

"Yes."

He leaned back in his chair, letting out a deep breath. "So that's what you were going to say that night on the phone but stopped."

She nodded her head.

"And being descended from the Goddess of the Horse gives you this ability?"

"Well, we have a lot of crossed lineage, you know how the gods were," Vi added. "But for the most part, yes it is a gift from Epona. Legend says she had the ability and passed it down through her bloodline."

"Protect it like my own," he said as if he was reassuring himself about something. "I understand now what you meant."

They looked at him as he leaned forward, taking Alanna's hand in his. "I will protect your secret like it was my own. I promise I won't tell anyone. You have my word."

They both smiled at him and in that moment Alanna felt like her heart was going to burst from her chest. "You're not upset, or angry?"

"Why on earth would I be angry?" He kissed her hand. "It explains a lot. I can also understand you not wanting people to know, and I know I'm new to the group, but are there more secrets like this? Do I need to prepare myself for something else? I get the feeling this is just the tip of the iceberg."

Alanna and Vi looked at each other. Then Vi nodded and said. "We will trust you with our secrets, but trust is a two-way street. Our secrets include my having many psychic abilities, that Alanna's mother, Eva, could talk to ghosts, her cousin Jenae is just starting to discover her telekinetic powers, and I believe that Alanna's dreams are psychic, or linked supernaturally in some way."

Alanna looked shocked. "Really? Telekinesis? When did Jenae discover this?"

"About two weeks ago. She's been moving and breaking things all over. I hate to leave her alone in the shop. She gets bored then all hell breaks loose."

Derek laughed. "Will you be able to do other things also?" he asked Alanna as she shrugged her shoulders.

Vi answered. "Most of us usually only develop one other gift, but my mother, Alanna's grandmother, had several."

Alanna tilted her head. "That's right . . . she had like five. I never really thought about how many she had."

"So your dreams, they really are premonitions?"

"Yeah, it looks that way." Alanna nodded her head.

Derek leaned back, running his hand through his hair. "Wow, this has been a hell of a week."

Alanna crossed her arms over her chest. "You wanted to date me," she said, sarcastically.

He stood up walking around the table, lifted her to her feet and pulled her into a hug. "Yes, I did." Then he stepped back "So could you do me a favor? Could you ask Tanner why he chews up everything?"

"I know why. He likes to keep his teeth clean. If you would brush them and give him some nice bones I bet he'll stop destroying things." She smiled up at him. "By the way he speaks in a British accent."

He looked shocked. "Tanner?"

"Yeah, he says 'ello, and telly, and crisps." She laughed.

He chuckled. "In my head, I always envisioned him talking like a surfer. Like totally rad dude."

"Nope, he's British. His old owner was a British ambassador that died and that's how he came to be in the pound. He told me the whole story."

Derek's eyes narrowed a little. "What else did he tell you?"

"Oh, not much, just that you think I'm the woman of your dreams and that you could live within my eyes." She extended her arms, presenting herself, lifting her nose toward the ceiling and fluttering her eyelashes.

He covered his nose and mouth with his hands "Yeah, I said that. Wow, you really can get a lot of information from someone's pet without them even knowing, can't you?"

She took his hands in hers, eyes imploring. "Are you really ok with this?"

"Well, you are very strange and unusual," he said and kissed her. "But you know how I love the strange and unusual."

"I'm glad, but apparently, I'm not as unusual as my cousin. Telekinesis, now that would be cool." Alanna felt a slight twinge of envy for her cousin's newfound ability.

Derek turned to Vi. "Hey, about a week ago my uncle said you threw a red crystal ball out the open door of your shop and into the street. He watched it roll down the hill and into the lake. He said you must have been really pissed about something. Was that a telekinetic thing?"

Vi closed her eyes, taking a deep breath. "That Jenae. She told me she sold that. Speaking of your uncle, I had a chat with him today. I understand you have a few family secrets of your own. If you don't mind, may I discuss them with you?"

He sat down, reaching over to hold Alanna's hand. "Does my uncle know about your abilities?"

"No, but he and I have been friends for many years and he suspects that I'm truly psychic. I speak without thinking sometimes, but today he and I talked about you, because you triggered certain wards I have around this house the last time you were here. Only someone with strong innate powers would spark those wards like you did." She hesitated for a second then asked, "Do you truly bear this mark Roger speaks of?"

Derek took a deep breath, letting it out loudly. They had trusted and confided in him; was he comfortable doing the same? More so, he wanted to know what his uncle had told her. "It's true that my family believes we have some kind of ancient curse passed down through the generations, and yes, I was born with the mark."

"May I see it?" Vi's curiosity showed in her voice as well as on her face.

He leaned back, considering her words, then stood up and pulled off his shirt, turning around. "It's there." He reached up, pulling his hair to the side to expose his birthmark. Vi stood up and looked closely at the mark on his shoulder blade but did not touch him. Derek closed his eyes and steeled himself for ridicule, apprehension or scorn. His past experiences with situations like this had not gone well, and that was with family. People who were supposed to love and care for him.

Apprehensively, he looked over his shoulder at Vi, her eyes completely fixated and fascinated by his mark. He swallowed, looking straight ahead once more. He had always been told to keep his mark a secret from outsiders, and that was one of the reasons he always kept his hair long enough to cover it. His brow furrowed, but if Uncle Roger had already told her of it . . . then maybe she knew things, and could help him learn more about it. He was hopeful and anxious for information and answers about something he had carried with him all his life. Mainly because he wasn't the only one in the family born with a mark regarding the curse. The more information he could get, the more he could understand why the curse had chosen him and his cousins to bear touches of it. The knowledge that this curse had its fingers wrapped around many of those that he loved and cared for haunted his thoughts.

"Those are runes," she said, with a hint of excitement edging into her voice. "Very old runes. Roger was right, they're overlapping or bound to each other. Thank you."

"Do you know what it means?" Derek asked, not meeting her gaze as he pulled his shirt on. His grandfather's warnings ran through his mind again.

"The last one is definitely Odin. The others I'll have to look up. They're old, very old. I'll be right back." She stood up, going to a door down the hall. They heard her open it and descend down a long stone staircase. Derek could have sworn he heard moving stones and then more stones sliding against others. He looked over at Alanna.

She knew what he was thinking and she shook her head. "It's best not to ask what's down there, she's touchy about it."

A few minutes later Vi appeared with an ancient, large and dusty leather-bound book. It looked like it would fall apart if you opened it. She sat it down on the table and gently opened it. Nemesis flew over and landed on her shoulder, looking down at the book.

Derek took in the sight of her with the raven on her shoulder, poring over the old text. A flash of memory went through his mind. It was of HugInn and MunInn, Odin's ravens. They had brought the god information and that's what Nemesis did for Vi. It was a scene he felt he had seen and been near before. He couldn't explain this feeling of déjà vu. Was his mind playing tricks on him?

She scanned a few pages, then eyed Derek. She turned a page, raising her eyebrows at the information she came across, then grabbed a pencil and paper from the desk behind her, drawing the design of his mark and pulling it apart, piece by piece, drawing each shape independently. Derek leaned forward, looking down at the text and symbols in the book but couldn't read them. It was in a language he didn't recognize.

Fifteen minutes later Vi leaned back and peered at him over the rim of her glasses. "According to this, your mark means Fire Warrior for Odin, or Warrior of Fire for Odin." She pulled her glasses off. "Translation is a tricky thing. The symbols overlap, so discerning the meaning can vary slightly. Roger said it was the mark of the 'chosen one'. I didn't realize exactly what he meant until now."

"Did he tell you anything else?" Derek looked down at the table.

"He told me that your great-great-grandfather, Oddvar, was the last in your line to bear the mark, and he was a seventh son of a seventh son, and that he died the death he did because of the power surrounding and contained within the mark and curse. He tried to gain control over the power, and failed. It caused him and your family great pain and destruction before he died. After the curse took hold of your great-great-grandfather, he became, well, not a very nice person, from what Roger says."

"He told you that?" The shock and hurt registered on Derek's face.

"Yes. He also told me that your grandfather went to great lengths to protect and teach you before he died."

"He died when I was twelve. All he taught me was a lot of ancient tales and superstitions, according to my parents." He looked away, resentment and anger edging into his eyes and tone.

"It is not my place to tell you what is truth and what is not, but a time will come when you will seek more answers, and I will help you as much as I can. But you need to trust your uncle, Derek. He may be tight-lipped, but he knows the truth even if he does not speak of it freely."

"He hasn't spoken freely in years. My parents won't let him. I used to ask but then he became very evasive. I wish he would talk to me about it, but you got more out of him in one afternoon than I've gotten out of him in the last fifteen years. He would never tell me even what the mark said, but I knew it was translatable, even though they told me it wasn't."

"Do not blame him. He doesn't speak of it to you because of a promise he made to your parents and your grandfather."

Derek seemed to brood for a moment. Should he tell them all the feelings that the mark seemed to stir in him at times? How much should he confide in them? It had scared his family so much that they refused to speak of it. No, now was not the time. He would get Roger to tell him the truth.

Vi narrowed her eyes, looking at him curiously. "At times, does your mark seem to move or burn?"

He was surprised she knew that. "No, of course not." He shook his head as he lied. He needed to discuss this with his uncle and then when he knew the truth, he would talk to Vi and Alanna about it.

"Good," she stated. "That would not be a beneficial thing."

He let out a long, frustrated breath. "Someday, somebody in my family is going to give me answers. I'm the one with the damned thing on my back." He reached up, rubbing his eyes. "But right now I don't know if my brain can handle much more."

Alanna reached over and touched his arm. "We should get back so I can check on Abbey."

He looked over at Vi. "Thank you."

"You're welcome." She inclined her head. "We all learn new things about ourselves every day. Look how much you learned today. Just think what you might learn tomorrow." She smiled.

"Gods help me," he chuckled, not too happily.

Alanna and Derek walked back to Treasure Grove. Along the way he asked her to describe what she heard, and she told him she had the ability to shut it out if she concentrated. Her grandmother had taught her how to control it, but right now it sounded like a full stadium with all kinds of voices around her. She didn't ask anything more about his mark and he was grateful for that. He was not in the mood to discuss it. They got back to the house, finding a large mound of dirt where the gopher hole used to be. All the surrounding flowers and small plants were mixed into the pile of earth.

Derek laughed. "Well, they covered the hole, that's for sure."

They walked into the kitchen and Emma met them. "What happened?" She threw her hands up. "I come back from the dry cleaners and look at all of this dirt! Tanner and Juneau are on the couch cleaning themselves like they haven't bathed in days, and I'm going to be vacuuming for a week!"

Alanna calmed her down by telling her what happened and that Derek now knew the family secret. Emma looked at Derek with a big smile and a sigh of relief. "It's strange at first, but you do get used to it. Eva was my best friend and she still unnerved me at times, talking to her dog and the animals around the house, and to ghosts." She patted him on the arm as she went to get her vacuum and Tanner came into the room.

"'Ello. The little one is asleep in her bed. She cleaned 'er wound well. It's not so bad." He sat down and started to clean his paw.

Derek walked over and knelt down. " 'Ello, Sir Tanner," he said in a fake British accent.

"What did 'e say?" Tanner tilted his head.

"He knows I can hear you. He also imagined you talked like a surfer."

"No. That would be 'is cousin, Lenny."

Derek looked over at her. "What did he say?"

"He said your cousin Lenny talks like a surfer."

"Yes he does." Derek scratched Tanners ears. "Lenny is a surfer. No doubt."

"Will you tell 'im to please buy me a clicker like yours?"

"He wants a remote with big buttons like ours so he can change the channels."

"Ok, buddy, whatever you want." He rubbed Tanner's head. "Just don't chew it up."

Juneau came into the kitchen, almost running. *"Emma is trying to vacuum me. Keep her away!"* She ran past them and out the back doors. *"That goes double for Dog Lover."*

Alanna watched her go. "Why is she so mad at you?" she asked him.

He stood up. "I don't know. She was hanging out in the bedroom this morning when I woke up."

"She's a bit annoyed 'cause 'e kicked 'er out last night. She wanted 'er own bed." Tanner said as he cleaned his side.

"Oh, she's upset because we tossed them out into the hall last night."

"And she blames me?"

"Well, I've never kicked her out before. She probably thinks that you're the reason for it."

"Is she the alpha?"

"She thinks she is." Alanna shrugged. "But I'm the alpha."

"You wish!" Juneau's voice came from outside.

"Yeah, she's on her high horse about something." Alanna frowned toward the open back doors.

"Well, is she going to shred my socks or something when I've got my back turned?"

"She might. She can be a little vengeful."

"So let me get this straight. Your dad, the cop, is ok with me here, but your cat has issues with it?"

"Yup, that's pretty much it. I'm going to get Abbey because she needs a bath."

"All right." He watched her go upstairs, then he looked around the kitchen. He thought for a few minutes then he went to his truck and got his tape measure.

Alanna came down the stairs with a protesting Abbey, taking her into the laundry room to give her a bath. Abbey meowed the whole time. *"I bathed!"*

Emma arrived in the laundry room with the blanket from the couch, not happy about the amount of dirt on it, just as Fintan came in through the laundry room door.

"Well. By the look on Emma and Abbey's faces, something happened," Fintan said the moment he saw them.

Emma left the room to go check on dinner while Alanna told him what had happened.

"Is Abbey ok?" he asked. "She sure has been getting into a lot of mischief lately."

"Yes, just a small cut on her shoulder." She reached up, wiping her brow. "Oh, and Derek knows."

"Knows what?"

"Everything about me," she shrugged, "Auntie Vi, and Jenae."

"Really?" Fintan raised his eyebrows. "How'd he take it?"

"He was very understanding. He promised he wouldn't say anything to anyone."

Fintan walked into the kitchen seeing Emma was looking into a tinfoil covered pan in the oven. Derek was at the table drawing on a piece of paper. Fintan went to the fridge and got out two beers, walked over to Derek and handed him a bottle. Fintan twisted the top off his beer then he clinked his against Derek's. "Hell of a day?"

"Yes, sir." Derek opened his, taking a drink. "You could say that."

Fintan pulled off his gun belt, hooked it and hung it over the back of the chair before sitting down and undoing the top two buttons of his uniform shirt.

"Just be thankful she can't talk to ghosts. That one can really get to you." He took a drink.

Alanna came over with an angry Abbey wrapped up in a towel. She rubbed her gently, drying her.

"Let me down, please?" Abbey struggled to get loose.

"Ok, here." Alanna put her down on the ground and she ran off down the hall.

Alanna looked from Fintan to Derek. "You two ok?"

Fintan winked at Derek. "Hey, everything is fine and dandy with me. I finally have another man around here that will understand my frustration and confusion." He drank.

Derek took a drink. "Hear, hear." They clinked bottles again and drank to that.

"Ok," she said with a hesitant note in her voice. "Glad to see you two are getting along, I think. I have to go change. I've got dirt all over my clothes."

"I'm going to do the same." Fintan stood up, tossing his gun belt over his shoulder. "Just a little heads up. If you ever want to surprise her about anything, and I do mean anything, don't say anything around the animals as they can't keep a secret." He went upstairs.

Alanna came downstairs and fed all the animals. Fintan and Derek were out on the patio having another beer. Fintan was relating a story about an encounter that Eva had with a ghost where she made him leave the hotel they had booked for a weekend up at Tahoe.

Alanna went over to where Emma was standing at the stove. "Emma, did something happen that I don't know about?" She gestured toward the two men. "Look at them, they're acting like old buddies."

"They have something unique in common now, and Fintan needs someone to talk to about . . . stuff." Emma cut into the pork roast to check it. "Don't worry, it's a good thing." She lifted the roast onto a plate. "Now, go bring them in for dinner."

Alanna walked out to the patio. "Emma says dinner is ready."

"Ok." Derek stood up as Fintan finished his cigarette.

As they ate dinner and talked, something occurred to Fintan. "When you came into the office today you said you thought that Brian's killer left the scene on a motorcycle. Did you dream about that also?" He took a bite.

"No, there was a witness that heard it leave," she said casually, offering Derek more potatoes.

"A witness?" Fintan leaned forward, his eyes wide at this information. "What witness?"

"Lois." She looked down, cutting her roast. "She's a cow in the pasture by the parking lot."

Derek started laughing, putting his hand over his mouth as Fintan looked at her and shook his head. "I can't put a cow on the witness stand."

Derek burst out laughing. "Sure you can, she can be udder oath." The two men guffawed.

"I could milk her testimony for all it's worth." Fintan grinned.

Derek smirked. "That's a bunch of bull."

Alanna gave them both a droll look.

Fintan cleared his throat trying not to smile as he asked, "Did she by chance see anything?"

"No, it was too dark. They were running away from the parking lot."

"Cowards," Fintan quipped.

Derek pointed his finger at him. "California scaredy cows."

The two of them started laughing again.

"You're not helping." Alanna eyed Derek.

"Sorry." He continued to grin as he ate. "I don't mean to be disrespectful."

She smiled a little. "It's ok. I guess when I say it out loud it is kind of funny."

"Udderly hilarious." Fintan laughed.

"Dad, you're not taking me seriously!"

"Yes, yes I am." He sat up straighter. "I will need that security footage you got from Tommy."

"I have it upstairs, I'll get it after dinner."

Derek didn't look up. "Does he have to wait till the cows come home to get it?"

He and Fintan snickered as Alanna shook her head and ate. They finished dinner and Derek helped her clean up. Then she went upstairs and got the DVD, showing them the part she had explained about where the headlight tracked Lori out of the parking lot.

Derek followed her into the kitchen as she put the animals' nightly treats into their dishes. She even set a dish down for Tanner.

"Yeah, num num!" Abbey came running into the kitchen, followed by the other three.

"Hummph, at least she remembered tonight," Juneau said with a mouthful, then she looked up at Derek. *"Why's he still here? Doesn't he have a home, a cardboard box or something? Why doesn't he leave? He needs to leave. What on earth does she see in him? He takes up a lot of room, he's got big tail-stomping feet and he takes his clothes off a lot. I don't like it. Not one bit,"* she grumbled as she chewed.

Tanner took a taste. *"Not bad. Needs salt."*

Jet looked up from her dish. *"If you don't want it, I do."*

Alanna went to the fridge.

"Do you want something to drink?" she asked.

"No, I guess I should be getting home." He leaned against the counter.

She reached in, selected a bottle of her favorite wine, and poured herself a glass. "Well, I am going to take this bottle of wine upstairs, run a nice hot bath in my overly large jetted tub and maybe put on some nice music." She sipped her wine, sighing a little.

"If you're trying to tempt me, it's working." He pulled her to him and kissed her.

"Good." She grabbed the bottle and another glass, pulling him seductively upstairs.

Juneau watched with narrowed eyes as they ascended the stairs. *"Damned dog lover."*

Chapter 22

Alanna awoke to Juneau standing over her pillow looking down at her. Her face was so close she could smell tuna. She blinked and rubbed her eyes. Derek was not in the room.

"Submit! Admit that I am the alpha!" Juneau leaned in a little more.

Alanna closed her eyes. "I'm not going to admit anything."

"This is unacceptable. You moved my bed! Moving my bed to one of the guest rooms is unacceptable. I have slept on that chest of drawers by the window since I was old enough to jump up there. That's my spot. This is not right! He is the guest, not me. He should sleep in the guest room. This is just not going to work." She sat down and backed her ears flat against her head.

Alanna sat up in bed, looking down at her. "Juneau, this is a really large house. You can't find one other spot to sleep at night once in a while?"

"No. That's my favorite. I like it there."

"You're going to have to compromise." She got up to go to the bathroom.

"Why should I compromise? He's the intruder." Juneau followed her. *"He has to go. He's troublesome and disrupting everything."*

"He's not an intruder or troublesome. He's my boyfriend and I'll have him over whenever I want." She ignored Juneau's rant, put on her robe and went downstairs.

Juneau sat on the bed watching her through narrowed eyes *"He will leave, or bow to my will!"* she yelled. *"Do you hear me? Mark my words he won't like it here, I'll see to that! He will fail in all attempts to have influence over me like he has you. You weak-willed human, you're obsessed with a damned dog lover! Have you lost your mind?"*

Alanna stopped short at the bottom of the stairs at the scene before her. Fintan and Emma were sitting at the kitchen table, drinking coffee and eating, while Derek was at the stove. She looked him over. He was in boxers and a black T-shirt. He looked around when he heard her come in.

"Morning." He smiled, flipping a pancake in the skillet in his hand. "Want some pancakes?"

Emma licked her lips. "They are simply wonderful. He makes his batter from scratch and puts brown sugar in it."

Fintan spoke up. "And walnuts if you want."

She walked over to the coffee. Derek leaned in and gave her a quick kiss. She looked down at the boxers and recognized them. She had given them to her dad last year for Christmas.

"Boxers?"

"Oh, yeah. I spilled batter on my jeans. They're in the washer. Your dad gave me these. They were still in the package." He wiggled his hips a little. The boxers had a Dodge Ram emblem on the back.

Fintan helped himself to another pancake off the stack. "I know you gave them to me, honey, but I'm a Ford man, and Derek has a Dodge."

She looked at him like his words didn't make sense.

Derek pointed at Fintan with the spatula. "He's so right about wearing them over your briefs. They are very comfortable. You're in your underwear, but you're not in your underwear. It's very freeing."

"See? That's what I've been saying all these years. They just don't get it." Fintan raised his hands in emphasis as Alanna walked over to the table and sat down.

She looked between the two men. It was strange, she had an uneasy feeling at first, but then she smiled. Derek felt comfortable . . . not just in the clothes, but here in her home, with her family. She sipped her coffee as he walked over and placed a plate of fresh pancakes in front of her and kissed her cheek.

"Tell me if you like them."

The front door opened and Andy called to them as he walked through. "Sheriff in the house!" He came into the kitchen.

"Mornin' Andy," Fintan said, motioning to a chair.

"Well, if this don't beat all." He looked Derek over as he got himself a cup of coffee. "Guess the flowers worked."

"Hey, Sheriff, want some pancakes?" Derek offered him a plate with a stack on it.

"Hell, yeah." Andy took it and sat down at the table.

Fintan sat back, rubbing his napkin over his mouth. "What's up?"

"We got the results back on the bodies in your air shaft." Andy poured syrup.

"Bodies?" Fintan, Emma and Alanna said in unison, shocked.

"How many bodies are we talking about, Andy?"

"Two. Female in her early twenties and her unborn infant." Andy took a bite.

"How long have they been down there?" Fintan drank his coffee with his brow furrowed.

"Sixty three years." Andy waved his fork at Derek. "These are great!" He looked over at Alanna. "You should think about keeping him."

She smiled, inclining her head. "Ok, I'll do that."

"Do you have any idea who the woman might be?" Emma asked.

Andy swallowed. "Yeah, we know who she is. She had on a silver wedding band with initials and a date engraved inside."

They all looked expectantly at him while he chewed in silence.

"Well . . . who is she?" Fintan finally asked.

Andy tilted his head and narrowed one eye. "You know that story that the kids tell about that old rickety bridge half a mile down from here? Old Parson's Bridge?"

Derek looked over saying, "Yeah, they say a demon lives under that bridge and he comes out every once in a while, dragging people down to hell without them dying, that their body and soul suffer an eternity of living hell they can't escape from. Kids dare each other to cross it."

Andy nodded his head. "That's the one. Do you know why the kids tell that story?"

"Mainly because many people have disappeared off that bridge and they have found abandoned cars with the doors open and no bodies."

"One car in seventy years, only one, but things tend to become exaggerated over time. Many people park by the bridge to fish so you do see cars there every so often, but only one car has been found abandoned with the doors open. That was sixty three years ago. That car belonged to a man by the name of Theodore Garrison. His pregnant wife, Candace, disappeared one night when she ran off the road at the end of the bridge in a rain storm, the storm washed away part of the road and the car slipped off the edge. They never knew what happened to her. She just disappeared. Until now."

"Candace Garrison is the body you found?" Emma asked.

"Yup." He grinned at Fintan. "Your old air shaft is the demon from hell," he rumbled.

Fintan let out a long, tired sigh. "You confirmed this?"

"The demon from hell thing? No." Andy gave a shake of his head. "But the remains, yes. By the way, I called Hank. He's coming out to cover the hole properly. He'll send you the bill." He took a big bite and chewed happily.

Alanna looked over at Fintan, re-stating what she had just heard. "So, she was pregnant, and out in the rain, when she fell in the hole?"

Andy nodded his head. Just then a cold shiver ran through her. Derek walked over, sitting down with his plate next to her. "You ok?" he asked, looking a little concerned at her reaction.

"Yeah, just something I dreamed a few nights ago that's made me feel a little uneasy." He put his arm around her shoulders, kissing the side of her head and then started to eat his breakfast. Emma got up and poured everyone some coffee, before cleaning up.

She took Fintan's empty plate and said, "At least the family will have closure now."

"Speaking of closure, you ready for tonight?" Andy asked Fintan.

Fintan took a drink. "We'll see."

Emma looked over at the men. "Meeting tonight?"

"Yeah. City Council has to decide about the budget."

Fintan looked down into his coffee. "Hopefully, this year they'll listen."

Andy let out a sardonic laugh. "Wishful thinking, bud."

"It's getting rougher out there, Andy, you've seen it."

"I know. Every weekend gets busier and summer hasn't even started." He took more pancakes off the stack. "Damned budget cuts."

"The festival is next month. We don't have enough staff as it is, not to mention that we've got that jet-ski company coming to do their promotion in six weeks. I'm just glad you got all the water." Fintan took a drink.

"Not quite fair since part of the lake is in city limits."

"Hey, you take the city parks and I'll take the lake."

"No thanks," Andy chuckled. "I heard that call come over the radio yesterday about the cellphone. So how'd you handle it?"

Fintan laughed. "I gave the guy Clay's number."

"Can't wait to hear him complain about that one."

Alanna looked over. "What happened?"

Andy gave Fintan a funny, wide-eyed look. "Yeah, Chief, what happened, do tell?"

Fintan smiled a little, looking down into his coffee cup. "There was this tourist in the park yesterday. Set his camera and cellphone down on the bench next to him and was feeding the squirrels. Next thing he knew, one of them jumped up and took off with his phone. Ran up a tree with it."

"Maybe it had to make a call," Derek offered.

Andy laughed. "Yeah, to his broker. Nuts are up, or down, however you look at it."

Fintan shifted his eyes over at Andy then rolled them. "Anyway, while he was chasing after one squirrel, another one took off with his camera. He didn't get far though. It was heavier, but he did manage to click off a few pictures while trying to drag it across the grass. So, he got hold of an officer and we had to get one of Buck's crews out there to retrieve the phone. It was damaged and scratched. The squirrel had dropped it and it was caught in some branches. So, the guy wants the City to replace it."

Andy's eyes laughed as he asked Fintan, "Did you arrest the perp?"

"No. Guy couldn't identify him out of the line up," Fintan quipped back.

"I actually heard Diane's description of him over the air. Short, fuzzy, mean and possibly armed with a stick." Andy laughed.

"Yeah, I have to talk to her about that. They actually had wanted posters of a squirrel up yesterday before I left. The whole station had fun with it and I'm sure I'll hear about it from Buck."

They finished breakfast while Fintan and Andy headed off to work. Emma decided to take the rest of the day off since no one was going to be home for dinner.

Alanna was brushing her hair when Derek appeared in her bathroom doorway.

"So, what are you going to do today?" she asked him.

"I have to go to the hardware store and get some stuff. There's a project I want to work on plus I have to go get my stitches out today. You?"

"I need to run up to Sacramento and get some painting supplies, then down to Lodi to buy a wedding dress." She smiled as she walked over to him.

His eyes widened. "Ah . . . Alanna, did I miss something?" Confusion was showing on his face.

She laughed. "I'm buying Sam her wedding dress as a surprise wedding gift."

"Oh, for a second there I thought . . ." She silenced him by putting her finger over his lips, then kissing him. He pulled back, tracing his finger over the neckline of her shirt. "I know you have your meeting tonight with your family, but you could give me a call after. Maybe I can take you to dinner if it's not too late?"

"Ok, I'd like that. We usually get done by seven or so if things go well." She kissed him and they hugged a little while before he collected Tanner and left.

Alanna spent the day running her errands. Thoughts of Derek kept her fairly captivated, but thoughts about her dreams and theory kept playing over and over in her mind also. What had made the person she suspected do what they did? There was a piece of the puzzle she was missing. Motive. Her father had told her that. Without motive they really couldn't prove anything. She trusted him when he said he'd look into it, but she got the feeling he was holding something back from her as well. She knew he hadn't told her everything about this case, and she had a nagging feeling it was something big.

Her newfound relationship with Derek seemed a constant distraction. She smiled; it was an awesome distraction though. Actually she was really happy. Happier than she'd been in ages. She spent a little extra time in the bridal shop because they had a nice lingerie section. She had called days ago and had them hold the dress that Sam had liked so much. She couldn't wait to see the look on her face when she gave it to her. When she did get her stuff home and put away she wanted to call Derek but it was already time for her meeting.

At six o'clock sharp she was in her Uncle Nevin's conference room with Vi, Jenae, and Nevin's sons, Colton and Magnus, who were joining them by teleconference. Nevin walked in, and the meeting began. Alanna took notes on her holdings, asking a few questions, but every once in a while when the conversation didn't pertain to her, she found her mind drifting to other things. Mainly Derek. The meeting went smoothly. Almost everyone was happy with the proposals. Vi wasn't too sure about the purchase of a company in South Dakota, but she agreed to go with Nevin's recommendation after Colton gave her a rundown on the numbers. It was a company one of his friends owned and he was trying to help him save it. In the end he convinced her that, if anything, it could be a tax deduction, but he said he had a gut feeling about it turning around with the right management. After all business was completed and the others were gone, Alanna stayed behind to talk to Nevin. She moved to a chair closer to him.

"So, I got the message that you had a question about your trust," he inquired.

"Do I still have to work at my job?"

"No, you have been there for almost two and a half years. The trust stipulates only two years." He shuffled his papers. "Out of curiosity, what are you thinking about doing? Vi mentioned to me you were weighing your options."

"I'd like to paint full-time."

A knowing smile broke out across his face. "I think that would be a good thing. You have true marketable talent. Just so you are aware, the gallery downtown close to Atherton Bookstore is for sale."

Alanna frowned. "Sharon's selling her shop?"

"Yes, her mother's health is failing and she wants to move to Indiana to be with her. She's not advertising the shop. She wants to find the buyer herself. She cares what happens to it, plus she wants to help her staff stay on if possible."

"But I don't know anything about owning a gallery."

"You don't have to, you can be the landlord, Sharon said she would keep in touch as a consultant and you could keep her current management staff, which just happens to include my wife's niece, but she's really good at what she does and has worked there for years." He smiled.

"Would you talk to her about purchasing it for me?"

He made a note on his legal pad. "I will do so tomorrow. Anything else?"

"No, I just wanted to know where I stood on things."

"All you have to do is wait until June first, the day you turn twenty five, and it's all yours. But please don't touch the principal. You have more than enough interest being earned each day to live on for the rest of your life if you don't go overboard."

"I will listen to you, Uncle Nev, I promise." She stood up and collected her things.

"Thank you for your confidence. I'll do my best."

She kissed him on the cheek then walked toward the doors of the conference room.

"Alanna?"

"Yes?" Her hand was on the doorknob as she looked back at him.

"You do know about the stipulations in the trust about prenuptials, right?"

"Yes, I am aware of them. Why?"

Nevin smiled. "I heard you have a new boyfriend."

"We haven't been seeing each other that long."

"It's not the length of time that concerns me, it's the intensity of the relationship. I'm your mother's brother, remember? I know how strong-willed and fervent the women in our family can be. So I'm just letting you know, that if you up and decide to elope to Reno or Vegas, I have a prenup for you. It's already made out."

She frowned, exasperation filling her tone. "What do you mean already made out?"

"It's just a precaution so don't get upset, but if you are serious about him he needs to know about it. Some aspects of your life will change when you get full control of your trust. This is a small town but your influence can be vast, and very important. Just be aware, and cautious." He gave her his that-is-all-but-I'm-here-if-you-need-me look. The whole conversation had caught her completely off guard.

"Ok," she said slowly as she walked out to her truck, feeling stunned. Serious? The word went through her mind. Serious. They had just starting dating, yet she did seem to have feelings for him. Was she serious about Derek so fast? What constituted serious? She definitely felt something for him, but trying to put it into words was difficult. She was waiting at a stop light as she pulled her phone out to dial Derek about dinner, but didn't. Suddenly her life seemed very complicated, with her job, Derek and all the deaths recently, plus what Nevin had said. Why couldn't things be simple? Normal? Because nothing about her or her family was normal, that was why.

The light changed. She drove straight to Derek's, feeling she needed clarification. When they talked to each other everything would seem clear. He was so understanding and intuitive. She pulled into the driveway just before seven thirty, and sat there for a few minutes. When she was with him everything else seemed to just melt away. She felt so safe, so warm, so complete. She was compelled by an unseen force she hadn't felt before she'd met him.

Taking a deep breath she got out of the car and walked to the door, rang the doorbell and heard his stereo going. Her heart skipped a beat when she heard his hand touch the knob. He opened the door as a big smile broke out across his face and he opened the screen door to let her in. She stood still for a second staring at him. In that moment everything left her mind. Nothing mattered except for him. She felt complete elation at seeing and being near him. It hit her like a ton of bricks, she needed him in her life. Forever. She smiled and stepped into the foyer.

"Hi," she said, turning to look at him while he closed the door.

"Hi," he said softly, turning quickly to press her up against the wall and kiss her fiercely. She dropped her purse, returning his passion. He picked her up in his arms and carried her over to the couch as she ran her hands through his loose hair. He laid her down, kissing his way down her neck. She closed her eyes, running her hands over his back pulling at his T-shirt. He raised up, stripping it off and throwing it to the floor as he started unbuttoning her shirt, becoming more passionate. She kissed his neck and shoulder. He pulled back a little, remembering to be the chef and host he always was.

"Are you hungry?" he asked, out of breath.

She nuzzled his neck. "For you."

"Ok, we'll order pizza later." He went back to kissing and unbuttoning her shirt.

At just before nine, they were sitting on the couch eating pizza and talking.

"So, how was your meeting? Any good fights?"

She shrugged. "No, it was peaceful."

He glanced sideways at her. "So, what happened that has you on edge?" He was starting to read her pretty well. She had something on her mind.

"Nothing." She looked down at the slice in her hand. How could she ask him about his feelings when she didn't know about her own? She was so content and confused all at once.

He nudged her a little with his elbow. "Something's up, I can tell." He put his pizza down. "You want to talk about it?" He turned, putting his arm along the back of the couch and giving her his full attention.

When he looked at her like that she felt like she was the center of his universe. She so wanted to ask him how he felt, but she didn't want to appear needy or desperate. Why did this have to be so complicated? Why couldn't she just put everything into words without sounding foolish or immature?

"It's nothing, really." She tossed her slice back into the box, wiping her hands on a napkin.

"Ok, if you say so."

"It's just . . ." She looked down at the couch, struggling with her emotions and sudden lack of vocabulary. Should she tell him what she was feeling? She wanted to tell him, but they had just started going out, and she was unsure of what she should or shouldn't say at this point. What was she feeling? Could she describe it without sounding stupid, or naïve? If he'd just tell her how he felt first. That would make everything easier, right? She let out a long breath.

íJust what?" He reached out his hand to brush her cheek.

"It's stupid." She shook her head. This was all too much too fast.

"At least tell me what it has to do with? Maybe I can help," he coaxed. "Alanna, you know you can tell me anything, right?"

"I know."

He looked deep into her eyes. "Please tell me? I want to know what's on your mind."

She truly did feel she could tell him anything, but how would he react? "Us," she said softly. She was so inexperienced at all of this relationship stuff. Were these feelings real or some kind of endorphin high from sex? She was not sure but she hoped they were real.

"Us, how?" he asked, his engrossed gaze making her pause for a moment.

She looked down, rubbing the hairs on his forearm with her fingers. "Derek, I . . . well, I just. . ."

He reached up with his other hand and lifted her chin so she would look at him.

"Just say it, whatever it is," he encouraged her softly. "Don't be afraid to tell me."

"Well, it's just . . ." Her brow creased.

"Go on," he encouraged, even though fear that she might be about to put the brakes on their relationship made his gut clench tight.

"It's just I have all of these emotions surging through me, and you said those wonderful things coming home from Aunt Vi's, and we seem, well, and the sex." She widened her eyes in emphasis. "It's amazing and I can't seem to get enough of it, or you for that matter."

"Ummhmm."

"But it's not just the sex. That's like the ice cream on top of the cake. It's more than that, so much more. I just can't seem to put it into words." She stopped, frustrated by her babbling.

"Try. I want to know what you're feeling, it really matters to me." He leaned his head a little. "Please don't be afraid to tell me how you feel. We agreed to be completely open and honest with each other, remember."

She smiled a weak smile, searching her vocabulary for a word or phrase that didn't sound clichéd. She failed to find one and settled on the honest truth. "This may sound weird, but when I'm not with you I feel like something is missing, like I didn't know I needed it, but now I do. When I see you my heart races, my stomach flips, and I feel overwhelming joy. When I'm not with you, I wonder where you are and what you're doing. It's weird. I can't concentrate on anything. I'm all tangled up inside. My mind is like complete mush."

"Ok, I get what you're saying. I've been feeling the same way, but for me it's a little different."

"How so?" She tilted her head, grateful he seemed to understand.

"I know what I'm feeling, there's no way of denying it," he stated.

"So, you've felt this way before?"

"No, not like this. This is more intense and consuming. More overpowering than anything I've ever felt." He reached up again, gently stroking her cheek. "Now, what is bugging you so bad? Did your family say something to get you upset?"

How could she approach this? *Should* she approach this? It was so soon; too fast, but yet what if? He said he felt the same, and he seemed to accept everything else about her fairly well. She looked up into his thoughtful eyes and swallowed the lump in her throat.

"If . . . if something was to happen between us, I mean later?"

He got a puzzled look. "Did they talk to you about that pre-nup thing?" he asked, getting a quirky smile on his face.

"How did you know?" She frowned at his knowing.

He laughed out loud. "Alanna, I don't think you realize how much your father worked me over before I asked you out." He continued to laugh as he held up his hands and started counting on his fingers. "He asked me how many women I've been with, how many of them I'd been serious about, how many times I've had unprotected sex, had I been tested for any and all S.T.D.s, how much I make each year and how much debt I have. He asked what my long term intentions are, and told me that if I even thought about getting serious about you that there would be a pre-nup, with no ifs, ands or buts. He said that he had to sign one himself, Bob had to, and so did your Uncle Nevin's wife. He said your uncle would have one drawn up the minute we kissed the first time and that he might make me sign one just to date you." He laughed a little. "I'm surprised he didn't demand to see my tax returns and medical records. Which I have prepared in case he does ask."

She was befuddled and mad at her dad. How had Derek he put up with all of that? "So that kind of thing doesn't bother you?"

"No." He leaned over, pulling her hand into his. "Alanna, I don't care about anything but you. I just want to be with you and make you happy. This has been the most amazing, eye-opening and interesting week of my life. You are definitely the most wonderful and fascinating woman I have ever met. Being with you makes me happier than I've ever been, in my life. I'd go through anything to be with you. If he wants an M.R.I., lie detector test, or colonoscopy, I don't care, bring it on."

"I want to be with you too, more than anything and I'm sorry my dad put you through all that."

"It was worth it. He's very good at his job."

"Being a cop or being my dad?"

"Both. It actually helped us develop an understanding of each other. I know where I stand with him and I now know where he keeps his shotgun, he made a point of telling me that."

"My family is very protective of our assets."

"Seeing as how you're their most precious asset, I can understand what all the fuss is about."

Her heart melted when she heard that.

He took a deep breath, pausing for moment. He felt he was going too fast, but he wanted her to know how he felt. He knew she was "the one". He felt it with every fiber of his being. He didn't want to rush her, push her or scare her, but he was going to put his heart out there and see if she caressed it, or crushed it. He wouldn't tell her everything just yet, but he would let her know where he stood.

"Alanna, I'm not a wealthy man." He paused. How much should he say? "I work hard for what I have, and I don't have much. My house is paid for, a gift from my parents when I graduated. I have some money in the bank, some in investments and I make decent money for someone my age, but really all I have to offer you is all my love and respect. It's not much in the big picture, I guess, considering what you're used to, but if you'll let me, I'll do everything I can to make you happy and I promise I'll never do anything to hurt you. But I want to be with you, for as long as you'll let me."

He watched for her reaction. He wanted to tell her more. He wanted to bare his soul completely to her, to tell her that at times the mark on his shoulder did move and burn, causing feelings of ancient evil to stir within him, and lately they were growing stronger. Could she accept him if the curse his grandfather told stories about was true? Would she fear him if what was deep inside him was his ultimate destroyer? He pushed all that out of his mind and focused on her.

Tears welled up in her eyes. She sniffed a little. "It's more than I could ever hope or want for." She started to cry.

He reached up, brushing away her tears. "Geez, I was hoping for a little happier reaction when I told you that I loved you. I was worried it was too soon, but I didn't expect tears."

She started to sob and he pulled her against him, letting her cry against his chest. He wrapped his arms around her and held her tight.

"They're tears of joy," she said between sobs.

"Well, I definitely won't forget this moment." He kissed the top of her head.

She pulled back, picking up a napkin to wipe her eyes and nose. "I'm so happy," she said as more tears streamed down her face.

"Could have fooled me." He used another napkin to dry her tears.

"No, really I am." She sniffed loudly. "I'm so happy . . . could just cry." She started sobbing again. He cupped her face in his hands, pulling her to him and kissing her deeply. She stopped crying as she felt a wall inside her crumble, breaking away and freeing her.

She kissed him back completely unrestrained, something he hadn't felt before. She held nothing back. He could feel that it was more than passion; it was with her whole heart that she kissed him. They stopped and their eyes locked together.

"I love you, Derek," she whispered, her voice and words surging through him.

"I love you too," he whispered back. He felt so warm, whole and unbelievably happy. He kissed her, beginning to push her down onto the couch when the doorbell rang. Then there was a loud knock a second later. The doorbell rang again, again and again.

"Are you expecting someone?"

"No, but at least they don't have a key."

The doorbell rang again. The next knock was almost a pound. He went to the door, turning on the porch light. Fintan was standing there with Andy and Buck.

"Derek, where's Alanna?" Fintan demanded.

He stepped back, letting all three men in the front door. Alanna had grabbed the blanket off the back of the couch, wrapping it around herself when Derek had answered the door. All she had on was one of Derek's dress shirts and her panties. Derek had his jeans on from when they had gotten the pizza delivered.

"Dad, what's going on?" She stood up, wiping the tears from her face.

He crossed the room in three strides, grabbing her gently by the shoulders and looking over her face and arms.

"Are you ok?" he demanded, seeing that she had been crying.

Andy and Buck stood back by Derek, who crossed his arms. It was apparent that Fintan was very worried about his daughter for some strange reason.

"I'm fine. What are you doing here?"

"Did he hurt you? You'd tell me if he hurt you, right?" Fintan insisted, his tone tinged with anger.

"What the hell are you talking about? Dad, Derek has never done anything to hurt me. Why are you here?" She moved to stand in front of Derek who reached down to grab his T-shirt from the floor.

"We had an anonymous call that there was a domestic disturbance at this address. The call came in just as I was leaving the City Council meeting. Every damned scanner in the parking lot went off with Derek's address being broadcasted."

"I'm fine, Dad." She took a step toward Fintan. "Really, I'm fine," she said trying to convince him.

"You weren't fighting or yelling?"

Derek smiled to himself. No, that's definitely not what they had been doing.

"Dad, it must be a different house." She moved beside Derek. "We're not fighting. We've never even have had an argument." She reached down, picking her jeans up from the floor as she looked at her father who crossed his arms.

"Why have you been crying then?"

"They were happy tears, Dad, really they were." She looked up at Derek, smiling at him.

Fintan gave her a skeptical look. "Happy tears?" he questioned.

"Yes, Daddy, happy emotional tears."

Tanner walked into the room and sat down by Buck. *"Why all the bobbies?"* he asked, looking around at the men in uniform.

Buck reached down and petted Tanner, looking around the room. "Fin, I don't think they've been fighting. Pretty boy there would be the one hurt if that was the case. Besides, it doesn't look like there's been any type of ruckus here, and the dog's not agitated at all."

Andy stepped further into the room, looking down at the pizza box and drinks. He picked up a piece of pizza, taking a bite. "This is still warm. People don't fight like that and then call for pizza."

Fintan looked around, still glaring. "Then what the hell was that call about?"

Alanna's cellphone rang; she recognized that ring tone, it was her house phone calling. She reached down by the door, picked up her purse and pulled out her phone.

Juneau's frantic voice touched her mind. *"Mom! There's someone in the house! It's a stranger, they're tearing everything up and Jet's been hurt!"* She meowed as loud as she could. *"They're headed toward the library. You have to get home and save the library!"*

"Oh my God!" Alanna yelled at Fintan. "Someone's broken into our house!"

She dragged on her jeans, discarded the blanket and ran out the front door after the four men and Tanner. "We're on our way!" she yelled into the phone, getting into the passenger seat of Fintan's squad car. Derek got into Andy's car with Tanner. Buck hustled to his fire chief's car to follow.

With sirens wailing and lights flashing, all three cars made it to Treasure Grove in record time. When they got through the gate they saw the front door was wide open. Fintan pulled to a stop, blocking the driveway, Buck and Andy behind him. Alanna was already out and running inside before he could stop her. She ran into the disheveled house and into the kitchen where she found Jet on the floor, unconscious or dead, she wasn't sure.

"Oh, my God! Jet!" She knelt down, feeling for a heartbeat. Fintan and Andy came in with their guns drawn. Fintan moved down the hall toward the den and Andy went up the front stairs. She felt Jet's heart beating, thank God!

Fintan came back into the kitchen. "Get back outside! Now!" he said in a hushed tone to Alanna while he moved down the hall toward the studio and ballroom. Derek came into the kitchen, kneeling down by Alanna. He lifted Jet up and carried her toward the front door. He got her out to the front lawn, and laid her down. There were other sirens coming up the road. He looked back for Alanna, but she wasn't behind him.

Alanna was searching for Abbey and Juneau. Suddenly, someone dressed all in black and with a ski mask grabbed her tight and pressed a knife against her throat. She was going to scream but the killer pulled back on the knife, pressing the sharp blade into her flesh, slicing it and bringing forth a stream of blood. Her heart clenched with fear and her breath hitched in her chest. Terror began to take hold of her. She moved her eyes over towards the front door. Derek seemed to appear inside the door frame from nowhere. For a second her mind left what the attacker was doing to her and went to Derek. His eyes! They were glowing . . . no, they were on fire! He seemed taller and bigger somehow, almost filling the entire frame of the door. He was changing right in front of her as his handsome features contorted to something furious, almost evil. God, what was happening to him?

Derek didn't even have time to think as he saw the woman he loved in danger with blood on the blade at her throat. He felt a huge dam within him burst and in less than a heartbeat it was as if his mark leapt to life, scorching his shoulder with what felt like the fire of more than a thousand suns that spread out from the mark, coursing through every vein of his body and causing everything in him to strengthen and burn with rage.

He felt twice as large and ten times as strong. His eyes became a living, flickering flame. He narrowed them as the uncontrollable rage engulfed him. His only thought was to save his woman and destroy the threat against her.

He let out a low, loud predator growl and rushed forward. His movements were a blur, faster than any normal human. He grabbed the assailant's knife hand, pulling it away hard, as he tossed Alanna to the side. She hit the wall, sliding to the floor. Derek was holding the knife to her attacker's throat before she even had time to look over.

Something inside made him want to kill this vile thing that had threatened his love. It was an overpowering animalist desire he didn't think he could control. His breathing was heavy and fast as he fought inside his mind for control of the rage. It felt primitive, this malevolent primordial instinct taking over his mind and body.

He closed his eyes and shook his head, trying to clear his vision and his mind. He looked over at Alanna and their eyes locked for a second, but a second was all it took.

She was sitting against the wall, watching him in wonderment. "Derek . . . baby?"

In that second he felt and heard all her love and concern for him and only then did he feel himself began to gain ground in the evil battle within him as the rage started to dissipate slightly, the reddish flames slowly leaving his eyes and his mind beginning to clear. Andy and Fintan came into the hall, guns trained on the killer. Derek was still breathing hard as he extended his steady, clenched hand towards Fintan to give him the knife.

"Take this or I'm going to kill the son-of-a-bitch," Derek growled in a low, inhuman voice.

Fintan took the knife from Derek's very reluctant grip as Andy reached down and cuffed the intruder, who was being held down by Derek's knee. Derek slowly stood up, his movements showing his internal struggle not to kill the assailant. He walked over to Alanna, lifting her up and pulling her to him in one swift motion. He held her tight while he felt the last of the fire leave his veins, his mark becoming still once more. He couldn't tell which of them was shaking the hardest. Fintan and Andy took the culprit outside. Fintan glanced over at Alanna to make sure she was ok.

Derek finally let Alanna go and she looked up at him and kissed him, with no fear or hesitation, only concern in her eyes. His curse was real, she knew that now, but so was her love for him.

She pulled back. "I've never seen anything like that before."

"I've never felt anything like that before."

"Are you ok?" They said it at the same time, then both smiled a little.

"Does it hurt much?" He reached up, touching the small cut on her throat. The moment he touched her it healed instantly. His eyes widened with shock and amazement at what he'd just done.

"No, it's not that bad." She touched the spot where it had been, not realizing that it was now healed. "I just hope everyone else is ok. I have to find all my girls."

"Mom?"

Alanna heard Jet's voice from outside. She ran to the front lawn to find Jet awake, but very groggy, with no bleeding and nothing broken, Jet tried to sit up.

"Mom, someone broke in. I tried to stop them. They hit me with .. . something. Where am I?"

"Jet, its ok, baby." She hugged her. "You're on the front lawn. Are you hurt real bad?"

"No, I don't think so, but I'm dizzy and my head hurts. Where are

the cats? I saw Juneau run for the office and Abbey jumped on the mean person's back before everything went black."

"She did?" Alanna stood up as Derek looked down at Jet.

"What'd she say?" he asked.

Alanna motioned toward Fintan's squad car. "She said Abbey jumped on the intruder and Juneau went toward the office, I have to go find them and make sure they're ok."

"Ok. You stay here, Jet." He petted her, not realizing that he was causing the bump on Jet's head to lessen as he touched it.

Jet lay back down and rested her head on her paws. *"Ok."*

Buck, Andy, Fintan and six other officers dealt with the aftermath of what had happened. Derek followed Alanna as she stepped past an officer and went into the kitchen. Drawers and cabinets were open and stuff was thrown on the floor. The house was a mess with books and things tossed everywhere. She moved down the hall to the office. She found Juneau there, crouched under Fintan's desk, among scattered papers, the phone and a lamp.

"Juneau! Are you ok?" She picked her up, cuddling her. "You're not hurt, are you?"

"I'm fine. You can put me down. Abbey ran upstairs. Have you seen her? How's Jet? How's the library? Did the books get hurt? Did they bludgeon the intruder? Did you know you're bleeding?"

"Jet's going to be ok. We'll go look for Abbey." She sat Juneau down with one final hug. "I'm glad I showed you how to use the one-touch call buttons." She motioned to the phone on the floor.

"Yeah, maybe we should invest in a security system so I don't have to be the one saving the day all the time."

Alanna laughed then told Derek what Juneau said.

"We'll always need you to save the day, Juneau. That's what geniuses do." He smiled.

"Now's not the time for scoring points, Dog Lover. We need to find my sister!" She took off down the hall toward the stairs. They followed her upstairs and found Abbey under Alanna's bed. She came running out when she heard Alanna calling her.

"Mommy! Mommy! Mommy!" She jumped into Alanna's arms. *"I was so scared. Not as scared as the coyote, but almost. Is Jet ok?"*

"I'm so glad you're ok. Jet's going to be fine." She sat on the edge of the bed, holding Abbey. "You could have been hurt."

Derek sat down and petted her too. "You were very brave by jumping on the intruder."

"Jet tried to stop the bad person. She bit its arm, then it hit her with the toaster. I jumped on its back and clawed and hissed. I even spit!" She rubbed her head under Alanna's chin. *"It pushed me against the cold box and I jumped on top of it. Then Juneau yelled that you were coming, so I ran up here. I think we need a bigger dog to protect Jet."*

Juneau jumped up to her cat bed, yelling down. *"We don't need another dog!"*

Alanna laughed, telling Derek what was said. "I need to go check on Jet." She carried Abbey out to the front lawn. Jet was lying there watching the officers and Fintan.

"Let me see your head." Alanna bent down next to her. She felt the small lump on the top of her head. "That evil moron hit my baby." She kissed Jet's bump.

"It hurts, but not as bad as it did. Can I have some frozen peas, please?"

Alanna laughed telling Derek what she said. They took her inside and got the peas out of the freezer, holding them to her head.

"That does feel better."

Tanner came running into the kitchen. *"Bloody 'ell, took forever for them to let me out of that car! Bleedin' bobbies! What did I miss? Is everyone all right?"*

"Everyone's ok, Tanner." Alanna reached over and petted him. "Juneau's upstairs if you want to go check on her."

"Crikey, I bet she 'as a tale to tell." He ran upstairs.

"I don't know if I'll ever get used to the British thing," Derek said.

Fintan and Andy came into the kitchen, looking around. "Is everyone ok? I assume you would have told me if one of them was hurt."

"They're ok. Jet got hit on the head, but she seems to be all right. Should I call Dr. Stuckey?"

"No! No vets! I'm fine. He'll want to take my temperature. And poke me. Look, my head's getting better. Don't call him!"

"Ok, ok. I won't call him, so calm down." She moved the peas back into place.

"We have a hell of a mess to clean up, interrogating to do, as well as a lot of paperwork." Fintan looked around and then checked his watch. 10:17 p.m.

"Why were they going through our stuff? What were they looking for?"

"I don't know. We're going to go downtown now and find out. I'm going to head to the station if you're ok. I trust Derek will stay with you?" He looked over at Derek.

"Of course, I won't leave her side." Derek put his hand on her arm.

Fintan moved over to Derek, extending his hand. "Thank you for everything, Derek." Derek stood and shook Fintan's hand. "I'm sorry for thinking you might have hurt her."

"It's ok, I understand. I think the call was to keep you away from the house."

"Yeah, we got that too. She sure was quick to defend you." Fintan smiled. "Her mother was that way too." He turned, gave Alanna a quick hug and then left the house.

Hours later, all the officers had left and Derek and Alanna had straightened and cleaned up everything that had been disturbed and broken. They were both exhausted. They didn't talk about what had happened with Derek. Alanna wanted to ask but he seemed really quiet, so she just let it go for the time being.

Fintan did not get home until almost dawn. He looked in the bedroom's open door to see Derek holding a sleeping Alanna close with Abbey curled up by her head. Jet and Tanner were on the floor by the bed. Derek opened his eyes when Fintan appeared in the doorway. He nodded at Derek as he heard Juneau's snoring, then went down the hall to his own room.

Chapter 23

Derek woke later that morning to something pecking at his earlobe. He looked up to find Nemesis standing on his shoulder and staring down at him. He closed his hand around Alanna's arm. "Alanna?"

She stirred slightly. "Umm, yeah?" She opened her eyes a little.

"I think your aunt wants you." He didn't move as Nemesis pulled on a strand of his hair.

"Mistress wants you, now." He pulled on Derek's hair.

Alanna looked at the clock. "It's 6:30 in the morning."

"She wants you, now." He gently pecked at Derek's shoulder.

"Hey!" Derek protested.

"Ok, ok I'll go." Alanna rubbed her hand over her face.

"He's the one she wants." He tilted his head, eyeing Derek.

"What about me?" She raised an eyebrow.

"You can come also." He walked down Derek's hip then flew towards the door, down the stairs, and landed to maneuver out the doggie door.

"What did he say?"

She rolled over, hugging her pillow. "That Aunt Vi wants you to come over."

"Me?" He sat up. "What about you?"

"I am not necessary," she said sleepily.

"He didn't say that," Derek said skeptically.

"He said you're the one she wants." She snuggled down.

"Well, come with me?" He kissed her cheek. "Please?"

"Ok." She rolled over, snuggling into his chest. "But not just yet. Give me a minute."

"Take all the time you want." He kissed the top of her head and held her close.

Vi looked at the clock. It was 7:10 a.m. when they walked into the kitchen, having left all the sleeping animals at home.

"Are you both ok?" she asked them as they sat down at the table.

"Yeah, just tired," Alanna said with a yawn. Derek was more alert than her.

"Here, have some coffee." Vi placed a cup of coffee in front of each of them. Then she put a plate of muffins on the table and sat down with her own cup. "So tell me what happened at 9:47 last night."

"Well, someone broke into our house."

"Ok, that's what led up to it, but what exactly broke the spell?" she asked expectantly.

"Spell?" Alanna asked.

"Yes, my dear, you know what a spell is," Vi said, anxious for details.

Alanna rubbed her hand over her face. "Yeah, but I have no idea what you're talking about."

Vi let out an exasperated sigh. "At 9:47 last night, a surge of power went through the ley line under this house, the likes of which I have never felt before. I can only assume that it meant that the binding spell that was on Derek is now broken, and it is broken . . . I can feel his power all the way from your house. What broke it?"

Derek and Alanna looked at each other and then at Vi. They were dumbfounded.

"Goodness, you two can be frustrating." She shook her head. "Did your mark move last night?" She looked directly at Derek.

He leaned back. "Yes, it did."

"May I see it?" Her request was actually more of a demand.

He stood up, pulling off his torn T-shirt as he turned around, moving his hair to the side. Alanna and Vi gasped loudly at the same time.

"What?" He looked over his shoulder. "What's wrong?'

"It's changed!" Alanna stood up and touched it. "It's all different."

"This is what I suspected." Vi stood up but she did not touch him.

"What's it look like!" Derek demanded.

"Well, it's actually really cool," Alanna said, tracing her finger over the design.

Vi reached over to her counter and pulled an ornate, silver hand mirror out of a velvet pouch. "Here, it's charged to me, but should not be affected by your power."

He didn't understand what that meant.

Vi held the mirror up so he could look over his shoulder at what was reflected. His mark had transformed into what looked like three triangles which were shaped like Celtic knotted horns, intertwined and surrounded by a circle of flames. The mark was very dark, like a deep, rich tattoo, and it shimmered! He grabbed the mirror which Vi didn't seem too happy about, moving it around to look from different angles. Each angle showed it to be a slightly different color. It was basically black, but if you moved slightly this way it had an orange tinge, and that way a red tinge, and moving up slightly it seemed more yellow. How was that possible?

He looked at it for a while. He had to admit that it looked a hell of a lot cooler now than before, like a detailed and intricately laced tattoo. He reached back and touched it. It felt the same. Last night his shoulder had burned worse than it ever had in his life and it had felt like his skin was crawling around on his back, but he hadn't been paying attention to it. He had been paying attention to Alanna and the situation that they had been in.

"What were you feeling before it moved?" Vi sat down.

He looked at Vi and sat down as he said pointedly, "Alanna was in danger and I had to save her. It was the only thing I cared about." He glanced back over his shoulder, then he put the mirror down and put his shirt back on.

"Was there blood drawn?" Vi leaned forward.

"Hers, not mine. There was a knife at her throat."

Vi looked over at Alanna, peering up at her neck. Then she raised her glasses to her nose, looking closer.

"I see no wound."

"I touched it and it healed instantly," Derek said softly.

Vi dropped her glasses as Alanna reached for her neck. "It did?" She continued to feel her neck.

"Yes." He looked down at the table. "I didn't say anything because of everything that was going on with you and the animals needing attention. Then you seemed to forget about it after I washed the blood off."

Vi leaned back in her chair and crossed her arms. "Tell me what you felt when your mark moved. Did it feel like a fiery rage consuming your entire body and mind?"

He narrowed his eyes. "Yes, that's exactly what I felt."

"His eyes did this weird flame thing." Alanna spoke up.

He turned to her. "They did what?"

"It looked like your eyes were on fire." Alanna stood up, grabbing a candle from the shelf along with a match. She lit the candle pointing to the flame tip as it flickered. "Like that. All around the iris of each eye."

"Living flame," Vi stated.

"Yeah, I could see the whites of his eyes and his pupils, but all the brown was little flickering reddish-orange flames. It freaked me out at first. I thought it might be painful for him, but it didn't seem to hurt him."

"Why didn't you tell me they did that?"

"I don't know. We didn't really talk much about anything that had happened. You seemed larger and faster when it all happened. I thought maybe I was in shock and imagining it."

"Inhumanly fast and strong?" Vi asked Alanna.

"Yeah. One second I had a knife to my throat and the next Derek had the knife, and they were on the floor and I was by the wall. I didn't even see it happen."

"I'm sorry I threw you against the wall. I just wanted you away from danger. No one has a right to hurt my woman." He reached over, caressing her shoulder.

A slow, wide smile crossed Vi's face. "Well, now we know what broke it."

They looked at her. "What?" Derek asked.

Vi smiled warmly and her eyes danced happily. "You're completely in love with Alanna and you feel deep within your heart and soul that she is the one and only woman put on this earth for you."

"Yes, that's true. I am very much in love with her and that's exactly how I feel." Derek reached over and held Alanna's hand.

Vi's eyebrow went up. "This type of binding curse is usually invoked to hold a person's powers to remain bound until they feel the most important thing to them is in jeopardy. Only then can the spell be broken, but it takes someone very strong and powerful or properly trained to control the powers once they are released." She leaned forward. "Tell me, did you kill the person that threatened her?"

"No." Derek looked over at Vi. "But it took everything in me not to. It was like that was my sole purpose and if Fintan hadn't come and taken the knife from me, I don't know what I would have done."

"Really?" Alanna gripped his hand lovingly.

"It was . . . like I had this lust for blood and wanted to see it on the knife and on my hands." He closed his eyes when he said it. He had not wanted to voice that. He slowly opened his eyes and looked over at Alanna. She leaned forward and kissed him.

"It must have been horrible. I'm so sorry you had to go through that," she said softly.

Should he tell her that it hadn't been horrible, it had been amazing, and in retrospect at that moment he had actually felt very powerful and almost invincible? "I was just glad I could control what I felt," he said as he brushed her cheek with his knuckles.

Vi eyed him curiously. "You need to go and have a very long talk with your uncle. Show him your mark and tell him what happened."

"But he won't talk to me about it," Derek said.

"Oh, he will now." Vi smiled knowingly. "The binding spell your grandfather put on you is broken. Roger is no longer obligated to your parents to protect you from the truth. He now has an obligation to teach you how to handle the truth, and all the power you just unleashed."

"What is the truth?" He raised his voice. "What the hell am I?"

"Why, my dear, you're a Berserker, a Fire Warrior for Odin." She said the last four words slowly. "And now your powers have been unbound, and you will have to learn to use and control them, especially when you get angry, or see your blood or blood of those you care for."

"I've heard of them." Alanna looked at Vi. "I thought they were just a myth, but all the characteristics seem to fit, except the healing of others thing."

"That would be a seventh son of a seventh son thing." Vi waved her hand dismissively. "Other powers may surface that don't fit the basic Berserker because he's a seventh son, but his genetics are from the ancient Norse gods and can no longer be denied."

"This is too much." Derek rubbed his hands over his face and head. "And you two talk about it like it's an everyday thing." His sarcasm was rampant. "Oh, and by the way this is my boyfriend. He's a mythical warrior for some ancient Norse god that can kill you if he gets too pissed, but if he doesn't kill you then he can fix you, so don't worry."

Vi gave him a sympathetic look. "I understand this is a lot to comprehend."

His mouth fell open. "A lot to comprehend? That would be an understatement, don't you think?"

Vi tilted her head. "But you accepted the fact that Alanna has gifts. Is it so hard to accept that you have some also?"

"It's just . . ." He put his head in his hands, leaning his elbows on the table. "It's a lot to deal with."

"May I suggest you take some time to adjust to what you have discovered about yourself, then relax and realize you are who you always were, just a new and improved version? Also remember that you have the unwavering and never-ending love of one of the most incredible people on this planet and she will help you through everything. Then talk to your uncle."

"You were talking about me, weren't you?" Alanna whispered. "The never-wavering love thing?"

"Yes, of course. Who else do you think I was talking about?"

"His mother?"

"Oh, please." Vi laughed. "Elsa is a decent enough person, but she's scared to death of what he is. She will cross herself five times and say fifty Hail Mary's when she finds out the spell is broken. She's the one who gave birth to a seventh son and believe you me, she has tons of guilt about him. Her fears have escalated over the years and she might keep her distance from him for quite some time once she finds out his powers are unbound."

"She's not going to be happy, that's for sure." Derek sighed. "She's never happy about anything unusual."

"Well, I'm happy." Alanna smiled at him.

"Really?" He looked at her like he didn't believe what she had just said.

"Derek, you're a walking myth!" she exclaimed. "You know how I love mythology."

He laughed, reluctantly. "You are so strange," he said and leaned over to give her a kiss.

"Actually, he is a proven legend, or a gift from the gods." Vi smiled. "Doesn't one of those sound better?"

"I like Fire Warrior," Derek stated. "It really sums up the intense feeling of it."

"You're my warrior and you light my fire." Alanna playfully batted her eyelashes at him.

"I'll show you what I can light." He reached over and pinched her thigh a little.

Vi was still smiling. "Well, I am glad you are both unharmed after last night. I knew the surge was from Derek, I just didn't know if he had control over it right away. Now I know. I didn't come over because Nemesis said there were many police cars and officers. I trusted Fintan to take care of it. If he had needed me he would have called."

"So you knew I had a binding spell on me and you didn't say anything?" Derek asked.

"Yes, I felt it the other day when you hugged me."

"Why didn't you say something about it when we were talking?" he asked, somewhat annoyed.

Vi noticed his reaction. "Binding spells are put into place for a reason. Most people don't know when they're bound. That's just how it is. Who am I to interfere with the fact that your family fears your powers enough to bind you? If I was to bind someone or place a geas on them, I wouldn't want someone else speaking of it. But you know about it now, don't you? It's better you found out this way and not by someone trying to remove the spell by force. Now that can do some serious damage."

He wondered what other things she knew about him being a Berserker that she wasn't telling him. He really didn't want to know any more today; he was exhausted and his head hurt from thinking. Today he just wanted to spend time with Alanna, and try to grasp everything that had happened and what he had just learned. And he wanted to take a shower . . . with Alanna.

On their way back to Treasure Grove, he told Alanna he didn't want to talk about the mark any more today. He needed time to let things sink in. She understood, and a little after eight they got back to her house to find Emma there. Fintan had told her everything that had happened before he'd left for work. She fixed them breakfast then started cleaning like a wind-driven storm. Derek said he had something at his house he wanted to show Alanna. Last night Fintan had sent an officer to his house to lock up, but he was anxious to get home and check on things.

When they got there he took her into the garage. On one side stood a beautiful black Harley Davidson Heritage Softail Classic, gleaming in the fluorescent lighting. It was parked on a large square of carpet.

"Nice bike," she said.

"Thanks. I love to ride. It's a great feeling." He shrugged his shoulders as he turned to show her a large cat tree condo that was on the other side. "So, do you think Juneau will like it?" It stood at least eight feet tall from the top to the bottom. It had ten different levels with tunnels and platforms, and at the very top there was a round platform with a raised edge and a soft cushion. There were ropes and toys dangling in places. Alanna was impressed. She had a few scratching posts around the house for the cats, but none that were this large and complicated.

"This is amazing. Did you make this yesterday?"

He walked over to it, putting his hand on it. "Yeah, I made one a few months ago for my sister's cats. It wasn't this large and it didn't have the little bed at the top, but it gave me a starting point. It's just some construction tubing, four by fours and carpet."

"And a lot of imagination." She looked down into one of the tubes that led to another platform.

"I figured when we kick her out of her bed, maybe she can sleep in the bed at the top of this. I just hope it makes her happy."

"Well, she should be. This is so neat."

He pulled over a step stool so she could inspect the top of it.

"That's so sweet of you to think of her and do something like this." She gave him a kiss after getting down off the stool. "It's pretty big and tall. How are we going to get it to my house?"

"It comes apart." He pointed to some large bolts. "I can remove this part, and put it back together there."

"You just keep amazing me with your talents." She put her hands on her hips.

He walked over to her, slipping his arms around her waist. "You have the amazing talents," he whispered in her ear as she giggled.

Fintan stood on one side of the two-way mirror watching Detective Mark Holmberg interrogate the killer. He looked across the room at the killer's eyes. There was no remorse there. No pain. No sorrow. Just cold, bone-chilling hate. The killer smiled. Mark leaned in and asked another question. The killer looked past him to the mirror.

"I still don't believe it was an anonymous tip," the killer said, eyes narrowed. "Whoever told you about the ring, their days are numbered. Mark my words, I'll see to it. I'll get my revenge on whoever ratted me out and my money. This isn't over!"

"Oh, yes it is." Fintan let out a long breath. He would never allow anyone here to know that it was Alanna who had told him about the crucial piece of evidence. He had put Mark onto the so-called anonymous tip the day before yesterday. Then the killer had broken into their house looking for something. He was waiting to find out what.

He walked down the small hall to the next two-way mirror. The killer's accomplice was in the next room, head down on the table crying, racked with guilt and anger. Oh, this was definitely over. He was just glad Alanna hadn't been hurt. He didn't know all the details about how Derek had saved her, but he knew all he needed to know for now.

This had been haunting her for a while now. She had stood face to face with the killer and had not even known it at the time. When she had realized her suspicions were justified she had trusted Fintan to put steel bars between them, and that's just what he was about to do for a very, very long time.

Derek changed his clothes, took the cat tree apart, loaded it in his truck, and followed Alanna to Treasure Grove. They pulled into the driveway and she parked in the garage. He used a hand-truck to move the largest part of the cat tree around to the back of the house and through the back doors and into the kitchen. Emma was in the kitchen when they came in.

"What is that?" She looked over at them, her eyes widening.

"It's a present Derek made for the cats." She helped him get it through the door.

"So, where do you want it?" he asked, looking around the kitchen.

"I think I want it right here by the sideboard." She indicated the wall behind the kitchen table.

"In the kitchen?" Emma asked, with a little shock in her voice. The thing was huge. She was going to have to vacuum it all the time. It was a giant cat-hair magnet. And so close to the dining table?

"Well, it's where we spend most of our time, and if you put it here, Juneau can look out the window." She pointed to the window beside the French doors that led to the backyard.

"Ok, if that's where you want it." Derek moved the sideboard to the left, and put the base of the cat tree down against the wall. He went out to his truck to get the rest of the structure, and his tools to put it together.

"What is that thing?" Jet asked Tanner as they sat in the backyard, watching Derek.

"It is a scratching post for the cats." He cleaned his paw.

"Why?"

"It 'as to do with mating." Tanner used his paw to clean himself, licking it and pulling it over his ear like a cat. *"And balance, order, and preventing chaos. At least that's what 'e said yesterday."*

"Strange." Jet tilted her head.

"Yes, I agree."

"Where's Juneau?" Alanna asked Emma.

"She's in the den." They found her watching a show on Arctic animals.

"Hey, Juneau," Derek said, leaning over the couch.

"Oh look. It has returned to torment me." She glared up at him.

"He's not here to torment you," Alanna said, petting her. "Be nice. He brought you a gift."

"He brought me a gift?"

"Yes, and he made it himself."

"Is it food?"

"No, it's not food." She picked Juneau up, handing her to Derek.

"I don't like to be held." She squirmed as he carried her to the kitchen.

"He built me a throne?" Juneau looked up at it, sniffing it.

"It's not a throne."

Derek lifted Juneau into the round bed at the very top.

"Sure it is. There's your own little spot." He smiled at her.

"Ohhh." She pushed the pads on her feet into the soft cushion and kneaded it under her claws. *"I like this and I can look down on all that I survey."*

Derek looked over at Alanna. "Does she like it?"

"Oh, yeah, she likes it. You have created an imperialistic monster."

Juneau settled down on the cushion. She looked down at Derek. *"This is a very nice peace offering. It will go far in leaning the negotiations in your favor. But do not take my enjoyment of it to mean that I accept you. For the time being I will allow you to stay, temporarily."*

"As long as she likes it." He reached up, petting her.

Abbey ran into the kitchen. *"What that?"* She came over and sniffed it. Then she reached up and dug her claws into the thick carpet on the side of a tunnel. *"It tickles my paws."* She darted into one of the tunnels and jumped from platform to platform. She ran all over it until she had climbed her way to the top. She looked up toward the top platform where Juneau was.

"I want up there." Abbey looked like she was going to jump toward Juneau.

"This is my spot! And only my *spot. You will not even think about coming up here!"* Juneau hissed.

"Mommy, make her let me up there." Abbey climbed on the platform below Juneau.

"That's her spot, Abbey. Just let her have it and you can play on the rest of it."

Abbey jumped toward a rope hanging down and batted at it with both paws. *"Ok."*

She ran all over the cat tree trying all the platforms and tunnels. Juneau leaned over the edge of her platform, watching her with a critical eye. If Abbey came anywhere near her top bed, Juneau hissed, *"Away!"*

Derek looked over at Alanna. "So what now?"

"It's only eleven thirty, but after last night I'm still tired. Do we have to go and do anything? I would really like to just hang out here and relax."

"You read my mind. I could use some recovery time myself," he said, stretching.

"There is one thing I want to do, though."

"What's that?" He wiggled his eyebrows.

She smiled. "Well, now that I've made my decision to quit the retail business, I think I'd like to type up my resignation letter."

He followed her into Fintan's office and she sat down at the computer and began typing. Abbey came running into the office and jumped up on the desk. *"Mommy, am I normal?"* She sat down on the desk by the monitor.

"Yes, you're normal. Why?"

"Juneau keeps telling Tanner I'm Abbey normal." She tilted her head, rubbing it against the monitor. Alanna laughed a little.

"What?" Derek asked from the chair on the opposite side of the desk.

"Juneau keeps telling Tanner that she's abnormal."

"Abbey, you're perfect just the way you are. Don't let her bug you," Derek said.

"What doing?" She sat down in front of the monitor, obscuring part of Alanna's view of the screen as she watched the cursor and letters on the screen and touched the movement with her paw.

"I'm getting out of the retail business."

Abbey turned and came closer to her. *"Don't do that, Mommy."*

She stopped typing and looked at Abbey's cute, furry face. "Why not, baby?"

"What if I need a new tail?"

Alanna laughed and told Derek what she had said. He smiled, picking her up for a cuddle while Alanna finished her letter. After she was done and it was printed, they went into the kitchen. She got two sodas and handed him one.

"Can I have a TV put on that wall there?" Juneau asked from her perch, pointing her paw.

"No, you cannot." Alanna stated.

"How about a book stand attached to the side here so I can read?"

"No."

She relayed to Derek what Juneau wanted and she could tell he was thinking about how he could attach one for her as he looked up at the top. Emma made them some sandwiches and they walked down the hall to the den to sit on the couch and watch a little TV while they ate. Then Alanna went upstairs to retrieve her book off her nightstand while Derek went to the library and chose a book for himself.

They sat at opposite ends of the couch in the den with their shoes off, rubbing each other's feet a little as they both read.

Hours passed. She loved the fact that she could be quiet with Derek; it was very comfortable. They didn't have to talk, they could just sit and read together. She came to a steamy part of her book. She looked up over the top of her book at him. She used her sock-covered toe to rub the lower buttons of his shirt. He looked up from his book, his brown eyes shimmering with a knowing look.

"Are you at a good part?" he asked in a low, sensual voice.

"Ummhmm." She rubbed her toe lower as she nodded her head in response.

He looked back down at his book with a grin which lifted up one side of his mouth. She slid a little lower on the couch, reaching her toe up to touch a higher button. She pulled her foot slowly all the way to his knee. Keeping his eyes on his book, his smile widened.

"Do you want to read to me?" he asked softly.

"No." She placed her book down and crawled slowly over on top of him. He closed his own book, laying it down on the floor. They kissed and cuddled for a while and then the phone rang. She heard Emma answer it. She came into the den to speak to them.

"Ah . . . I have to run to the butcher for your father. I'll be back in a little while." She left the room. They heard her exit the laundry room and get in her car and leave.

They went upstairs to the bedroom.

Later, Alanna came downstairs to her art studio and closed the door when she heard Emma start vacuuming in the den.

Sam and Nick walked in the front door a few minutes later.

"Al?" Sam called out. There was no response. They walked into the kitchen. Nick opened the fridge to get a beer, and had a good look at the cat tree.

"I'll go find her, I want to hear everything that happened." Sam headed upstairs. She came to Alanna's bedroom door. It was slightly ajar. She pushed it open. Derek was standing by the bed with his back to the door. He didn't hear it open. He dropped the towel he had around his waist. Sam's eyes widened as she beheld his glorious naked backside. She pulled the door shut, but not all the way. Derek turned and looked at the door. He felt like he was being watched but the door was closed. Sam paused a second, then she eased it open again for a second peek, closing it again quickly. Derek turned again to see the door closed. Damned if he didn't get the strangest feeling. He continued to get dressed.

Alanna came down the hall and into the kitchen to find Nick sitting at the table.

"Oh, hey Nick."

"Hey there, Sam's looking for you." He gestured toward the stairs. Alanna headed up the staircase as Sam was coming down. Sam came to a stop, placing her hand on Alanna's shoulder. Sam closed her eyes then opened them slowly.

"Girl, that man has a butt like a Greek statue. He's absolutely perfect."

Alanna frowned as Sam's words sunk in. Sam had seen Derek naked! A streak of fury and jealously ran through Alanna at lightning speed.

"Sam! What were you doing in my room?" Alanna pushed her hand off her shoulder.

"I'm sorry, I always go into your room."

"The door was closed. Didn't you knock?" Alanna followed her into the kitchen.

"Sorry." Sam looked into the fridge, getting a soda.

Nick looked up from his beer. "What's going on?"

Alanna scowled. "She saw Derek naked."

"She what?"

"Just his butt," Sam shrugged as she sat down at the table. "It was an accident," she smiled sheepishly with downcast eyes, "the first time."

"What?" Alanna almost yelled.

"I couldn't help myself," Sam said defensively, taking a drink. "He's built really well."

Nick gave her a scolding look. "How many times did you look at him?"

"Twice."

"Sam!" Alanna actually stomped her foot. "I can't believe you would deliberately look at Derek's naked butt."

At that moment Derek came down the stairs and into the kitchen. He was pushing his long, damp hair behind his ears. "What about my butt?" he asked as he entered the room.

"Sam saw your naked butt!" Alanna said angrily.

"I thought I heard the door open." He narrowed his eyes at Sam. "Don't you know how to knock?"

Sam threw her hands up in surrender. "I'm sorry. Next time I'll knock."

"There better not be a next time," Nick said, pointedly.

"Damned right," Derek agreed.

"It's not right, not right at all!" Alanna said, still angry.

"It's not, but if it makes you feel any better, I've seen his naked butt too," Nick said, taking a drink.

Derek laughed. "Yes, he has."

"When?" Sam asked.

"We played football together." Nick and Derek looked at her. "We had to shower."

Juneau leaned over the edge of her bed on the platform. *"I've seen his naked butt also."*

Alanna glared at her and sat down with a thump. "Well, I guess we'll just have to start a club since there are so many of us," she said with angry sarcasm.

Emma walked into the room just then and smiled. "What kind of club are you starting sweetie?"

"The 'I saw Derek's naked butt' club," Sam said with a smirk as Alanna glared hard at her.

Emma stopped by the counter and turned. She tilted her head as a smiled played at her lips. "And how do I join?"

Nick laughed as Derek rubbed his hand over his face, blushing slightly.

"You don't," Alanna said sternly. "No one else gets to join . . . ever!"

Derek smiled, reaching up and touching her flushed cheek.

"You're jealous." He was touched.

"No, I'm annoyed." She crossed her arms over her chest again.

Emma asked curiously, "So, who here has seen Derek's naked butt?"

Everyone raised their hand. Even Juneau's paw raised up from inside her bed on the platform.

Emma looked around. "Well, now I really feel left out."

Derek looked up at her. "Don't." He raised his voice loudly in announcement. "Hear ye, hear ye, henceforth, no one except for Alanna MacLachlin shall ever see my naked butt!"

Fintan cleared his throat loudly. Everyone turned to see him standing in the doorway to the laundry room. They all, even Alanna, started laughing at the look on Fintan's face.

Chapter 24

Fintan passed silently through the kitchen and went upstairs to change as everyone else laughed. The mood lightened in the kitchen after that. Alanna was still a little mad but it didn't show . . . much.

She and Derek relayed most of the details of the night before to Sam and Nick. They left out the parts about Derek's mark, but Alanna did make him out to be the hero. Sam said "Holy crap!" a lot. Fintan came back downstairs in his boxers, opened the fridge and got out a bottle of beer and the large package of meat in butchers paper Emma had brought home. He grabbed his favorite knife and cutting board, taking them to the table. Then he went back to the fridge and got a bottle of Alanna's favorite wine. He opened it, poured a glass and walked over to the table, handing it to her.

"Thanks, Dad."

"No, thank you." He placed a hand on her shoulder, looking lovingly and gratefully into her eyes. "I'm so glad you're ok, and thanks to your suspicions and theory we were able to put her away for three murders."

"Three?" everyone said in unison, looking at Fintan.

"She killed Cecilia and Lori also."

"Holy crap!" Sam said, again. "I can't believe it." She looked at Alanna in astonishment.

Fintan washed his hands then sat down, unwrapped the large beef tenderloin and began to trim off the fat. "So, for everything you've been through, I thought I'd make your favorite dinner." He smiled at Alanna.

"I still can't believe it was Kristina," Sam said. "And to think I felt sorry for her losing her mother and all, and here she was the one that killed her! What a sicko!"

"Did she tell you why she killed all of them?" Emma asked, sitting down at the table.

"Finally, after hours of interrogating her." He talked while he trimmed. "When we took her in last night and started questioning her about the murders she wouldn't talk. It took some time, but after a few well-placed comments she began to confess. Her lawyer advised against it but she informed all of us, including her lawyer, that one day she will get out and make us all pay. Her partner found out the truth and confessed her part in it all. That's all we needed to get a confession out of Kristina.

"She has real anger issues and when she found out Zara had confessed she really became unhinged. At first she wasn't talking at all, she wouldn't answer our questions, so we carefully used the ring against her." He pointed his finger at Alanna. "The ring you pointed out to me, that was one-of-a-kind and very significant to her." Fintan looked around the table. "When she did confess, she told us the whole story. She seemed to be very proud of her skills as a killer."

"What on earth made her kill so many people?" Emma asked. "Including her mother?"

Fintan carved as he launched into his story. "Well, apparently it started years ago when Brian Parker was in college. Lori Morgan and Brian had gone to college together and had been an item for a brief time. Lori got pregnant but she didn't tell him: He was involved with Karen by that time, and Lori decided to keep the baby.

"She never told him and gave birth to Kristina. Years later they met again at a company convention. They started having an affair. She transferred to the Lodi store to be closer to him. They were hatching a plan to run away together but they needed funding for their escape. With each of them being a manager of a store, they had access to millions of dollars each year so they came up with a plan to embezzle the funds.

"Brian was a wiz at computers and manipulating numbers and documents, and he was good friends with his boss so he was able to talk his way out of a lot of questions when they came up. They had also created over fifty dummy companies to launder the funds, then the money was transferred into offshore accounts. They needed the accounting office managers to be in on it to cover their tracks, so they enlisted Cecilia and her daughter, Zara. With their help, they were able to siphon hundreds of thousands of dollars unnoticed. Cecilia was very creative and smart. Apparently her ex-husband had taught her a lot about that kind of stuff. Maintenance and supply accounts were the ones they focused on mostly."

A look passed between Alanna and Sam, both thinking maybe Dave wasn't that crazy after all.

Fintan continued his story. "Brian had the account numbers to three accounts, Lori had the other three account numbers, Cecilia had the passwords to three of the accounts and Zara had the other three. I guess this kept them all honest, as honest as thieves can be. What they didn't count on was Kristina. She had known that Rick Morgan was not her real father, but that he had raised her as his own. Then Lori got pregnant again. Rick knew it wasn't his and that she was having an affair.

"Kristina overheard them arguing one night after her brother Cameron was born. She followed Lori to the casino and saw her with Brian. She confronted her mother when she was on her way to the parking lot that night. Lori told her the truth about Brian being her real father, which only fueled the fire of Kristina's anger. Lori told her that she could come with them when they left.

"Brian had found out about Kristina being his and had given Lori his mother's ring to give to her. She was, after all, his first-born. Lori tried to give her the ring that night but Kristina became enraged and fought with her, telling her she was going to expose them all and make her pay for hurting Rick and destroying their family. She threatened Lori with a gun then she chased her from the casino and caused Lori's accident. The sad thing was that she didn't mean to kill her mother, she just wanted to make her stop hurting Rick. But when she confessed, she was so cold, callous and detached.

"After her mother had told her about the embezzlement, she decided to get close to Zara and Cecilia. She had the three account numbers from her mother but she wanted it all. She felt that after a lifetime of lies and deceit she deserved it. She felt Brian should die, for having never been there for her and causing her family so much pain and hurt.

"She had a good alibi for the night she killed him. She had to work at her store in Lodi until almost midnight. No car can make it from Lodi to Aurum in less than forty minutes on the main roads, but a motorcycle on the back roads can make it in half the time if you break all the speed laws. She killed Brian and took his cellphone because that's where he kept the other account numbers, Zara had told her that.

"They were more than just friends by then but Zara didn't know that Kristina was going to kill her mother. Zara thought her mother really did die of an accidental allergic reaction. Kristina had made it look like an allergic reaction by coating the rose stems with Benadryl so when Cecilia poked her fingers on the thorns, she would ingest it. It took just a small amount for her body to react, then she let the paramedics finish the job by giving her more Benadryl. She said she watched the whole thing. We wouldn't have been able to pin that one on her but once she started confessing we just let her talk. She was actually proud of the way she had killed Cecilia. Who the hell kills someone with a rose thorn?"

He cut the meat into steaks.

"After the memorial service, they were going to head across the border and then fly off together forever, but Kristina wouldn't leave her baby brother, Cameron. She was going to take Cameron and leave Rick some money. Kristina never even shed one tear while she confessed. I thought Zara was going to come through the wall when she found out Kristina had killed her mother. She gave Erin a black eye trying to get to her." He sighed deeply. "It's been one hell of a day." He looked at Alanna. "She said she broke in here to get back something you had of Cecilia's."

"All I had of hers was her bracelet, and I gave that to you."

"When did you find the bracelet?" Sam asked her.

"Abbey found it that day we went to Cecilia's house after she died."

"And you didn't say anything?"

Alanna waved her hand at Fintan. "He told me not to."

"I don't think it was the bracelet. She removed the bracelet and threw it in the bushes the night she killed Cecilia, hoping someone would find it outside. We think it has something to do with the accounts that the embezzled funds went into. Zara said they were looking for the passwords that Cecilia had to the other three accounts."

"Well, all I found of hers was the bracelet. Could the information on it have been the passwords?"

"I don't think so. Like I said, she didn't keep it."

"Well, I don't have . . . wait!" Alanna jumped up from the table and went to her purse on the counter. Fintan stopped cutting as everyone watched her pull the tattered paperback out of her purse. "This was Cecilia's. Mr. Beckman let me have it as a reminder of her. It was one I gave her for her birthday." She thumbed through it. There were three underlined, highlighted passages marked in the book. "Dad, do you think that this has the passwords she was looking for?"

"I hope so. When did he give you that book?"

"On Monday, the day I noticed the ring on Kristina's finger. She was standing there when I told Zara I had a book of Cecilia's."

"Put the book in a plastic baggie and set it on the counter so I can take it in."

She did as he said. "If this is why she broke in she would have never have found it since I had it with me in my purse."

"So Brian was killed by Kristina, his illegitimate daughter?" Emma asked, trying to understand everything. "And she killed her own mother and Cecilia? And all for money?"

"Yes." Fintan stood up, carrying the meat to the counter by the stove where he got his large skillet out of the cabinet. "A lot of money."

Alanna looked over at Sam. "I knew I had seen that ring before. Mrs. Parker had told me she had given it to Brian. It took me a while, but I remembered seeing it on Lori's hand on the steering wheel in my dream. I knew there was something I was missing when I suddenly remembered seeing it on Kristina's finger the day she was carrying the box of Cecilia's things. It just took me so long to put it together. And I only put two and two together when I saw a garnet ring in a store window downtown."

"But you finally did put it all together." Derek leaned over and kissed her. "That's what's important."

"He's right." Fintan seasoned the steaks and started frying them. "They could have been out of the country before we could have brought them in on embezzlement charges. We were working on that angle, thanks to Mr. Beckman. He knows his numbers and they weren't adding up. They were going to be gone in just a day or two but they needed those passwords. Plus, I think if Zara had found out that Kristina had killed Cecilia, she wouldn't have hesitated to kill Zara also. She was prepared to but she screwed up when she broke in here. She knew we didn't have an alarm system and she couldn't figure out how we got here so fast."

"We do have an alarm system and her name is Juneau." Alanna smiled up at the paw and tail hanging out of the bed at the top of cat tree.

"And my fee is one large TV on that wall." The paw pointed.

"Every killer makes mistakes and her biggest one was in coming here," Fintan said.

Everyone was silent. Fintan looked over and smiled. "So, who's up for steak au poivre?"

Chapter 25

Alanna awoke the next morning in her bed with Derek beside her. She reached over and brushed his hair away from his face. He smiled, opening his eyes.

"Good morning, sexy," she purred.

"Ummm." He pulled her to him, cuddling her. "Good morning. How are you doing? You had kind of a rough night."

"I'm better. Sorry I woke you." She'd had a nightmare where she was shot and drowning. It had seemed so real and she had woken him up when she bolted upright, clutching her chest.

"That's ok, it seemed like a really bad nightmare."

"It was."

He smiled. "So, would you like to go somewhere today?"

"Ok, where?"

"I don't know. Let's just hit the highway and see where it takes us. Maybe Yosemite?"

"Sounds fun." She kissed him.

"I have to run home first, but then I'll be back and we can head out. Ok?"

"Ok." She watched him as he got up and dressed. He kissed her goodbye and left.

She got dressed and headed downstairs. She poured herself a cup of coffee and then stepped out onto the patio. Fintan was in his boxers, T-shirt, cowboy boots, and his old straw cowboy hat, riding his lawn mower around the trees, cutting the grass. He loved to ride that thing. They had a yard service that came once a week, but he still liked to cut the grass every now and then. She saw the earbuds in his ears as he bobbed his head to a song he liked.

Emma came out and stood behind her. "So what do you and your young man have planned for today?"

Alanna sat down at the patio table, glancing at the headline of the *Aurum Town Crier. Killer Caught. Police Solve Three Murders.*

"I think we're going to go to Yosemite." She drank. "We might get a room for the night."

"That sounds nice." Emma sat down next to her. "May I ask you something?"

"No, Emma, you can't join the club." Alanna gave her a warning look.

"You've already said that. I was just noticing how you've been acting and looking at Derek." She patted Alanna's hand. "Just between us, right now, if he was to ask you to spend the rest of your life with him, what would you say?"

Alanna was shocked. "The wedding dress in the guest room is for Sam, Em."

"I know that. Just be honest with me and answer the question."

She leaned back, knowing why Emma had asked: She was making a point.

Alanna knew what she felt now. She could put it into words. One word: Love . . . deep, heartfelt, joyous love with that wonderful sprinkling of lust. She was completely in love with her Fire Warrior. She didn't know what their lives together would hold, but she hoped desperately that it would be a long one.

She smiled. "Yes," she said softly.

Emma raised an eyebrow. "Well, it's good to know that love can still work its magic. You two have been seeing each other, what, a week now? It took me longer, a whole nine days." Emma laughed, standing to go into the house. "By the way, did I tell you I'm willing to pay membership dues?"

"Emma!" Alanna exclaimed over her shoulder. "Stop that!"

A short time later, Alanna was dressed in jeans, a tight T-shirt and a zippered hoodie, standing by the hood of the Porsche in the driveway. The gate to Treasure Grove opened to reveal a rider dressed all in black leather on a sleek black motorcycle. The rider pulled up in front of her.

He gracefully dismounted, leather pants and jacket hugging his amazing body. He approached her, unbuckling his helmet. In one swift motion, he pulled the helmet off and tossed it onto the soft grass. Derek's hair fell loosely around his head and shoulders. He came close to her, pushing into her as she leaned back against the fender of the car, and he kissed her. She reached up, starting to unzip his black leather jacket. She saw his bare chest become exposed underneath and let out a small cry of delight,

"God, I love déjà vu," she whispered as she grabbed his hand, pulling him toward the house. She closed and locked the bedroom door behind them. A few minutes later Juneau was placed gently outside the door.

"What? You can't take a little constructive criticism?"

Reviews

If you enjoyed *Cat 'n' Dog Get Retailed* please consider leaving a rating and review on Amazon and Goodreads. Reviews and feedback are important to an author, as well as other potential readers, and would be very much appreciated. Thank you.

A sneak peek at what's Coming Soon –
Cat 'n' Dog Get Drenched

Alanna MacLachlin felt the steel crossbow arrow pierce through the fabric and padding of her neoprene ski vest, and embed itself deep into the tissue of her still beating heart. Her eyes widened in pain and terror as she gasped for air, the force of the impact pushing her off the back of her jet ski and into the cold, dark water of the lake.

Blood flowing from the wound seeped into the water surrounding her as she moved, painfully trying to keep her head above the surface. Blood and water filled her mouth and lungs as she began to lose consciousness. Her legs and arms felt very heavy, as if weighted down.

Her heart tried to beat one last time as she felt the smooth wet coils of a snake slip around her neck and start to tighten. Her eyes closed slowly as she saw the head of the serpent slide past her face then past her ear. Her limbs stilled as her head slipped quietly beneath the dark, smooth surface of the moon's reflection on the water.

If you would like to be kept updated of new releases, please click 'Follow' on Lilli Lea's author page on amazon.com and amazon will send you details as soon as books become available.

Acknowledgements

I want to thank all those people who helped make this book happen. You know who you are and a special thank you to you all.

My heartfelt thanks to Karen Perkins and Louise Burke at LionheART Publishing House. You are my unsung heroes. Thank you for everything.

Huge thanks to my friend Ross González for doing the cover art. You rock, Ross!

To my niece Jennifer Brockman, you get the biggest thank you of them all. If it wasn't for you the seed for this story would never have been planted, watered (with mead, lots of mead) or harvested. Thank you for being there on the other side of the wall when I would yell "Quack", "Yo?" and "Trebuchet!" You are the most wonderful influence and inspiration in my life and I thank you for your laugh and constructive criticism. And . . .the piñata stick you hit me with to get me going on this.

About the Author

Lilli Lea is a flannel wearing squirrel lover that has had a passion for writing her whole life and has been creating adventurous works of literature since 2007. Within the last decade she was transplanted to Sioux Falls, South Dakota from Lodi, California with her husband and their four-legged furry children. She has proudly worked for Walmart for the last twenty three years, which has helped develop the *Cat 'n' Dog* series. She loves spending time with her family, friends, and furry ones. When not writing or working she enjoys numerous hobbies that include reading, keeping up to date on way too many television series, going to the movies, visiting and hiking national parks, and zombie target shooting.

www.ingramcontent.com/pod-product-compliance
Lightning Source LLC
Chambersburg PA
CBHW070431120726
47910CB00003B/740